'They took risks for us all the time. We can't just let them rot.'

Slaney sighed. 'In this business we all take risks of one sort or another. And we know what the consequences are if we get caught.'

'If I got caught what would we do?'

'That's different, Charlie. And you know it. You're a British subject – a British officer.'

'So what would we do?'

'We'd look who we'd got of theirs and try and negotiate an exchange.'

'So why don't we do it for my people?'

'What do you suggest?'

'We try to do an exchange.'

'Oh, for God's sake, Charlie. Your people are Germans. We'd be admitting that we use Germans for cross-border intelligence. They'll probably get no more than a year inside. We can look after them when they come out.'

'They'll be tried as spies, that can get them up to ten years. Maybe more.'

'Look, Charlie. I know it's upsetting when these things happen but it's part of the game. You win some you lose some.'

Also by Ted Allbeury,
and available in Hodder and Stoughton paperbacks:

Show Me a Hero
Other Kinds of Treason
The Dangerous Edge
The Reaper
A Time Without Shadows
Deep Purple
A Wilderness of Mirrors
The Crossing
The Seeds of Treason
Children of Tender Years
The Judas Factor
No Place to Hide

About the author

Ted Allbeury was a lieutenant-colonel in the Intelligence Corps during World War II, and a successful executive in the fields of marketing, advertising and radio. He has been writing since the early 1970s: he is best known for his espionage novels but has also published one highly successful and highly praised general novel, *The Choice*, and a short story collection, *Other Kinds of Treason*.

The Line-Crosser

Ted Allbeury

CORONET BOOKS
Hodder and Stoughton

First published in Great Britain in 1993
First published in paperback in 1994 by Hodder and Stoughton
A division of Hodder Headline PLC

A Coronet paperback

10 9 8 7 6 5 4 3 2 1

British Library Cataloguing in Publication Data

Allbeury, Ted
Line-crosser
I. Title
823.914 [F]

ISBN 0 340 60302 X

Printed and bound in Great Britain by
Cox and Wyman Ltd, Reading, Berks.

Photoset by Rowland Phototypesetting Ltd,
Bury St Edmunds, Suffolk.

Hodder and Stoughton Ltd
A Division of Hodder Headline PLC
338 Euston Road
London NW1 3BH

My wife has just had a liver-transplant and is doing well. This is to say thanks to our GPs Drs Rob and Gill Johnson and to the liver-transplant team at the Royal Free Hospital in Hampstead. Thanks not only for their skill and experience but for the kindness and caring that covered several years.

It was Dr Burroughs who set in motion the team: Mr Rolles, the surgeon, Drs Caroline Marshall and Jonathan Appleby, the anaesthetists. After the transplant it was Sister Alison Ibbetson and her colleagues in the Intensive Therapy Unit, Dr Thompson, the Registrar, and his team of young doctors and the nursing and care staff of Hassall Ward. We are particularly grateful to Linda Selves as transplant co-ordinator for her help at every stage.

And last, but definitely not least, our grateful thanks to the National Health Service that made it all possible.

Ted Allbeury

The treason past, the traitor is no longer needed.
Pedro Calderon de la Barca

PART ONE

PART ONE

CHAPTER 1

They had sent Willoughby to talk to her. To make one last effort to dissuade her. Because Willoughby was handsome and only a couple of years older than she was.

As she poured out the drinks for them he glanced around the room. It was elegant and light. White paint and pale blue decoration with touches of gold on the pillars and covings. He couldn't really imagine Johnny Tarrant in that setting but it fitted her perfectly.

She wore a white cashmere sweater and a black skirt. There were small diamanté bows on her black shoes and she was more than pretty, she was beautiful. And she knew it. Long blonde hair way below her shoulders, heavy-lidded blue eyes, a neat nose and the pouting mouth of a teenager. She looked about twenty-one or twenty-two but he knew from the 'P' file that she was actually twenty-eight.

As she turned to hand him the drink his eyes went for a moment to her big firm breasts and when he looked back at her face she was smiling, obviously aware of where his eyes had lingered. When she sat she crossed her long legs so that her skirt rose half-way up her thighs.

'Was it Slaney who sent you?'

'He asked me to have a word with you, yes.'

'He's a creep that man.'

'What makes you think that?'

'He's an old woman. A prude and a hypocrite.'

'Never struck me like that.'

3

'He pretends to be indifferent to attractive women. But he isn't. He danced with me at one of the Harrises' parties and believe me he's as horny as they come.'

'He's a very shrewd man all the same, Mrs Tarrant.'

She smiled. 'Not if he thought you could talk me out of it at this stage.'

'Was there a stage when he *could* have talked you out of it?'

'Who knows? But threatening me with the Official Secrets Act wasn't a good first move.'

Willoughby nodded. 'You never signed it, did you?'

'Of course not. Why should I? I wasn't in your filthy racket. Thank God.'

Willoughby sighed and then said patiently, 'It's not filthy, Mrs Tarrant. It's as much part of the establishment as the diplomats, the police and the law courts. We have to deal with unpleasant people but that doesn't make us unpleasant too.'

'How long have you been in the racket?'

'Four years.'

'Straight from Oxford?'

'Cambridge actually.'

She shrugged. 'Like Philby and the other two.'

'Same university but no more than that.'

'Well, tell Slaney no dice.'

'Could I ask you a frank question, Mrs Tarrant?'

She shrugged. 'Go ahead.'

'Why do you want all this court business? It could be done discreetly. We could have seen to that.'

'You should speak to Johnny about that, not me. He could have gone along with it. Instead of which he wants to defend it. Every bloody word.'

'You could have got a divorce without all those allegations. That's what's made him fight it. Pride.'

'Like hell. It isn't pride, it's bloody-mindedness. He wants to humiliate me.'

'I don't think he does. I've spoken to him and that's not my impression. He sees it as deliberate . . . a kind of persecution or harassment.'

'What sheer crap. He's got a persecution complex, that's his problem.'

Willoughby smiled diffidently. 'There are others who see it as harassment too.'

'What's your first name?'

'Hugh.'

'Can I call you Hugh?'

'Please do.'

'And I'm Jenny, but you must know that already.' She smiled. 'All those silly files.'

'I do.'

'Look, honey, I'm paying my lawyers good money and it's their advice that it should be done the way they've chosen. If you want to stop the fight then tell Johnny just to accept my statement. Let him play the gentleman for once instead of the boy from the back streets. Who cares what I say about him? It's all true anyway.'

'The press are bound to make a song and dance about it. It's got everything they want.' He paused. 'You're very young, Jenny, and very beautiful. It isn't your image at all.'

'Are you married, Hughie?'

'No. I'm afraid not.'

'Girl-friend?'

'A few, but nothing serious.'

The big blue eyes looked intently at his face. 'Did Slaney tell you to try and get me into bed?'

'Good God no.' But there was no surprise on his face at the question and she guessed it had been at least discussed. But he was SIS, a professional, and his grey eyes looked back at her calmly and unblinking for a few moments before he spoke again.

'Is there anything we could do that would avoid the court case?'

'Like what?'

'We would pay your legal costs and a cash recompense.'

'Johnny will have to pay my legal costs anyway. And nothing will satisfy me after what he said about me except me putting the record straight.'

'He said it in anger. You know that.'

'He said it. And he said it in front of other people. That's all that matters to me.'

'I understand from our legal people that it leaves you open to be questioned in court. It cuts both ways.'

She shrugged. 'So be it. He's going to lose anyway.'

Willoughby stood up slowly. 'Thanks for the drink, Jenny. I'd better go.'

As they stood in the hall, by the door to the steps and the street, she looked up, smiling, at his face. '*Did* Slaney tell you to get me into bed?'

For a moment he hesitated and then he said, 'Of course he didn't.'

Still smiling she said, 'Will you give him a message from me?'

'Of course.'

Her slim arms went round his shoulders, her soft mouth on his and she could feel his hardness against her belly as her tongue slid into his mouth. A few moments later she released him, laughing softly at his confusion.

'What's the message, Jenny?' he said quietly.

'That was the message, Hughie.'

And she opened the door, smiling as she watched him walk hurriedly down the steps and across the road.

Slaney pushed his heavy glasses back up his nose as he stared across his desk at Hawkins, the staff legal adviser for SIS.

'Johnny Tarrant's not going to be much use to me for a long time after this is over.'

'What's he been working on?'

'He's been in charge of penetration of extreme left-wing groups.'

'You can give him a desk job surely.'

Slaney shrugged. 'Sure we can, but it's a terrible waste of an experienced agent.'

'There's no way we can stop her. She's determined to put him through the mincer.'

'The parts in her statement that you've marked as having a security aspect, can we stop just those?'

'I'm afraid not. Once she's in court she can say what she likes so long as it's relevant.'

'Will the court accept them as relevant?'

'Most of them. It depends on how her counsel frames the questions.'

'Have you spoken to her counsel?'

'You bet. But he says she's adamant. Won't tone it down under any circumstances.'

'Do you think he's really tried to persuade her. Does he realise the seriousness of what she's up to?'

'I'm sure he does but he can't go beyond advising her. She's the client, and unfortunately for us what she's saying could well be considered as relevant.'

'Would it help if I really put the heat on Tarrant so that it goes through undefended?'

'First of all I don't think you could persuade him not to defend. She's going to skin him alive for every cent he's got. He's practically paranoid about it. I mean that. And just her petition alone would blow all Tarrant's cover sky-high.'

'Fancy being married to a bitch like that.'

Hawkins smiled. 'It would have its compensations, my friend.'

'You've met her?'

'No, I've just seen the file photographs. She's gorgeous.'

'Will that help her in court?'

'Of course it will. It always does. How much, depends on the judge.'

'Who is he?'

'They haven't listed it yet.'

'So nothing can stop it going ahead?'

'Nothing short of drastic moves against her personally.'

'You mean something that prevented her from appearing in court?'

'Even that may not stop it. Her petition would be enough. There's forty or fifty pages that read like a mixture of *Fanny Hill* and *Brighton Rock* with a touch of Eric Ambler.'

'Can we ask the DPP to help us?'

'To do what?'

'To clear the court. Have it heard in camera and put reporting restrictions on it.'

'We might be able to do that. I'll ask. But it would alert the press immediately.'

'That bitch will alert them anyway.'

'Do you want me to make an application?'

Slaney took off his glasses and wiped his eyes with a Kleenex and then used it to clean the lenses of his glasses. He put them back on slowly and sighed.

'Yes. But get the DPP's people to do it. Not us.'

'I'll let you know what happens.'

Slaney nodded. 'Do that.'

It was eight o'clock when Slaney got home and there was a whisky on the hall table waiting for him. As he walked into the sitting room his wife smiled.

'A fellow named Hawkins called. Said to tell you the DPP said no. He said you'd need a drink.'

'How's it been, sweetie?'

'He gave me some different pills. A different drug. He says it could help in the long run.'

'Would you like to go out for dinner?'

'Let me do us an omelette.'

'*I'll* do us an omelette, you just stay right where you are.'

Slaney leaned over and kissed her gently as he stood up and made for the kitchen, his glass in his hand.

As he put on the striped pinafore and opened the fridge he tried not to think how it must feel when a woman has had both breasts removed and then they tell her it was too late but with the treatment she'd got somewhere between nine and eighteen months to live. It had been like a nightmare for the first few weeks after they discharged her from the hospital. That was four months ago and she'd lost ten pounds in that time.

As he cracked the eggs into the red plastic bowl he closed his eyes and said one of his quick silent prayers. There were never any words, he just thought a prayer. If there was a God he'd get the message. He didn't believe in a God but he was a good administrator who instinctively planned for all possible eventualities. But the unspoken, imagined prayer gave him a few moments' peace. Even the problems and crises of his daily work were a relief from the mental treadmill of how to deal with the situation in his home.

Willoughby shared a flat with one of his contemporaries who worked for the Soviet desk, a section that had been controlled by Tarrant before the legal chaos had developed. The office had had no objections to the sharing arrangements. Porter was too obviously macho for any suspicions of a sexual relationship. Despite the strict rules they gossiped freely about their office colleagues and the operations they were concerned with. They were both in their early thirties but they seemed younger than their years. There was an air of beer mugs and rugby clubs about them, and their cynicism was more a pose than a reality.

Porter grinned. 'What was she like?'

'A real doll. Better than the file photographs.'

'Did she actually say she wanted you to screw her?'

'Not in so many words but she really wanted it. No doubt about it.'

'I wonder how Johnny Tarrant got stuck with a bitch like that?'

Willoughby pointed at his beer. 'I don't think much of this keg.' He paused and looked at Porter. 'What d'you say? Oh yes, Johnny Tarrant. I guess it was sex, and who could blame him? Have you seen him at all since this started?'

'A couple of times. He's like a bloody zombie. I was filling him in on the current operations and I swear he never heard a word. Just stared at the window. It's a bloody shame.'

'What's he like?'

'Johnny? He's a real professional. Cool and efficient. Tough as old boots and with all the moves worked out in advance. Just like a chess master.'

'What's he like as a chap?'

'Hard to say. He's friendly as long as you do your job well but he can be very acid if anybody fumbles the ball.'

'D'you like him?'

'You bet. I'd be very happy if I thought I could end up like him.'

Johnny Tarrant only half listened to the news headlines as he sipped his coffee and ate the single piece of buttered toast.

As he stood up he looked around the flat. It wasn't really a flat. A poky little kitchen. A small toilet and shower and the one room with its divan bed not very well disguised as a couch with a couple of silk cushions. Two wicker armchairs and a glass-topped coffee-table were the only new pieces of furniture in the room. There were no pictures on the walls and no books on the empty shelves. On the cast-iron mantelshelf was a cheap digital clock and a small plastic model of a Westland Lysander.

He sighed as he looked around the room. He had moved in two weeks ago and he knew that this was how it was going to be for a long, long time. This tatty room was now his home. Then he looked down at his suit, a light grey gaberdine suit with narrow, faint chalk stripes. Almost without thinking he walked over to the larger of the two leather cases lying open on the bed. Maybe it didn't matter what suit he wore, but it could be that a light-coloured suit might be considered as showing disrespect for the court or the occasion.

He changed hurriedly into a dark blue suit and swapped over his keys, wallet and coins. He was panting, breathless, when he finally stood ready, and he closed his eyes, aware and afraid of the indecision that seemed to have infected his mind for so long. He had never been indecisive, nor afraid, before, but these days he clutched at the most ridiculous straws. Reading the fate of Scorpios in the *Evening Standard*, treading furtively on the joins in the paving stones, wondering what lay behind the things that people said. Fearing their antagonism if they said too little but suspecting that they were only embarrassed or covering up if they chatted too readily.

As he got to the door he looked around the room again and it was then that he remembered the bundle of papers on the coffee-table. Stiff, creamy paper with its sheets held together by the pink ribbon threaded through the punched holes. It was folded twice but its stiffness left it lying open like a trap for some small animal. He went back for it, thrusting it into the inside pocket of his jacket.

He waved down a taxi in King's Road aware that it was

an extravagance. He knew that he had to get back to the thinking of the old days when taxis were only for desperate emergencies. There was one of the royal coaches turning out from the gates of the Royal Mews as the taxi slowed down in Buckingham Palace Road. It seemed a long time ago when he had paced up and down that piece of road before he went in to the investiture. Then standing outside the palace gates with Jenny as somebody photographed them looking at the medal in its open case. The three narrow white stripes on the purple ribbon of the Order of the British Empire. Despite what he'd said at the time he'd been quite proud of it. Apart from his commission and promotions it had been the first mark of approval that he had ever received from any form of authority.

They had married three weeks later, before he went back to the embassy in Warsaw. He'd been twenty-three and she was just nineteen. 'Pongo' Wallace had been his best man and a witness. Her mother had refused to come to the wedding.

CHAPTER 2

She was standing at the far end of the corridor, outside the court-rooms, nodding as the taller of the two men spoke to her. The other man was Martin, her solicitor. Their solicitor once, but now just hers. In Tarrant v. Tarrant. He guessed that the taller man was her counsel.

It was her birthday next month and she would be twenty-nine years old. But as he looked at her she looked much the same as she had looked the day he had first seen her at that club. She had one of those faces that improve year by year. It was probably those big blue eyes with their heavy lids and long lashes that did it. When they looked at you it was like being hypnotised. And the full sensuous mouth, its lips always slightly open, the glint of white teeth in the centre. She was wearing a black tailored suit edged with black braid. And she wore a hat. It was what Martin would have advised her to wear to court to give her an air of vulnerability, as if she were a widow rather than the plaintiff in a divorce case. And the tight white sweater that emphasised her beautiful breasts. Part of the reward a man might get for helping her in her hour of trouble. He felt the sour taste of bile in his mouth as his anger and frustration surged through him. And he prayed that she would look his way and see him. And walk across to tell him that it wasn't going to happen. That she was coming back to him because he was the only man she'd ever loved.

Then he was aware of Sellars looking at him as if he were waiting for an answer to some question.

'I was daydreaming. What did you say?'

'When you're giving evidence they'll try to provoke you. Try to make you angry. Don't rise to the bait no matter what they say. They want the court to get the impression that you're violent and quick-tempered. It's an old dodge but all too often it works.'

'I'll do my best.'

Sellars looked at him, shaking his head. 'Not your best, Johnny. Just don't respond at all. Just remember, she goes on first, and she'll be cool, calm and collected. The patient, forgiving wife who finally threw in the towel. Violence, drunkenness, unfaithfulness, jealousy and finally driven from the marital home. You've seen the stuff in her statement and you've seen the affidavits. It'll all be used, and it's up to you to stay calm.'

'How do you think it'll go, Sellars?'

Sellars shrugged. 'You never can tell. It's unfortunate that we've got old Rawlings. He's very susceptible to a pretty face.'

Tarrant nodded without speaking. It had happened often enough. It sometimes seemed as though the whole world was susceptible to that particular pretty face. Then his heart leapt she turned her head and looked at him. For a moment or so they looked at each other and then she turned away, putting her hand on Martin's arm, smiling up at him as she said something that made him smile. The bitch. To hell with her, there were plenty of other pretty women. He'd live the life of Riley. Free and independent at last. Then, driven by one of those terrible impulses that sometimes swept aside his reason he turned to Sellars.

'I don't believe she wants it, you know. Maybe I ought to go over and have a word with her.'

Sellars took a deep breath, hesitating before he spoke.

Not wanting to hurt but anxious to avoid any sort of incident.

'I shouldn't do that, Johnny. Just stay calm. Even if she's granted a decree there's three months before it's made absolute. You've got a good case. Let's not rock the boat.'

'You really think I *have* got a good case?'

'Of course I do or I would have advised you not to defend it. The courts can recognise provocation when they hear it. Why not pop downstairs and have a cup of tea? I'll come down for you when they call us.'

'I'll just hang on, Sellars. They might want to talk to us. Some last-minute change of mind. You know what women are.'

Sellars took his arm gently, turning him so that they walked slowly towards the stone steps that led down to the main hall. At the top of the steps Sellars stopped.

'Listen carefully to what I say, Johnny. This isn't just a divorce case. It's your career. You know that as well as I do. Your people have spoken to me. They'll stand by you whichever way it goes but if you cooperate it'll make a big difference.'

Tarrant shook his head. 'They don't understand, Sellars. I'm sick of taking a beating from her.'

'Johnny. Listen to me. They're on your side. They know that she's a first class bitch. They're no fools. They understand. They're on your side.'

'I wish I could believe you.'

'Would it really make a difference?'

Tarrant sighed. 'You don't know what it's like, Sellars. She twists them round her finger. I haven't a friend left.' He paused. 'Even Tony Martin's sided with her.'

'He's not. That's ridiculous. He's just doing his job.'

'That's not true. Tony Martin was my friend long before I knew her. We were at school together. But he's acting for her not me.'

15

'That's because she went to him first.'

'He could have turned her down or recommended someone else.'

'He'd have no grounds for doing that. He's a professional.'

'Rubbish. He's a man and she gives him that smile and sticks out her tits and that's it.'

'I happen to know that he not only doesn't like her, he detests her. He didn't like her when you were married to her. He thinks she's a phoney and a liar.'

'You're just saying that to cool me down.'

'I'm not. He told me so.'

For a long time Tarrant was silent, then he said, 'D'you mean that? You're not just calming me down?'

'Of course I mean it. He's not fooled by her story nor impressed by her attractions. Nobody is.'

Suddenly the tension of months ebbed away and Johnny Tarrant said quietly, 'What do you want me to do?'

Sellars took a deep breath and said slowly, 'I want you to go home. I don't want to put you on the stand. Let her have her fling. Treat it for what it's worth. Nothing. She'll be granted a divorce but the moral victory will be yours. She's set her heart on seeing you on the stand being put through the mincer. Don't give her that last pleasure, Johnny. Do what I ask.'

Tarrant nodded. 'You'll let me know what happens?'

'Of course.' He looked back at the younger man's face. 'It's time to get back to normality, Johnny. Learn the lessons and call it a day.'

'Thanks for what you told me. I wish I'd known before.'

'It was a gross breach of professional etiquette to tell you about what Martin told me. But it needed to be said.'

Sellars watched the young man walk down the wide stone steps and across the hall to the doors that led to the Strand.

16

CHAPTER 3

Powell knew exactly how he wanted it to go but he'd had a word with Slaney first. Protocol required that courtesy on several grounds. Firstly, Slaney was Tarrant's present boss, secondly they were taking Tarrant away, and thirdly, and more importantly, Slaney had been involved in the Foster business right from the start. But Slaney had gone along with Powell's intentions without any obvious resentment.

It meant arranging the meeting with Mitchell and Willis somewhere away from Century House and he'd taken a small room at the Reform where they could talk freely. Or as freely as their natural caution allowed. He ordered a cold buffet for them so that they wouldn't need a waiter. There were a couple of bottles of both white and red wine available. Run of the cellar stuff, and a coffee percolator on a trolley with the appropriate bits and pieces. Powell had family money behind him and that gave him an instinct for watching the pennies even if they were SIS pennies.

They sat in leather club armchairs around a low, glass-topped coffee-table, and when he had checked that everyone had had a bite or two he set the ball rolling. He was a grade above the other two in the hierarchy and he was just about to say, 'You've seen . . .' when he realised that what he was about to say would sound patronising. Got to be 'we' not 'you'.

'I expect we've all had a chance of considering the

sitreps on the GDR.' He smiled, rather frostily. 'Looks like somebody's turned the tap from simmer to boil. And I thought we ought, perhaps, to think about our friend "F".'

He looked at the other two, satisfied that he'd sounded as if their views really mattered. It was Willis who responded, frowning as he said, 'Who set that up originally?'

Powell shrugged. 'I guess it was Slaney, but it was a desperate solution for a desperate problem.'

'So what's the problem now?'

Powell smiled. 'The same as it always was.'

'Tell me.'

It was Mitchell who intervened. He'd been part of the Berlin team when it all happened. 'First of all we've no idea where he is and more important we've got the usual problem we have with double agents – whose side is he really on.' He paused as he poured himself a coffee. When he looked back at Willis he said, 'Usually we've at least a chance of talking to the man and trying to form a judgment. We haven't seen our friend since he went over the Wall.'

Mitchell shrugged. 'So why don't we just carry on as we've been doing?'

Powell took over again. 'Because things are falling apart the other side of the Wall. Sooner or later he'll have to make up his mind where he belongs. Us or the KGB. From the information we're getting we probably only have months to influence him.'

'Does he matter all that much?'

Powell frowned. 'He's the only real asset we have who could provide information about the other side.' He paused. 'I have in mind sending someone to see if they can find him and give us an idea of how things stand.'

'Who've you got in mind?'

'Tarrant.'

'How much would you tell him?'

'As little as possible. Just enough to head him in what I hope might be the right direction.'

Mitchell shook his head slowly. 'Slaney won't like all that stuff being raked up again.'

Powell shrugged. 'I shall warn Tarrant to be very diplomatic.'

'Have you any idea of which way our friend will jump if things fall apart in East Germany?'

'Not a clue. That's what we need to find out.'

'Could mean another body going down the Swanee.'

'So be it.'

Willis stood up and strolled to the window, looking out before turning to look at Powell.

'Why Tarrant?'

Powell had been waiting for it. 'He's tough, he's experienced, and he speaks good German and passable Russian. And he's a good judge of people.' Conscious of Willis's lifted eyebrows he shrugged and added. 'Of men anyway.'

'How much is it a device to get Tarrant out of the mainstream for a bit?'

'He just happens to be uncommitted at the moment,' Powell said sharply, and Willis took the hint. 'What can I do to help, Tony?'

Powell said a little too quickly to sound spontaneous, 'I'll need funding arrangements in Berlin and . . .' looking at Mitchell, '. . . he'll need documentation from your section.'

Mitchell looked puzzled. 'Why doesn't he use our facilities in Berlin?'

'He won't be attached to them. He'll be on his own.'

'Have you told him yet?'

'No. When I have I'll get him to talk to you both direct.'

Powell moved on to the Special Section budget reviews that were up for consideration in two months' time. Willis and Mitchell were well aware that Powell was chairman of the sub-committee that decided their budgets. There was no hint of any connection with their previous discussion but as the two of them shared a taxi to Victoria Station Willis said, 'What do you think that was all about?'

Mitchell smiled. 'You're kidding.'

'I'm not.'

'Well the bit about Tarrant will mean that Powell can claim that he discussed the operation with us before it was initiated. So if it goes down the pan the responsibility is ours as well as his.'

'But we neither agreed nor disagreed. He didn't even ask if we agreed.'

'But neither of us said we disagreed.'

'How could we? I don't know enough about what he has in mind to even comment.'

Mitchell laughed softly. 'You could write him a considered memo that puts on record that you disagree.'

'I don't necessarily disagree.'

Mitchell laughed. 'Precisely. Neither do I.'

Powell had gone out of his way to show a friendliness to Tarrant that was not entirely genuine. In his code Johnny Tarrant had got what he asked for. The woman was a slut. Admittedly she was a singularly beautiful slut but that was no excuse. A man didn't have to marry that kind of woman to get what he wanted. Bad judgment. But Tarrant was an efficient field-officer and in Powell's view that was what mattered. All that training and all that experience could not be wasted because of one rash action. And Powell shared the view of several senior SIS officers that any man who chose to be a field-officer was suspect anyway. Despite the façade of the cool loner they were, in fact, nearly always over-emotional and reckless in their private lives.

He pointed to the chair. 'Make yourself comfortable, Johnny.' And as Tarrant sat down Powell looked him over. He certainly looked calm and more alert. Maybe the storm really had blown itself out.

'Before we get down to business, Johnny, let me say that you have the sympathy of all of us for the problems you've been having over the last few months. I think you dealt with them in a very sophisticated and sensible way. It's a great temptation to fight one's corner but it seldom pays once the lawyers are involved.' He nodded briefly. 'Anyway, well done.' He paused and smiled. 'Let's turn to a more worthwhile subject – your career.' Powell leant back in his leather chair. 'D'you remember one of our chaps called Foster?'

'I've heard the name but I didn't know him. There was some cock-up in Berlin, wasn't there?'

Powell pursed his lips. 'That's one way of describing it, I suppose. It was a bit more complicated than that. And it certainly wasn't a cock-up. Let's say there was a difference of opinion between Foster and our people in Berlin at the time. Foster rather took it to heart.'

Tarrant raised his eyebrows. 'What's that mean when it's translated?'

Powell smiled. 'Put crudely – Foster walked out.'

'And?'

Powell shrugged. 'That's the problem. We're not sure about what happened after that.'

'When did all this happen?'

'Just over a year ago – back-end of '87.'

'Why the sudden interest in him now?'

'To the best of our knowledge, or to be more precise our best guess is that he's somewhere in Germany. We don't even know which Germany – West or East. Could be either. Things are getting out of hand the other side of the Wall and we need to know where he is for several reasons. There are . . .'

Tarrant interrupted. 'What makes you so sure that he's in Germany anyway?'

'At this stage I don't want to go into that.' He paused. 'Apart from security problems our reading of the situation could be misleading.'

'And when I find him?'

'Ah yes. When you find him.' He paused and looked at Tarrant. 'One of the reasons why you were chosen for this mission was that you've got a good nose for . . .' he just managed to avoid saying 'deceivers' and changed it to '. . . for phoney agents. We want you to locate him but not contact him. Do a full surveillance, life-style, habits, friends, contacts, finances – that sort of thing. When we give you the go-ahead to contact him we'll come to the crux of the matter. With the present unrest . . . whose side is he going to end up on? Ours or theirs. He isn't going to tell you the truth. You've got to know enough to decide for us what we should do.'

'Do about what?'

'Deciding whose side he's on and what to do about it.'

'You think he might want to come back?'

'It's possible.'

'Have there been any approaches that way from him?'

'No, none.'

'And if he wants to come back?'

Powell smiled. 'Sufficient unto the day etcetera.'

'Who was in charge of the British operation when he walked out?'

'Slaney was in charge.' He paused and took a deep breath. 'There are others around who were in Berlin at that time. I'd rather you left Slaney out of it. For the moment anyway.'

'Why is that?'

'He's got problems at the moment. We don't want to add to them unnecessarily.'

Tarrant shrugged. 'If that's how you want it. When do you want me to start?'

'Soon as you can but take a few days' leave before you

go.' He paused. 'You'll be on your own. Facilities are opening a bank account for you in Berlin and Mr Mitchell has been told to provide you with any documentation you might need.'

Powell stood up and Tarrant knew that he was being dismissed. But Powell walked with him to the door. 'There's a rather skimpy briefing file for you with my secretary and there's a day and night number in the notes that you can use to contact me whenever you feel it's necessary. Best of luck.'

In the outer office Powell's secretary handed him a large but thin envelope and asked him to sign a receipt for what was described as 'Miscellaneous 504'.

As he took the elevator to his own floor he was well aware that Powell had described it as a 'mission'. 'Mission' was the official euphemism for an operation that didn't work out. It sounded like a wild-goose chase. Or was it Powell and Slaney getting together to give him something to occupy his mind? Something that was vague and probably pointless? A touch of mystery here and there to exercise the brain?

Tarrant got a coffee from the machine and went to his small office. He always had small offices. He wasn't at Century House often enough to warrant anything elaborate. He hung his jacket over the back of his chair and broke the seal on the envelope, tipping the contents onto his desk. The photographs slid out first. There were three of them, and half a dozen A4 pages of double-spaced typing.

He turned over the photographs but there was nothing on the back to identify them. One was obviously a family snap. A man and a woman and a young boy, standing in a garden all of them looking impassively towards the camera. The second was a man in his twenties in uniform. In his best barathea, a lieutenant with an Intelligence

Corps badge on his cap. The kind of photograph that
people had done when they'd just finished their training
at Templer Barracks. And the last was a square photograph, a full-face, the kind that goes on an ID card. Dark
hair, dark eyes, bushy eyebrows, a strong jaw, a determined mouth and a broad blob of a nose. It was obviously
taken more recently than the other photograph. There
was a tension about the eyes and the mouth.

There was a copy of a birth certificate that showed that
Foster was born in August 1952 in a military hospital near
Hanover. Father's occupation – regular soldier, a sergeant
in the Royal Corps of Signals, British Army of the Rhine.
Mother Helga. There was a school report from King
Edward's School, Aston, Birmingham, that indicated that
Foster had been a very bright pupil. There was a photostat
copy of a newspaper clipping from the *Birmingham Mail*,
September 1970. Charlie Foster the eighteen year-old son
of Councillor Eddie Foster had turned down a place at
Aston University to follow in his father's footsteps in the
Royal Corps of Signals. His mother, Ingrid Foster, was a
language teacher at the Ursuline Convent in Erdington.

The other pages read more like an obituary than an SIS
report on a missing agent. But it did record that Captain
Foster had come into conflict with the head of the SIS
team in West Berlin. A conflict which appeared not to
have been resolved when two weeks later Captain Foster
had not reported for duty and when his accommodation
had been searched it looked as if it had not been occupied
for several days. A check had been made at Tegel and it
was noted that Foster had booked a British Airways flight
to Dublin via Heathrow. A further note indicated that the
seat on the flight had not been taken up.

There was nothing about an enquiry into the incident
but a report had been made to MI5 from which no action
was recorded. As he pushed the papers back into the
envelope and shoved it into the bottom drawer of his desk

he knew that his first reaction to Powell was correct. It was a cock-up. It stank of a cover-up and he realised that even the report itself was continuing the cover-up. He was onto a loser. Either that or it was the brass's idea of a bit of therapy to take his mind off the happenings of the last few months.

He looked at his watch and then dialled Powell's number on the internal phone. Powell answered himself and when Tarrant asked him how long he'd got on the assignment Powell said 'as long as it took'. He also said that ample funds were available and any facilities he needed at Century House were also available. Thinking about the call to Powell as he took a taxi back to the dump in Fulham he wondered if maybe he was wrong. You didn't get unlimited funds and a full run of facilities unless they meant business.

He picked up the mail at his room and read it as he waited for the kettle to boil for his tea. There was a reminder from the library in Chelsea about an overdue book, an offer to quote him for double-glazing, and a couple of letters from people he knew offering condolences about the divorce. One from a man whom he had always disliked made the dislike even more obviously warranted by 'regretting the sordid details that he had read in the *News of the World*'. There was a statement from the bank that showed him more in credit than he expected. The last letter he opened was from his solicitor. At the meeting at the court to decide the question of maintenance the judge had ruled that Jenny was young and healthy and perfectly capable of providing for herself. A nominal one pound a week would be awarded her so that the matter could be reopened if necessary in the future. Costs had been awarded against him but it was only likely to be a few hundreds.

As he put the tea-bag in the mug and poured in the hot

water he wondered what he should do to celebrate. She would be livid at the court's decision. She had expected to wipe him out financially and despite what his own people had said about things being different these days on maintenance he'd taken it for granted that she'd succeed. As he sipped his tea, he smiled to himself as he imagined her reaction to the news.

He collected all his belongings and packed them into two suitcases. There was no need for him to stay any longer in that miserable dump. He'd drive down to his father's place and spend a couple of days resting and sorting himself out. It wasn't far from Birmingham and he could drive over and talk with Foster's father.

CHAPTER 4

There was a Granada estate parked beside the barn and he eased the MG in behind it. He could see his father standing talking to a woman by the farmhouse door. His father acknowledged him with a wave and he guessed that he didn't want to be disturbed because he was talking business.

His father was a handsome man who older women said looked like Jack Buchanan. Tall and elegant, he had a charm that seemed to work on both men and women. And it would be reasonable for a stranger to guess that he was an actor, but in fact, his father had been a sergeant in SAS and was then commissioned in the Intelligence Corps because of his languages. He never talked about what his work had been but Johnny assumed it must have been SIS or something else like it. There were people in Century House who had talked to him about his father. Anecdotes that emphasised toughness rather than charm. When he retired he and a colleague had built up a prosperous business in selling sports cars and eventually were given a Jaguar dealership. And now, in his sixties, he lived off the profits of the car business but spent his time and earned more money selling antiques which were stored in the stables. He watched as the woman sat down on a wooden bench at the side of a garden table. She took a cheque book from her handbag and made out a cheque, waving it in the air to dry the ink before handing it to his father. They walked together towards Johnny and his father introduced her to his son. As she turned to go to the Granada she said, 'When can you have it delivered, Tommy?'

'How about tomorrow morning?'

'That would be fine.' She smiled. 'Time for me to break the news to Arthur.'

'I'll buy it back from you at the same price any time you want, my dear.'

As they stood watching the woman drive off Tarrant's father said, 'There goes a George III mahogany bureau bookcase with swan-neck pediment on ogee bracket feet.'

'How much does that set her back?'

'Five thousand pounds.'

'Would you really buy it back if she wanted you to?'

'Like a shot. I buy only the best but I buy it hard. And I sell at less margin than most dealers would. My customers know that. If she wanted to dispose of it she could get more than I've charged her, even from a dealer.' He smiled. 'And what are you doing here?'

'A couple of days' rest and recuperation if that's OK.'

'You don't even have to ask – you know that. Your room's always there.'

They had eaten at the village pub and walked back to the farmhouse.

'Coffee?' his father said, smiling. 'Only instant, I'm afraid.'

Johnny smiled back. 'I'm used to instant. I rather like it.'

When his father came back with mugs of coffee they watched the late news on TV until the station closed down.

'How d'you like my white MG?'

'Magnolia, not white. Sounds like the tappets need adjusting. I'll do it for you tomorrow. How long have you had it?'

'A couple of months.'

'What happened to the Mustang?'

'Jenny was going to claim it as hers so I flogged it.' He shrugged. 'That was a mistake.'

'Why?'

'The court decided she was young and healthy and quite capable of supporting herself. They awarded her a nominal amount only.'

'How nominal?'

'A quid a week. Which is the least they give. But I've got her costs and mine to pay.'

'How much?'

'Just a few hundreds.'

'And how about you? How are you making out?'

He sighed and shrugged. 'I'm getting by.'

'And the job?'

'They were very decent but they've put me onto something different. It means I'll be spending most of my time in Germany for the next few months.'

'You going sideways or down?'

Johnny smiled. 'Neither so far as I can tell. I think the new job is meant to occupy the mind – take it off other things.'

'Can burn you up these things if you don't put them behind you.'

'Did it burn you up when Momma walked out?'

'For a time it did. You never entirely forget that piece of your life. That's the problem with that sort of woman. They're bad but they ain't all bad. Well-meaning people try to comfort you by running them down, and you end up realising how wrong their judgments are and it's kinda sad. You end up wanting to defend somebody you despise for entirely different reasons.'

'You never talked to me about it.'

'She was your mother. I knew you'd have your own views about her. Why should I spoil it. Anyway, like your girl she had her points.'

29

'Like what?'

His father smiled. 'They were both very pretty. They must have had something or we shouldn't have married them. We must have loved them for something. So let it ride. Forget them.'

'Do you ever think about her?'

'Yes. On her birthday and at railway stations.'

'Why railway stations?'

'Like you I was away a lot, so there were lots of good-byes on railway stations. And some nice welcomes too. It can't be much fun being married to a guy who leaves home in the morning and the next thing you hear from him is a phone call from Stockholm or Bonn.'

'Other wives get by.'

'Sure they do. But they're intelligent. They've got more interests than just screwing or going to parties.' He smiled. 'You and I chose them because they were real beauties. Long legs and all the trimmings. But we kidded ourselves they had virtues they didn't have. And maybe we weren't such great prizes ourselves.'

'You're a very honest man.'

'If you kid yourself you've had it.' He stood up. 'Time for kip. See you tomorrow.'

He turned as he got to the door as if he were going to say something, then smiled, raising his clenched fist as he left.

When his father had left Johnny made his way to the kitchen. It was still a typical old-fashioned farmhouse kitchen except for the Aga cooker. The farm had been 400 acres but his father had bought only the farmhouse and five acres of paddocks for his wife's horses. The stables were now used to house cars and antiques but once they had housed Gabby's horses. His father had left them there for a year in case she came back but one day he'd walked down there before he went back to university and the doors stood open, creaking on their hinges in the wind and, inside, the stables had been cleared of straw and tackle. His father had never told him, nor had he ever asked, what had happened to make him bring it to an end.

He made himself a glass of warm milk and honey and leaned against the heavy, oak table sipping the drink slowly as he thought about what his father had said. Other people had commiserated with him and criticised Jenny, but even knowing that she'd lost out on the settlement hadn't really been a consolation. But although he had said so little his father had shown him how to draw a line under it all and start again. What had seemed like a tragedy had become just an episode from which you learned some lessons about life and yourself. How to have a heart and a mind that was a bit bigger than other men's. Not dodging the issues but looking at the facts so that you learned something out of the mess. In half an hour his father had done more than all the others. Showed him how a real man dealt with such things. He felt strangely calm and ready to get on with his life again.

CHAPTER 5

Tarrant turned off the M6 early to avoid Spaghetti Junction and made his way through Erdington to Sutton Coldfield. He had checked hotels with the RAC and the one they recommended was near Sutton Park and not more than ten minutes' walk to Foster senior's home address. After booking in he had a beer and a sandwich in the bar and checked the street map.

The house was right at the edge of the park. A four bedroomed detached house that was obviously well cared for. The young woman who answered the door seemed to be a servant and she told him that Mr Foster was at the shop on The Parade. It had a Foster Electrics sign and was next to a café. Not more than a ten-minute walk.

The shop itself was double-fronted, one window displayed refrigerators and washing machines and the other a wide selection of radio and TVs. The double entrance doors were wide open and as Tarrant walked inside a young man asked if he could help.

'I'd like to speak to Mr Foster.'

The young man looked around and nodded towards a man who was showing a lady a TV set. 'That's Mr Foster. He won't be long.'

The young man walked over to Foster and spoke to him. He looked at Tarrant, nodded and smiled before he turned back to his customer.

According to the file Eddie Foster must be sixty-two or sixty-three, and apart from being heavily built he looked

33

fit and young for his age. His hair was still black and there were no jowls at the rather pugnacious jaw. Well dressed in a blue three-piece suit and well-polished black shoes he looked a typical successful businessman. He walked with his customer past Tarrant to the door and saw her out before turning to Tarrant.

'What can I do for you, sir?'

'I wanted to talk to you, Mr Foster.'

Foster smiled. 'That's what I'm here for. How can I help?'

'Is there anywhere we could talk privately?'

'Of course. Is it hire-purchase you're interested in? We do our own financing.' He smiled. 'Saves us both money.'

Tarrant followed him to a small office and Foster opened the door and waved him inside, closing the door behind him.

'What was it you were interested in?'

'I wanted to ask you about your son. Charlie.'

For long moments Foster stood looking at Tarrant's face, his eyes unblinking until he turned away and looked towards a small window where there was a begonia in a plastic pot.

When he turned back to Tarrant he said quietly, 'Show me your ID.'

'I'm not a police officer, Mr Foster.'

'I didn't think you were. I've been through all this caper before.' He paused. 'So what are you?'

'I'm from one of the government services.'

'MI5?'

'No.'

'The other one?'

Tarrant shrugged. 'It's only a routine enquiry. We'd just like to close the file.'

'What is it you want to know?'

'I just want to talk with you about Charlie.'

'Did you know him?'

'No. I'd heard of him vaguely but I never met him.'

'Your people looking for Charlie? That what it is?'

'They'd like to make contact with him some way.'

'Why?'

'Like I said. To clear it up once and for all. Write it off.'

'How long have you been with these people?'

'About ten years.' He paused. 'Do you know where Charlie is, Mr Foster?'

'No, I don't. And if I did I shouldn't tell you. If he wanted to make contact with you people he'd do it direct.'

'If I contacted him would you be interested in knowing where he is?'

'Are you one of Slaney's men?'

'I worked for him at one time but not at the moment.'

'What's he got to say about Charlie?'

'I don't know, I haven't talked with him about it.'

'Why not?'

'He's got some personal problems and they asked me not to bother him.' He paused. 'I'm not sure, but I think his wife has got cancer. That's what I heard, but it was only office chatter.'

Foster was silent for a few moments. 'Are you in a hurry?'

'No. I came specially to see you.'

'Where you staying?'

'At a hotel. I think it's called The Yenton or something like that.'

'I'll take you back to the house. We can talk easier there.'

'That's very kind of you.'

'I'll just tell my manager I'm off. Hold on.'

When he came back Foster took him through a back door into a service yard. There were two small vans with the shop's name on them. Foster's car was an old, but beautifully preserved Rover 90 which still smelt of leather as Tarrant got in the passenger seat.

It took less than five minutes for them to arrive at the house. Foster took him inside and Tarrant followed him into what was obviously a study.

'Tea, coffee or a beer?'

'Tea would suit me fine if it's convenient.'

'Sit down. I'll go and tell the girl.'

When he was alone Tarrant looked around the room. The furniture was obviously expensive reproduction but the only personal effects were the books and he stood looking at them. There was a whole row of Left Book Club books. At least a couple of dozen. A translation of the Koran and several biographies of Marx and Lenin and a few titles on the history of the Soviet Union. Two books of German poetry and a copy of Palgrave in a leather library binding. A few novels from the thirties and forties. Four Arnold Bennetts including the Potteries novels. A German bible and a book on comparative religions. A biography of Field-Marshal Montgomery and one of Rommel. There were two or three histories of England including Carr's and Trevelyan's. And then Foster came back in and Tarrant turned to watch him as he put a tray with tea-things on a low table. Foster pointed at one of the leather armchairs.

'Make yourself comfortable. You a reader, mister?'

'Just thrillers, I'm afraid. My name's Tarrant. Johnny Tarrant.'

Foster stopped with his cup on the way to his mouth.

'Tarrant. Tarrant. I knew a Tarrant. In BAOR. He was 30 Corps or 21 AG. Handsome chap; Max, was it?'

Tarrant smiled. 'Sounds like my old man. But his name was Tom.'

'That's it. Tommy Tarrant. He was in Field Security in Hanover or was it Brunswick?'

'I don't know. He never talks about those days.'

'Married a dancer or a singer.'

'That was his first wife. It didn't last long. Then he married my mother. She was what they called a society girl. That lasted longer but she left him some years ago. He's got an antiques business now.'

'Good for him. I'm on my own too. My wife, Charlie's mother, died a year ago. Nobody else'd ever take her place with me. She was very fond of the lad. Wanted him to be an academic like her father. German she was. They kicked up a hell of a stink when I wanted to marry her. Enemy alien and all that crap, and me in Signals Security. Pompous bastards. But I wrote to my MP. I don't know what he did but it worked the trick. Her father taught history at Göttingen University. Lovely man.' Foster paused for a moment and then said, 'Who else have you talked to about Charlie?'

'Nobody. You're the first.'

'Did they tell you why he walked out on them?'

'No. I gathered there was some sort of cock-up in Berlin.' He smiled. 'But if we walked every time there's a cock-up there'd be none of us left.'

'They were fools. They could have done what he wanted and that would have satisfied him.'

'What was it he wanted?'

Foster opened his mouth to speak and then decided against it and just shook his head. Then he said, 'Talk to the others who were in Berlin at the time.'

'Anyone in particular?'

'Try Shelley or Malins. They're still there in Berlin.'

'Charlie obviously told you what had happened.'

'Yes. He came here for a couple of days when he was arguing with them. He told me about it. I spoke to Slaney and warned him but he just said that Charlie telling me about it was an offence in itself. Quoted the Official Secrets Act at me. I hung up on him.'

'Did Charlie tell you what he was going to do?'

'Not really.'

'What's that mean?'

'He hinted.'

'What did you say to him?'

'I advised him not to do it. So did his mother. She was still alive then.'

'Did Charlie have a steady girl-friend?'

Tarrant saw the quick suspicion in Eddie Foster's eyes as he said, 'Why d'you ask that?'

Tarrant shrugged. 'Just to get a picture of the man. He wasn't married so maybe he had a girl-friend somewhere.'

'He reckoned that marriages didn't go well with his kind of work.'

Tarrant smiled. 'He was right too.' He stood up. 'Thanks for your cooperation, Mr Foster. I'll let you know if I'm able to locate Charlie.'

Foster offered him a lift but the hotel was only a short walk away. Foster saw him to the door and gave him directions to the hotel. But as Tarrant walked past the entrance to Sutton Park he turned back and followed a signpost that said, 'Wyndley Pool'.

There were few people about in the park. It was that in-between time when mothers with small children had gone home and the evening strollers were only just leaving work.

He sat watching a mallard with her brood of ducklings on the pond. There had been no point in prolonging his interview with Eddie Foster. There had been clues enough in what he'd said and more in what he hadn't said. He knew where his son was or he'd have wanted to be kept informed about him trying to locate him. And wherever Charlie Foster was his father knew that he was OK. He wasn't worried about what his son was doing. And he obviously resented what Slaney had done in Berlin. The answer was in Berlin. Eddie Foster was a straightforward man, an honest man. He had probably told no lies, he just hadn't given anything away. But Tarrant felt that whatever Charlie was doing his father didn't really go along with it. It was something he had become reconciled to since Charlie had been away.

There was no need to stay overnight and back at the hotel Tarrant paid his bill, checked out and headed back to his home.

His father was out when he got back but there was a note on his bed that said he would be back by 11 p.m. and he was to phone a man named Powell who had phoned during the day.

He used the phone in the kitchen and dialled Powell's number.

'Powell.'

'Tarrant. I had a message to call you.'

'Ah yes. I should have mentioned this the other day when I briefed you. When you're talking to people about our friend, especially the people in Berlin, don't let it be known that you're looking for him or that we're concerned in any way. Let it be just casual stuff. You're interested personally or maybe it's a belated exercise to ensure that such a thing doesn't happen again. I leave it to you. Just make it low-key.' He paused. 'How'd you get on with old man Foster?'

'How did you know I'd seen him?'

'Your father said you'd gone to Birmingham. I just put two and two together.'

'He wouldn't talk but I'm sure he knows where Charlie Foster is.'

'Does he now? Anything else?'

'He blames Slaney for what happened. He's very bitter about it.'

'Ah well. What's your next move?'

'I'll go to Berlin at the weekend.'

'Best of luck.'

'Thanks.'

Tarrant smiled as he hung up. Powell sounded a bit edgy. He wasn't the kind of man who wished people luck.

The next day Tarrant went down to the village shop with a shopping list that his father had made out. When he got back he saw that his father's Jaguar had gone and there was another car parked in front of the cottage. It was a car he recognised. A green Morgan with a personalised number plate with the prefix TM. It was Tony Martin's car.

The front door as usual was open and he walked though to the living room.

Tony Martin was looking out of the window and turned to look at Tarrant as he closed the door behind him.

'Hello, Johnny,' he said quietly. 'Your father said I could wait.'

Tarrant nodded and pointed at a chair. 'Sit down.'

When they were both seated Tarrant said, 'If it's about Jenny and money you're wasting your time.'

Tony Martin smiled briefly. 'It is about Jenny but it's not about money.' He paused. 'I contacted your solicitor and explained what I wanted to talk to you about and he agreed that I could see you if you agreed.'

'If it's some legal thing you should talk to him not me.'

'In a way it's legal but not in any adversarial way.'

Tarrant shrugged. 'So what is it?'

'How long did you know Jenny before you married her?'

'About a month. Give or take a few days.'

'Can I ask you why you married her?'

Tarrant shook his head. 'God knows. I was just a fool.'

'You're nobody's fool, Johnny. And never have been. There must have been a reason.'

'OK. She was very beautiful.'

Tony Martin smiled. 'You'd had dozens of pretty girl-friends, Johnny. It must have been more than that.'

'Maybe. Who knows?'

'Why do you think she divorced you?'

Tarrant's face flushed with anger. 'You took her statements. You should know.'

'I didn't believe what she said,' Tony Martin said calmly. 'Neither did the court nor anybody else.'

'So why did you go along with it, knowing it was a pack of lies?'

'I didn't *know* anything. I just didn't believe what she said.'

'Why did you take her on in the first place? You were my solicitor and my friend long before she was around.'

'I had my reasons.'

'What were they?'

Martin hesitated. 'Do you promise not to use what I tell you in any way?'

'If you want.'

'She had been to two solicitors before me. They told her frankly that they didn't believe her, and that she would stand little chance in court.' He paused. 'When she came to me she was in a desperate state. I was afraid that she might do something stupid.'

'Like what?'

Tony Martin shrugged. 'Let's say something desperate.'

'Don't bullshit me, Tony. She's as tough as nails. All she wanted was to do me down and grab all she could.'

'Why do you think she wanted to do that?'

'God knows. Wanted pastures new, I guess.' He paused. 'Why do *you* think she did it?'

'A mixture of jealousy, lack of self-esteem and loneliness.'

'What the hell makes you say that? Jealous of what?'

'You're an attractive man, Johnny. The girls always fell for you. She recognised that. She was an attractive girl and she was used to men making passes. It gave her a cynical view of how men behaved. She liked the attention she got. She knew she could get anything she wanted from a man. She thought it must be the same for you with other girls.

41

And as you were a man you'd take what you could get.'

'I've never played around with anyone else since I first knew her.'

'You never did know her, Johnny. That was the real problem.'

'I don't understand.'

'Tell me what you thought was her background.'

'Her father was dead. He was a heart-surgeon. Her mother was wealthy and snobbish. Jenny had been to a finishing school in Geneva and had played at being a fashion-model, but her mother had threatened to cut off her allowance if she continued in the rag-trade.' He waved his hand. 'That's about it.'

'Did you ever meet her mother?'

'No. She disapproved of me, apparently.'

'You believed all that?'

'More or less.'

'You never checked up on her?'

'Of course not. For Christ's sake, if you start treating your friends like they were KGB you'd soon have no friends.'

'Fair enough.' Tony Martin paused. 'Now the facts. Her mother's in a home for alcoholics. Her father was a book-maker's clerk. He was beaten up and died in prison when he was doing seven years for incest. The family never had two pennies to rub together. Jenny was a so-called glam-our model. Girlie magazines and the like. Was a hostess in a club when she met you. The flat which you moved into was provided for her by a man named Harris. Special-ised in high-value bank robberies. Just finishing a three-year stint in the slammer for aggravated GBH.' When he saw Tarrant's face he said, 'Sorry, Johnny. But you'd have found out sooner or later.' He sighed. 'With a background like that you create a fantasy world as a kind of armour against the world. Seems that once she realised that you actually cared for her and weren't just after her body, she didn't have the guts to tell you the truth. She thought about it, but as time went on she didn't dare in case it rocked the boat.'

'So why clobber our marriage and me?'

'You were away a lot and you never told her much about what you did. She thought you were tired of her. It had happened before in other relationships. I think when she started the divorce action it was no more than a bluff to make you pay attention to her. Stop leaving her alone. But with that sort of person the fantasy takes over and she began to believe her own scenario of her life with you. Once on the tiger's back she daren't get off.'

For a long time Tarrant was silent. Then he said, 'Why are you telling me this?'

'I never liked her. I thought she was dangerous. I don't know why I thought that. I had no justification. But I felt that because you so obviously loved her that I must be wrong. You were no fool.' He paused. 'You did love her, didn't you?'

Tarrant nodded. 'Yes. I guess I did.'

'So tell me why you loved her?'

Hesitantly Tarrant said, 'She was beautiful and she seemed to love me. She seemed kind of innocent, very dependent on me. Sometimes I thought I was almost a substitute father.' He shook his head slowly. 'Strange when I look back on it. But once she started on the divorce jag she got my adrenalin going. If she wanted a fight she could have one.' He frowned. 'She seemed so wilful. So destructive.'

'And what do you feel about her now?'

Tarrant shook his head. 'You didn't answer my question – why you're telling me all this about her.'

'She's in a bad way, Johnny.'

'You mean she wants money?'

'No. She made no application for money. I put in for her costs and a minimum maintenance. That was just routine. Me, not her. She changed her mind every five minutes about claiming maintenance, but in the week before the day in court she was adamant that no support claim should be made against you.'

'So how's she in a bad way?'

'All the adrenalin has been used up, Johnny. It's down-to-earth time. No longer the centre of attention, and all the time in the world to realise what you've done. And what you have done is to ruin your own life and thrown away the only worthwhile relationship you've ever had.' He looked at Tarrant for several moments and then he said quietly, 'She's in a deep depression. Several people, including me, have tried to talk her out of it. But to no avail. She's lost a lot of weight but what it really amounts to is that she is weighed down by obsessive remorse. Remorse for what she did.'

For long moments Tarrant was silent and then he said, 'Why are you telling me all this?'

'Because I think you're the only one who could bring her back to normality. She talks about nothing but you and the harm she has done you.' Tony Martin half-smiled. 'I'm tired of hearing about you and your virtues. It's like a litany, Johnny. It goes on and on all the time.'

'What could I do, for God's sake?'

Tony Martin shrugged. 'If you could bring yourself to do it, tell her that you forgive her.' He paused. 'You don't have to mean it.'

'Why do you think that would do any good?'

'I got a psychiatrist friend of mine to talk to her. He thinks it would work.'

'Where is she living now?'

'My secretary has given her a room. She lives in Pimlico. Just a small flat.' He paused and then said, 'Just see it as no more than a good deed. You don't need to be involved.'

'I'll think about it, Tony. I'll think about it.'

*   *   *

44

Two days later Tarrant contacted Tony Martin and, accompanied by Martin's secretary, Pauline, he had taken a taxi to the small flat in Pimlico.

He was shocked when he saw her sitting on the chair in her bedroom in a dressing-gown. He had assumed that Tony Martin's description of her had been to induce him to see her and that sooner or later she'd be angling for money. But if anything Tony Martin's account had been underplayed. She had lost a lot of weight and her pale face was like the faces of children he'd seen in news flashes of refugees. It was a little girl's face. No make-up but the same big eyes, and a nerve flickered by her left eye. And despite the summer sunshine her body trembled as if she had an ague.

He sat down on the edge of the bed, facing her, unsure of what to say.

She took a deep breath and said softly, her voice shaking. 'Thanks for coming to see me, Johnny.' She paused. 'I didn't know he was going to contact you. I swear I didn't.'

'It doesn't matter. I'm sorry you aren't well.'

'You must hate me.'

'Forget it, Jenny. These things happen. People get upset and they go off the deep-end. Once you get lawyers involved it gets out of control.'

She shook her head. 'I was a fool and I deserved what I got. I just wanted you to know that I was sorry for what I'd done. I just asked him to tell you that.'

'There were faults on both sides, honey. There always are. When it gets to divorce it all gets blown up and exaggerated.'

'Are you still with your old job?'

'Yes.'

'Are you off on your trips again?'

'In a few days. I've been down at my father's place.'

'It makes a difference having a father to fall back on.'

He nodded. 'Tony told me about your background. I wish I'd known.'

'Another pack of lies. But I was scared you wouldn't want me if you knew the truth.'

'It was other people, not you, Jenny. Any man who'd be put off by that wouldn't be worth having.'

He saw the tears running down her cheeks. 'I wish to God it had been like my fantasy world.' She shuddered suddenly. 'In the end you come to believe your own lies. But sooner or later . . .' She shrugged helplessly. 'Will you drop me a line sometimes? Just to say hello?'

'On one condition.'

'What's that?' She said it so eagerly that it made him ashamed.

'That you forget all this divorce business. It's gone. It's over. There's no hard feelings on my part.'

'You don't mean that, do you? You're just being nice because I'm so . . .' she shrugged '. . . so down.'

'That's rubbish, kid. Gone. Forget it. Just get well again. That's all that matters.'

He stood up slowly, taking her limp hand in his as he leaned forward and kissed her lightly on her forehead.

'Don't fret any more, girl. Forget it. All of it.'

She looked up at his face. 'And you'll send me a post-card sometimes?'

He smiled. 'Sure I will. We'll keep in touch.'

He heard her sobbing after he had closed the bedroom door behind him.

At Paddington station he paid the florist to send her some flowers through Interflora. When the florist asked for his preference in flowers he said anything except red roses.

Two days later Tarrant was having coffee with his father after their evening meal. He was off to Berlin the next day.

'Where've you been staying these last few months?'

'I had a grotty room in Fulham, all I could afford with the payments I was making to her.'

'Have you wrapped it up now?'

'Not yet. I'll write to the landlord when I get to Berlin.'

'Leave me the details and I'll clear it up for you. Make this place your base until you've decided what you want to do.'

'Thanks. I didn't want to stay there a minute longer when I knew she wasn't able to skin me.'

'How long will you be away?'

'I've no idea.' He shrugged. 'It's just a missing person job. I suspect it's just something to keep me occupied while they decide what I'm going to do once the dust has settled.'

His father nodded. 'When the chips are down they're not such bastards as people say.' He smiled. 'They look at your virtues and then your vices and work out how to cash in on both of them. They know what they're at most of the time.' He stood up. 'You going by train?'

'Yeah.'

'I'll drive you to the station and I'll check out the MG for you while you're away. What time's your train?'

'Nine fifteen.'

'OK, I'll call you at seven.'

CHAPTER 6

Half an hour before they were due to land at Tegel Tarrant opened his briefcase, took out the envelope from Facilities and walked down to the forward toilet. With the door bolted he checked the contents. There was a New Zealand passport in his name and a UK passport with his photograph but in another name. A thousand D Marks in used 10 DM notes and a thousand Ostmarks. A bank account at Deutsche Bank holding 15,000 D. Marks and a bank card and a receipt for a three-month rental of a flat in Kant Strasse with two keys on an Air France tag. He knew the flat, he'd used it before when he'd done jobs in West Berlin. It was spacious and comfortable and had two double bedrooms and a sitting room big enough for small meetings, with TV, telephone, answering machine and an ICOM transceiver.

He tucked them all back into the envelope and went back to his seat. The lights for seat-belts had come on and the captain was pointing out that they could see Berlin to starboard as he banked over East Berlin to come in to Tegel.

He took a taxi from the airport to the Savoy and walked down Fasanenstrasse, turning into Kant Strasse. The flat was over a boarded-up shop and nothing much had changed except that there was now a fax machine. There were the basics in the refrigerator and the place was spotlessly clean. Tarrant liked Berlin, he knew his way around and he'd always been successful there on past operations.

He unpacked his case and took out the clothes, laying them on the bed until he found the small plastic box that protected the Opto frequency counter. With the counter switched on he checked the obvious places, the telephone, the lights, the radiators, above the windows, and all plugs and sockets. Finally he switched it to boost for a general reading. But there was nothing. The place was clean. But old habits die hard. Half an hour later he took a taxi to Tauentzien and strolled down Marburger Strasse to the post-office and then back to the door by the club. There were two bells and he pressed the one with a card that just said 'L'. The buzzer sounded and he pushed open the door, closing it behind him before walking up the carpeted stairs to the top floor. He stood in front of the observation lens in the door and it opened immediately.

She was grinning and obviously pleased to see him, flinging her arms round his neck and kissing him eagerly before she drew back her head to look at his face. 'What on earth are you doing here, Johnny?'

He smiled. 'Can I come in?'

She laughed and waved him in, closing the door behind him.

'Your face is thinner – what've you been up to?'

He looked around. It all looked much the same. He turned to look at her.

'And you're as beautiful as ever.'

She grinned. 'And you're still the same old bullshitter. D'you want a drink?' She paused. 'Don't tell me you're still on cold milk.'

'If you've got some, yes. If not, a fruit-juice.'

'Sit down. You know where everything is.'

He looked around the room. It was very Brit. Laura Ashley. And despite her name Leni Mundt was from East Croydon. The Mundt was left over from a disastrous marriage to a self-styled impresario when she was seventeen and desperate to be in show business. The marriage had lasted four months. He had a German passport but Tarrant guessed he was a Turk, one of the *gastarbeiters* who started on building sites but ended up as pimps. From the photographs she'd shown him he could understand her gullibility. The Clark Gable face, the white Mustang and lashings of gold. Then the drama of sudden debt and his life in danger, the usual pimp's scenario. Just a couple of months obliging a few rich friends of his and they'd be straight. But when it got to the whips and black leather she'd walked out on him. There was a barely discernible knife scar from her left ear to her shoulder that had enabled her to get a divorce, and since then she'd learned the lesson. If she was going to be nice to rich gentlemen it would be for herself. She had been a 'hostess' at a number of Berlin clubs and now had a client list that gave her independence. But she took no lovers and she lived alone. He had known her for years and they had a genuine affection for each other. On his side because she was very pretty and good company and on her side because he treated her as his girl-friend, not a hooker. She wasn't the proverbial tart with a golden heart but she had a heart.

When she came back with his glass of milk and a can of Coke for herself he said, 'Is the downstairs flat occupied at the moment?'

'No. It's been free for a week.'

'Can I take it on?'

'Rents have gone up a lot, Johnny, with all the refugees from the east coming in.'

'Whatever the going rate is, Leni. No problem.'

'Let's say two hundred a week, OK?'

He reached in his jacket pocket and opened his wallet, counting out a thousand D Marks before he handed them to her. 'If I need it longer, is that OK? Payment in advance.'

'That's fine, Johnny. Tell me what you're doing these days. How's that doll of a wife of yours?'

'That's over. She divorced me a month ago.'

'I'm sorry about that. She must be crazy.'

He shrugged and smiled. 'Who knows? You free for lunch tomorrow?'

'That would be great. Where shall we meet?'

'I'll book a table at Kempinski's for one o'clock, OK?'

'Great.'

He stood up and walked to the door. 'It's done me good to see you, Leni. It really has.'

The next morning he phoned Waring who was in charge of the SIS detachment in West Berlin. He arranged to meet him at the Olympiad at 11 a.m. He knew Waring from his last posting in Berlin. He was both efficient and cooperative but he wasn't in charge when Foster did his flit.

Waring met him at the security post and stood there waiting patiently as the guards went through the high security checks.

In Waring's office he was waved to one of the armchairs and there was a Thermos of coffee for him to help himself.

'Powell phoned me on the scrambler that you were coming but he wasn't very forthcoming. I gather you're going to have a recce around the time when Foster went off into the blue. I was here at the time but Slaney was in charge and the line-crossing networks were kept under tight security.' He paused. 'How can I help you?'

'Tell me about Foster. What kind of chap was he?'

Waring smiled. 'I guessed you'd ask me that and I thought about how to describe him. He was tough and highly motivated. Worked all the hours God sends and I believe his network brought in a lot of useful data. Mainly order-of-battle, weaponry and public morale. He gave them all he'd got. And I think that was part of the problem. His network were devoted to him. Would do anything he asked. When three of them were picked up on the other side he was ready to take any risk to free them. But Slaney wouldn't go along with it. Neither would London. There were rumours flying around for about a week that there was a massive row going on with Foster in the middle of it. Then it seemed to die away and we all thought it had been settled to Foster's satisfaction. About three or four days later I heard he'd done a bunk. A lot of to-ing and fro-ing between here and London and then we all got on with our respective jobs.'

'Are there others here now who were here in those days?'

Waring thought for a moment. 'Just Sanders and Richards as far as I know.'

'What about the records for that time?'

'I think London took most of them but there may be some around. Ask Jane, who keeps our records.'

'D'you mind if I talk to Sanders and Richards?'

'Not at all. Help yourself.' Waring stood up. 'If you need anything let me know.' He paused. 'I was sorry to hear about your domestic problems. Seems to be par for the course in this job.'

Freddie Sanders had obviously not been told about the new interest in Charlie Foster and was cautious in his response.

'I didn't know him all that well, Johnny. We were quite a big unit in those days and I was mainly concerned with subversives on this side of the Wall.'

'Where do you think he went to?'

'God knows. Could be anywhere.'

'Where would you go if you were doing that?'

Sanders frowned as he thought about the question, then shrugging he said, 'I'd need to know why I was doing it. He must have been guilty about something because even if he'd got some chip on his shoulder he could have resigned the service in the normal way.' He shrugged again. 'Why make a mystery of it?'

'Any idea of what he could have felt guilty about?'

'There was talk about a row with Slaney because of some sort of cock-up in Charlie's network. Who knows? Whatever it was died down inside a week or so.'

'When did Slaney leave Berlin?'

'About a year after Foster left. He was promoted but went back to London.' He paused. 'Back to Foster. If he was in some sort of trouble with London and he wanted to lie low for a bit I guess he'd be in Germany somewhere.'

'What makes you think that?'

'He was absolutely bilingual. Germans took him for a German and there's not much people could do to him here. He'd just fade into the background.'

'Well thanks, Freddie. If you think of anything else Waring knows where I can be contacted.'

As Tarrant walked down the corridor to Richards' place Waring came out of his office and walked towards him.

'When you asked me in my office what sort of man Foster was I knew he reminded me of someone.' He smiled. 'I just realised who the someone was.'

'Who?'

'You. Not in appearance but in personality, in character.'

Tarrant smiled. 'Tell me more.'

'Like I said, he was tough and efficient, A bit of a tiger if his people didn't bring home the bacon. But on the other hand I'd say he was emotional underneath all that. Inclined to rush in sometimes and not assess the risks beforehand.'

'Is that really how people see me?'

'Not necessarily. That's just me. And both sides are virtues in my book. That's what our game is all about.'

Tarrant shrugged. 'Could be worse, I guess. I'll have to think about it.'

Waring laughed softly and punched Tarrant lightly on his arm. 'If I was up a back alley in the dark I'd rather have you with me than anyone I can think of.'

Tarrant smiled. 'Or Charlie Foster, of course.'

Waring smiled and turned back to his office.

When he knocked on Stan Richards' door he heard a shouted, 'Come in, for Christ's sake.'

Richards looked up angrily and then broke into a smile.

'Come in, my boy. I heard you were snooping around. Grab a chair. How are you?'

'I'm fine, Stan, how're you?'

'God knows.' He leaned back in his chair and tossed his ball-point onto the blotter on his desk. 'I'm on neo-Nazis. At least that's what they call them.' He waved his arm. 'They're just bloody yobbos. Football hooligans. They're no more Nazis than I am. And all the fuss we and the Krauts make about them makes them feel important. Interviewed by bloody television reporters and the press they strut around like pouter pigeons.'

'What's the cure, Stan?'

'I'll tell you what the cure is, boyo. It's a girl with a pram.' He leaned forward, sighing. 'Anyway, you're not here to cure my blood-pressure. What can I do for you?'

'Charlie Foster. Tell me about him.'

'I'll tell you this, pal. There was nothing wrong with Charlie Foster. It was that bastard Slaney was the trouble. A cold fish if ever there was one. Should never have been allowed to be operational. He was made for a desk in Century House. A very small desk too.'

Tarrant smiled. 'Now tell me about Charlie Foster.'

'What? Oh yes. Good chap, but a bit of a romantic. Queen and country and all that crap. He ran his network efficiently and he cared about 'em too. Some of them got nicked over the other side. Charlie wanted to ride to the rescue. Slaney said he was crazy and London said the same but a bit more diplomatically. Then all of a sudden the shouting all died down. Seemed like Charlie had accepted their reasoning. I was on leave when he skipped and I thought he'd had a breakdown or something and he'd end up in some bloody hospital or maybe just walk back in.' He shrugged. 'How wrong can you be? Why are they so interested all of a sudden?'

'Just tidying up the files. Closing it down.'

Richards shook his head. 'OK. You ain't saying, but you don't have to bullshit me. You wouldn't be here if they didn't have some bloody good reason.'

Tarrant smiled as he stood up. 'If they have they ain't told me.'

Richards laughed. 'What the head don't know the heart don't grieve about. I wouldn't put it past 'em.'

'Where does Jane hang out?'

'Jane? Who's Jane?'

'Records.'

'Ah yes. Of course.' He grinned. 'Just your type, boyo; lovely pair of knockers.' His grin faded. 'I'm sorry, Johnny. How crass can you get?' He sighed. 'I apologise. As always, leaping before thinking.'

'It's OK, Stan. No offence.'

'Back to Jane. Next floor down, you need a pass to get down the stairs. The name's on her door. Jane – what is it, for Christ's sake? – ah, yes. Jane Morgan. Best of luck. Come and have a meal with us. Dolly would be delighted to see you.'

Jane Morgan had been pleasant and amiable but she had insisted on phoning Peter Waring before Tarrant was allowed even supervised access to any records. But there had been no problem and when she hung up she opened the security gate that gave onto the shelves of files.

'Let me tell you about the system. All records are on the computer database but only very brief details. But there are references to files and documents. If they exist. The base is recorded in names of people, ours and the other side. Code-names, Operation names. Places and standing orders. There's a self-help function that you can call up on the screen. If you want hard-copy you'll need written permission. And you can't make notes, OK?'

Tarrant smiled. 'Can I ask you for help?'

'Of course. But I'm very busy at the moment. See how you get on.'

She led him over to an IBM PC and switched it on. Then she pointed to a ring-binder beside the computer. 'Those are the lead words. Try one while I'm here.'

'It's just a name.'

'OK. Type it on the keyboard, it can be upper case, lower-case or mixed.'

'What's that mean?'

'Capitals are upper-case.'

Slowly Tarrant pecked out FOSTER, the screen fluttered and words came up – EXTEND IDENTIFI-CATION.

'Put in the person's initials or first name.'

Tarrant typed in CHARLES and almost as soon as he had done it the screen displayed – LONDON RECORDS. Then a second line came up. REMOVED THIS DATA-BASE DECEMBER NINE 1989.

'Bad luck,' Jane Morgan said. 'Keep trying.'

Tarrant sat at the keyboard and she said, 'If you're given clearance for hard-copy you just put in the password and press HC. OK?'

Tarrant smiled. 'Thanks for your help.'

'You're welcome.'

Back at the Kant Strasse flat Tarrant lay on his bed and thought about his day. He had taken two hours off at lunchtime for his date with Leni and he'd drawn money from his bank account and hired a BMW on his official

Visa card. His findings from the computer were what could be officially described as a nil report. Just one speck of gold among the dross. A list giving the actual names, code-names and locations of six members of Operation CROWBAR. Foster's line-crossing operation. He had to wait until tomorrow for Waring to OK him having hard-copy. There had been three names asterisked, one of them a female. And gossip said that three of the network had been caught. He wondered too about Waring's analysis of his character, and his likening him to Charlie Foster. He shook his head to dismiss the thoughts and shaved and changed, had dinner at a restaurant on the Ku'damm and then walked down to the Bleibtreu Club. Manuella had moved on to pastures new, nobody knew where but there was another equally pretty and equally well-endowed young girl. He took her out for a drink and then back to his place. It was in easy walking distance of the club but when she left in the early hours of the morning he hailed a taxi and paid her fare back to the club. She didn't finish work until 6 a.m.

CHAPTER 7

There was only one frame of hard-copy from the computer that Tarrant wanted and Waring had cleared it immediately.

It was the basic details of Foster's network. Nobody in the present set-up had any idea how many had been in Foster's network. There were seven names. Real names and sometimes cover-names. All with a code-name. Waring agreed with him that the asterisked names could well be those who had been caught. They were at least a starting point. Two addresses were in Berlin and the third, the female, was in East Berlin. An address not far from Humboldt University.

The first address was for a Martin Laufer, code-name Kern. He checked the street on his *Reise und Verkehrsverlag* street map. It was in Charlottenburg not far from the S-Bahn station. It was in walking distance of his Kant Strasse flat.

He made himself a ham sandwich and a cup of coffee and sat watching the news on RTL. Bonn had announced that the so-called 'welcome payment' for refugees from the east was to be increased from 30 to 100 D Marks. He switched off the TV and headed for Charlottenburg. It wasn't an area he knew well and he asked a taxi-driver at the station for Leonhardtstrasse. He wondered why the driver smiled as he gave him directions. But as he walked on he realised why he got the smile. It was an area of night-clubs, strip-clubs and sex shops interspersed with restaurants and cafés. The address was difficult to find because there were no numbers on many of the places.

He had a coffee at one of the cafés and asked the waiter where the number was. The waiter had no idea but said he'd ask the manager. He came back a few minutes later. 'It's three doors up, a blue door, but he says the teenage hookers aren't there until six o'clock.'

Tarrant gave him a tip and left.

The place with the blue door was between two strip-joints. There was no number and no name, but there was a bell and he pushed it tentatively. A couple of minutes later, after no response, he pushed the bell again and a few moments later a woman in her fifties dressed in black opened the door.

'We're not open yet, dear. Come back in an hour, OK?'

'I'm looking for a Herr Laufer, madam. Herr Martin Laufer.'

'Who are you? Are you a cop?'

'My name's Francis. Johnny Francis. I'm a New Zealander.'

'And who's this Laufer?'

'I just want to contact him, nothing special.'

She looked him over silently and then said, 'You'd better come in.'

He followed her up a wooden staircase onto a landing with a well-worn carpet and then along a corridor and he realised that the place must extend over the top of the next building. There was a smell of cooking and the faint sounds of Elvis singing 'Blue Suede Shoes'.

The woman opened a door and waved him into a small room. 'I'll be back in a couple of minutes. Make yourself comfortable.'

It was more a cubicle than a room and it was obvious what it was used for. There was a single bed with a lot of cushions and a satin cover and several strategically placed mirrors. There was a bunch of plastic flowers in a vase on the cast-iron mantelpiece over a gas fire and a couple of *Playboy* centre-folds tacked up on the plasterboard wall. There was a small set of drawers by the side of the bed and a lamp with a pink shade.

Then the door opened and a man came in, staring at Tarrant as he slowly closed the door behind him. He was big built with a blue seaman's jersey with its sleeves rolled up to show his strong hairy forearms, one tattooed with a schooner in full sail and the other with a flag that Tarrant didn't recognise.

The man said, 'She told me you're looking for someone. What's going on?'

'Nothing's going on. I was given this address for a man I met a long time ago.'

'How long ago?'

'Just over four years or so.'

'Where d'you meet him?'

'At the crossing at Friedrichstrasse.'

'Which side of the crossing?'

'The East side.'

'What were you doing there?'

'Just looking around.' He shrugged. 'We had a drink together, chatted a bit and we exchanged addresses. That's all.'

'What drink did he have?'

Tarrant shrugged. 'We both had coffees.'

'Where did you have the drinks?'

'At a pub called *Zum Letzten Instanz*.'

'And his name?'

Tarrant stood up. 'What is all this? Has he done something? Is he around or not?'

The man pushed Tarrant firmly but gently back until he was sitting on the bed.

'You got your passport on you?'

'No. And it's no business of yours.'

The man folded his arms casually and leaned back

against the door, looking at Tarrant. Then he said quietly, 'Do you know a man named Kern?'

It was several seconds before Tarrant decided how to respond. He said, 'Yes, he was a close relation to Martin Laufer.'

The man nodded slowly. 'My name's Laufer. Georg Laufer, I'm his elder brother.'

'Do you know where he is?'

The man shook his head. 'No. I could never find out. You're not a New Zealander, are you? You're a Brit and you're something to do with what my brother was doing.'

'What was the last you heard of your brother?'

'I heard he'd been arrested in East Berlin and charged as a spy and an enemy of the State.'

'That's the last you heard about him?'

'No. About six months after that I got a note from him.'

'What did it say?'

'It said he was OK and not to worry.'

'Are you sure it was from him?'

'Yes. It was in his handwriting.'

'Have you still got it?'

'Yes.'

'Could I see it?'

The man nodded and left the room. He was back in a few minutes and he handed Tarrant an envelope. He took out the paper inside. The message was exactly what the man had said. And it was written on a page torn out of a standard British Army issue report pad with its faint blue squares. There was no point in passing it to Forensic. He put it back in the envelope and handed it back to Laufer's brother.

'Could you spare the time to talk to me about your brother?'

The man looked at his watch. It was a Rolex but the steel-link strap had been changed to black leather.

'I've got about half an hour's work getting ready for the

evening trade but after that – as long as you want. I'll take you to my rooms if you'd like to wait. There's plenty of booze.' He shrugged and smiled. 'If you'd like a young girl for company that's easy fixed.'

Tarrant smiled. 'I'd settle for a coffee or a glass of milk, if that's possible.'

Georg Laufer grinned. 'Makes a change anyway. Let me take you to my place.'

Laufer's place was on the next floor and was surprisingly civilised. The furniture was old-fashioned but obviously well made and expensive. There was a bank of Technics Hi-Fi and all the CDs and cassettes were of classical music. There were books on politics, sailing and seamanship and on a glass-topped coffee-table was a coffee-table book of nudes by André de Dienes.

Tarrant was standing by the window looking at the men going into a sex cinema when there was a knock on the door and a girl came in carrying a tray with a glass of milk and a cup of coffee. She was young and pretty and topless and instinctively Tarrant looked at his watch. It was 5.55 p.m. and she smiled back at him as she put the tray on the coffee-table. She swished a neat backside as she walked to the door where she stopped and looked over her shoulder at him. 'I'm Joanna and I work here every day including Sundays.'

'You're very pretty, Joanna. I'll remember that name.'

She smiled again as she went out.

Ten minutes later Georg Laufer came in and sat down opposite Tarrant, pointing at the empty glass. 'You really do drink it then?'

Tarrant nodded and smiled. 'Tell me about Martin.'

'He worked as an engineer on the U-Bahn, on the signals network. He often had to do work on the other side because those bastards wouldn't lift a finger to keep the railways running. He didn't make much money but it was a safe job and it was what he liked doing.' He stopped.

'Before I say any more you got to level with me about who you are and what you're doing. I don't want more harm to come to Martin than he's already got.'

'It's best you don't know my name Georg. I'm a Brit and I work for an organisation like the German BND, the *Bundes nachrichten Dienst*.' He paused. 'Did you ever hear Martin talk about a Brit named Foster?'

'Talked about him to me all the time. Hero-worshipped him.'

'Did he tell you what he did for Foster?'

'Not much. Sort of gave him information about things the other side of the Wall. Messages and so on.'

'And what happened to Martin?'

'God knows. He went off to work one morning, same as usual and he never came back.'

'Where do you think he is?'

'I just don't know. In some jail on the other side, I suppose. But that doesn't fit with his letter to me. I reckon they found out what he was doing and they collared him.'

'Has anyone else heard from him?'

'Not so far as I know.'

'Did he have a girl-friend?'

'Several but not a steady girl.' Georg shrugged. 'I guess he saw enough of what goes on here to put him off. He liked his independence.'

'If I find out where he is, are you interested in knowing?'

'You bet. He's the only relative left. And we were good friends despite being brothers.'

'What happened to Foster?'

Laufer looked surprised. 'No idea. I didn't know anything *had* happened to him. I went to the British Army people about my brother but they said they'd never heard of him or Foster.' He paused and looked at Tarrant. 'I knew they were lying but there was nothing I could do.'

'And you think he's still there, somewhere in East Germany?'

'Well he wouldn't need to send me a note if he was this side of the border.'

'Who told you he'd been arrested?'

'Someone showed me a cutting from an East Berlin newspaper. It gave his name. There were two others arrested at the same time but I don't know if they were pals of Martin. One of them was a female.'

'Have you made an attempt to trace him?'

'No. I wouldn't risk going over the other side.'

'Have you told anyone else about the note?'

'No. Not a soul.'

'Has anyone else ever asked you about where your brother might be?'

Laufer thought for a moment and then said, 'I'd forgotten all about it until you asked but a couple of months after Martin got arrested there was a chap came asking about him. Said he was a reporter, but he wasn't. Didn't even speak proper German. A foreigner of some kind.'

'A Brit?'

Laufer smiled. 'No. We don't count Brits as foreigners. They're *gastarbeiters*, like the Turks. No, this chap was some kind of Slav. Could have been Polish.'

'A Soviet?'

Laufer shrugged. 'Could be. I can't tell one from another.'

'What did he ask you?'

'Was Martin my brother? What was he like as a kid? What were his hobbies, did he have any pets as a kid? Why was he arrested?'

'And what did you say?'

'Just odd things about when he was a kid. Nothing of any use to anyone. And I said he'd probably been arrested because some bloody Stasi didn't like his face.' He smiled. 'I don't think he liked that and that made me suspicious and I sent him packing.'

Tarrant stood up. 'I'll keep in touch, Herr Laufer. My name's Johnny. Thanks for your help.'

As Tarrant walked back to the flat he felt that he had learned a lot. But he wasn't sure what it was. He suspected that Laufer's foreign visitor wasn't Stasi but KGB, checking on Martin Laufer's background, comparing it with what he'd told them. Looking for discrepancies. Looking for lies that could be part of some pre-planned cover story. It looked as if the three network members were still in jail or Martin Laufer would have at least contacted his brother again.

He phoned Leni and told her that a film she had always wanted to see, *Un homme et une femme* was being re-run at a small cinema on the Ku'-damm, would she like to see it tonight? She hesitated for a moment and then said she'd love to see it but she had to be back at her place by 11 p.m. That was no problem and he said they'd go to the early show and there would be time to have dinner after.

As he hung up the phone rang. It was Powell asking how it was going. He was noncommittal. He'd only been active for a few days and it wasn't usual for the brass to start stirring the pot so soon. But it was a good sign, in a way. At least it meant that the operation was for real.

As he shaved and changed, his mind was on Leni. Way back when she was a hostess he'd slept with her regularly but things had changed for both of them since those days. Not that she was any less desirable but he was conscious that she had a separate life now. A life he wasn't part of. He liked her and admired her independence but he was a friend now and instinct told him not to try and revert to their old relationship.

She had enjoyed the film and had cried at the sad parts and cried again at the happy ending and was as lively as ever when they were having dinner at a small restaurant a few doors away from her place in Marburger Strasse.

When they were at their coffee she reached out her hand and put it on his as she said, 'Did you get hurt very much about the girl?'

He hesitated, then said, 'Enough to be going on with.' He sighed. 'I don't really know.' He paused. 'What made you ask?'

'Because when I needed it you cared about me. And I care about you.'

'I'm getting by, honey. I'm OK.'

'Are you on holiday in Berlin or is it work?'

'Work.'

'That's why you rented the flat.' She smiled. 'A hideaway.'

'Kind of. I'd better walk you home.'

'No. It's OK. My . . . er . . . friend might be waiting.'

'I'll phone you next week some time.'

She leaned over and kissed him. 'Thanks for a nice evening. *Tschüs*.' She picked up her handbag, waved to the owner of the restaurant, who smiled and nodded as she walked to the door.

CHAPTER 8

The address in East Berlin was in one of the small streets near Humboldt' University and the third address was in Wilmersdorf. Some instinct made him decide to try the East Berlin address first.

He went in through Checkpoint Charlie on the New Zealand passport and walked up Friedrichstrasse to Unter den Linden. It was the first time that he had been in East Berlin for nearly two years and there seemed to be more tension in the atmosphere. Groups of people talking together, groups that would have been broken up in the old days and moved on by the *Volkspolizei* or security police in plain clothes. There was a long queue for oranges at a fruit-shop and there hadn't been oranges in East Germany for at least twenty years.

The small street of the address was a row of old-fashioned houses opposite a builder's yard. Tall, narrow houses with three or four storeys. They looked as if they had been damaged in the Allied air-raids and then repaired rather than rebuilt after the war. The house in the address was only a half-dozen houses down from the main road and it had a handwritten card by the bell that offered lodgings for females only. When he rang the bell the door was opened almost immediately by a large, middle-aged woman in a flowered dress and a pinafore. She looked at him aggressively.

'What do you want? I don't allow male visitors in the house.'

'I'm looking for a Fräulein Bayer. Ursula Bayer.'

'There's nobody here of that name.'

'This was her address at one time. Perhaps you know where she is now.'

Tarrant saw two young girls on the stairs behind the woman.

'Nothing to do with me where she is now. Who are you anyway? You're a foreigner, aren't you?'

Tarrant shrugged. 'I just wanted to contact Fräulein Bayer. Nothing more.'

'Well, can't help you. On your way, mister.'

And with that she closed the door. Tarrant walked slowly up the narrow street towards the main road. As he stopped at the corner he heard the sound of someone running towards him. He turned to look. It was one of the girls who had stood behind the woman. In her early twenties and very pretty, her face flushed from running. She was panting, trying to get her breath back before she spoke.

'I heard you asking about Uschi, Uschi Bayer.'

'Do you know where she lives now?'

She smiled. 'You're her lover, aren't you? The old woman spotted your accent. She's afraid of you people and the Stasis.' She smiled and shrugged. 'I guess we all are.'

Tarrant smiled. 'You've nothing to be afraid of from me, I promise you. You knew Uschi, did you?'

She nodded. 'Yes. She was a student in her fourth year when I started at Humboldt. She had a room next to mine at the house.'

'Is there somewhere I could take you for a coffee?'

'There's a café by the tennis courts.' She pointed. 'It's terrible coffee but we could have an ice-cream.'

'Let's go. You lead the way.'

As they walked along he asked her what she was studying at the University.

'Russian and English.'

He smiled. 'Putting your bets on both ways, yes?'

'I don't understand.'

'Just a joke. Not a very good one.'

'What happened to you two way back?'

'Let's wait until we're having our ice-cream.'

The café was spotlessly clean but with almost nothing to offer, but when he offered them DeutschMarks there were cream cakes and *strudel* and the coffee was instant but drinkable. They sat inside and the café was almost empty. She ate hungrily at the *strudel* and he passed across the cream cakes to her side of the small table.

'Aren't you going to eat anything?'

'I had a good breakfast.' He stirred his coffee as he said, 'Tell me about Uschi.'

She looked surprised. 'She told me that you had got her released when those bastards arrested her.' She shook her head. 'Espionage they said. She was conspiring against the State. Fools. She was just a student.'

'Are you a member of the Party?'

'Good God, no. They wouldn't have me even if I wanted to be.'

'Why not?'

'Because of my father.'

'Tell me about him.'

'He was SPD. He was an official. When the Communists took over they merged the SPD with the Party. But he refused. Said he was a Social Democrat and not a Commie and never would be.'

'What happened?'

'He was taken before the People's Court.' She shrugged. 'The usual crap – Enemy of the State.'

'Then what?'

'Found guilty.' She looked away for a moment before looking back at Tarrant. 'They never told us what had happened to him, and we've never heard anything about him. It's not allowed to make enquiries about prisoners who are Enemies of the State.'

'Tell me why you thought I was Uschi's lover.'

'I saw Uschi about two months after she was arrested. She was only in the prison for a month. She said that someone, a man, had arranged for her to be released and she now had a job at a bookshop. I saw her again about two months later. She seemed very happy. She was working for some government department.' She smiled. 'And she told me about you. She said she lived with you at a flat near Alexanderplatz. She said you were an important man with lots of privileges. And you could buy things at a government shop for top people in the Party and the Soviets.'

'Did she tell you my name?'

She frowned as she tried to remember. 'I'm not sure. Is it Sasha?'

'Do you know where she lives now?'

'I assumed she was still with you.' She frowned and said softly, 'I've made a ghastly mistake, haven't I? You aren't Sasha are you?'

'No. But don't worry, you've not made a mistake. If Uschi needs help I can help her.'

'You're not a Russian: what are you?'

'I can't tell you. You don't need to know. Let's just say that I'm on the other side. But you must promise me not to tell anyone about what either of us has said. You understand?'

'Yes. I promise. But I'm scared. Tell me why you're looking for Uschi.'

'I'm not looking for Uschi, but she knows a man who I want to contact. From what you've told me he could have been the first lover. He knew her well. He was a foreigner and I think perhaps it was he who got her out of prison.'

'Was that man an Englishman?'

'Yes.'

'And you're an Englishman too. I recognise the accent now. I just assumed you were Russian and that your accent was Russian or Slav anyway.'

'Was Uschi pretty?'

'Yes. Very pretty. Blonde, long hair in a double braid. Average height. Good figure and very intelligent.'

'You liked her.'

'Yes. She was my best friend.'

'Any idea where the flat near Alexanderplatz was? The street maybe?'

'I've no idea. She wouldn't talk about her life except in general things.'

'Where do her parents live?'

'I don't know. But I think they're in West Berlin, not over here. She just came here as a student.'

'Why here?'

'Because she too was taking Russian. The best tuition in Russian is at Humboldt. They even take West Berliners because the West Berlin government pay in hard currency for their fees.'

'Is your mother still alive?'

'No. Her life revolved around my father. She lasted about four years and then gave up the ghost. The hospital said it was some unidentifiable virus . . .' she shrugged '. . . it wasn't of course but doctors don't believe in broken hearts.'

'How do you get by, yourself?'

'I've got a State scholarship at the Humboldt and I get a small allowance for my board and lodging.'

'Boy-friend?'

She shook her head, smiling. 'When they find out that your father is classed as an Enemy of the State they back off quickly.'

'So why tell them?'

'I don't, the woman at my lodgings is an informant for

the Stasis. She tells them. She wouldn't be allowed to rent rooms if she didn't cooperate. They're into everything. Nothing's too small or insignificant.'

'What did Uschi tell you about the first man – the one you think got her out of jail?'

'I got the impression she knew him before she was arrested and that they were more than just friends. She was very cautious. She didn't say much. But from the little she said he wasn't local – he wasn't a German – I'm sure of that.' She sighed. 'He must have cared for her a lot to even try getting her out of prison when she'd been arrested on espionage offences.'

'Maybe he was a Party member?'

She laughed softly. 'You're kidding. A Party member wouldn't have lifted a finger for someone arrested for espionage.'

'Why do you think they thought she was involved in espionage?'

'God knows. What could she know? She was just a student like me. She didn't know anything that people on the other side would be interested in.'

'What are you going to do after university?'

She shrugged. 'Who knows. I'll be told what I have to do. We don't have any choice.'

'Why do you talk with me? Why do you trust me?'

'I was just thinking that. You must be a mind-reader. I don't know. Just instinct.'

'Feminine intuition.'

She smiled. 'Yes. Gets us into lots of trouble. Hearts not heads.'

'It works pretty well. The trouble only comes when you ignore it because you want whatever it is or whoever it is so much that nothing else matters.'

She laughed. 'Maybe. And how about you? Tell me about you. Why did you talk with me? I could have been a Stasi informant.'

He smiled. 'Feminine intuition. Hearts not heads.'

'You're a romantic, aren't you? A faller in love all over the place. Leaping before you look.'

He laughed. 'But you trust me.'

She nodded. 'Yes, I do.'

'Would you do something for me?'

'What?'

'Ask around about Uschi. Just gossip.'

It was several moments before she answered and then it was fairly non-committal. 'I'll see what I can do. Where can I contact you?'

'How about we meet here this time next week?'

'OK. I'd better go or the old bag at my lodgings will wonder what I'm doing.'

'I don't even know your name.'

'It's Ingrid. Ingrid Schumann. And yours?'

She smiled as he hesitated. 'Johnny. Just Johnny, OK?'

'OK.'

'You go and I'll hang around for a bit. Take care.'

'You too.'

Peter Waring had too many operations going to want to spend time trying to find out what Tarrant was up to but he was ready to cooperate if it didn't interfere with his work. When Tarrant had phoned him he suggested a sandwich and coffee meeting at mid-day in his office.

He was on the phone when Tarrant came in and he waved towards plates of sandwiches and a Thermos of coffee on his desk, and the visitor's chair. When he hung up he said, 'Something's going on on the other side of that Wall. I wish I knew what it was.'

'What sort of thing?'

'Not for repetition but I've had feelers from two high-up Stasis in the last week. And . . .' he shrugged. 'How about your game?'

'Not a lot of progress but when I was talking to old man

Foster he suggested I spoke to a guy named Malins and one named Shelley. He said they were around in Charlie Foster's time. Where can I find them? Are they still with you?'

'Shelley's still with me. He's on the drugs operations.'

Tarrant looked surprised. 'How are we involved in drugs? Surely that's SIB's manor?'

Waring shrugged. 'Not when the drugs are being pushed by the Stasis on behalf of the KGB.'

'Why should they be interested in pushing drugs?'

'Gets you informants. Gets you agents of influence – politicians, smartarse diplomats. Gets you commercial and industrial secrets.' He smiled. 'And of course they're not above a bit of private enterprise on the side.'

'Can I talk to Shelley?'

'Of course. He's in the building right now. You can see him after we've finished. Help yourself to the sandwiches and coffee.'

'What about Malins?'

Waring leaned back in his chair, munching at a tomato and egg sandwich and Tarrant realised that he was playing for time before he had to talk about Malins. Finally he said, 'Malins took early retirement. But he *is* still in Berlin. Runs an import/export business and a travel agency. At least that's what he calls it.' He paused. 'I'd be very cautious if I were you in talking to him.'

'Tell me why?'

'I was never too happy about friend Malins. I've got to admit he did a good job. A real ferret and tough as old boots.'

'What was wrong with him?'

'He was a crafty bugger and mixed with a tough criminal element. And when he was applying for early retirement I did a bit of checking on him. Not with our people but with the Germans. Malins had bought four properties. A house and three small office blocks and he'd got four different bank accounts. None of them with Brit banks. They wouldn't give me details but it was obvious we weren't talking about a couple of thousand D Marks. More like several millions. And I guess he had connections the other side of the Wall.' He sighed. 'I told London but they let his application go through. Gave him a decent reference – not that he needed it.'

'Where's he hang out?'

'He's got an office and an apartment on the Ku'damm over a travel agency. He owns the building and the travel agency. His house is in Grunewald right on the river.' He reached for a scribbling block and a pencil and said as he wrote, 'These are the two addresses. But like I said – keep your cards close to your chest when you talk with Malins.' He tore off the page, folded it and pushed it across his desk to Tarrant. 'I got a call from Powell this morning. Slaney's wife died last night. He wants me to go over for the funeral.'

'I'm sorry to hear that.' He paused. 'What was Slaney like when he was here?'

'He was OK. Went by the book. They say he lacked imagination but who knows? – except for the cock-up with Foster I gather it ran pretty much as you could expect in this place. Berlin's always been understaffed and underfunded, bearing in mind what we're supposed to cover.'

'Where can I find Shelley?'

'I'll walk you down to his place.' He smiled. 'Don't be surprised by his appearance. If you're in drug circles you've got to take on the protective colouring.'

Shelley was in his early forties. Tall and lean with a sallow complexion and a two-day stubble. He wore a gold ear-ring in his left ear and his eyes seemed to be looking at something in his mind that was far away. He shook hands and pointed to a wooden chair.

'Why are you interested in Foster? I thought it had all been wrapped up long ago.'

'It's just routine.'

Tarrant saw Shelley's quick grin at his recognition of the lie.

'So – friend – how can I help you?'

'Foster's old man said you could tell me about his son's disappearance.'

'Did he now? Well . . .' he leaned back, smiling '. . . what is it you want to know?'

'Anything . . . what do you think happened?'

'Well Charlie Foster ran a network into East Berlin. I understood that it was rated highly but that's only scuttle-butt. Some of his people got knocked off in East Berlin. Charlie had some crazy idea of rescuing them. Slaney and London said no way – there was a blazing row between Charlie and Slaney. Lasted about a week and then suddenly all was back to amiability on both sides. About a week after the reconciliation Charlie lit out. That's about it.'

'Any idea where he went?'

'Could be anywhere.'

'Where would you have gone if it had been you?'

Shelley smiled. 'Interesting question.' He closed his eyes thinking, then he said, 'Bi-lingual German. Brought up in Germany. I'd have stayed in Germany. Fixed myself some credentials before I left. Maybe as a West German national.'

'How would you live?'

'God knows. Back home I could work for a security firm but here they're too strict to get by.' He shook his head. 'I don't know.' He laughed. 'I guess I'd get into the drug business.'

'And why would you have left in the first place?'

'Yeah. Why? I guess bloody-mindedness, anger at not getting my own way . . .' he shook his head '. . . could be anything.'

'One of his network arrested was a girl. D'you think he could have been involved with her?'

'Screwing her, you mean? I shouldn't think so. More the romantic type.' He shrugged. 'But you never know these days. We've all got our little fantasies bottled up in our heads. And we don't let on. I've given up guessing what makes people tick.'

'If you think of anything, could you contact me through Peter Waring?'

'Sure.'

Jane Morgan was standing looking at the computer screen when he went into Records. When she turned and saw Tarrant she cleared the screen and walked over to the counter.

'What can I do for you, Mr Tarrant?'

'I'd like to see a couple of files, please.'

She smiled. 'Your wish is my command. What are the files?'

'"P" Files for Mr Shelley and Mr Malins.'

She shook her head. 'Sorry. Nobody has clearance for "P" files of serving officers except Mr Waring personally and he doesn't have discretion to give clearance for anyone else to see a "P" file. He'd have to refer to London if you insisted on a need to see them.'

'Who in London?'

'Head of Personnel, Chief Archivist *and* Mr Powell. Deputies not acceptable.'

'OK. Thanks. I'll leave it for now.'

CHAPTER 9

Tarrant was surprised when he arrived at the travel agency that was Malins' address. He was sure that the flat over the offices had been an SIS safe-house when he was previously in Berlin. There was a door alongside the entrance to the agency and Tarrant hesitated but went through into the agency.

There were three young women at separate desks and Tarrant asked the nearest one where he could find Herr Malins.

'Have you an appointment, sir?'

'No, but if you give him my name I think he'll see me.' He smiled amiably.

'What name shall I say?'

'Johnny Tarrant. Century House. London.'

She pressed a single button on a white internal phone and then spoke.

'Herr Malins. I have a gentleman at my desk who would like to see you. He gives his name as Johnny Tarrant of Century . . . yes, sir. Right away.'

She hung up and smiled. 'Please follow me, sir.'

He followed her up two flights of stairs and a small dapper man was waiting for him beside an open door. He was smiling. 'You must be Tommy's boy. Come on in.' As Malins led him into a large, well-furnished office Malins said, 'I seem to remember you were here in Berlin a couple of years ago.' He waved to a leather armchair. 'Do sit down. A drink?'

'A coffee would suit me fine.'

Malins phoned down for two coffees which were brought in by the time Malins had taken off his jacket and lit a cigar.

'Now, my friend. What can I do for you?'

'I wanted to ask you about when Slaney was here and the Foster business.'

'I hear Slaney's lost his wife, poor chap.'

'You're very well informed.'

Malins smiled. 'Have to be in my business. Anyway, what is it you want to know?'

'Anything you can remember about what happened.'

Malins shrugged. 'Just the usual cock-up all round. I don't know whose fault it was. Six of one and half a dozen of the other. Slaney misjudged Foster's feelings. But he didn't know all the facts. And what Foster wanted wasn't in Slaney's power to give. Nor anybody else's either. You got two good chaps at logger-heads, getting angrier every minute. And in the end Foster does a moonlight flit.'

'But I understand from other people that whatever their differences were they were resolved after a few days.'

'Well they were wrong, weren't they? If it was all settled Foster wouldn't have walked out.'

'So you blame Slaney?'

'Not really. He was sticking to the rules.' He shrugged. 'Foster didn't like the rules.'

'What did he want that Slaney wouldn't agree to?'

'Some sort of deal that would release the three people of his network who had been nicked over the other side.'

'Why was he so intent on freeing them?'

'He was Sir Galahad riding to the rescue.'

'Would you have done that?'

'No way. There wasn't a deal to be made. They were in the bag. End of story.'

'Somebody hinted that maybe he was involved with the girl. What do you think?'

Malins was silent for a moment. 'That's a new angle. Could be, but I doubt it.'

'Why do you doubt it?'

'If he'd got something going with the girl he would have pulled her out of the network and not risked her neck.' He paused. 'Who gave you that angle?'

'No one person. I just put a lot of small pieces together and found it a possibility.'

'You're a pretty shrewd bastard, aren't you?' Malins was smiling.

'What makes you think that?'

'Slaney didn't think of it. Neither did anyone else.'

'But you knew, didn't you?'

Malins laughed. 'Maybe.'

'Was that what you meant when you said Slaney didn't know all the facts?'

Malins ignored the question. 'Why are they so interested in Foster all of a sudden?'

'Just routine. They'd like to close the file.'

Malins grinned. 'Don't bullshit *me*, pal. I was in the business, remember.'

'Where do you think he went?'

'I've no idea.'

But he said it too quickly and too positively and Tarrant knew he was lying. Maybe he didn't know exactly where Foster went but Tarrant knew Malins was lying when he said he had no idea. He had known things that Slaney didn't know and he'd never volunteered what he knew.

Tarrant smiled. 'My turn to say don't bullshit me, pal. I'm still in the business. Why not tell me what you think?'

Malins was silent for a few moments and then he said quietly, 'D'you ever take advice, Tarrant?'

'Depends on the donor.'

'Well let me tell you you're walking around in a minefield. And your bosses in London knew that before they sent you. Who sent you anyway?'

'Powell.'

'I might have guessed. Smooth as butter and crafty as a monkey.' Malins stood up. 'Anyway, think on as they say in Bradford where I come from. Think on.'

And Tarrant knew that the meeting was over. As Malins showed him to the door Tarrant said, 'Can I chat with you again if I make any progress?'

'Would be my pleasure, friend. Give my regards to your old man.'

Back at the flat there were two messages on the answer-phone. One from Leni inviting him for a meal that evening at her place. The second was from Powell to say that the funeral of Slaney's wife had been well attended and well conducted with eulogies by both an Archdeacon and a well-known actress recalling Mrs Slaney's days in stage musicals as a soubrette. There was a slight pause on the tape before Powell went on to suggest that he kept well away from Malins.

As he dialled Leni's number he wondered who was keeping Powell informed. He didn't see Waring as a likely stooge for Powell.

They were sipping coffee together on the soft leather three-seater, the bunch of red roses that he had brought her in a crystal vase on the circular coffee-table.

'How often do you go into East Berlin?' He asked as casually as he could.

'Funny you should ask me that, I meant to ask you last time we met – why is it called Checkpoint Charlie? Who the hell was Charlie?'

Tarrant laughed. 'It's not somebody's name, it's army jargon. When soldiers talk on radios or telephones to one another they always spell out names of people and places in a phonetic code, because using normal spelling can lead to mistakes. An F can sound like an S. So they have a special alphabet they use. There are three checkpoints that the military use – A, B and C. So it's Checkpoint Able, Checkpoint Bravo and Checkpoint Charlie.' He smiled as he looked at her face. 'You look disappointed.'

'I am. I thought it would be something romantic. Some special man.'

'So back to my question, how often do you go into East Berlin?'

'Fairly, often. About once a week. But as I'm German I have to go through the Friedrichstrasse checkpoint.' She paused. 'Why do you ask?'

'Just out of interest.'

She smiled. 'Liar. Are you playing your old games again?'

'Of course not.' He paused. 'As a matter of fact I'm just looking for someone. Nothing more.'

'And you think he or she might be the other side of the Wall?'

'I'm beginning to think so. I hope I'm wrong.' He looked at his watch and then at Leni. 'You got time for a drink with me at *Dschungel* before you go to your club?'

She shook her head slowly. 'I'm on early tonight. Some other night if you ask me again.'

They chatted for another ten minutes and then he left and walked back to the *Gedächtnis Kirche* and watched the kids on roller skates in the *platz*, glancing up at the Mercedes star over the Europa Center before he moved on.

Back at the flat he watched the news on Sat Eins as he undressed. Stopping to watch the shots of near riots in the streets of Leipzig. He could just make out a hand-painted sign hoisted on a pole that said simply – *40 Jahre Qualen – wir fordern freie Wahlen* – after 40 years of torment we demand a free vote. And there was another rough placard that said – *Produzieren statt spioneren* – make goods not spying. It didn't seem possible that crowds like that could assemble in East Germany without bringing out the tear gas and water cannon. And as for those posters, they must have a lot of guts to wave those around.

He moved to the kitchen and made himself a hot chocolate. As he sat at the table he thought about Malins' warning. Was it a warning or just an attempt to scare him off? And why should an ex-spook like Malins want to do anything to put him off looking for Foster? When you've been in the business you would know that that kind of gambit makes you more determined than ever. The bit about Foster and the girl fitted neatly into the vague stuff that Ingrid Schumann had told him. But if so, who was lover number two?

Tarrant spent the next day sorting out the notes he had made of his conversations with various people, and trying to assess their significance. It became obvious that, in fact, the information he had got from Ingrid Schumann was the most revealing. According to her, Uschi Bayer had had two lovers and almost certainly the first one had been Foster. But the second wasn't a Brit and wasn't a German. There was also the problem of her designation of both men as 'lovers'. If she had just meant the man was a friend, a man friend, she would have used the word *freund*. If she had meant more than that she would probably have used *liebchen* the old-fashioned word for sweetheart but she'd used *liebhaber* and that was 'lover' and all that the word implied. Bed, sex, the works. And commitment.

If Uschi Bayer and Charlie Foster were lovers why so soon afterwards was there a second lover? Was the first relationship over because Charlie Foster had disappeared? And Malins' point was valid – if Foster had really loved Uschi Bayer he would have pulled her out of the network rather than risk her being caught. It had been done before. You just fiddled the Imprest Account so that she got paid and gave her some sinecure like Information Collator.

And as for the second man, East Germany was swarming with foreign workers from the Warsaw Pact countries and the Middle East. He must have a good job or he wouldn't be living around Alexanderplatz.

Also Malins had made pretty clear that there was a relationship between Foster and the girl. But if Malins knew that, why hadn't Slaney known it? He was almost prepared to dismiss Malins' warning of mine-fields as no more than a dig back at his erstwhile employers. Most ex-SIS people either hated the organisation or loved it. Maybe it was significant that the haters were usually field agents and the supporters were desk-types.

He stood up, stretched and switched on the hi-fi as he walked towards the window. He smiled as he recognised the tune they were playing on British Forces Radio. It was *'Smoke Gets in Your Eyes'*. Could be the signature tune of this operation.

As he stood at the window Tarrant remembered Peter Waring's comment that he and Foster were much alike in attitudes and temperament. Tough and efficient. So what? Emotional. Inclined to rush in without assessing the risk. That was how they weaselled out of their share of responsibility for some cock-up you'd got into because they'd pressed you to go ahead with some operation without giving you time to plan it carefully.

Tarrant groped for the alarm with his eyes closed, switched it off and sat up in bed wondering whether to shave first or have a coffee. He opted for the shave and walked to the window in his bath-robe, the shaver in his hand. It was his day to go over the other side again to meet the girl. He didn't expect much from her but it was a useful contact. She might have remembered something she hadn't mentioned to him about Uschi Bayer. And it was only then that he realised that it was snowing. Just a few wisps of snow to remind Berliners that it was, after all, the last week in November. Indian summers didn't last for ever.

It was two hours later when he went through Checkpoint Charlie on a British passport but not in his name. When he reached the café by the tennis courts there was a notice saying that it was closed until the first of April. He looked at his watch. He was on time but he was the only person there. A few minutes later a woman with a child in a push-chair strolled past. He walked slowly to the far end of the courts and then back to the café. The snow was beginning to settle and he turned up the collar of his leather jacket. There was a girl walking towards the café but it wasn't Ingrid. He watched her walk past and then she stopped and turned and then walked slowly and hesitantly back towards him. She was almost past him when she stopped and looked at his face as she said softly, 'You're Johnny, yes?'

He nodded and she said, 'I was on the stairs with Ingrid when you came to the house. She's afraid to meet you here. She's waiting for you at Alexanderplatz.'

'Where in Alexanderplatz?'

'By the ticket office in the station.'

'Why is she afraid?'

'She'll tell you. I must go.'

She turned abruptly and walked away from him towards the main road and he stood there watching her until she was hidden by the buildings.

He walked up Karl Liebknechtstrasse but as he got to Alexanderplatz he realised that the girl hadn't said whether Ingrid would be at the U-Bahn station or the S-Bahn. He tried the S-Bahn first and it was very busy but he saw her straightaway, by the ticket office, wearing a red woollen hat with a bobble on top, a red and white striped scarf and a fake leather coat.

When he reached her he realised that she was shivering. He didn't know whether it was because of the cold or because she was frightened. He took her arm and led her towards the cafeteria.

'Are you OK?'

'Yes. But I can't stay long.'

'I'll get us some soup.'

'They won't have soup.'

He smiled and sat her down at a table. 'They will for dollars.'

It was tinned soup but quite good and he made her eat both bowls of soup before he asked her what the problem was about meeting him.

'I think the woman at my rooms told the police or the Stasis that I had run out of the house and spoken to a man who wasn't a German.'

'There's thousands of men in East Berlin who aren't Germans. I could be a *gastarbeiter*.'

She smiled wanly. 'You don't look like a *gastarbeiter*.' She paused and then said, 'I've found out where Uschi lives. I don't think it's good news for you.'

'Tell me anyway.'

'She lives in a flat over the shops by the market hall on Karl Liebknecht. She's married. That's what scares me.'

'Why should that scare you?'

'Because she's married to a Soviet. And she works as a typist at the Soviet HQ at Karlshort.' She paused and looked at his face. 'He's a KGB officer.'

'D'you know his name?'

'No. All I know is that he's about thirty. Very good-looking.' She shrugged. 'Is this any good to you?'

He nodded. 'Yes. How did you find all this out?'

'I've got a girl-friend at the Housing Office. She owes me some favours. But she was scared when she found out that Uschi's man was a Soviet. She wouldn't help me any further.'

'How did you find out what he looked like?'

'I went to the building and I saw him come out and get into a car with army plates and he was wearing a uniform.' She paused. 'It was a KGB uniform.'

'How do you know it was KGB?'

She smiled. 'Everybody knows what a KGB uniform looks like. It's got blue piping on the collar, the cuff of the jacket and brass buttons with the KGB symbol on them.'

'Anything else?'

'Yes. Yesterday Uschi phoned me at my rooms. Why, after all this time? She must have been told I had been asking about her. She just chatted. Said she was married now. Didn't say it was to a Soviet. Said she was very happy and had a good job.' She took a deep breath. 'I think some official must have been told that I've asked about her. I said I'd wondered what had happened to her after what I'd read in the paper and she laughed and said it had all been a silly mistake.' She paused. 'I'm scared, Johnny. Am I being silly?'

It was several moments before he replied. 'No. You're being very sensible.' He paused. 'Tell me, what are you going to do when you get your degree?'

'I've no idea.'

'What would you like to do?'

She shrugged. 'Anything that will earn me money to live on. Maybe teaching.'

'Have you thought of West Berlin?'

She half-smiled. 'Everybody dreams of West Berlin. Most of those who've tried are dead.'

'Would you go if you had the chance?'

'Like a shot.'

'Have you been missing lectures?'

'No. I'm doing a project at the moment.'

'What's the project?'

'A film treatment of *War and Peace*.'

'Is there anywhere we could meet in future?'

She thought for a moment. 'Do you know where the Huguenot Museum is?'

'Is that the one in Platz der Akademie?'

'That's the one. There's the new Concert Hall and the street beyond the cathedral is Französischestrasse. There's a café there – the Arkade Café – I've got a girl-friend who works there. A lot of tourists use it. We could meet there and Gerda would take messages for me. Ask for Gerda and I'll warn her that a friend of mine might phone for her to contact me.'

'Have you got time to go there with me so that I can meet her? It might be easier all round if you hint that I'm one of your boy-friends. A bit old but rather useful.'

She laughed. 'You're fishing for compliments.' She stood up. 'Let's go.'

At the café he sat alone at a table while Ingrid talked to her friend. There were glances towards him and some laughing between them but Tarrant was interested to see that Gerda worked on the check-out, and alongside the cash-register was a telephone.

When Ingrid joined him at the table she said softly, 'It's all OK. You're Johann. I've got a café card with the telephone number. They close at ten at night but she has a room over the café and I've got her phone number there. Here she comes. I'll introduce you.'

When the introductions were over they'd had pastries and coffee and Tarrant had paid in ever-welcome D Marks. She left before him and they had arranged to meet in two days' time.

CHAPTER 10

Tarrant checked in his notes for Keller's phone number. He had worked on two jobs in the past with Max Keller. They got on well together and were much the same age. And Keller was BND, the West German intelligence service. Twice he reached out for the phone and then drew back his hand. Finally he dialled the number and Keller's secretary answered.

'Can I help you?'

'I'd like to speak to Max Keller, please.'

'Who is that speaking?'

'My name's Tarrant. Johnny Tarrant.'

'I'm not sure if he's available. Let me check.'

There were a few moments of silence and then Keller was on the line.

'Hi, Johnny. How are you?'

'Fine. Can I come and see you?'

'Sure. When?'

'Now, if it's possible.'

'OK. You know where I am.'

'Still at the old place?'

'Yes.'

'About ten minutes.'

'OK. See you.'

Keller's place was at the back of a bookshop near the Europa Center. The shop and its flow of customers provided good cover for Keller's visitors. Access to his suite of rooms was through a door marked 'Private – Special Editions', a description which sometimes led to awkward encounters between Keller's receptionist and elderly gentlemen who assumed that the description was a euphemism for Hamburg's more advanced erotica.

Keller was in reception when Tarrant pressed the bell beside the door and he came to the door himself, smiling as they shook hands.

'I wondered when you'd be paying me a visit.'

Tarrant looked surprised and as they walked together into Keller's office he said, 'How did you know I was in Berlin?'

Keller grinned and pointed to a chair as he moved behind his desk. 'A little bird must have told me.'

Tarrant needed time to decide whether in the light of what Keller had just said it was wise to broach the subject he had in mind, and he diverted the chat to Keller's family and their recent holiday in Jamaica. It worried him that Keller already knew that he was in Berlin. He was quite sure that neither London nor Waring in Berlin would have informed the BND.

It was Keller who finally cut through the chit-chat.

'Have you decided yet, Johnny?'

'Decided what?'

Keller smiled and shrugged. 'Decided to talk about whatever you came here to talk about.'

'Tell me, Max. Off the record – how did you know I was here?'

'I was told you were here.'

'Who told you?'

Keller shook his head slowly. 'Nobody you know. It was a coincidence.' He looked at Tarrant. 'Is it all that secret?'

Tarrant didn't answer. He decided to plunge in. 'I wanted to ask your advice on getting somebody across from East Berlin.'

'Willing or unwilling visitor?'

'Willing.'

'Do they want to go back later?'

'No.'

'So why ask me? Your people at the Olympiad do it often enough.'

'This isn't anything to do with them.'

Keller's eyebrows went up. 'You mean it's freelance stuff?'

'Not exactly. It's official but nothing to do with Waring's people.'

'Sounds interesting. What sort of timing have you got in mind?'

'In the next couple of weeks. But I'm not sure of the timing yet. But if it was necessary it would be at very short notice.'

'You got spending money if it's needed?'

'Yeah.'

'Does it have to be East Berlin to West Berlin or would some other route be acceptable?'

'Like what?'

'Like Helmstedt or a bit more south. The Harz say.'

'I'm not sure at the moment, but I guess that would be OK.'

Keller leaned back in his chair. He was a big man and it creaked ominously. 'We'd better go on the record, Johnny. I'd need to get clearance from Pullach and they'd need a reference point in London.'

'That would be Powell.'

'Is he still doing the same job? The Soviets.'

'Yes. So far as I know. He briefed me but it's a bit outside his usual area.'

'Is the body male or female?'

'I'm not sure yet. Depends on what happens.'

For a few moments Keller was silent, his head turned to look at a framed photograph on the wall. A large aerial photograph of the centre of Berlin at the end of the war. The skeletons of buildings flattened by bombing and shelling so that they looked like rows of decayed teeth. When he looked back at Tarrant he said quietly, 'You paid a visit to Malins a few days ago. Can I ask why?'

'I wanted some background information from him.'

'You're being very cagey, my friend, for someone who's looking for cooperation.'

'What more do you need to know?'

'Who the target is. Nationality. What it's all about. Diplomatic repercussions. Why not the locals?'

'There'd be no diplomatic comeback. Let's say it's an internal service matter. I can't say more.'

'Was it about this you saw Malins?'

'Indirectly, yes.'

'You want to watch your step with that guy. He ain't a Berlin fat-cat by sticking to the rules. He's into very dangerous games.'

'It was just past history I wanted from him. Just peripheral stuff.' He smiled. 'The kind that's classified as "anecdotal" in official reports.'

'Let me have a word with my masters and I'll get back to you.'

'I'm not at the Olympiad offices.'

Keller smiled. 'I know. You're at the place in Kantstrasse.'

As Tarrant walked back to the flat he wondered who had tipped off Keller that he was in Berlin. And he wondered how Keller knew about his visit to Malins. Old habits die hard and he always kept an instinctive watch about being followed. But he hadn't expected any local interest in his visit and his precautions had not been aimed at avoiding real surveillance.

*   *   *

Keller phoned Michaels at Pullach and told him of his meeting with Tarrant, and after a few moments of silence Michaels said, 'What do you think, Max? Are we about to get our lines crossed with Century House?'

'It looks like that to me. He said it was internal and that fits. And he said his visit to Malins was about past history. Who else could it be but our friend?'

'And you think it's him he wants to get out?'

'It fits. It fits.'

'What do you suggest? Do we hold hands with him? See how the land lies.'

'I think we've got no choice. We cooperate. But we don't mention our interest in the matter. He's obviously on a fishing expedition.'

Michaels laughed. 'So are we. But it sounds like he's made more progress than we have. If he leads us to our friend so much the better. Once we've found where he is we can take over. We've got the resources and it sounds like Tarrant's playing the Lone Ranger.' He paused. 'Anyway, keep me in touch.'

'I will.'

Keller looked at his watch. Tarrant wouldn't have got back to the flat yet. He'd let him sweat for an hour.

PART TWO

CHAPTER 11

The door opened and a private in battle-dress called over to the man sitting at the bench turning the dial on a rack-mounted metal-cased receiver.

'Sar'major wants to see you in his room sa'r'nt.'

The man at the bench nodded, switched off the radio and the Swedish Aga wire-recorder, and stood up, reaching for his forage cap in case the sergeant-major wanted to make it formal. He didn't think he would. They were both technicians and their jobs didn't go with a strict adherence to the army's rules and regulations.

He knocked on the CSM's door and walked in. CSM McNay was a small dark-haired man with a red face, black hair and bright, alert eyes.

'Sit down, Eddie.'

When he was sitting McNay said, 'This interview with the CO. You sure you want to go through with it?'

'Yeah. I do.'

'They won't agree. You know that?'

'Why not? It's OK to marry a German now.'

'Maybe for infantry types but not on this job.' McNay shook his head. 'This is top security work you're doing, my boy.'

'They could transfer me to routine signals at 5 Div or 30 Corps.'

'Not after the work you've been doing here.' He shook his head slowly. 'You're committed. You signed that piece of paper – The Official Secrets Act.' He paused. 'What's wrong with our girls anyway? There's plenty of pretty ATS crumpet down at HQ.'

'Nothing wrong with them, I just want to marry this girl.' He hesitated and then said, 'There's no regulations now against marrying local girls. I won't be the only one.'

McNay shrugged. 'OK. If that's how you want to go he'll see you at 1600 hours on the dot.'

Sergeant Foster went back to his radio and switched on. As he waited for it to warm up he stood looking out of the window of the wooden hut across the valley. Where the farmhouse with the white walls was bathed in the late autumn sunshine was the start of the Russian Zone. Duderstadt was barely three kilometres from the border and Number 3 SSU, Special Signals Unit, was deployed in a cluster of wooden huts monitoring all radio communications by the Soviet military on the other side. His job was to monitor all their frequencies and switch on the Aga wire-recorder whenever there was any traffic. He had no idea what the messages contained, that was the task of HQ in Göttingen. He was a fast reader of Morse but the signals he recorded were not only in code but were based on the Cyrillic alphabet. But Sergeant Foster was a conscientious operator and he worked diligently the dozen frequencies that were his responsibility.

When he signed off and another sergeant took over he went back to his room and shaved again and boned up his regulation boots until they shone like a good soldier's boots should shine. He had done well in the army, and had the campaign ribbons for the Desert War, Italy and Germany. He liked the comradeship of the army and the army liked him. He was a quick-learner and totally reliable.

When he was ready he walked outside to the open shed that housed the motor-cycles and the 15 hundredweight van. At twenty-three years old he was still delighted that he had been allotted his own motor-cycle, a 500 cc BSA in standard army camouflage colours and tuned to give an extra 10 mph over the official top-speed. He was careful as his foot went down on the starter to avoid getting any marks on his canvas gaiters. He let the engine run-in for a few moments, eased in the clutch slowly and stopped at the guard-room to check out. He'd be back at 2300 hours as usual when he wasn't on night-shift.

'Sit down, sergeant-major.'

When McNay was sitting Major Ryan said, 'You had a chat with him, I understand.'

'Yes, sir. But he seems determined to go ahead. Said he'd ask for a transfer to non-security duties.'

'We need him here. All that training and all that experience can't be just thrown away.'

'What was the report on the girl like?'

'I got Field Security to give me an independent report. There's nothing in that we could use. Her father was in the Nazi teachers' union but they all were or they'd have lost their jobs.' He shrugged. 'All I can do is play it tough and try and bluff him out of it.'

'There's something I ought to mention off the record, sir, if that's OK.'

'Go on.'

'I've heard third hand that he's written to his MP about his application.'

'He has, has he? Thanks for warning me. Cheeky bugger. I shan't mention it but I shan't forget it either. We can teach Master Foster a lesson in our own sweet time.' He shook his head. 'I don't like barrack-room lawyers.'

There had been all the formalities of a CO's interview. Being marched in by the CSM, stamping of boots, salute, cap off and then the CO pointing at the chair and nodding dismissal to the CSM.

'Well now, Sergeant Foster. You asked for an interview regarding your application to marry an enemy alien. A German. Yes?'

Foster shuffled uncomfortably. 'She's just a girl as far as I'm concerned, sir.'

'Why her, sergeant? What's wrong with all our girls at home? Or here, for that matter.'

'Nothing wrong, sir.' He paused. 'The 30 Corps bulletin said that troops could marry local girls provided there was no security aspect.' He paused again. 'So far as I know there isn't any security problem. She was barely ten when the war started.'

'It's not your young woman who's the security problem. It's you, sergeant. You spend your time monitoring Russian military communications. Maybe you don't know what's in the traffic but you know what we do and what we're here for. Your work – the whole of this unit's work, is top secret.'

'Maybe I could be transferred to Div or Corps signals and do normal traffic.'

'I can't imagine the people at 21 AG going for that. A skilled and valued tradesman lost for the sake of marrying a German girl. And I don't feel I could pass on such a request. We're not 5 Div or 30 Corps – we're 21 Army Group.'

'Can I respectfully request an interview with the Commandant of Royal Corps of Signals at 21 AG, sir?'

'No. The matter is closed, sergeant, but you may raise the matter again in a year's time.' He paused. 'The young woman's not pregnant, is she?'

'No, sir. Would that make a difference?'

'Where did you meet the girl?'

'She was serving tea at the NAAFI canteen in Göttingen.'

'How long have you known her?'

'Nearly a year.'

'You think that's long enough to make such a decision?'

'Yes, sir. I knew I wanted to marry her after a couple of months but she wanted longer to make her mind up. She didn't want me to have problems.'

'What kind of problems?'

Foster shrugged. 'From the kind of people who call all Germans Nazis or Krauts. And problems with my job.'

'Does she know what you do?'

'Just that I'm Royal Corps of Signals. But she knows that I want to stay in the army.'

'Why do you want to stay in the army?'

'Because I like it.'

'Why?'

Foster shrugged. 'The friendships, and my work. The army's my family.'

'You're an orphan, aren't you?'

'Yes, sir.'

'And you're quite sure about the girl? For better or worse?'

'Yes, sir, quite sure.'

For a few moments Major Ryan was silent, looking directly at Foster.

'All right, sergeant. I'll endorse your application and that means that you can marry the girl any time thirty days from today's date.' He stood up. 'I can only wish you well, but . . .' Ryan pointed a finger at Foster '. . . don't, repeat don't, ever discuss any aspect of your work with this unit with anyone, including your wife – understood?'

'Yes, sir . . . and thank you, sir.'

Six weeks later Sergeant Edward Foster was married to Ingrid Maria Schultz in a church in Göttingen. There were no members of her family there. A dozen friends of hers, as many colleagues from Foster's unit, and Major Ryan had given away the bride. Her father had approved of the marriage but was worried that his brief and enforced membership of the Nazi Party's teachers' union might be an embarrassment. He was assured that nobody would ever know but he had always been a shy man and Ingrid thought that despite the fact that he was a well-respected lecturer at the university he might be scared to make a speech at the reception.

Sergeant Foster had no home in England and after travelling to Hanover where there was a British Consul they got a British passport for Ingrid Foster and moved on to spend their honeymoon in Amsterdam.

Married quarters accommodation was found for their return to Duderstadt. Their son Charles Foster was born in a military hospital in Hanover in the autumn of 1952.

When his son was two years old his father-in-law gave them his house in Göttingen. The town had not suffered greatly during the war and the house was in a pleasant suburb, roomy enough to house them all comfortably. The old man doted on his grandson, wheeling him in his pram to meet his cronies in the local park. He had been checked by the local Field Security Section and cleared of any Nazi involvement that mattered and he was given a part-time lecturing post back at the university. He got on well with his son-in-law and was thankful that their marriage had provided security for his daughter in those first grim years in post-war Germany.

Despite their differences in character, background, and up-bringing, Eddie Foster and his wife found their marriage entirely satisfactory.

When the boy was five years old his mother suggested that it would be better for him to attend the local German school rather than the one that was available for children of the occupation troops and Military Government. It would give him two languages and a better curriculum. So at school the boy spoke only German and at home he spoke English. Eddie Foster picked up enough German himself to get by, but it was more of a gesture towards his wife and her father than an interest in the language itself.

Young Charlie Foster was a bright pupil and he benefited too by absorbing the solid practicality of his father and the imagination and tendency to romanticism of his mother. His relationship with his grandfather became very close. The old man talked to the eight-year-old boy as an equal, telling him about Germany before the war and before the Nazis.

When the boy was ten years old his life changed drastically. His grandfather died and his father had finished his time in the army and it had been decided that they would move to England. Although his marriage to a German girl had not finally been opposed Eddie Foster had never been promoted. Most of his contemporaries were now either commissioned or Warrant Officers. He never showed any resentment at being passed over, he was now a highly skilled technician and that would stand him in good stead when he left the army. And that was what mattered to him. Although they never talked about it his wife was well aware that he had been punished for marrying a German girl and it was one more proof of the love of a man who was not given to displays of emotion.

Eddie Foster left with a glowing reference from his commanding officer and an enthusiastic letter of introduction from an officer at BAOR to a friend of his who was looking for a service manager for his chain of shops in Birmingham. After a short interview he was engaged at a salary that was three times what he was earning in the army.

They rented a house in Erdington and Eddie Foster was at work the following Monday.

It took almost a year before Charlie Foster and his mother felt at home in England and in that time they grew closer together, taking comfort from each other's difficulties in a strange land.

It was easier for the boy, who was absorbed in getting accustomed to his new school. He won a scholarship to the local grammar school and later he was offered a place at the university. It was a disappointment to his mother when he decided to join the army instead. There had been no persuasion by his father who would have much preferred him to go to university and had pointed out the narrowness of army life compared with what a university education would provide. But at nineteen years old he said, logically enough, that if he didn't like the army then he could leave after three years and apply again to go to the university.

Charlie Foster signed on for his three years in the Royal Corps of Signals and because he was bilingual he was posted after his initial training to a unit in West Berlin that monitored the radio traffic of the East German armed forces and the security police, the Stasis.

After only three months he was promoted to sergeant and shortly afterwards he was called to a meeting with his CO, Lieut.-Colonel Ramage. Ramage's appointment had not been on the grounds of his technical knowledge of radio but because he was a shrewd assessor of men. In a high-security unit that was of prime importance.

'Ah, sergeant, come in.' Ramage smiled. 'Do sit down.' He paused. 'I thought it might be useful for us to have a little chat.'

'Yes, sir.'

'Are you happy in your work in the unit?'

'Yes, sir.'

'You've made a number of very sensible suggestions about the operation. You've obviously given a lot of thought to how we go about our monitoring job.'

'Not really, sir. They were fairly obvious improvements.' He shrugged. 'I guess new boys have a different perspective.' He smiled. 'I don't suppose it will last.'

Ramage smiled too. 'We're hoping it will. And that's what I wanted to talk about.' He paused. 'There was talk of putting you up for a commission. How'd you feel about that?'

'I'd see it as a great compliment, sir.'

'You'd have to go on an officers' training course but I don't see any difficulties for you there.' Ramage looked intently at Foster as he went on. 'There's just one problem I think I ought to mention. I won't beat about the bush. I'm told that you spend most of your free time with Germans rather than your colleagues. Is that a fair comment?'

For a moment Foster was silent, then he said, 'Yes, I think it is fair comment.' He shrugged. 'My background was gone over before I was posted here so I expect it's all in my "P" file. My mother is German, or was, until she married my father. I was brought up in Germany. Until I was about ten or eleven. I went to a German school not an army school so that speaking German is as natural for me as speaking English. I'm interested in what's going on politically in this country but I could stop those contacts if it was thought undesirable.'

Ramage nodded. 'That's a sensible approach but what I said wasn't a criticism. As you probably know, the information we gather is passed on elsewhere. And the people responsible have noticed that you put your own comments on your material. Others do that too but they lack your knowledge of the country and the people. The people concerned would be interested in taking you over. How do you feel about that?'

'Are these the people at the Olympiad?'

'Yes, do you know any of them?'

'No. I just know about them. Very vaguely.'

'How vaguely? What do you think they do?'

'I assume that they're intelligence. MI6 or something like that.'

'Fair enough, but I have to say that what they do is a bit more to the point than our rather passive role here in monitoring. Would that suit you, do you think?'

'I can't see why not if they think I'm suitable.'

Ramage half-smiled. 'I think we can safely assume that they've looked at you fairly intensively and we wouldn't be talking right now if they had any doubts. Shall I arrange for you to meet them and have a talk?'

'Yes, please.'

Ramage stood up and as he walked to the door of his office with Foster he said, 'The officer you'll be meeting is a fellow called Slaney. Don't know much about him. Used to be in Beirut.'

The interview with Slaney was only one of several, not only with Slaney but with other officers. He was sure that they already knew the answers to many of the questions they asked him about himself and his parents, especially his mother. There were the usual personality tests and a medical check-up. He wasn't given any indication of their findings but after a week-end of conversations in a country house in Kent he was told that he had been accepted. His army service was terminated and he was now a civilian and a member of SIS. After a six-month training period he would be posted to West Berlin or Rheindahlen.

Foster was impressed by the training programme. There were five others on the course which covered surveillance, handling agents and the street craft of dead-letter drops and communication. There were special modules that applied to only one or two course members and in Foster's case they covered East German politics and East German intelligence and their KGB masters. A separate module on the organisation and identification of East German and Soviet military and their equipment. Foster was not required to attend either the radio course or the main language refresher course as his German was bilingual and up-to-date. For the period of those two modules he was given a crash course in Russian. Good enough to hold a non-technical conversation in Russian and to read Russian documents. There were practical tests of all the elements of the course and Foster's enthusiasm and quick intelligence were noted in his final report. The programme had actually taken eight months because of the Russian language course and during that time he had not been allowed any contact with his parents. But he was given two weeks' leave before his posting which was to Berlin. Although he was now officially an officer of SIS the records still showed him as an army officer with the rank of captain in the Royal Corps of Signals. An administrative precaution in case he sometime needed to be in uniform, to give him easier access to East Berlin.

He spent his leave with his parents, helping his father decorate the shop in Erdington which he had rented for his own retail shop selling radios and TVs. They had a farewell meal together at the Kardomah Café near the cathedral.

For a year Charlie Foster learned what it was really like. Learning that it was people who mattered. Learning that you had to earn your network's loyalty. Neither rank nor charm would do it. He had spent the time with two different networks. One was run by a quiet self-assured man who seemed to know what would motivate the various people who worked for him. The other was a network that was run by a rather wild, gung-ho officer who asked a lot of his people but rewarded them with the knowledge that he would never let them down.

One other thing that he learned in that year was that the men on the other side of the Wall were just that –

men. Men who were sons, fathers, uncles and husbands. There were always going to be men on both sides who thrived on violence and ruthlessness. But they were in the minority. And they seldom proved successful in commanding other people's loyalties.

The networks that were run by SIS Berlin into East Berlin depended mainly on expert observation. It could be no more than a new type of track-link on a Soviet tank, a change of regimental insignia on the Red Army guards at Die Wache that indicated that a new unit had taken over, or the financial problems of a guard at Checkpoint Charlie. A sergeant from a Red Army tank regiment who no longer played for a local team could indicate that his unit had been moved elsewhere. It was a giant jigsaw and the thousands of small pieces that seemed so insignificant to a casual observer could end up giving a picture that would affect a policy decision in Century House or the Foreign Office.

When Foster was finally given his own network he recruited them all himself. As much care was taken in recruiting couriers as the agents themselves. To Foster they were all vital links in the chain. His three couriers serviced seven agents. Agents who actively provided information on military dispositions, new services equipment, economics, local politics, public morale, imports and exports. The network ran smoothly and provided a wide spectrum of vital information to those whose job was to evaluate life the other side of the Wall.

CHAPTER 12

Foster had gone through the checkpoint in plain clothes, using an Irish passport, and with a camera slung around his neck. It was late afternoon and there were already a few young prostitutes hanging around the fountain. The chalk-mark was still there on the stone facing the statue, and it hadn't been crossed through. That meant that the dead-letter drop hadn't been checked.

He took a few snaps of the fountain and then strolled to the Centrum, East Germany's show-place department store. As always it was busy with shoppers, including American GIs and a few British soldiers. The glassware, crockery and bedding were cheap and of reasonable quality, but most of the goods displayed were shoddy, badly made and old-fashioned. Clothing made of synthetics processed from Romanian oil. He made his way slowly around the store and stopped at the counter where they sold ladies' scarves, poor copies of Hermès and Chanel, the colours already fading where they caught the sun in the bay window where they were displayed.

There was only one assistant, a middle-aged woman who seemed in no hurry to serve him.

'The girl said the new scarves would be in today.'

She leaned back against the display case, arms folded, her attitude faintly aggressive.

'Which girl's that?'

'I don't know her name. Blonde girl. Young. Been here for at least a year. Works afternoons.'

'She didn't turn up, they transferred me from souvenirs.'

'Is she poorly – the girl?'

The woman shrugged, indifferent and uninterested.

'Who knows? She didn't come in, that's all I know. I got commission in souvenirs and nothing here. Nobody buys this rubbish except tourists and GIs.'

'Any idea when she's coming back?'

She just shook her head and turned to look at a pigeon on the windowsill behind her.

He walked slowly through the store and out into Alexanderplatz, uneasy and apprehensive. A no-show happened from time to time. Illness, work, some domestic crisis could disrupt things. But two no-shows at the same time were more than just a coincidence.

There was a telephone kiosk by the travel bureau and he dialled the number, listened for two rings, hung up and dialled again, letting it go on ringing. After ten rings it cut off abruptly and he hung up. He knew then that the network was in trouble. The three of them were not informants but cut-outs. Routine carriers of messages and instructions. People who served the dead-letter drops. But they were his pipeline to the people who really mattered, and without them the network couldn't operate efficiently. It would mean taking risks. Direct contact with informants. People whose lives would be put at risk. But before he could plan anything he needed to know what had happened.

He found out what had happened when back in West Berlin he heard the news on DDR radio that evening. Three people had been arrested by State Security and charged with espionage for foreign powers. A woman and two men.

It was only the next day when the East Berlin news media gave out the names of the 'enemies of the State'.

The last paragraph of the item hinted that the three spies had been working for the American CIA. That hint was the only hope he had. If they didn't know who the three were working for they probably knew very little. Somebody must have shopped them. It didn't look as if the arrests came from long-term surveillance. He would have to find out what Slaney suggested they should do about them.

It was mid-evening before Slaney could see him and when he went in his office Slaney was on the phone but he waved him to one of the chairs in front of his desk. When he hung up he pushed aside a pile of files and looked at Foster.

'I hear you've got a problem, Charlie.'

'Yeah. I wondered if you'd had any thoughts about it.'

'You mean about replacements?'

'No. I mean about getting them out.'

Slaney looked surprised and was silent for a moment.

'How long will it take you to replace them? They were only cut-out couriers – weren't they?'

'They'd been working for us for nearly a year.'

'I don't get the point.'

'They took risks for us all the time. We can't just let them rot.'

Slaney sighed. 'In this business we all take risks of one sort or another. And we know what the consequences are if we get caught.'

'If I got caught what would we do?'

'That's different, Charlie. And you know it. You're a British subject – a British officer.'

'So what would we do?'

'We'd look who we'd got of theirs and try and negotiate an exchange.'

'So why don't we do it for my people?'

'What do you suggest?'

'We try to do an exchange.'

'Oh, for God's sake, Charlie. Your people are Germans. We'd be admitting that we use Germans for cross-border intelligence. They'll probably get no more than a year inside. We can look after them when they come out.'

'They'll be tried as spies, that can get them up to ten years. Maybe more.'

'Look, Charlie. I know it's upsetting when these things happen but it's part of the game. You win some you lose some.' He paused. 'What did you tell them when you took them on?'

'I gave them the standard guff. If they were caught they were on their own. We'd swear we'd never heard of them.'

'Well then.' Slaney looked at his watch. 'I'll have to go, Charlie. Let's talk about it in the morning.'

'What time?'

'I don't understand?'

'What time in the morning?'

'Oh.' He waved his hand distractedly. 'Let's say nine.' He stood up. 'Have you got any idea how they were rumbled?'

'Somebody grassed is my guess.'

'You could be right. Three at one go isn't usual. I'd guess they picked up one of them and they gave him the works and he shopped the other two to save his own skin.' He shrugged. 'It's been done before, Charlie. These people we use aren't knights in shining armour. They aren't really on our side, you know. Most of them hate our guts.'

'So why do they risk their lives?'

'You know why as well as I do. Money, privileges, a bit of mild excitement, maybe a need for self-importance.' He shrugged. 'Not to mention the chance of having a dig at the Russians who they hate even more than they hate us. Now I must go, Charlie.' He smiled. 'See you at nine. Sleep on it. We'll work something out.'

* * *

Foster walked slowly back to his office and unlocked the
metal filing cabinet and took out three files. Sitting at his
battered desk he drew a yellow-paged notepad out of the
drawer of his desk, pulling off the cap of an Edding felt-
tipped pen and laying it beside the pad. The first file was
titled 'Operation Paintbox' in black Letraset. The second
just said 'Stasi – Stadt Mitte' and the third had a typed
label marked 'Relevant KGB'.

For two hours he leafed through them again and again,
making brief notes on the yellow pad. But he concentrated
on the second and third files. When he finally put the
files back and locked the metal cabinet he stood beside it
leaning his elbows on its top. The grey paint was heavily
scratched and the drooping remains of a begonia in a
plastic pot had scattered the browned florets into a glass
ash-tray.

He rested his chin in his hands as he stared at the large-
scale street map of the centre of Berlin. There were three
blue pins and seven red pins stuck into the cork board.
The blue pins were the couriers and the red pins were his
informants. Without the couriers there was no way he
could find out if any of the agents had been picked up
too. Not unless he went over himself and broke the security rules by contacting one of them himself.

The three had already had one night in prison and by
now they'd probably been handed over by the Stasi to the
Soviets. Laufer probably wouldn't talk. He was a tough
cookie and his cover was good. Klein would talk. He was
probably the first in the bag and he'd have talked the first
time they clubbed him. He closed his eyes as he thought
of the girl. Poor Uschi. So young, so pretty and so trusting.
And so loving. He sighed and wondered if that was why
he had recruited her in the first place. No emotional
involvement with people you used as informants, they had
said on all the training courses. He hadn't meant it to be
any kind of involvement at first but he liked her. And

then it had been affection. Genuine affection. He'd never made a pass at her. They'd kissed and cuddled but nothing more than that. And he'd kidded himself that as he didn't sleep with her it didn't count as involvement. The same long, blonde hair and blue eyes as his mother. What the Germans called '*Ein echt deutsche Typ*'.

The brief knock on the door before it was flung open startled him. He half-turned and saw Shelley standing there. Black leather jacket and black leather trousers both liberally encrusted with metal studs. He stood there in the open doorway looking across at Foster.

'What you doing here at this time of night?'

'Nothing really.'

'Come and have a beer and a sandwich.'

'I'm too knackered. I need some sleep.'

'OK, we'll go to Maxi's place. Five minutes' walk. Come on. Stop farting about.'

In fact they'd had vegetable soup and a Wiener Schnitzel. And when the coffee came Shelley said, 'Are you fretting about your dopes who got caught?'

'They weren't dopes. Just ordinary people but not dopes.'

'I read some of your reports.' He paused. 'I got the feeling you were fond of the girl.'

'What made you think that?'

'Don't know. Just the old bells ringing, I guess. Am I right?'

'Partly. She was a very nice girl. Really nice. I liked her a lot.'

'What did Slaney say?'

'He couldn't care less. Just wanted to know how long before I could get replacements recruited and trained.'

'I heard him talking to Miller at the club. Said you'd got some idea of trading a couple of Ossies for your people.'

'What did Miller say?'

'Was kinda neutral but said it was worth considering.'

'Have we got any we could trade at the moment?'

Shelley shook his head slowly. 'Forget it, Charlie. Slaney would never agree. He got burned that way when he was in Beirut.'

'What was he doing there?'

'Much the same as you. Running an intelligence network. Two of his people were kidnapped by one of the groups. I can't remember which one but they were fanatic fundamentalists taking their line from Tehran.'

'What happened?'

'The other side came up with a shopping list for an exchange that started with AK 47s through to an armoured car and engine spares for a personnel carrier. There was no way anybody was going to agree to that. Not even Slaney.

'The bargaining went on for three weeks and it was finally agreed that the deal would be done with a truck full of medical supplies for the refugee camps. The truck would deliver the supplies to a named camp at an agreed time. They would hand over our two Arabs and we'd drive to our Embassy and that would be that.'

'So what went wrong – they didn't return the two kidnapped Arabs?'

'Oh yes they did. The truck driver disappeared into one of the bombed buildings and the two men were in the back of the truck. Naked, with their throats cut and buzzing with blue-bottles and maggots. The quack said they'd been dead for at least ten days. It was Slaney and a chap named MacArthur who found them.' He reached for his cigarettes and said, 'Bear that in mind when you're talking to Slaney.'

'How long ago was this?'

'Three, four years, something like that. But for Slaney it was yesterday and always will be. The time when he persuaded others to bend the rules and he got a bloody nose. And as far as London's concerned his arse was out in the snow for at least a year.'

'Any suggestions as to how I could help my people?'

Shelley looked away and then signalled to the waitress to bring the bill. And then he turned to look back at Foster.

'Tell me what *you* think could be done.'

'Like I said, we could contact them and offer an exchange of their people we've got in jail.'

'They wouldn't be interested, Charlie. They're not that kind of people. They know that any Stasi or KGB stooge we've pulled in isn't of any great importance. They assume they'll have talked, so why should they bother?' Shelley smiled wryly. 'They might settle for Slaney, of course.'

Foster didn't smile. 'What about money or TVs or VCRs?'

'By now they'll be controlled by the KGB not the Stasis. KGB guys can buy anything they want on the other side. That's one of the perks of the job. You know that.'

'What about letting me put a snatch squad together and having a go?'

Shelley sighed and leaned back in his chair as he looked at the bill, gave the waitress a fifty D Mark note, telling her to keep the change but to receipt the bill. When she'd left, Shelley folded the bill and put it in his inside pocket.

'Forget it, Charlie. It's one of those things that happen in this game. Just get some new bodies or you'll lose your agents through lack of contact.' Shelley stood up. 'Let's go. I've got a raid in a couple of hours. We can share a taxi to the Zoo. I'll drop you off there.' He put his hand on Foster's shoulder. 'Get some sleep before you see Slaney tomorrow. And play it cool. It's not the end of the world.'

CHAPTER 13

Slaney shook the rain off his coat and hung it on the hook behind the door before he turned to Foster and pointed to a chair. He dried his face with a handkerchief and then wiped it over his hair before he sat down behind his desk.

'Well now, where were we?'

'We were talking about my people who've been arrested.'

'Yes. I had a word with London last night. They were sorry of course. Sent their condolences but they don't feel there's any action we can take at this stage.' He paused and took off his glasses and reached for a Kleenex, cleaning them slowly. 'They've got a lot on their minds at the moment. But they're concerned that you should keep your network live. We need all we can get from the other side of the Wall at the moment. They were much impressed by the material you've been providing.' Slaney took a deep breath. 'They'd be prepared to transfer a couple of the cut-outs from Scorpio if that would help.'

'They won't fancy taking over where the previous cut-outs have been nicked.'

Slaney shrugged. 'They don't have any choice, Charlie.'

'Why not?'

'Dicey backgrounds. They owe us. Plenty.'

'The morale of my agents won't be too good right now.'

'Maybe it's worth you popping over yourself and making clear that we shall go on supporting them and that we value their cooperation.'

'And when they ask what we're doing about the cut-outs – what do I say?'

'Tell them we want to let the dust settle before we make any move.'

'For Christ's sake, these people trusted me – all of them. But they're not fools – they'll know I'm lying.' He shook his head angrily. 'I want something done for my couriers – quickly.' He stood up and standing there glaring at Slaney he said quietly, 'Or I'll organise something myself.'

'Like what?'

'That's my business.'

'Sit down, Charlie.' Slaney's face was flushed with anger. 'Now listen very carefully, Foster. This is no longer just a friendly chat. I'm talking to you officially. Your network is not some private army you've put together, it's part of our intelligence operations in Berlin. It's a nuisance that your three people have been taken but you might ponder on whether perhaps it was some carelessness on your part that made them vulnerable. Too much of the old pals act and not enough attention to the rules of the game. You're a professional. You've had months of training. You've done a good job up to now.' He wagged a finger at Foster. 'Don't – repeat don't – spoil your record. We don't bargain with the other side at this level and we don't play James Bond games either. When they've served their time we'll see what we can do for them.' He slapped his palm sharply on his desk. 'And that's the end of the matter, Charlie. Take a couple of days off. Calm down. And report to me when you're in the right frame of mind to carry on with your good work. And there'll be no hard feelings on my side.'

For a moment or so Foster was silent, then he said, 'Could I ask for this to be considered by Century House?'

Slaney stood up. 'You go too far, my friend. It's time you came down to earth. Who the hell do you think you are? Get back to your work or take some leave. But don't ever raise this matter with me again. Understood?'

Foster nodded slowly. 'Understood, Mr Slaney. Understood.'

Back at his rooms Foster sat at the small desk in the living room. Making notes on a pad, crossing through words and whole sentences. Screwing up page after page as he read and re-read his attempts at making his case. It was four a.m. when he gave up. There was no case. No case that either Slaney or London would accept. Time and again he wrote those words. 'Forget it. There is no case.' But he knew it wasn't true. There was a case. Loyalty to people who had been loyal to you no matter what the cost. No matter what the consequences.

Then he did what his training had taught him to do. Make out the case for the other side. He used the official words and jargon but it only took four lines. As he pulled the sheet from the typewriter he read it carefully. Twice. Even in his own words it was decisive. SIS never offered deals to the other side when an agent had been taken. No matter how senior he may be. Deals would be considered in some circumstances when the initial offer came from the other side and for one reason or another was considered valuable enough. This protocol was instilled in all agents at the start and end of their training. There were no exceptions.

He burned all his notes in the kitchen sink and washed the black remnants down the waste pipe, running the water for fifteen minutes before he turned off the tap.

It was beginning to get light when he lay on the bed and slept in his clothes.

Foster spent the morning looking through both West and East Berlin newspapers from the date when his three people had been arrested. But there was nothing beyond the first short report of their names and the charges brought against them.

He spent the afternoon looking through the shelves of files on the East German secret police, the Stasis. It looked as if the arrests would have been carried out by *Abteilung X* which went under the description *Aktive Massnahmen*. And it was when he was looking through the names of their organisation in East Berlin that he thought of the radio intercepts passed on by his old monitoring group. He phoned one of his old colleagues and asked what Stasi frequencies they monitored and what sections they covered. There were several hundred frequencies that were randomly monitored and only a dozen with round-the-clock coverage. Four of those frequencies were for *Abteilung X*. Two of those frequencies covered the area called Stadt Mitte where his people had worked.

He took a taxi across to his old HQ in the big house in Grunewald. His old friend Garrett was a lieutenant now but quite ready to bend the rules for a mate. Nobody had ever actually said that individual SIS people couldn't refer to Security Signals' files.

They chatted for a few minutes and Foster was duly impressed by the banks of new equipment. AR 3000 scanners and ten ICOM R 9000s all fitted with auto-recorders linked to Revox tape-recorders with over-sized reels. There was a new section of four R 9000s coupled to M-7000 decoding terminals each with its own monitor and Epson printer.

'What do you need the M-7000s for?'

Garrett shrugged. 'They use a lot of RTTY for official communications to Moscow. And the Stasis use it a lot. 'What is it you're looking for?'

Foster explained without going into his conflict with Slaney, and Garrett took him to a row of steel shelving.

'Stasi stuff for the Stadt Mitte is all on this shelf. Covers two months and then it's moved over to main storage on *fiche*, if there's anything on your people it should be here. It's up-dated daily.'

'Wouldn't you have sent anything on those arrests to SIS anyway?'

'Depends. They're arresting scores of people every day. We may not have seen any significance in a particular arrest.'

'Do you still have the IBM 370?'

'Sure we do.'

'Does this Stasi stuff go on the computer?'

'Yes. Takes two days to get it on.'

'Is it programmed for name traces?'

'Yes. There's a list of trace categories pasted on the IBM. Just follow the code listing. There's a help-line if you need it. I'll leave you to it. Anyway, you know your way around.'

For six hours Foster ran the three names through the data in the computer. He found only one name. The girl's name. But it gave a reference match to a series of tracings of monitoring sessions. When he checked the transcripts he could see why they had had no significance for the evaluators. There were no details of the charges. Just the girl's name and address and the dates of Stasi surveillance reports. But what it did give was the name and location of the Stasi officer concerned. As Foster had surmised he was *Abteilung X*, a Leutnant Kolbe stationed at an address near the Library. And that was all he needed.

It was 10 p.m. when he got back to his office at the Olympiad and after checking in he went straight to Archives and searched the main directory for where Stasi personnel information was held.

There were a dozen bulky files but he breathed a sigh of relief that the system provided an alphabetical listing of names. There were few recorded names with ranks below major but all names relevant to *Abteilung X* and *Abteilung III* were recorded whatever their rank.

Abteilung III was responsible for under-cover espionage agents in embassies, consulates and other official organisations in foreign countries.

Leutnant Ernst Kolbe rated only a couple of short paragraphs. He was thirty-five, unmarried. Had done a year in the *Volkspolizei* before being recruited into the Stasis because of his police experience and his fluent Russian. He was the leader of a team of six responsible for counter-espionage in the central districts of East Berlin. Had been a member of all the usual communist organisations from youth onwards. Was rumoured to be homosexual but a handwritten note suggested this was unfounded. Lived alone in Stasi accommodation for unmarried officers. Had a degree in History from Humboldt University. No known close associates. He had been a Stasi officer for seven years. No known hobbies or special interests. SIS evaluation made him slightly above average Stasi in potential.

To be slightly above Stasi average was no accolade. Stasi officers varied widely in both experience and intelligence but the vast majority were time-servers who relished their authority over the population and exercised it ruthlessly in a thousand petty restrictions on personal liberty. They were not much more than the natural inheritors of the old Nazi Party system of *blockleiters* who spied on and informed on the inhabitants of every building in every city of the Third Reich. Petty tyrants who were feared and loathed by one and all. Despised even by the people who used them.

Satisfied with the fruits of his trawl through the monitoring records he went back to his rooms. He typed out his request to Slaney for an interview at Century House and kept a carbon copy.

In his office the next morning his request was delivered back to him in an official envelope. It was his original request, date-stamped with the date and time of receipt. It was crossed through heavily enough to have torn the paper in two places and scrawled across the space below his signature was written 'Request refused' in capital letters, and Slaney's signature.

CHAPTER 14

Slaney was stirring his morning coffee when the phone rang and he saw the red light flashing on the scrambler. He pressed the two buttons simultaneously and put the receiver to his ear. The voice on the phone was so loud and so angry that he couldn't hear what was being said because of the overload on the diaphragm.

'I'm sorry – I can't hear you. There's some kind of distortion on the line.'

'Is that you, Slaney?'

'Yes. Is that Tony Powell?'

'Too bloody true it is. What the hell's going on at your end?'

'I don't understand.'

'This fellow Foster. Talking about us throwing his people to the wolves and . . .'

Slaney broke in. 'I'm sorry, Tony. I'll get him in and deal with him at once.'

'He's here, you bloody fool. At Century House. Talking about going to the press. Why haven't you dealt with him in Berlin? For Christ's sake, don't you even know where your people are?'

'I told him to take a couple of days off to calm down. I didn't suggest he came to CH.'

'I bet you didn't. Anyway. I'm shuffling him back to you. You deal with him, my friend. If he talks about going to the press tell him we'll kick his arse from here to breakfast.'

'How did you respond to his story?'

Powell seemed to calm down a little. 'A bit of Land of Hope and Glory, a bit of Henry V at Agincourt and plenty of sugar in his tea.'

'And you're sending him back here.'

'He's gone to see his parents and I've told him as tactfully as I can that provided he's back with you by Friday noon latest he won't be posted AWOL.'

'And he was satisfied with that?'

'How should I know? That's your worry.'

'How do you want me to deal with him?'

'Oh, Jesus.' His voice rose again. 'Haven't I made myself clear? It's up to you to deal with him. But I don't want any drama here in London or in Berlin either. Be a bit tactful. Find some compromise.'

'Including what he wants – some sort of exchange?'

'Don't be ridiculous.'

And the phone was slammed down.

Back at Century House Powell straightened his tie as he said to Harris, 'Sometime in the next two or three months put your thinking cap on and find me a way of getting Slaney back here behind a desk where I can keep an eye on him.'

'Early retirement maybe?'

'No. It's my fault for picking him in the first place. Got a good track record until that cock-up in Beirut. Must have affected him more than we realised. More than I did anyway. Went rushing into trouble with those bloody Arabs and can't forget it. Plays it by the book now and the book don't work in places like Berlin. Especially with chaps like Foster. Struck me as quite a tough cookie. Intelligent too. But just a touch *naive*.'

'Do you want me to have a word on the side with Slaney?'

'No. Let him get on with it. Teach him a lesson.' He

paused. 'However – might be an idea for you to check that Master Foster heads back to Berlin, and to let Slaney know when he's arriving.'

Slaney went himself to Tegel to meet in Foster's flight. They sat for about ten minutes in the airport coffee bar and Slaney was as amiable as he could bring himself to be. Foster seemed calm but noncommittal when Slaney said that they would work something out together.

The following day Slaney had asked Foster to use his knowledge of conditions behind the Wall to evaluate the reports of the networks that worked into Leipzig and Dresden. Foster didn't seem enthusiastic about what was obviously intended as a compliment and was meant to be seen as an olive branch. It was too late for olive branches. Foster had made up his mind what he was going to do. It may not work, but at least he'd try. It depended on how the people on the other side reacted. His father had said it was crazy but his mother had been sympathetic. If it didn't work out nobody, except perhaps himself, would be any worse off.

Back at his rooms that night he collected the things he wouldn't need and took them to a locker at the Zoo Bahnhof, and booked himself a single room at the Remtor in Marburger Strasse. He took it for three nights, but slept that night at his own place.

CHAPTER 15

He used the phone in the Tourist Office. There was no problem getting an East Berlin number on that line as they were constantly booking accommodation for tourists who were spending a couple of days in East Berlin. There were three rings before the phone was picked up at the other end and the man just gave the number.

'I want to speak with Leutnant Kolbe.'

'Who's speaking?'

'It's a personal call.'

'Hold on.'

There was the sound of the receiver being put down and he heard the man say, 'Call for you, Leutnant. Says it's a personal call.'

There was the clicking of the call being transferred and then, 'Kolbe, who's calling?'

'I'd like to meet the Leutnant.'

'What about? And who are you?'

'Cooperation.'

'Where are you calling from?'

'From West Berlin.'

There were a few moments' silence.

'Tell me about the cooperation.'

'That's what I want to talk to you about.'

'I'll think about it. Where can I contact you?'

'You can't. I'll meet you today on your side of the fence.'

More silence.

'OK. Where shall we meet?'

'You know *Zur Letzten Instanz*?'

'Yes.'

'You name the time and I'll meet you there.'

'OK. Two p.m. inside. How shall I recognise you?'

'I'll be wearing Levis and Reebok trainers.'

'I hope for your sake you're not wasting my time.' He paused. 'And be alone or the meeting's off.'

'That goes for you too.'

Foster heard the phone being hung-up and walked out slowly into the sunshine. It had gone better than he expected. He'd thought there might be more red tape, a need for time to contact somebody back at Normannenstrasse.

He had a ham sandwich at an Imbiss kiosk on the Ku'damm. When he looked at his watch it was 12 noon. He took the S-Bahn from the Zoo Bahnhof to Bahnhof Friedrichstrasse, the crossing for pedestrians only. He used the Canadian passport and there was no problem. He changed more D Marks for Ostmarks at the money exchange on Georgenstrasse by the station. There was no way he could have been identified and followed but he walked around for ten minutes and with no sign that he was being followed then took a taxi from the station to Alexanderplatz.

It was exactly 2 p.m. when he went up the steps of *Zur Letzten Instanz*. The bar was used mainly by people from the nearby arts and drama centre. Wine upstairs, beer downstairs, and in the summer a small beer-garden outside. At this time it was half empty and Foster took a table near a window that looked out on the street. He looked around the bar but saw nobody else alone and when a waitress came over he ordered a beer. He had almost finished the beer when a man came in dressed in a dark green cotton jacket, a blue shirt and grey trousers. The leather belt with its brass buckle was identification enough. After looking around he walked over to Foster's table and pulled out a chair. As he sat down he said, 'Kolbe, you're younger than I expected.'

Foster smiled. 'You too.'

'Let's go upstairs, it's usually quieter.'

In fact there were only two other people in the upstairs wine bar and Kolbe led Foster over to a table in the far corner.

When they were both sitting Kolbe said, 'What's the cooperation you're offering?'

'Is Colonel Wagenbreth still the head of *Abteilung XI*?'

Foster saw the surprise on Kolbe's face and then suspicion taking over.

'Who the hell *are* you?'

'I'm in the same business as you are.'

'BND?'

'No.'

'Kripo?'

'No.' Foster paused. 'There's something I want from your people and I've got something to give in return.'

'You know that attempting to bribe a government official is a criminal offence in the DDR.'

Foster smiled. 'It is in the Federal Republic too. I'm not offering a bribe I'm offering my services to you people in exchange for something I want that will cost you nothing.'

Kolbe put his hands flat on the table as if he were about to stand up. But he stayed sitting as he said, 'I think we'd better discuss whatever this is in my office with other people present.' He shrugged. 'That's as far as I can go.'

'I didn't expect you to give me an answer without referring my proposition to Normannenstrasse or maybe Karlshorst. But it's better if I explained it to you first.'

'Why Karlshorst?'

'Because the KGB will be interested.'

'Let me make a phone call first.'

Foster shook his head slowly. 'No way. We either talk here or I leave and I'll contact somebody else at Normannenstrasse.'

'Why did you choose me to contact?'

'I'm not carrying a gun, I'm going to put my hand in my pocket for a piece of paper with three names on it. OK?'

Kolbe nodded. 'OK.'

The names were written in block letters on the face of a white envelope that Foster pushed across the table to Kolbe who looked at it for a few moments and then back at Foster.

'What are these?'

'You don't recognise the names?'

'No.'

'They're the names of three people your unit arrested a few weeks ago.'

'What were they charged with?'

'Espionage. Enemies of the State.'

Kolbe shrugged. 'There's too many to remember. Espionage is just a catchall description. We sort them out later.'

'These were my people. They just carried messages. They weren't important.'

'Go on.'

'I'd like them to be released.'

Kolbe half-smiled. 'You've got a bloody cheek, my friend. Once they're in the system nobody short of Honecker himself could get them out. Why should we release criminals?'

'Because what you get in return is far more valuable.'

'Why are you so interested in these people anyway?'

'They were my people. Small-time people in my network. They just carried messages. They had no idea what was in them.'

He saw the disbelief in Kolbe's face.

'You must be Foster.' Frowning, he said, 'But SIS never use German nationals as officers.'

'I'm not German. I'm British.'

'You speak German like a German.'

'My mother was German. I grew up in Germany.'

'And your people want to do a deal for these people?'

'No. Just me.'

'But why, if they were just couriers? Why do they matter so much?'

'Because they aren't spies. They're just people who thought they were doing the right thing.'

'So how can you do a deal if your people aren't interested?'

'I'm offering you my services. I'll work for your people for a year.'

'Doing what?'

Foster hesitated for a moment, then shrugged and said, 'Almost anything, but nothing against the British.'

'Are you kidding?'

'No. I'm very serious.'

Kolbe slumped back in his chair still looking at Foster. 'My people will never believe all this.'

'Maybe I should meet them.'

'You'd do that?'

'Of course.'

'Aren't you scared that we might just collar you? Catching an SIS officer over here could get a nice promotion.'

'Then you'd lose all the benefits you'd get from cooperating with me.'

'How much time have you got today?'

'As long as you want.'

'Let me phone HQ and see if they're interested.'

'No silly games, OK?'

'Not by me anyway.'

'OK. Go ahead.'

As he waited Foster wondered what their reaction

would be. They would assume from the start that it was a plant. An attempt by SIS to infiltrate the Stasis. But he'd rehearsed the scenario in his mind and he was pretty sure that he could convince them in the end that it was a genuine offer. It would be interesting to see if they referred it to the KGB. A lot would depend on what level they dealt with it. The more senior the level the more likely that they'd be interested. But Kolbe was beginning to be interested and that was a good sign. And he hadn't shown all his cards in talking to Kolbe.

It was almost fifteen minutes before Kolbe came back and sat down facing him.

'Sorry I took so long but you can imagine it wasn't easy to put it over. Anyway, cutting it short they'll see you in about half an hour. The guy's a major and very suspicious.'

'They think it's a plant, yes?'

'Yes. That's about it.'

'Where are my people now?'

'I checked. The two males are in the prison at Cottbus and I couldn't trace the girl.'

'Is the major coming here?'

'No. He wants us to go to his office at HQ. At Normannenstrasse. He's sending a car.' He paused. 'Don't be surprised if they don't go for your idea.'

Foster smiled. 'I didn't expect a red-carpet reception.'

Kolbe sighed. 'Let's go. The car will be outside by now.'

The car was a black Lada and the driver was in uniform with an ominous bulge of a weapon on the left-hand side of his jacket.

Neither Kolbe nor the driver spoke as the driver threaded his way through to Karl-Marx-Allee, turning off at Frankfurter Allee ignoring the main entrance in the sprawling complex of old and new buildings that was the headquarters of the *Staatssicherheit*, the Stasi, in the

Democratic Republic. They stopped at a sub-entrance and the driver got out and walked to the guard-room and Foster could see him showing a paper to one of the guards. When he came back he drove a couple of hundred yards to a small parking area and waited for Kolbe and Foster to get out of the car.

A man was waiting for them inside the glass door and Foster was searched very professionally as Kolbe waited and watched. They were handed over to a middle-aged woman who took them to a small elevator and up to the top floor. She signalled for them to wait in a small office, knocked on a heavy door and went inside. A few moments later she came to the door and waved them inside.

It was a large office. Swedish style teak and chrome and a thick carpet. The standard picture of Honecker on the wall behind the big desk. There were two men, one in uniform and the other in well-cut casual clothes. Foster saw a yellow file cover with his name on. It seemed encouragingly thin.

The officer told Kolbe to take a seat in the far corner and then pointed to a chair in front of his desk for Foster. He sat down behind the desk and the other man sat away from the desk.

'Right,' the officer said, 'you've been telling fairy stories to young Kolbe. Now try them on me.'

'It's very simple, major. I would like these very low-grade people from my network who were arrested over here to be released. And in return I will work for your organisation for a year.'

The major was a large man, good-looking in a coarse sort of way and he leaned back in his chair until it creaked.

'What kind of shit are your people peddling this time?'

Foster didn't reply and the major leaned forward resting his arms on the desk, his big hands clasped together, his grey eyes looking intently at Foster's face. It was an old-fashioned interrogator's move and it only disturbed new recruits. But there were a lot of medals on the tunic.

'You want those criminals to go over to the West, yes?'

'No. I just want them freed and their records destroyed. Two of them are local people not West Berliners.'

'What's the point in all this?'

'They aren't important, they aren't criminals and they certainly aren't spies.'

'You told friend Kolbe that your people wouldn't agree to this, so why are you disobeying their orders?'

'I think we should have tried to do a deal to get them released. We've done it before, for Brits.'

'Kolbe tells me your mother was German.'

'Yes. She was.'

'I'd have taken you for German. Never met a Brit who spoke German like a German.' He paused. 'You must have been very useful to them.'

Foster shrugged. 'I've been doing it for some years.'

'You're in the radio monitoring unit, aren't you?'

'No. I left them some years ago. I've been running networks into East Berlin since then.'

The major glanced briefly at the civilian and then back at Foster.

'Tell me why you really want these people released.'

'I've told you already. They were my people. They were loyal to me. They deserve my help.'

'So we set these bastards free and you slide back into West Berlin and we never hear from you again, while you dine out on the story of how you fooled the Stasis.'

'No. Not at all. I'd stay here in the DDR. I'll work here.'

He saw the surprise on the major's face but it was the civilian who spoke.

'Herr Foster, do I understand you are deserting from your SIS unit and proposing to work for us – here in East Germany?'

Foster nodded. 'Yes. But I wouldn't work against my own people.'

'Who would you work against?'

Foster shrugged. 'Anybody. It doesn't matter to me.'

'The Americans? The West Germans?'

'Yes.'

The civilian stood up slowly and looked at the major. 'I'll take over, Franz. I'll be in touch later.'

The major stood up and the civilian turned to Foster. 'We'll have a little chat, Herr Foster, and see if we can sort something out. My name's Hartmann. Peter Hartmann.'

Hartmann chatted about the German tennis-players, Becker and Graf, as he drove the white Mercedes through the side streets to a large house in Wilhelmsberg. There were big wrought-iron gates and a gardener opened them for the car. There was a well-kept lawn on each side of the gravel drive that curved round to the front of the house itself.

As they walked to the house Hartmann said, 'I'm sure you'll understand if I warn you that our friends will have you under surveillance, even while you're with me. I thought I should mention it.'

CHAPTER 16

The house was big and well-cared-for. It was faced with some kind of white stone and it looked as if it might have been a rich merchant's house that had been bomb-damaged and restored. Hartmann led the way into a tiled hall and through to a large living room. It was well furnished with antique furniture and a Steinway boudoir grand in the far corner near a stained-glass window.

Hartmann pressed a bell and signed to Foster to take one of the armchairs. When a male servant came Hartmann told him to bring them both coffee.

While they were waiting for the coffee Hartmann got them talking about football, seeming to be well informed about the popular teams in the Bundesliga. He smiled as he said that he supported Cologne. When Foster asked him why Cologne, Hartmann waited until his man had left after putting down the coffee things on a tray on the low table between them.

'Like you I was brought up in Germany but my father was a Russian. A Red Army officer. My mother was in Berlin when the Germans surrendered.' He shrugged. 'They had an affair and she went back to her parents in Cologne where I was born. I have always used my mother's name.' He stood up slowly. 'Make yourself comfortable – but don't go outside the house. I've got a few calls to make.'

Foster poured himself another cup of coffee and looked around the room without getting up. Hartmann was a strangely attractive man. Easy to talk to. And that was a useful talent for an intelligence officer. But Hartmann had a sort of easy-going charm that didn't go with what Foster knew of Stasis. There were film actors like Hartmann. Cary Grant and David Niven, Rex Harrison in *My Fair Lady*, and that Frenchman, Maurice Chevalier in *Gigi*.

He stood up and walked slowly around the room. The pictures were all modern with a couple of lush nudes that looked like Annigoni originals. The newspapers and magazines on a long table were mainly Russian. There was no music on the piano and Foster tentatively lifted the keyboard lid, and sat down on the stool. He put his right hand on a chord and struck the notes. He had never played a Steinway before but it was a wonderful, mellow sound. He looked to see that he was still alone and then he played. He played all those old German tunes that his mother loved so much, the *shmaltz* of Vienna and the popular songs of post-war Germany. He was playing *Drunt in der Lobau'* with lush chords when he suddenly stopped. It was crazy, he must be out of his mind, playing the piano in the middle of bargaining with people like the Stasis. It was Hartmann's voice that interrupted his thoughts.

'Don't stop. I was enjoying it.'

Foster turned to look at him. 'It just struck me that it was crazy sitting here playing like I was at home when we are discussing serious things.'

Hartmann smiled. 'Come over here and let's talk.'

When Foster was seated Hartmann said, 'There are one or two questions I need to ask you.' He paused. 'But before I do perhaps it would be only fair to tell you that I'm not a Stasi officer, I'm KGB.'

Foster was surprised but he made no comment and Hartmann said, 'I've checked on some of the Stasi files. Can I ask you if your main interest is the girl who was arrested, Uschi Bayer?'

For a few moments Foster was silent, then he said, 'I was concerned about all of them but particularly the girl. She's very young and I liked her a lot. She depended on me.'

'Were you lovers?'

'No. But I cared about her. I think she liked me too.'

Hartmann nodded. 'What kind of work for us did you have in mind?'

Foster shrugged. 'Anything you want as long as it's not against the Brits. Your radio monitoring system is very low-grade. I could up-date it.'

'What about a network into West Germany?'

'Stasi or KGB network?'

Hartmann raised his eyebrows. 'Why does it matter?'

Foster smiled. 'The Stasi networks go for numbers not quality. Far too expensive on people and money and all they produce is gossip not intelligence. It's just firing birdshot.'

'What about KGB networks?'

'Too thin on the ground but where you've got assets they're well-placed and well-controlled.'

'Just one more question before we eat. Were you expecting to go back to West Berlin tonight?'

'Yes. This was meant to be just a preliminary discussion.'

'But you meant what you said about moving here into East Berlin.'

'Providing my three people are released, yes.'

'I'm afraid that going back to West Berlin won't be possible. We've already gone too far for that.'

'But my clothes and my money are out there.'

'We'll either get them for you or reimburse you. You have to consider yourself more or less under arrest.'

'On what charges?'

Hartmann shrugged. 'We could find a dozen charges. Not that we need to.'

'And if I don't choose to cooperate any more?'

'Let's not go into that at this stage.'

Foster stood up. 'You'd better put me in jail right now. I don't intend cooperating under pressure.'

Hartmann frowned. 'Do sit down, Foster. There's no question of you going to jail, you'll be staying here at my house for a couple of days while you and I sort things out.' He looked at Foster. 'I must remind you, Herr Foster, that you do not come here as a plenipotentiary. You come as a man who chooses to desert from one intelligence service to its rivals.' He put up his hand to silence Foster. 'For a good reason. An unselfish reason. But – and I emphasise this – you have no rights here. You are dependent on our evaluation of your proposals. So far you have done quite well and I suggest that you should reflect on what would have happened if one of our people approached your old friends with a similar proposition and behaved as though he were dictating the ground rules.' He stood up. 'Now. Let's put this aside for a time and eat.' He walked to the door and Foster followed him.

The food had been good. Duck in cherry sauce followed by a fresh fruit salad. And the talk had been about America and American politics. After the coffee Hartmann said, 'I'll be away for a couple of hours. Play the piano or take a book up to your room. Make yourself at home.' He smiled. 'My people will take good care of you.'

Hartmann used the special 'secure' suite at the Soviet Embassy for his call to Moscow. He had used Litov's direct line but he'd had to hold on for nearly five minutes while Litov's deputy got him out of a meeting. Litov was a Georgian from one of the small towns outside Tbilisi, but most people assumed that it was the genes from his Armenian mother that had given him the subtle, contriving mind that had made him a General in the KGB when he was only in his early forties. Litov's brief ran wide and deep in Dzerdzhinski Square but his special area was the devising and control of special operations that didn't fit with the KGB's vast bureaucratic structure. Hartmann had been Litov's man in East Berlin for two years and had a string of wise decisions and operations that gave him an unusually close relationship with the General. He was a trusted man and the KGB top brass didn't go in much for trust. When at last he came on the line he said, without introduction, 'Another bloody reorganisation meeting.' He paused. 'What's your problem?'

'No problem. I've got an SIS man. Willing to come over. I want your approval to use him.'

'Tell me more.'

For five minutes Hartmann went over the details of what had happened and there was a long silence before Litov responded.

'What's so special about him?'

'He's a real gem. A strange mixture. Half Kraut half Brit. With experience of electronic surveillance and of running a network. Tough in a quiet sort of way but malleable. It's difficult to describe. A man who's shown that he's willing to risk his own skin out of loyalty to people who worked for him. People who don't really matter. Three non-active casual couriers.'

'And what do you want to do with him?'

'I want to let him comment on our radio surveillance. Equipment and procedures. After that pick his brains on our penetration of the West Germans.'

'Go on.'

Hartmann laughed. 'What makes you think there's more?'

'Because I know you, my friend. If that was all you wanted you'd have got on and done it without contacting me.'

'When he's proved himself I had in mind using him as my liaison with the Stasis at operational level. Non-executive but all-seeing.' He paused. 'If you know what I mean.'

'Yes, I know exactly what you mean.' He paused. 'You're sure you can control this fellow?'

'Yes. Played the right way I think I can make him as loyal to us as he was to his three stooges who were picked up.'

'OK. Go ahead. But don't rush it. And keep me informed.' He paused. 'Did you hear that Gavrilov's gone?'

'No. When?'

'Yesterday. The new man is slowly killing off the dinosaurs. Not a time for the old guard to ask for favours. Bear it in mind.'

'I will.'

Hartmann waited for Litov to hang up and then hung up himself. He lit a cigarette and sat there thinking about what Litov had said. It was always wise to do that no matter what relationship you had with the man in Moscow. Go over it word by word and look for a second meaning. When Brezhnev died in 1982 and Andropov had taken over, the KGB had looked forward to even more power from its old boss, but four years later Andropov was dead and it was Chernenko's turn and the big freeze came. And now only a year later they'd got the new man, Gorbachev, and nobody seemed to know which way the cat would jump. The consensus was that things were going to change. But nobody would forecast whether they would change for better or worse. He hadn't taken the title of President, he'd made Gromyko President and was ruling the country as General Secretary. He was only in his middle fifties and a staunch communist, but the impression was that he was going to be a reformer. And when reformers were in power you needed to know who and what was going to be reformed.

He phoned for a coffee and turned his thoughts to the

new development. It was an interesting scenario. Taking on an SIS man and gradually turning him into his mole inside the Stasis. He had sometimes thought of doing it himself but he'd been around too long for them to accept him as anything other than KGB. And his KGB rank would be against him. You shouldn't have a mole right at the top. One step down you got a wider picture. Carefully controlled Foster would be a real asset. Ideal background and experience, a genuine contributor and an ideal character and personality. Shrewd and tough but faintly old-fashioned. A character out of Thomas Mann.

He looked at his watch. It was just after ten. He'd better get back to the house.

Foster was aware that he was being discreetly watched. The house servants wore civilian clothes but they were obviously soldiers. The straight backs, the tendency to march rather than walk and standing to attention when he spoke to them. He tuned the radio in the sitting room to US Forces Radio in West Berlin and the second item was a report on the conviction of ex-US Navy officer James Walker for operating an espionage ring for the Soviets. Foster had read the confidential files on the Walker case. Walker had made huge sums from the KGB, but he was a macho slob whose appetite for teenage girls had eventually led his jealous wife to denounce him to the FBI. Foster switched off the radio and moved to the piano.

He played quietly without being aware of what he was playing until one of the servants came up to him and asked if he would play a Beatles' tune for him – he asked for 'Yesterday'. As Foster played it he thought of the words and wondered if they were significant. '*Yesterday – all my troubles seemed so far away . . .*' As he played the last few chords he had his first real doubts about what he was doing. He closed the piano and went up to his room, standing at the window looking down at the garden.

There were artificial lights at the feet of some of the trees that threw long shadows of leaves and branches onto the lawns. He heard a dog bark in the shadows below the window and the crunch of boots on gravel. And then the metallic clatter of what sounded like the loose magazine of an AK 47. For the first time in that eventful day he felt low. But he didn't know why. It had gone more or less as he expected. Better still when Hartmann had taken over. He seemed quite civilised. He had half expected them not to let him go back into West Berlin, and had thought that he might even end up in a prison cell. So why should he feel depressed to find himself in these luxurious surroundings? And it was only then that he realised that he wasn't depressed, he was lonely and vaguely homesick. Homesick both for his father and for his routine life at the unit. He shook his head, half-smiling in disbelief as he turned and walked to the bathroom. He had noticed earlier that there were all the usual bits and pieces including a toothbrush and toothpaste alongside a razor and an old-fashioned shaving brush.

There was a knock on the door as he came out of the bathroom and before he could call out the door opened and Hartmann was there, standing in the open doorway leaning against the door frame as he looked around the room.

'Well, my friend. Have you made yourself at home?'

Foster shrugged. 'Maybe not at home. But I'll survive.'

'Are you too worn out by the day to talk?'

'No.'

Hartmann closed the door and walked over to one of the armchairs and sat down. He waved towards one of the other chairs but Foster sat on the edge of the bed.

Hartmann took a deep breath and exhaled slowly. 'Too many cigarettes.' He paused. 'I've spoken to Moscow and I think we can accommodate you.' He smiled. 'With a bit of give and take on both sides.'

'What does that mean?'

'Problem number one is that we can't trace where one of your people is at the moment. Have to search the records. He was in jail in Cottbus assembling cameras for Praktika. But he was moved on somewhere. We can't trace where. Just a question of time. The other two – the girl and the man named Laufer, Martin Laufer I can get released tomorrow, but they'll have to stay this side of the border. You'll understand why, I'm sure.'

'That's fair enough.'

'And then there's you, Herr Foster. First of all I want you to look at the Stasi radio surveillance unit and tell me if it can be improved.'

'Will they agree to that?'

Hartmann smiled. 'Yes. I'm sure they will.'

'Who will I be reporting to?'

'To me personally. And coming down to sordid details you'd be paid in local currency at the same rate as a KGB captain with additional payments for languages and specialist knowledge. You'll have a quite pleasant house with a maid and cook. And a car. Not a Merc, I'm afraid, but not a Trabbi either. Probably a Lada.'

'And when do I start all this?'

'I've got files and handbooks for you to read about the Stasi set-up so that you know the ropes and know how it works. And I'll talk with you about the KGB relationship with both the Stasis and the East German government. Say a week or ten days and meantime you'll be based here.' He paused. 'You look doubtful or surprised. Which is it?'

Foster shrugged and smiled. 'Surprised.'

'Why are you surprised?'

'*You* surprise me.'

'Why, may I ask?'

'You don't fit my picture of a KGB officer.'

Hartmann laughed. 'We're not all Genghis Khans, you

know.' He paused and said quietly, 'That's a stereotype that died five, six years ago. Our masters slowly realised that those grim-faced men were out of date. You don't get invited to embassy parties in the West if you aren't just a little bit civilised. So they started casting their net a little bit wider.' He shrugged. 'Your thinking is part of the problem. You don't see us as people. You don't remember that Tchaikovsky, Rachmaninov, Chekhov and Tolstoy were Russians. And our people are the same. We don't talk to each other as nations. We shout. Abuse based on fear and ignorance. Saves us from all the bother of thinking and understanding. And that provides the excuse for us to build up armies and weaponry that could wipe out the whole world ten times over. So like you we stick to our prejudices. Cardboard enemies. Never fellow human beings who might have longings for a better life.' He smiled. 'Here endeth the sermon.'

For long moments Foster was silent. 'There is a difference, colonel.'

'Tell me.'

'We don't torture and kill our own people because they disagree with our system.'

Hartmann smiled and said softly, 'When were you last in Mississippi, my friend.'

Foster didn't reply and Hartmann stood up and walked to the door, where he stopped and turned.

'We need a new name for you. A German name. Any ideas?'

'How about Schultz?'

'Why that?'

'It was my mother's maiden name.'

Hartmann thought for a moment. 'OK. Schultz it shall be.' He nodded at Foster.

'Sleep well, my friend.'

And then he was gone and Foster was alone. He undressed slowly, putting his clothes on one of the chairs.

As he lay in bed in the darkness it was like when he was a child waiting for his mother to come in with the hot-water bottle to put by his feet before she tucked him up and kissed him goodnight.

CHAPTER 17

A servant roused him from his sleep the next morning. The colonel expected him for breakfast in half an hour. He looked at his watch and was surprised to see that it was nearly 9 a.m.

When they got to the coffee Hartmann nodded towards a long table at the far side of the room. 'Read those files. You've got two days to familiarise yourself. I'll be back this evening if you've got any queries.'

There were a dozen files laid out on the table each with a number stencilled on the cover. None of them was very thick and on top of the first file was a folded sheet. He drew a chair up to the table and unfolded the sheet. It was a schematic diagram of all the departments and sub-departments of the Stasi organisation with a note for each on its function and the names of senior officers. It was the same as the copy he had checked over at SIS a few days earlier. The title spread across the tops of both pages said simply *Struktur der Hauptverwaltung Aufklärung (HVA) des MfS*.

The files gave outlines of the different departments and their functions. They included espionage against the British and the United States, surveillance of East German troops, frontier control, control of the civil population, radio interception, specialist surveillance, a forensic and photographic section, recruitment and training, liaison with the Politburo of the DDR, translators and interpreters, espionage against the West German armed forces, NATO and the European Commission.

By late afternoon Foster had read them all. There was little apart from details that he didn't already know, but he noted that the files did not cover the section that was responsible for liaison with the KGB at Karlshorst.

Just after six o'clock there was the sound of a car and the shouting of orders and a few minutes later Hartmann knocked on the door and came into the room. He smiled as he saw Foster lying on the bed.

'Don't tell me those Stasi files sent you to sleep.'

Foster swung his legs over the edge of the bed so that he was sitting up facing Hartmann.

'I left the files on the table.'

'You read them all?'

'Yes.'

'D'you learn anything new?'

'No.'

Hartmann smiled. 'So no questions.'

'Just one. There was no file on the section of the Stasi that liaises with the KGB.'

Hartmann said sharply, 'You don't need to know about that.' Then he smiled and relaxed. 'I'm going to freshen up, then we'll eat and after that I want to brief you about your time with the radio people.' Hartmann walked to the door then stopped and turned. 'The girl and the chap named Laufer were formally released today. But I've given orders that Laufer must stay here in East Berlin but in return he'll get accommodation and a job to suit his skills.'

'Thank you.'

'Another thing. I've taken over a house for you. Small but pleasant enough. It's in Friedrichsfelde not far from the Stasi HQ.'

*　　*　　*

After they had eaten Hartmann ordered coffee to be brought to the sitting room. Foster saw that the files had gone.

When the coffee had been brought, Hartmann said, 'Am I right in thinking that there was nothing you didn't already know in those files.'

'More or less. A few details, mainly changes of officers' names.'

'Do your people have moles inside the Stasis?'

Foster shook his head slowly. 'I told you I wouldn't talk about my previous set-up.'

Hartmann shrugged. 'So be it. Let me tell you about your first job with us. You'll be introduced as a consultant. You can see anything you want, and ask any questions you want. If they try to find out who you're reporting to or your background you don't answer. Be tough with them.'

'What do you want me to look at particularly?'

'Everything. Equipment, procedures, anything that you find inefficient.'

'People?'

Hartmann hesitated for a moment, then said, 'No. Have opinions but don't make any comment.'

'How long do you want me to take?'

'As long as you need.'

'And how do I report on what I find?'

'Tell me when you're ready and I'll arrange a meeting for you to report verbally to me and another KGB officer.'

Foster smiled. 'Do I have to be tactful – diplomatic?'

Hartmann shook his head vigorously. 'No. Definitely not. This is a test of you as well as them so far as I'm concerned.'

'What name do I use?'

'Your new name – Schultz.'

Foster looked at Hartmann. 'Why did you keep your mother's name when your father was Russian?'

Hartmann was silent for a few moments and then he said, 'Because my father was a soldier, and I was born because he raped my mother. She found out his name but she wanted nothing to do with him.'

'But you have to be a Soviet citizen to be an officer in the KGB.'

'The commander of my father's battalion gave my mother an official note about the facts. That allowed me to take Soviet citizenship if I chose.'

'Why did you choose to be a Soviet?'

'Because in occupied Germany it was better to be a Russian than a German.'

'And you don't hate them for what they did to your mother?'

'You can't hate a whole nation because of what one man does. Your people raped German girls, so did the Americans and the French. It's what happens to the losers after a war. The Wehrmacht and the SS raped and killed in the campaign in the Soviet Union.' He shrugged. 'Ask your father, he was here in those post-war days.'

'How do you know that?'

Hartmann smiled. 'I checked up on you. Take it as a compliment. I had to call in a couple of favours.'

'Why bother?'

'Because you impressed me and I thought you could be valuable if you were treated properly.'

'Let's hope you're right.'

Hartmann stood up, stretching his arms. 'I'll drive you over to Normannenstrasse about 9 a.m. tomorrow. They'll have a Lada for you but you'll come back here until your own place is ready in a few days.' He stood up. 'See you about 7.30 tomorrow.'

Hartmann had taken him to the big block in the Stasi HQ that housed most of their radio and telephone monitoring. It was a much bigger operation than he had expected and he realised that SIS had substantially under-rated the Stasi monitoring operations.

He had been introduced as Schultz to a dozen departmental and specialist section heads. They had all been told that he was an independent consultant who had been ordered to carry out an audit of the whole operation. From their attitude he guessed that he was not only unwelcome but that he could expect only very limited cooperation.

In the afternoon he had been taken to the Soviet's military installation in Karlshorst which housed the large KGB directory staff. He was photographed and later given an identity document in both German and Russian that showed him as being a senior civilian employee of the Soviet Kommandatura.

Back at the house they had a sandwich and coffee and then Hartmann had driven him back to Karlshorst where he had signed for a 1984 1200 Riva Saloon, one of Lada's more reliable models. He was also given a driving licence and a card that entitled him to draw petrol and have his car serviced at the Soviet army transport section which was also in Karlshorst.

It was after dinner that evening that Hartmann told him that a housekeeper had been moved into his house to prepare it for when he would move in. Hartmann also gave him a thick wad of Ostmarks and a pass to the privilege shop where Soviet officials could buy both local and foreign goods.

'I've arranged for one of my young men to move into the house with you. He'll see that things run smoothly and he won't interfere in any way.'

Foster smiled. 'Is he army or KGB?'

'KGB. A lieutenant. Speaks excellent German. Well educated. Moscow University. Father a politician.'

'Sounds like what we call a minder.'

'What's a minder?'

'A kind of bodyguard who keeps you out of trouble.'

Hartmann smiled. 'I guess that's a fair description.' He stood up. 'By the way, if you want to communicate from time to time with your father I will see that your letter gets through without showing where you are. Your letters would be censored of course.'

Foster shook his head. 'I shan't want to contact him until I'm more settled. He wasn't very pleased with what I intended to do.'

'Your people the other side of the Wall have kept it damped down. I understand Slaney has an idea of what you have done but the official word was that you had had a nervous breakdown through overwork.' He paused. 'Do I know you well enough yet to ask you again why you did it?'

Foster was silent for long moments and then he said, 'It was a mixture of reasons but I suppose the deciding factor was something that Slaney said when I begged him to do a deal for my people. After a lot of hedging he said – "Why bother, they're only Germans." I never liked Slaney. He was an efficient officer but he was an upper-class snob. He saw people like me as useful peasants.'

'Would he have done an exchange if you'd been caught?'

'Probably. But only because I know too much. He'd assume that you people would beat me up and that I'd talk. But he would have resented having to do it.'

Hartmann said quietly. 'Did you expect to be beaten up?'

'If I'd been left to the Stasis – yes. But I insisted from the start that I wanted to talk to a KGB officer.'

'What's the difference?'

Foster smiled. 'A KGB man would recognise straight away that I was a valuable property. Stasis are just glorified policemen. Typical Gestapo types. No imagination.'

Hartmann nodded but not necessarily with approval. 'Interesting.'

* * *

For some reason that wasn't explained the move to his own quarters was postponed until he had completed his inspection of the Stasi monitoring set-up. It was three weeks before he told Hartmann that he was ready to report. He was told that a meeting would be arranged with Hartmann and another KGB officer in two days' time. The meeting would be at Hartmann's house. The officer was a KGB lieutenant-colonel and was from Moscow. But nothing was said about his role in the KGB. His name was Nikolas Granov.

CHAPTER 18

The three of them had eaten lunch together. Hartmann, Granov and Foster. Granov was a tall, thin man in his early forties. He spoke passable German but said very little. From the little he said Foster guessed that he was an academic of some kind. He searched for the precise word, speaking slowly and carefully and he seemed to avoid looking at Foster directly. The conversation was mainly about books and music. He had recently seen a performance of Gliere's *The Red Poppy* in Prague and was enthusiastic about Czech musicians. The only time he actually looked directly at Foster he smilingly confessed to being very fond of Britten's 'Simple Symphony', especially the pizzicato movement.

When the meal was over Hartmann led them to a room that Foster had not seen before. It was obviously a study and office combined. The walls lined with books and on a teak desk were various pieces of electronic equipment and three phones. One a red one which Foster assumed was a scrambler line to Moscow.

They sat at a long table and Hartmann nodded to Foster.

'Tell us what you found.'

'Let me deal with equipment first.' He paused and looked from one to the other. 'I was surprised at both the quality and extensive range of all the equipment. In fact the only . . .'

Hartmann interrupted. 'Forgive me for breaking in but

I'd like to talk first about what sort of cooperation you received.'

Foster hesitated for a moment and then smiled as he said, 'As you would expect in any large organisation it was a bit mixed. The technicians were wholly cooperative.' He shrugged. 'They were proud of their equipment and their maintenance record. They were quite frank about the down-time on the mainframe computers. It was properly recorded as breakdowns when it applied.' He smiled. 'A commercial installation very often hides its down-time as routine maintenance.

'Section heads and department heads ranged from total cooperation to almost pathological obstruction. But none of it was any real hindrance. The obstruction wasn't related to the function of the section but to the character of the man concerned. Those on the defensive would have been exactly the same if they had been running a factory making spanners.' He smiled. 'They didn't want outsiders passing judgment on their tried and proved operations.'

Granov said quietly, 'Did they attempt to find out who had given you the authority to check them out?'

'Not seriously. I had been introduced by Colonel Hartmann and I think they were more interested in what he does than my role.'

Hartmann said, 'What did you tell them about me?'

'Nothing. I said quite truthfully that I had no idea what your work is.'

'Were they satisfied by that?'

Foster smiled. 'I'm sure they weren't but they didn't probe beyond that. At least – only one tried to pursue it.'

'Who was that?'

'A Frau Lange who is in charge of personnel records of engineering staff.'

Hartmann raised his eyebrows. 'Why do you think she was so interested in my work?'

Foster smiled. 'I don't think she was interested in your

work at all. I think she fancied you and wanted to find out if you were married.'

'Good God,' Hartmann said. 'Do continue your report.'

'My only criticism on the technical side is that you should have a big mainframe computer to analyse check-words.'

'What does that mean?'

'You get masses of computer print-out every day. You'd need hundreds of people to read it and more to analyse it. So you feed in check-words to the computers and it looks for those words and does a separate print-out of any section where those words appear. You sometimes need to put in extra check-words even in that print-out to make sure that you aren't wasting time.'

'And we don't do this?'

'Oh yes. You do it but only when one of your main-frames is not occupied on other processing. You need a stand-alone computer for check-words. Moscow use a number of big ICL number-crunchers and they could specify what the Stasis need. Moscow buy direct from London, claiming that they are needed for industrial reasons.'

Hartmann nodded. 'OK. Carry on.'

'I then looked at how their resources were used and that is where I would recommend that you examine the operation very carefully.

'Their monitoring of NATO and West German forces is way out of date. Looking through their frequency lists for monitoring they are only scratching the surface. They are working not more than five per cent of the available radio traffic.'

Granov said, 'Why are they so lacking?'

Foster hesitated. 'At the risk of causing offence I have to say that too many people and resources and too much time and budget is being spent on petty domestic surveillance.'

Hartmann said softly, 'Could you justify that comment?'

'I think so. Eighty per cent of your resources and time are being spent on worthless domestic surveillance. There are literally hundreds of thousands of files on citizens – files that are seldom referred to. I came across dozens of cases at random that were pointless but time-consuming.'

'Give us an example.'

'A woman complains to a neighbour that her kid has never seen a banana. She's classified as a subversive. They bug her phone and every room in her flat. To do that secretly a false fire alarm is given. The whole block of flats is evacuated. Two or three hundred people. The surveillance goes on for years. Tape-recorders, typing transcripts of domestic chatter are recorded and preserved. The card on the file shows that the contents have never been looked at. Not even once.' He paused. 'And there are thousands of examples you could find. They have had to take over four large extra buildings just to house that sort of file. You could have built a new hospital with that money.'

There was a pause as Foster waited for a response but Hartmann just said, 'Anything else wrong?'

'Nothing technical.'

'What else then?'

'Low morale below the top. Middle ranks and lower ranks reckon that they have no chance of promotion without doing favours for the bosses.'

'What kind of favours?'

'Building work, decorating. First-rate electronics technicians painting the kitchen of some section boss. And in at least two sections there was sexual harassment. Sleep with the top brass or don't expect promotion. Or maybe not even keep your job.'

Foster saw Hartmann and Granov exchange brief glances and then Hartmann said, 'Anything else?'

'No. Nothing worth commenting on.'

Hartmann nodded. 'OK. We'll see you later. I've booked us seats at the *Staatsoper* tonight.' He looked at Granov and smiled, 'Not Gliere, I'm afraid. All Tchaikovsky but the Junior Kirov and they tell me they're very good.'

When Foster had left, Hartmann and Granov moved to the armchairs set around a small circular glass-topped table.

Hartmann looked at Granov. 'Well, Nikko, what do you think?'

'Competent, tougher than he seems, got an obvious chip on his shoulder.'

'About what?'

'Typical socialist. Justice for the workers. An instinctive suspicion of bosses and authority. You could use him, I'm quite sure of that.'

'Why so sure?'

'He's a born hero-worshipper. Looking for a role model. You could be that role model.'

Hartmann looked away, towards the windows and then back to Granov.

'Why me, Nikko? Why me?'

'Who knows. But you told me he asked you if he had to be diplomatic about the Stasis and you said no. You wanted the truth as he saw it. Yes?'

'Yes.'

'Can you think of any German who'd risk his life criticising the Stasis?'

'No. And all too few Soviets too. But how does that make me a role model. Is that just part of your new psychology?'

Granov laughed. 'There's no such thing as new psychology. We just learn more as we go along. For me I don't go on theories. I just learn as I go along. You or anyone else as intelligent as you could do the same if they had the same opportunities of exploring as many people's minds as I do. I just see the same patterns come up again and again. And like the Stasi surveillance I file it away. But unlike them I look at my files continuously. My experience tells me that this young man needs someone he can trust. Someone he can rely on. Somebody as strong as he is. Somebody he can respect.'

Hartmann took a deep breath. 'I'll bear it in mind, Nikko. Meantime, you know where your room is. I'm going to freshen up.'

As Hartmann got to the door Granov said, 'There's just one other thing, Peter.'

Hartmann turned to look at him, surprised.

'And what's that, Nikko?'

'You could also do him great harm.'

For several moments Hartmann stood there, looking not at Granov, but at something far away. Then he turned without speaking and opened the door. Hesitating for a moment when it was half shut behind him and then closing the door slowly and quietly.

After the theatre Hartmann had taken them to the *Ganymed* on Schiffbauerdamm. In deference to Hartmann who was obviously known there they were given a table by a window that looked out onto the Spree.

Apart from the Singapore duck with red cabbage, the wine and the plush, genteel environment, Hartmann had surprised them with his knowledge of the history of the place. Back in the 1920s it had been the most elegant bordello in Berlin and once upon a time Bertolt Brecht and Helene Weigel had been regular patrons of the restaurant.

Foster was seeing Hartmann for the first time away from his official background and he found him to be more sophisticated and outgoing than he had been back at the house. He wondered if it was because they were with Granov who seemed to be drawn out of his reticence by Hartmann's easy-going but obviously well-informed talk of poets and novelists. Several times Hartmann had drawn Foster into the magic circle by asking him about English writers. Not the usual Russian enthusiasms for Dickens and Shakespeare but modern writers like John Osborne and Kingsley Amis. Both of whom Hartmann saw as political writers. Writers of protest.

When they got back to the house Hartmann had insisted that Foster played for them all the Gershwin, Irving Berlin, Jerome Kern and Cole Porter that he could remember. It was 4 a.m. before they finally went to their rooms. But it was another hour before Foster slept.

Half-way through his report to Hartmann and Granov he had realised that they were not really interested in the points that he raised. It was like those questions they asked when he was doing his army training. Questions that you find out later had no correct answer but were merely to probe your mental reactions to situations calling for decisions that had some sort of moral conflict built in to them. It had all seemed comparatively relaxed but it was obvious that Granov was not really interested in the vices and virtues of the Stasi monitoring operation. It was some kind of test but he had no idea as to whether he had passed or failed.

Hartmann and Granov had talked for an hour together the next morning and finally Hartmann had asked the question that mattered.

'Will you back me in Moscow, Nikko?'

Granov smiled. 'You don't need my backing. You know that. They've given you a free hand. You can use him how you like.'

'I'm asking for your opinion. Off the record, if you want it that way.'

'My opinion about what?'

'Oh for God's sake, Nikko. For using him to run a network into West Germany.'

'OK. Let me be devil's advocate for a moment. You've got networks into West Germany already. Why do you need another?'

'Because the existing networks are virtually useless. They're amateurs. They're not Moscow trained. And they're Germans. The information they send back is gossip and rumour and half of it they've picked up from newspapers. We've had no more than six or seven really successful agents in West Germany in forty years. And they've all been Moscow trained. A year, sometimes two. These people I've got have had a month at the Stasi school. They think that sleeping with some elderly secretary in Bonn makes them into James Bonds. They are a waste of time.'

Granov smiled. 'And you still haven't mentioned Moscow's other reason for giving you a free hand.'

'What reason is that?'

'Our friends the Stasis.'

'Moscow told me not to discuss that with anybody. Did they discuss it with you?'

'Briefly.' He paused. 'They want you to have a mole inside the Stasi set-up. Yes?'

'Yes.'

'They didn't tell me why the sudden interest in our friends.'

Hartmann sighed. 'With all the changes going on in Moscow and unrest in the Warsaw Pact allies Moscow is concerned about the unrest here in East Germany. They want to know how much we can rely on the Stasis if there's a show-down.'

Granov smiled wryly. 'And how much they can rely on Honecker and his gang.'

'Exactly. So back to Foster. Do you back me on that?'

'Yes. But not in writing. I'll give you a favourable comment when I get back.'

'Do you want me to keep you informed?'

'No way. These things don't interest me.' He shrugged. 'I'm just one of Dzerdzhinski Square's tame psychologists. A humble worker at the rock-face of deception and . . .' He shook his head.

'And what?'

'I was going to say betrayal but the betrayals are not mine. I just supply the rationale for others. But even I demand some justification these days.'

Hartmann smiled but said nothing. Granov was not the humble figure he had described. He was Chebrikov's personal adviser and you didn't get to be any kind of adviser to the head of the KGB unless you had a tried and tested track record. But it was obvious that Moscow hadn't told Granov what the real role was that they had in mind for Foster. It was a sign of the times that they had agreed so readily and that it had been put on a 'need to know' status. Somebody in Moscow had been looking in his crystal ball and finding some disturbing answers in the very near future. Maybe it wasn't just Foster who was under examination by Granov. You never could tell with Moscow. Perhaps he too was being looked over. There was no litmus paper that would change colour to indicate loyalty, and with all the changes in Moscow now that Gorbachev was General Secretary all the pieces of the Kremlin jigsaw puzzle had been shaken up once again. It was like an American song he had heard and remembered from a trip to New York – 'There's gonna be changes made'. He always enjoyed his times in New York. The arguments, the discussions, putting the world to rights in dimly-lit bars in the Village with a wonderful stride pianist playing Fats Waller into the early hours of the morning. Landing at Sheremetyevo always made him feel that somebody had switched off all the lights.

CHAPTER 19

The next morning as Foster looked out of his bedroom windows he saw that there had been a heavy fall of snow in the night and he realised that it was only a month from Christmas. Christmas 1987. It would be the first Christmas that he had not been with his father for at least a couple of days. He would be busy all day in the shop and at night he would be working out the details for the January sale of cookers and refrigerators. Sometimes he envied him the routine of his life. Always knowing how the days would be spent, the highlight for his father a trip down to Villa Park to see the Villa play. Hartmann had said he wanted a talk with him mid-morning and he wondered what it would be about.

They were in Hartmann's study and Foster sensed that the KGB man was avoiding coming to the point. They had talked about the summer holidays when they were children. Foster at Weston-super-Mare and Hartmann at a villa on the Baltic. But eventually Hartmann said, 'I want to brief you on what we have in mind for your new role, but first of all another small matter.' He smiled. 'I'd planned what I thought might be a pleasant surprise for you, but having thought it over I decided that maybe I ought to tell you about it first.'

Foster smiled. 'Sounds interesting.'

Hartmann shrugged. 'Maybe.' He paused. 'Your girl courier – Ursula Bayer – I thought it might make you feel more at home in your new place if she was your housekeeper. I talked to her about it and she was obviously delighted.' He paused again and looked at Foster. 'How about you?'

Foster looked surprised. 'A generous thought. It suits me OK.'

'You'll be working mainly from the house and of course you'll have what you call your "minder" there permanently.'

Foster nodded but made no comment.

Hartmann shifted uneasily in his seat, leaning forward as he said, 'The operation is top-secret and it would be a disaster if it were leaked. For that reason it was decided that despite its extent and complications it had to be done by one man. It requires experience in two different aspects of intelligence. Experience that would not normally be available in one man.' Hartmann looked at Foster. 'I'm sure that you're aware that our attitude and treatment of you has been unusual. And it is no reflection on your talents if I say that the reason for our reactions is that you happen to combine the two different areas of expertise that we need. The operation was approved two months ago but there has been no suitable candidate for us to consider.' He shrugged. 'You're just what we need.'

'What is it you need?'

'Somebody with enough experience of computers and radio to use all the Stasi facilities without them knowing what he's doing combined with experience of recruiting and running a network of agents.'

'And who or what are the targets?'

Hartmann sighed as he stood up, walking slowly to the door and then turning to walk back slowly to Foster, standing there silently looking at him for long moments. Then, avoiding Foster's eyes Hartmann said, 'A variety of targets. For now, let's say, the West Germans, especially the BND, the neo-Nazis here in the DDR and the Stasis themselves.'

'That would take a team of at least twenty. Technical evaluators, researchers and unlimited access to all available records. It would take months to set up before we even started a penetration operation.'

Hartmann shook his head. 'Just you, my friend. You should be flattered.'

'Why?'

'That you're the only one we trust to do it.'

'And access to records?'

'Unlimited access to all Stasi files.'

'Is this why you had me look over their operation?'

'Partly. At least you know where to look.'

'Can I copy files? – it would have to be on a computer and floppy-disks.'

'Anything you want. Tell me what equipment you want and I'll see you get it.' He sat down on the sofa beside Foster. 'A lot depends on this operation – for me especially. And others.'

'Who are the others?'

'Just two men. Men in Moscow. KGB men.'

'Is this official – the operation?'

Hartmann hesitated. 'Official enough.'

'Why not a Soviet to do this work?'

'There was nobody suitable at the moment.'

And for the first time in their relationship Foster knew that the KGB man was lying.

'The Stasis will do everything they can to hinder me.'

Hartmann smiled. 'They won't know what you're looking for. Take files you don't want as well as those you need. You don't need me to tell you how to handle it.'

Mid-day he drove the Lada, following Hartmann's car. It was snowing again. The house he was to occupy was only a few minutes' drive from Hartmann's house. It was a smaller version of Hartmann's place with red tiles on the roof and blue shutters. He pulled up at the doors of a double garage alongside Hartmann's car.

There was a porch over the door of the house and as they stood there Hartmann said, 'Neither the KGB man nor the girl know anything of your operation. Just tell them you are doing research for me.' As Foster nodded Hartmann took out a bunch of keys from his briefcase, handed them to Foster, holding one of them separately. 'These are your keys. When your work-room is ready it will have special security.' Then he smiled. 'Let yourself in. They're expecting you.'

Foster's reunion with Uschi Bayer had been both brief and stilted, both of them acutely aware of their changed circumstances; eager to talk about what had happened to each of them but restrained by the presence of Hartmann and Sasha Tolstoy the young KGB officer.

The house was well furnished and on three floors. The whole of the top floor was his. A sitting room, a bedroom, bathroom and a study with a desk and table. The heavy door to the study was steel in a metal frame and with two complex locks and a dead-bolt. When he left, Hartmann said to him quietly, 'Lieutenant Tolstoy will check the house for bugs twice a day, he'll let you use the detector yourself on your rooms.'

After Hartmann had left, Foster found Uschi Bayer in the kitchen. She was blushing as he looked at her, smiling.

'Are you OK?' he said.

'I'm fine.' She paused. 'Why did you do it?'

'Do what?'

'The colonel said you offered to work for them if they released me and the other two.'

'That's right.'

'But why? Why did you do it?'

'Because the charges brought against you were ridiculous. You were no more enemies of the State than the East German politicians who sneak across the border to buy Western goodies.'

'But your family and your job. Your whole life.'

Foster smiled. 'Don't worry. It'll be all right. Tell me about you. What happened?'

She shrugged. 'They came for me at the University. They took me to a Stasi place and kept asking me questions about what I did and who my contacts were. I refused to answer any questions and it was obvious that they knew all they wanted to. Somebody had talked already.'

'Who?'

'I think it was the man you had at the library.'

'Why do you think that?'

'They talked quite openly about Laufer, the railway worker, but they never mentioned Braun.'

'It doesn't matter any more. They've released Laufer and given him a job this side of the Wall.'

'They told me I was to work here for you. I didn't have any choice.' She paused. 'Do you mind?'

He laughed. 'Of course I don't. I'm glad you're here. Somebody I know. How about you? Do you mind?'

'I'm delighted. I shall enjoy it.'

'Have you met Lieutenant Tolstoy?'

'Yes. He's OK. He does what the colonel tells him.' She laughed. 'He does what I tell him too.'

'Have they put any restrictions on you?'

'No.' She smiled. 'The only one I have to please is you. I can get anything for the house. I can come and go as I please. I've got a nice room here.' She shrugged. 'I'm very lucky.'

'What do you do in the evenings?'

'I've only been here for two weeks but most evenings I visit one or other of two families I've known a long time. Two very different families. One very simple but very gentle and kind. And the other is kind of academic. Always arguing and discussing. Putting the world right.'

'I'd like to meet them. Both of them.'

She looked embarrassed and then said quietly, 'What should I say you are? They're bound to ask.'

'I'm a computer consultant to the government.' He shrugged and smiled. 'And what's more, I really am.'

'Tell me when you're ready to eat. And what do you want to do for Christmas?'

'Christmas?'

'Yes.' She smiled. 'Next week.'

He shrugged and smiled. 'I'll leave it to you.'

In his work-room he sat at the long wooden table and wrote out a long list of the equipment he needed and drove round to Hartmann's place to hand it over. The KGB man read it through and then looked at him.

'I don't understand computers. Is this equipment easy to get?'

'Most of it is standard stuff. I've marked a couple of non-standard items. If they can't get them I'll tell them how to get hold of them from suppliers in Frankfurt.'

'OK. Leave it with me.'

By the end of the week all the equipment was available and Foster spent a day wiring it up and testing it. When Hartmann called in that evening he told him that he was ready to start. Hartmann used the house phone and spoke to several people at Stasi HQ and arranged a meeting for the next morning.

CHAPTER 20

There were four Stasi men at the meeting with Hartmann and Foster and as Hartmann told them that Foster had authority for access to all Stasi files their resentment was all too obvious.

It was a man named Kurth who expressed their resentment.

'With respect, comrade colonel, this man is being given access to files that are not only top security grading but which are not available beyond our own sections. Where in some cases we ourselves do not have access authority.'

'I'm aware of that, Herr Kurth. If you want to dispute my instructions you should contact General Ustinov at KGB HQ.'

'I'm just pointing out the situation, comrade colonel.'

Hartmann smiled. 'Thank you, Herr Kurth.' He looked around at the four of them. 'Any other questions, gentlemen?'

There was no response and Hartmann stood up. 'Herr Schultz will be reporting directly to me on a daily basis. I shall appreciate your enthusiastic cooperation.'

As they walked back to where the cars were parked side by side Hartmann said, 'When they call me comrade colonel I know the bastards are going to try and make trouble. Don't compromise. If you don't get what you want immediately, phone me, don't wait for our evening meeting. And go back in there now and get started.'

* * *

Foster spent the rest of the day noting details from the indexes of the areas that interested him. The indexes covering high-level Stasi informants, neo-Nazis and Stasi contacts in West Germany. He found a reference to files on SIS Berlin and added them to his list.

The information had already been input to dozens of floppy-disks. He reckoned that it would take two full days to transfer the information to hard-disks that were compatible with his own equipment. Fortunately most of the Stasi equipment was based on standard hardware and software.

All day he was ignored by Stasi staff but he was aware that they were trying to find out what interested him. He checked on several indexes that didn't interest him just to confuse them.

He took his notes back to the house and locked them in his work-room before going down to the kitchen for a coffee.

He smiled when he saw the Christmas tree in the living room, complete with tinsel and paper decorations. He took Uschi Bayer for a meal at *Zur Goldenen Gans*, a pleasant restaurant that was part of the Grand Hotel on Friedrichstrasse. They had chicken soup followed by venison. It was the first time in her life that Uschi had eaten in a real restaurant.

When they were looking for Foster's car she suggested that they called in on the way home at the family Mundt.

On the way to the Mundts' place, a flat in a workers' block, she warned him that they were very simple people and rather old-fashioned in their attitudes to life. As they drew up at the tower-block he reminded her that his name was Schultz and that he came from Nieder-Sachsen. His father and mother lived in Austria.

The small apartment was on the third floor, which had originally been accommodation for a married couple but was now housing four people. There was a kitchen which was also for eating in, a living room and two bedrooms. The toilet had a wash-basin but no bath, but the rent for the flat, which was the equivalent of £3 a week, included four free passes to the public baths. The flooring was a cheap plastic from a factory in Leipzig.

Old man Mundt was in his sixties, an electrician at a local factory making cardboard boxes. A lifetime member of his union but not interested in politics. Seemingly just glad to be alive and have a safe job, and devoted to his family. A devotion that was practical rather than overly emotional. Frau Mundt was several years younger, a plump, laughing woman who spent her days making children's clothes at a local factory. Her wages just enabled them to survive but she enjoyed the company of the other women working on the sewing-machines. Karl, who was in his twenties was an apprentice at a large garage and his sister, Paula, was sixteen and still at school.

When Foster and Uschi arrived the TV was switched off and it was obvious that she was treated as part of the family. Foster was made welcome but with a politeness that was also a reservation of judgment. His only proven virtue was that he was Uschi's friend.

When they learned that Foster's work was with computers they were obviously impressed, Frau Mundt looking across at Uschi with an approving nod for the new boy-friend. The men talked football and the women about shortages of fruit and toilet rolls and after about an hour it was time for them to leave.

In the car on the way back she said, 'What did you think of them?'

'They reminded me of my parents. Not had so many chances as my parents but good, hard-working people, uncomplaining and not expecting much from life.'

'Tell me about your parents.'

He sighed. 'It's better if you don't know, Uschi.

Anyway they're just straightforward, ordinary people. Doing their best.'

'Were you the only child?'

'Yes.'

'Do you miss them?'

'In a way I do, but I can cope. But I'm sad for them. They miss me and they don't really understand why I've done what I have.'

'How is it you speak German like a German?'

'My mother was German. I grew up in Germany. I went to school here.'

'Will you ever go back?'

'I've no idea. I've just got to wait and see how things turn out over here.'

'Sasha says the colonel is very pleased with you.'

'Who's Sasha?'

'The KGB lieutenant.'

'What's he like?'

She shrugged. 'He's OK. He's no problem.'

A week after Christmas he met the Westphals, her other family friends. A sharp contrast to the Mundts. Both strong Party members but their sons Frederik and Johan were a strange mixture. Disagreeing with their parents on almost everything. Resentful that they couldn't travel in the West and openly critical of the old men who ran the State. Eager to quote gossip of corruption and nepotism but tolerated by their parents provided they didn't air their views outside the home. The father taught German history at a local High School and their mother was an important official of the Party's women's section. They saw their sons' attitudes as no more than the typical defiance of the generation war. Despite their differences they were a lively, sharp-witted family who made their disagreements seem academic rather than real.

*   *   *

In that same week Foster had started his task of transferring the information he had identified, from floppy-disks to hard-disks. And that had meant using the Stasi equipment at Normannenstrasse.

He did this work at night when there were fewer Stasi people on duty and the computer area was only on stand-by.

During the day, back at the house, he checked the hard-disks and formatted another disk for the next night's work.

After ten days he had recorded everything that he needed. But that was only the beginning of his work. He had around 50,000 files on his records and they would probably yield not more than a hundred files that were of use to his operation. But his most useful discovery was the codings that identified the nature of the contacts on each file. Codings that indicated status, vulnerability, and code-names. Codings that would save him days of useless file-reading.

He routinely reported to Hartmann every day but because of working nights he saw little of Uschi Bayer and Sasha Tolstoy. The first night that he was at home Uschi had been invited to the Westphals for a vegetarian meal. She had phoned and asked if Foster could come with her. No problem. It was to be an evening of open discussion and so long as he joined in he was welcome. The subject for discussion was the arrest of members of the East German social democrats who had assembled in Berlin on 17 January to commemorate the murder of Rosa Luxemburg and Karl Liebknecht. The arrested people had been deported over the border that day into West Berlin.

The discussion was already under way by the time they arrived. The whole family were there and a middle-aged married couple who both worked at the Party HQ in Dresden.

Herr Westphal was waving his arms around as they

settled on to the floor between his wife and son Johan. His indignation was almost uncontrollable.

'Why should people want to remember dinosaurs like Luxemburg and Liebknecht? They died fifty years ago – or more.'

'Nearly eighty years actually,' shouted Johan. 'And they didn't die – they were murdered by Wehrmacht officers.'

Westphal turned on him angrily. 'Karl Liebknecht was a bourgeois, a lawyer – and a social democrat, not a Party member.'

Frederik joined his brother. 'But Rosa Luxemburg was a Party member. She was in prison for years because she wouldn't renounce the Party. Wasn't she worth remembering?'

'Why not celebrate our own heroes – those we know – like Pieck and Ulbricht. The living not the dead.' He paused. 'What do you think, Herr Schultz?'

Foster hesitated for a moment and then said, 'Maybe we ought to remember what Rosa Luxemburg said – "Freedom is the freedom of those who think differently".'

Frau Westphal moved in to smooth the ruffled feathers. 'Moscow always remember Rosa, my dear.' She looked around. 'The food's on the kitchen table. Let's go.'

On the way home Uschi said, 'What did you make of all that? I've never seen Otto so worked up.'

'Didn't you get what his real problem was?'

'No. What was it?'

'Those people were arrested and then shoved over into West Berlin, which is what most people in the GDR are longing to do. Their punishment was a reward but he daren't complain on that score.'

'Why not?'

'Because the Party faithful always portray West Berlin as a living hell so you can't say the punishment itself was unfair.' He paused. 'It was very revealing.'

'Of what?'

'Of his own secret thoughts – that West Berlin is a better place to be.'

'Is it?'

Foster shrugged. 'Depends on what you want. If you want freedom and democracy then yes. But you have to pay the price.'

'What's the price?'

'You have to think for yourself. Make your own decisions. Some people are happier doing what they're told to do.' He paused. 'How did you come to meet them?'

'I gave Johan Russian lessons. I got bored with it and I passed the job on to Sasha.' She shrugged. 'He needs a few pennies.'

As he was locking the car she turned to look at him, and said softly. 'I never said thank you for setting me free.'

'All that matters to me is that you *are* free.'

She kissed him on the mouth and as his arms went round her she pressed her firm young body to his and drew back her head to look at his face. 'Do you want to sleep with me?'

For a moment he didn't reply, then he kissed her again and released her. 'Yes, of course. You're very pretty and I always cared about you a lot. But we'll wait. I don't need rewarding. But you give me a kind of peace just being here. Something sane and gentle that's nothing to do with my work.'

He walked her to the door with his arm around her waist. As he opened the door she screamed and pointed. Lieutenant Tolstoy was lying at the foot of the stairs. His face was deathly white except for a raw red wound along his cheek. As Foster bent over him and pressed his finger below his jaw he felt the pulse and Tolstoy groaned. There was a smell of ether on his clothes.

Foster turned to the girl. 'He'll be all right. Phone the

colonel. Tell him what's happened while I check the house. We'll need an ambulance.'

As the girl picked up the phone Foster went up the stairs to his rooms. The outer wooden door was splintered, the lock hanging loose. Whoever it was had tried to open the door to his work-room the same way but the steel frame and door had held and an attempt had been made to make a hole in the breeze-block wall, but the network of perforated steel between the blocks had been too much.

When he went back downstairs Hartmann was already there.

'They tried to break into my work-room but they didn't make it.'

'Are you sure?'

'Quite sure.'

'I've ordered a KGB ambulance for our friend here.' He paused and looked at Foster. 'Did you smell the ether?'

'Yes.'

Hartmann turned to the girl. 'Go to bed, Fräulein Bayer. Forget all this. We'll deal with it.'

Reluctantly she walked to the stairs and Foster realised that she was still scared. He walked with her to her room and checked that it had not been disturbed before he went back to Hartmann.

Two men in para-medic whites were lifting Tolstoy onto a wheeled stretcher. They rolled it to the front door and down the two steps to a waiting estate car with KGB number plates and a wooden ramp leading to the open rear end of the car. Hartmann and Foster watched them drive off.

Hartmann leaned against the wall. 'OK. What's your guess?'

Foster smiled. 'Same as yours.'

'You got any particular man in mind?'

'I'm afraid not.'

'Where did you go tonight?'

'Some friends of Uschi, a family named Westphal. Both parents keen Party members.'

'By invitation?'

'They invited Uschi and I just tagged along. They didn't know I'd be going.'

'I've arranged for a KGB Special Investigation Unit to look it over. They should be here any minute.'

'I'll make us a coffee.'

As Foster spoke he heard the sound of car doors being closed and Hartmann went to the door.

It was nearly 6 a.m. and beginning to snow when the squad had finished checking inside and outside the house and questioning Foster.

As Hartmann was leaving, he said, 'They tell me that there are plenty of latents and it seems that one of your neighbours reported a dark blue Lada parked across the road for nearly an hour. But she called the *Volkspolizei* and they hadn't been informed that your place was a secure house. They didn't send out a patrol car. Just logged the call.' He sighed. 'Get some sleep, my friend. I'll be around about mid-day. We'll get the bastards who-ever they were. And the ones who gave them their orders.'

'What hospital are they taking the lieutenant to?'

Hartmann shook his head. 'Forget him. He'll be all right in a couple of days.'

CHAPTER 21

Foster woke the next morning to the sounds of hammering and when he went to the window he could see men building a wooden shed near the gate from the street. It was almost finished and a man was paying out cable from a drum and laying it loosely along the side of the drive towards the house.

He dressed and shaved and knocked on Uschi's door on his way downstairs. There was no reply and when he walked into the kitchen there were two women there. A woman in her fifties, plump and homely, nervously touching her grey hair as she saw him and then turning to look at the other woman who he guessed was in her late twenties. She smiled as she said, 'Fräulein Bayer is taking a few days' leave and Frau Kramer . . .' she nodded towards the older woman '. . . and I, have been asked to take over. My name is Gala. Would you like breakfast?'

'Just coffee and toast would be fine. Is Fräulein Bayer upset?'

The girl smiled. She was very beautiful. Tall and slim with big dark eyes, a neat nose and a full mouth. 'I don't think so. It was the colonel who felt she might be better away for a few days. He will be coming to see you at mid-day.'

'What's all the hammering for?'

She shrugged. 'Just a place for a couple of watchmen to see you don't have another break-in.'

He took the tray with the coffee and toast into the living

room and switched on the radio before settling down on the couch with his breakfast. The radio was tuned to Moscow's 'Peace and Progress' radio station's news in German. A former professor had just been elected as President of Haiti, many thousands had been made homeless in Tian Shan province in China and in County Armagh Irish freedom fighters had killed four members of the British army of occupation. The Soviet forces in Afghanistan had assisted the ruling government in its efforts to bring peace and democracy to the area of Kandahar.

He stood up, switched off the radio and walked upstairs to his room. The locks on his work-room were stiff from the battering the door had received but they slid open with a little manoeuvring. He switched on his ICOM transceiver to the BBC's World Service. It was an interview with England's football team manager discussing the pros and cons of the long-ball game and the possibility that a sweeper might be brought into the line-up for the international game against the Poles. Almost without thinking he tried RIAS the American radio station in Berlin and then the West Germans' WDR in Cologne. The Americans were concentrating on the leader of a pop group who was giving a concert that evening in Berlin in aid of a German children's charity and WDR were engaged in a solemn discussion between a director of Deutsche Bank and an opposition politician about the real meaning of inflation and the significance of something called the Lombard rate.

As he switched off the set it struck him that for a few moments he had listened in to what four major powers thought was really important that day. Moscow and Soviet propaganda, football for the Brits, generosity funded by rock and roll by the Americans and money for the West Germans. Like the Gospels said – 'Where your fortune is, there will your heart be also.'

*   *   *

It was mid-afternoon before Hartmann arrived, looking strangely worried but trying to conceal whatever was troubling him.

'The girl, Uschi Bayer, were you lovers?'

'No. I told you that when you first questioned me.'

'But since, since you were at this place?'

Foster smiled and shook his head. 'No. Does it matter anyway?'

'Not really. It makes my bit of domestic gossip easier to announce.'

'Sounds intriguing.'

Hartmann shrugged and smiled. 'She went to the hospital this morning to see Tolstoy. She phoned me and I gave her a permit.' He paused. 'It seems they want to get married. Love at first sight apparently and last night's little drama brought it to a head. I said it would depend on your wishes.'

'It's OK with me. When's the big day?'

'As soon as possible. She's in the family way.'

Foster laughed and shook his head. 'I'd no idea. They must have been very discreet.'

'She was very worried that you would think she was ungrateful for what you did for her.'

'No way.' He paused and looked at Hartmann. 'Any news on last night?'

'Only negative news.'

'Like what?'

'I assumed it was your old friends back at the Stasi monitoring unit. But it wasn't.'

'How do you know?'

'Let's just say I know and leave it at that.'

'Who else would know about me?'

'That's what I'm trying to find out.'

'Any clues?'

'Yes. But they don't fit.' He paused and looked at Foster for several seconds before he went on. 'There's some pretty strange things going on in this country at the moment.'

'What kind of things?'

'I don't know. It's just a feeling. A new kind of anger at us, groups of people who seem to be planning, waiting for something to happen.'

'What kinds of people?'

'Neo-Nazis, dissidents, subversives, the Stasis themselves. A lot of liaison with groups in the West. And meetings between groups here and in Hungary and Austria. We think that the West Germans are funding dissident groups over here. Maybe even providing weapons.'

'For what purpose?'

'Just stirring up trouble.'

'What do Moscow think?'

Hartmann smiled wryly. 'They suggested I should take a holiday. Victim of stress. Give them their due they've put a small team together to run through every scenario from an armed uprising against the Soviet occupation to NATO forces coming over the border.'

'What are the symptoms that make you feel this way?'

'More and more recruitment and activity by the National Front. Public meetings in defiance of the law. Openly wearing their swastika armbands and screaming Hitler slogans.'

'But they're just thugs looking for a fight. They're not a political party with policies.'

'They preach Germany for the Germans. Foreigners out. More and more people are attending churches. The churches are packed every Sunday. The black-market is big business. Across-border trade. International. Ordinary members of the public demonstrating against shortages and corruption.' He stood up and walked over to look at the piles of print-out on Foster's work-bench. But he wasn't really looking at them. Finally he turned and looked at Foster.

'Despite what they say Moscow are scared.'

'Why?'

'Because it's all falling apart. Gorbachev and his *glasnost* and *perestroika* have lifted the lid off and they can't get it back on again. People are openly criticising and he can't prise the hands of the old men off the levers of power. He can make policy statements until he's blue in the face but nothing changes. It's crazy to think that all those guys are going to give up their power and their privileges without a struggle.' He paused. 'It's strange, it's a mirror image of things here. Churches crowded, ordinary people demonstrating, the black-market thriving.'

'But you and I know that these things go on all the time, Colonel. This is our background. We live with it and experience tells us that most of our fears are never realised. We look for treachery and subversion. We become paranoid.' He smiled. 'We use paranoia as a therapy.' He paused. 'Or is there more to it this time than you've told me?'

'What makes you think that?'

Foster shrugged. 'In this business you get an instinct. Little bells ring, little red lights flash. You don't know why. But you know something's wrong.'

'That's the difference between you and me. One of them anyway. I'm a planner, an organiser, but you're a doer. My career could sometimes be at stake but not my life.'

Foster laughed. 'That probably means that your worries are more likely to be a quite accurate analysis of the situation than paranoia.' He paused. 'Tell me about the girl who calls herself Gala.'

'Galina Michalevya Leonov. She's twenty-six or seven. Moscow University, excellent linguist, sophisticated and well travelled for a Soviet.'

'And her background?'

'Father is one of the top film directors in Moscow and her mother was a well-known singer. Opera. She died two years ago in a car accident in Rome. Both of them highly respected and neither of them political.'

'And the girl herself – what does she do?'

'She's KGB.'

'Why did you choose her for this place? She seems over-qualified for the job.'

Hartmann smiled. 'Uschi was OK but I thought you needed someone a bit brighter. Gala has a wide circle of friends, creative people. You hardly know East Berlin and the GDR and it's time you had some life apart from your work.' He paused. 'She knows about your background but not about your work for us. I told her you were doing research for me.'

For a few moments Foster was silent and then he said, quietly, 'When are you going to tell me what my real brief is?'

Hartmann stood up. 'When you've got your initial work done we'll talk again.'

Looking from the window of his living room he saw that the 'watchmen' turned out to be uniformed and armed Red Army soldiers under the command of a sergeant, and Foster wondered what kind of intruder warranted such protection for him.

Inside his work-room he felt in no mood for work and he stood looking at his work-bench, twelve feet by two feet of hardboard covered in white vinyl and supported at two feet intervals by angled struts. Above the equipment was a row of a dozen electric sockets and another half-dozen sockets at the far end where there were neat piles of computer print-out. There was a computer with facilities for twin floppy-disks and ports for a hard-disk drive, a port for a modem and two laser printers. An ICOM transceiver stood beside a Sony ICF-2001D next to a tele-phone, a modem and an AR-3000 scanner.

He felt in no mood to tackle the work he had planned

for the day and he moved over to where the print-out of the main indexes had been pinned to a cork board on the wall. There were a dozen categories of information and a few files that were not really part of his programme. There was one that caught his eye as he hung his jacket over the back of the chair. Its title was – 'SIS Berlin/Federal Republic'. He hesitated for a moment then noted down the file number and moved back to the computer area.

The first page that came up on the monitor screen was an index and the next five pages were a brief description of the typical functions of an SIS unit outside the UK. Two further pages described the general activities and locations of several SIS premises in West Berlin. There were photographs showing the entrances to several West Berlin buildings suspected of being SIS bases. There were two pages of addresses that were suspected of being safe-houses, contact points and sub-stations. Another three pages showed photographs and locations of suspected SIS dead-letter drops in East Berlin.

The descriptions of the general functions of SIS were no more than translations of so-called 'histories' of MI6 by self-styled British historians. Grand collages of conjecture, surmise, opinion and guesswork, sprinkled with a few out-of-date facts and names. The main theme always that SIS was incompetent and run by traitors. Long-serving officers were posthumously libelled. A few retired colleagues responded with angry letters to *The Times*. But SIS itself never reacted. If the British public were persuaded to see them in an unfavourable light, the KGB knew better.

The information on SIS Berlin was surprisingly accurate and up-to-date so far as names and appointments were concerned, but the details of both past and current operations were patchy. The files' strength was in the background detail of personnel, some of it previously unknown to him about people he knew. Quite deliberately he

TED ALLBEURY

kept the report on himself to the last. He read it through slowly and was amazed at the details it gave of himself and his parents. It could have been his SIS 'P' file – not that he had ever seen that. It gave no details of his operations but it indicated accurately his general areas of responsibility.

The last entry stated that he had left the service, and it gave the exact date, and claimed that he had been given a dishonourable discharge because of conduct likely to endanger the lives of associates. He had wondered how they would react to his disappearance. He had expected some sort of fudge like a transfer or ill-health but they had really gone for maximum damage with minimum information. With that in the record he wouldn't even make security for a suburban store. They would guess that he'd defected but they couldn't be sure. They wouldn't want to acknowledge a defection and Legal had probably warned them that if he hadn't defected and popped up somewhere the right side of the border he could probably make a fortune out of a libel or slander case.

There was a box at the bottom of all the pages marked 'Source'. The source on most of the SIS Berlin pages was 'MÖWE' – Seagull in English. Somewhere in the miscellaneous files had been a register of informant code-names. It was 'eyes-only' Amtsleiter General Schumann who was responsible for all Stasi counter-intelligence against the Brits, the Americans and NATO.

It took him nearly an hour to trace the file on his disks. He scrolled it slowly through the alphabet to 'M'. Alongside MÖWE were three consecutive nine digit numbers and that meant three separate pages of information. And it meant accessing a different disk.

The first page was headed '*Strengste Geheim. Abteilung 1x General Major Schutt.*'

There were only a few lines on the page.

196

Code	MÖWE
I.D.	MALINS Roger Frederick
Contact points	Tel. 9801476/Autoverkauf
	GERHARD/Zoo
Subjects	Bundesnachrichten Dienst/SIS Berlin
Grade	AA.

(more)

The following two pages were single-spaced details of dates of meetings, locations, subjects discussed and payments made. The entries covered a period of two years and over fifty meetings.

The subjects discussed were only briefly described with references to fuller reports on separate files. But they showed quite clearly that the Stasis had been kept well informed of personnel and locations of the BND, the West Germans' intelligence service. Not only in Berlin but in West Germany in general. Targets of the BND operations in East Germany were general rather than specific.

Similar information was given covering SIS personnel and operations in East Berlin and East Germany, with particular emphasis on line-crossing networks. But it was clear that Malins had only vague knowledge of such operations apart from the network he ostensibly ran himself.

Half-way down the third page Foster read the details of Malins' betrayal of his network. It seemed that Braun, Foster's courier who worked at the library, had contacts with a porn-shop in West Berlin where Malins had some financial interest.

Three entries further on was a brief meeting where Malins had passed on the information that Foster had been dismissed from the service. The last meeting was only two weeks previously.

For a few moments he sat looking at the monitor screen

and then he leaned over, switched on the printer and then pressed two keys on the computer keyboard that would activate the printer. When the three pages of hard copy had been printed he took out the disk and switched everything off at the mains switch.

For several minutes he sat at his work-bench thinking. He felt neither anger nor disgust at Malins' treachery. It was part of the business they were in. Then he reached for the three printed pages and tapped in the digits on his pocket calculator for the payments received by Malins. Most payments were of 25,000 D Marks and they came to a total of 1.4 million D Marks. Almost half a million pounds sterling. The Stasis had either been ripped-off by Malins or he was passing more information that wasn't reported in the details of the meetings. It could mean that they were so short of contacts in West German and British intelligence that they needed to ensure that they kept him happy, no matter what the cost. What ever it meant he would sleep on it.

Hartmann put the pistol on the table together with an envelope.

Foster looked surprised. 'What's that for?'

'For you.'

Foster smiled. 'Who chose it?'

'The sergeant-armourer at Karlshorst. Why?'

'Did you tell him what it was for?'

'Not specifically. I just asked for a personal weapon.'

'That's a Ruger .357 Magnum.'

'So?'

'It's too big and heavy to carry around and far too powerful for anything I would need.'

'What do you want then?'

'If I have to carry a gun then a Walther PPK or a Beretta would be more suitable.'

'Write down what you want.'

Foster looked at the KGB man. 'What makes you think I need a gun anyway?'

Hartmann shrugged. 'Just a hunch.' He paused and pointed at the envelope. 'That's a permit for you to carry a personal weapon.'

'Thanks for the thought but I don't need a gun. I can look after myself.' He paused. 'Tell me about the hunch.'

'I've a guest at my house. I want you to meet him. Come for dinner tonight. Bring Gala with you. About eight.'

Foster opened his mouth to speak and then, seeing the look on the Russian's face he decided against pursuing his question.

'Who's the visitor?'

'A man from Moscow. A very important man.'

'KGB?'

Hartmann smiled. 'Wait until you've met him and you can decide for yourself.'

On the drive to Hartmann's place he asked Gala if she knew Hartmann's visitor.

'I think he came to our house a few times when I was just a kid but I haven't seen him since.' She looked at his face as he drove. 'He's a very powerful man. Tough. Not like the colonel.'

'Is he KGB?'

'He told me not to answer any questions about the visitor.' She paused. 'But watch what you say. He's been around for a long time.'

The man sitting on the settee was in his late fifties. Grey hair in a crew-cut, bright blue eyes, and a face that had lived a lot of life. He was wearing slacks and a black rolled neck sweater. His chest, shoulders and arms belonged to a wrestler and when Hartmann presented Foster the man just nodded towards an armchair at the side of the settee.

As Foster sat down the man stared at him for long moments before he said, 'I've never liked defectors. A man who betrays his country is a coward.'

He looked as if he expected a response but Foster said nothing.

'So why should we trust you?'

'You don't have to trust me, comrade. And I haven't betrayed my country and you know that.'

'A few months ago you were a capitalist and now you're a communist, yes?'

'I'm only interested in politics when it concerns my work.'

'And what do you think of the Stasis now you've seen them close-up?'

Foster shrugged. 'In some ways they are more efficient than I expected but they're not an intelligence organisation.'

'Why not?'

'They are really only concerned with intelligence inside the GDR. But that could be because the KGB want it that way.'

'You ever been to Moscow?'

'No. I've never been to the Soviet Union.'

'What do you think of our new fellow – Gorbachev? And all this crap about *glasnost*?'

'I think he means it.'

'And you bastards can all sit back and relax and wait for the Soviet Union to collapse.' He paused. 'Or are you all waiting for the chance to cut our throats and get it over with?'

'I can't imagine any circumstances when the West would attack the Soviet Union without being attacked first.'

'So who do you get to do it? The Germans, the Czechs, the Hungarians – who?'

'And the Soviet occupying forces just stand by and watch them do it?'

'The revolutionaries would get their reward. Dollars,

recognition, independence – the World Bank and the IMF ready to give them anything they asked.'

The blue eyes stared angrily at Foster but he looked back defiantly. He was sure that the Russian was trying to goad him into losing his temper but he'd played those games too many times to lose his cool for the sake of winning an argument.

'So what do you say, my friend?'

'I'd say that Secretary Gorbachev has done more in the last few months to make war impossible than any other Soviet has done in the last fifty years.'

'So why is he so popular in the West and criticised daily in the Soviet Union?'

'You know the answer to that as well as I do.'

'So tell me.'

'Maybe there are others in Moscow who would welcome a conflict.'

'And who are they? – tell me. Go on tell me.'

'People like those who sent the Red Army into Afghanistan.'

'Two million Russians died in World War Two, remember that.'

'Stalin killed more than two million Russians before the war had even started.'

Foster saw the anger in the man's eyes but it was only for a few moments and then the Russian turned to Gala.

'And how's that renegade father of yours? Still making films for the intellectuals instead of the workers?'

The girl laughed, 'Of course, my dear. Two special prizes for the last film. One at Cannes, one in the USA. And in Kiev they queued all night for a seat at the cinema to see it.' She pointed a finger at him, laughing as she said, 'You have to remember, darling, we are all intellectuals now.'

The Russian smiled, an indulgent smile. She really was very beautiful.

During the meal the Russian seemed a different man. He said his name was Serov. Igor Serov. His whole personality seemed to have changed. He asked Foster about politics in Britain and the views on the Soviet Union of ordinary people. He seemed extremely well-informed about both British and US policies and politicians. He was not only friendly but he listened intently to all that Foster said. Eventually he got down to what Foster's views were on communism and Christianity.

Foster thought for a few moments and then, smiling, he said, 'It's an interesting question, comrade Serov. In my opinion they have one thing in common. Either of them would work if it wasn't for people. We're the problem. And if we face the facts as they are nobody has ever tried either of them. In the Soviet Union you have Bolshevism not Communism. Privilege and power for a few and misery for the rest. And in the West nobody lives by the teachings of Christ.' He shrugged and smiled. 'Disappointing, but a fact.'

Serov looked at Hartmann. 'You've got a stony-hearted cynic here, comrade.'

Hartmann smiled and said amiably, 'Let's just call him a realist.'

Serov frowned and shrugged, turning back to look at Foster.

'And what are your feelings about the Soviet Union?'

'I never think about it. I think about Russians not Soviets. The system is like most such systems, corrupt and tyrannical.'

'And Russians?'

'Tchaikovsky, Rachmaninov, Glazunov, Tolstoy, Chekhov, Solzhenitsyn. Boris Pasternak said it all in *Dr Zhivago*.' He smiled. 'And of course the KGB's own team – Moscow Dynamo.'

Serov actually smiled. 'And the Americans?'

'Exactly the same as Russians.'

'How d'you make that out, for God's sake?'

'You're both the same. Big on families, big on kids, show-offs. Both got to be first and biggest whether it's the Olympics or outer space. And as individuals both kind and generous. But wave a flag and you can send 'em crazy.'

'And the Germans?'

Foster shrugged. 'Much the same. Schubert, Brahms, Thomas Mann. The same old mixture as the others. Good guys, bad guys.' He looked at Serov. 'You have to remember, comrade Serov, that it wasn't Nazis who ran concentration camps, it wasn't Soviets who raped women in Berlin and it wasn't capitalists who killed villagers in Vietnam.'

'So who was it?'

'Men. Just men. They didn't have to do it. All this crap about just carrying out orders is bullshit. You don't *have* to do it.'

'And if you refuse you get shot yourself for disobeying an order.'

'OK. But they can't shoot everybody. Not all men are cowards.'

'You're a strange man, Herr Schultz. You obviously have your own views on life. And it must have taken some courage to come over the border.' He paused. 'I listened to a recording of your original interview. You said if we released your people you would work for us for a year.' He paused again and looked at Foster. 'And what happens after the year?'

Foster knew instinctively that it wasn't a casual question.

'I'll have to see how things go. So will you people.'

'Would you consider staying if we made it attractive?'

Foster knew very well that it wouldn't just be his decision. He had the trappings of being free but he would be in no position to just go back to the other side unless it suited the KGB to let him do it. He shrugged as he said,

203

'Possibly. But it would depend on what I was required to do.'

Serov nodded. 'Of course.' He leaned forward, resting his large hand on Foster's knee to help himself get up from his chair.

She put her hand on his arm as he drove out of Hartmann's place. 'What's the time?'

'About eleven.'

'How about we go to a club for an hour?'

'What club?'

'The Blue Parrot. It's just behind Alexanderplatz.'

'Is that what you want?'

'Yes.'

'OK.'

'Turn left at the next light and it's straight on back to the town Mitte.'

The man at the door swept the bead-curtains aside for them. Gala was obviously known. There were several tables set around a small area for dancing and a bar along the length of the far wall. There were five steps down to the floor level and a man in a blue denim shirt and jeans kissed Gala on both cheeks, Russian style, and waved them in the general direction of the tables.

The lighting was dim but the music was loud, a tape of Genesis coming from a quartet of massive speakers. The smoke swirling around the pink lamp shades above them was not all from tobacco.

Gala took him over to a table where a couple were waving to her. They were both actors and obviously old friends of Gala. The man was in his late thirties and the girl in her twenties and they were celebrating two-month contracts at the Volksbühne. The talk was all of theatre and films and much gossip about Gala's father's latest skirmish with Moscow. There had been a TV interview with her father on Moscow's main station and apparently every other word had been deleted as he angrily criticised Moscow's attempts at censorship of his film, *A Letter to the Politburo*.

Gala introduced him to half a dozen other friends of hers. Painters, photographers and musicians. They left just after midnight.

As they came up the stairs she slid her arm in his and said, 'Let's walk around the Platz, it's so beautiful at night.'

They walked over to the fountain and sat on one of the concrete slabs. The spotlight was still on the statue and the big globe on top of the TV tower was still illuminated.

She turned to look at his upturned face. 'What did you think about Serov?'

'Like you warned me, he's tough. But there's a lot more to him than that.'

'Tell me.'

'It's hard to describe. He makes me think of those nature films of a lion or a cheetah crouching, with its tail swishing as it concentrates on its prey. Ready to pounce. He listens intently to everything that's said, absorbing it, to be digested later.' He paused, frowning. 'I can't imagine anyone pulling the wool over those laser eyes.'

'I've heard a lot of people describe him but that's the best description I've heard. Most people just dismiss him as a fanatic or a monster. But he's not either.'

'What does he do?'

'I don't know.' She shook her head. 'Don't look so disbelieving. I really don't know. He was a general in the Red Army at one time and people who knew him then said that his role was to look ahead three or four years. To forecast what changes will happen in the world situation and suggest how the army would need to respond. People said he was so good at crystal-ball gazing that he was taken over by the politicians and removed to the Kremlin so that they could benefit from his talents.'

'Who is his boss?'

'Rumour says he doesn't have a boss. He's totally independent. All sorts of people call on him for advice but if he doesn't like them they get nothing. Certainly the Kremlin use him – or think they do. He has contacts, cronies, everywhere. He not only knows what's going on everywhere but he knows what's going to happen before it happens. My father told me that Serov said Gorbachev would be the next Secretary-General when most people had never heard of him.'

'What's his relationship with Hartmann?'

'I don't think there is an official relationship – mind you, I'm only guessing. But Serov has a kind of circle of contacts in all sorts of places – buddies. These people are special – a kind of secret inner-circle. My father calls them "The Chosen". He's one of them. So is Hartmann. These are relationships where you can really say what you think with no possible comeback. No taboos, political or otherwise.'

'Why did he want to see me?'

'Hartmann thinks you're something special. My guess is that Serov was looking you over. Testing you out.'

'For what?'

'Don't play dumb – you know damn well what for. He thinks you could be one of the "The Chosen".' She stood up. 'Anyway. You'll soon find out.' She reached for his hand and he stood up. 'We'd better find the car.'

They had talked for over an hour and as Hartmann poured them another whisky Serov said, 'Time to decide, comrade. What do you think?'

'You first.'

'No way. What are the advantages?'

'The most important is that he's a neutral figure so far as they're concerned. Not a Soviet, not a German and not Stasi or KGB.'

'And after that?'

'That's it for me.'

'No. Number one is the man himself. He's credible and he's loyal. If we can convince him about what we're planning he won't be just a messenger, he'll be a contributor.'

'So when do we proposition him?'

'Tomorrow.' He paused and pointed a finger at Hartmann. 'There's one other vital advantage that fellow has – he understands politics, but he doesn't inhale. The same with religion.'

'How do we convince him?'

'I've got something in mind. I'll think about it overnight.'

'Are you holding out on me?'

'Yes.'

'Why?'

Serov laughed. 'Because I'm not sure you'd agree with what I have in mind.'

CHAPTER 22

There was a note beside his plate on the breakfast table. Hartmann and Serov would be over to see him and his set-up mid-morning.

They arrived about 10.30 a.m. and he heard them talking to Gala and the housekeeper downstairs. When they arrived at his work-place it was a different, amiable Serov who held out his hand.

'Can you spare us a few minutes to show us your operation?'

'Of course. Can you pull up a couple of those folding chairs?'

When they were seated Foster turned to Serov.

'What I have done is extract from Stasi records the details of all contacts that they have outside East Germany.'

'What kind of contacts?'

'West German politicians of all parties. Government officials and administrators. A few members of the BND, West German intelligence. Officers and officials of NATO. Various United States citizens, both military and civilian. Top union officials. Key people in transport. Members of the *Kriminal Polizei* and the *Grenz Polizei*. Diplomats and staffs of all embassies in West Germany. There is also quite a considerable file of miscellaneous contacts in the West. Business people, members of foreign communist parties. And individuals in Britain and the

USA who have been willing to pass information for one reason or another.'

'And the objective?'

'To select about twenty suitable people for a network to operate a high-grade penetration in West Germany. And in the course of building that network to recruit at least a dozen people, probably from neutral countries, as agents of influence. People who can subtly influence Western media and decision makers.'

'How long will it take?'

'The agents of influence about six months. The network will have to build up slowly. A year before it's really effective. But I'll lay out a total plan in case someone else has to take over.'

'Have you got somewhere we can talk more comfortably?'

'There's a sitting room downstairs.'

Serov looked at Hartmann over Foster's shoulder and Hartmann almost imperceptibly shook his head.

Hartmann said, 'Let's go back to my place. We can use my study.'

They were sitting in leather armchairs around a low coffee-table with a glass top and a bowl of fresh fruit in the centre. There was a china coffee-pot and the bits and pieces.

It was Serov who poured the coffee and handed the cups around.

'We talked yesterday about what happened when you'd completed your year working for us. You thought any more about that?'

'No.'

'Have you any strong personal reasons for going back to England?'

'There's just my father.'

'No girl-friend?'

'No.'

'Tell me – are you a queer?'

Foster looked surprised. 'No. Why the hell did you ask that?'

'So far as we know you haven't had sex since you came over. You didn't sleep with Uschi Bayer, did you?'

'No. But what if I'd said yes – I'm gay?'

'No difference. I just need to know.'

'Did you ask Captain Tolstoy if I'd made a pass at him?'

Serov smiled. 'He'd have told us without being asked. Standing orders.' He shook his head. 'It's just routine. Another coffee?'

Foster shook his head. 'I'll help myself when I want it.'

'Back to our subject. What do you think our attitude will be if you decide to call it a day when your year is up?'

Foster shook his head. 'No comment.'

Serov looked at him, eyebrows raised. 'You want me to stick *my* neck out, yes?'

'I'd like to know what it's all about.'

Serov was aware of the irritation in Foster's voice. 'You'll understand why I've been beating round the bushes when I've finished. You'd do the same if you were in my place.' He leaned back in his chair. 'There's something we'd prefer you to do for us rather than what we've been talking about so far – the networks into West Germany and so on.' He sighed. 'I hardly know where to begin.' He paused. 'Last week, March 12, there was the Spring Fair in Leipzig. There was a large public demonstration demanding the right to travel outside the GDR, four hundred people were arrested. The government kept it out of the media but people saw it on TV if they had sets that could get West German TV. We have reliable information that the Hungarians are going to remove the barbed-wire that marks the borders with Austria. All the signs are building up that there's going to be trouble all over East Germany. Starting in Leipzig and Dresden. In two weeks' time there's the East German elections and unless the votes are fiddled the opposition will win. Honecker and his gang will be thrown out. The Stasis swear that they can keep it all under control. We don't think they can. What do you think?'

'Depends on Moscow's attitude to Honecker.'

'Go on.'

'When Secretary-General Gorbachev paid his official visit to East Germany it was obvious that he was more popular with the people than Honecker. And it was equally obvious that he didn't want to be identified with Honecker and his government. It's only since Gorbachev's visit that there have been street demonstrations. If Honecker lets the Stasis attack the people, how will Moscow react?'

'Well, we've been doing a bit of crystal-gazing and we aren't sure which of the likely scenarios is going to be the actual one. What is worse is that we don't like any of them. Every option seems to lead us into a minefield. Maybe we're too close to the problems. That's where you can help us.' He paused. 'That's if you are willing to help us. There are four constituents of the problem, and you are independent from all of them. We are not.'

'Tell me the four constituents.'

Serov marked them off on his fingers. 'You're not a Soviet, you're not a West German, you're not an East German, you're not a Stasi. And one extra benefit – you're not an American. But you know a hell of a lot about all the pieces of the jigsaw that make up the problem.'

'So tell me the problem.'

'It worries me deeply to even discuss our problems especially with someone who is not a Soviet. But we can't have it both ways. You not being a Soviet or belonging to any of the other parties concerned is why we need you. But you can imagine that it grieves me to discuss the failings of our system.

'Let's start with Moscow. Gorbachev is a popular world figure now but at home he's got more enemies than friends. All those *apparatchiks* who've never had it so good are going to lose their privileges and there's all the old die-hards who don't want change. That means we can't rely on the Red Army or any of the armed forces. And there are others who'd like to take over. That's problem number one. Will he last? Will *glasnost* and *perestroika* last? And if not – what comes after?

'Next we've got the East Germans. They may love Gorbachev but that's because they see the chance of independence from Moscow. Gorbachev might pull back all the occupation forces and leave the East Germans to get on with it. But there's a snag. Nobody loves Honecker and his cronies. All the indications are that there's going to be some sort of uprising by the population. Honecker's been told but he doesn't believe it. Says anyway the Stasi could hold it down. Honecker's only worry is that if there's too much loss of life the West Germans would use it as an excuse to come in to settle it once and for all. I've seen a NATO paper on the possibility of that happening and the inference was that unless the Soviets came in to save Honecker and his gang NATO would back the West Germans. The way things are I can tell you Moscow wouldn't lift a finger to save Honecker.

'Then we come to the Stasis. They could decide to anticipate the trouble and clamp down on the trouble-makers. Firing squads, arrests – the usual routine – and so frighten the civilians that all thoughts of some kind of uprising are put on the back-burner or abandoned altogether.' Serov paused and looked at Foster. 'Not a pretty picture, my friend.'

Foster nodded. 'Agreed. How many people in Moscow agree with your scenario?'

'A lot. The problem is – we aren't sure what to do about it. So Colonel Hartmann and I would like to take out a little insurance policy that covers all eventualities.'

'What sort of insurance policy?'

'You, my friend.'

'Nobody in Moscow's going to give a damn about my views on anything.'

'Maybe not. But Hartmann and I will and we can make people in Moscow at least listen. And maybe, act before it gets out of hand.'

'I'm flattered, comrade Serov. But I still can't see how I can help you.'

'You realise that if things go wrong and the wrong people succeed that you could go down with the rest of us. They'd show no mercy.' Foster opened his mouth to speak but Serov held up his hand. 'I want to make you an offer before you decide.' He paused. 'If for any reason you don't want to be involved in this mess we will release you right now from any deal you made with us. We'll provide you with funds and a passport for any nationality you specify and we'll take you anywhere you want to go. Any country you choose. You can be away in three days. No hard feelings on either side. No records here. It never happened. Neither we nor the Stasis ever heard from you.'

'And if I stay?'

'Your own Brit passport back to you. A second Brit passport in another name. Genuine – not forged. A Soviet passport in the name of Schultz and a document from the KGB that makes you untouchable unless things go very wrong in Moscow. If it all works out peacefully then you can do and have anything you want. No limit.'

'You're a very shrewd man, comrade Serov.'

'What makes you say that?'

'You knew which way I'd go before you made the offer. It was a genuine offer and I appreciate it. And I'll stick around as long as I can help.'

Serov stood up, obviously relieved and pleased. 'Let's eat.'

For five hours they had talked of what they wanted him to do. It had a strange logic to it. For them the missing piece of their puzzle was what the Americans and the Brits would do in all the variations of the troubles they could see ahead. He would advise them on what he thought the West's reactions would be to Moscow's moves and counter-moves. At what point would they be prepared to abandon the newfound detente with Moscow and cash in on the turmoil in Moscow and East Germany.

They had obviously had this in mind from the first days after he had come over. The information he had gathered from the Stasi records was their insurance. The names of West Germans who were Stasi informants, contacts inside the BND, diplomats, journalists, business people who could be persuaded to use their influence or risk being exposed and ruined. There was enough evidence of treason and double-dealing by hundreds of people in all of the constituents of the problem to bring down every government concerned. And he guessed that Hartmann and Serov had collected similar material covering every aspect of Soviet authority including the KGB itself.

It was early evening when Foster got back to his place and Gala was waiting for him in the hall.

She smiled. 'They rang through to say you were on your way.' She paused, looking at him with her head to one side. 'You look tired, let's have a drink and then go out for a meal.'

She took his arm and led him into the sitting room. She was amused when all he wanted was an orange juice. She handed it to him and then walked over to the small set of drawers where the TV stood. When she came back she handed him something wrapped in chamois leather.

'Mind, it's heavy. A man came, said it was from the colonel. It feels like a gun.'

He unfolded the covering slowly to reveal a Beretta, covered in oil. Instinctively he took out the clip and pulled back the breech. They were both empty and he smiled faintly as he laid it on the table beside him.

'Why are you smiling?'

'It reminded me of an old army saying.'

'Tell me.'

'The armourer sergeant always said, "You're gun's your best friend. You should keep it clean, bright and slightly oiled." He looked at her smiling. 'I guess it's the same in the Red Army. But too much oil.'

'You don't seem interested in it.'

'I'm not.'

'Why not? He wants to be sure you can defend yourself.'

'I don't need a gun to do that. They don't understand. But they mean well.'

'So what do you do if somebody shoves a gun in your back?'

He laughed. 'I'd take it off him.'

'But how?'

He shrugged. 'I'll show you some day. I'll teach you how to do it. Meantime if you ever pull a gun on someone keep at least three feet away. Only idiots shove it in your back.'

She sat looking at him for long moments. Then she said quietly, 'They don't understand you, do they?'

'What makes you think that?'

'Because they're men. They've asked you plenty of questions but none of the right ones.'

He smiled. 'So you ask me the right ones.'

'OK.' She paused and looked at him. 'What do you think about just before you go to sleep at night?'

He was silent for what seemed a long time as she waited, then shook his head and said, 'Ask me another.'

'Did you have a girl-friend before you came over?'

'Over the years I had several but nothing very serious.'

'Did you sleep with them?'

'With two I did.'

'Were you in love with any of them?'

'I liked all of them – but how would you define love?'

She shrugged. 'Do you miss anyone from those days? Your parents perhaps?'

'I sometimes miss my father.'

'Why him? Were you very close with him?'

'Not consciously, but looking back I guess we cared about each other. He didn't want me to come over.'

'Why not? What reason did he give?'

'He said the sacrifice was out of proportion.'

'Have you thought since that maybe he was right?'

He shrugged. 'It had to be done.'

'Why?'

'I couldn't just leave them to rot in jail for just carrying messages about meetings and dead-drops. They did it out of loyalty rather than conviction or reward.'

'What did you offer them as their reward?'

'Money for the two men and West Berlin for the girl when she finished university.'

'That was Uschi?'

'Yes.'

She smiled. 'And you and I will be going to her wedding in two days' time. And she marries the enemy.'

'Is that what it is?'

'It is.' She paused. 'Hartmann tells me you're going to stay on working with them – him and Serov. Is that true?'

'Yes.'

'He told me they'd given you the chance to walk out on them right now. Is that true too?'

'Yes.'

'You're making a mistake. Can't you see that?'

He smiled. 'Tell me about it.'

217

'Don't you realise, you don't have a life? No friends.
Not even casual acquaintances. You don't go out. You
just work, like you're serving a prison sentence. Getting
through the days. No outside stimulus. Nothing to look
forward to. No nice surprises. Nothing. It's like you've
retired from life.' She frowned. 'Don't you have any
ambitions, any hopes – any dreams?'

'I get by, Gala.' He smiled. 'But thanks for thinking
about me.'

'What did your mama call you when you were a little
boy?'

'Charlie, or Karl when we lived in Germany.'

'OK, Karl it is from now on. I'm going to make you
part of the human race – noticing whether it's spring or
winter, whether it's sunny or snowing.' She paused. 'I
asked my father once what he'd learned about life and he
thought for a few moments and then he said, "Always
remember that this is Take One, and honey, there ain't
no Take Two." And I'm saying that to you.'

For a few moments he said nothing, and then he said,
'Why are you bothering about me, Gala?'

'If I didn't know you better I'd say you were fishing for
compliments. Take me out to eat.'

He smiled. 'Give me an hour. I need to make some
notes.'

'OK. And speaking of notes our friend tells me that
you play the piano like Fats Waller. Will you play for me
sometime?'

He nodded. 'Of course I will.'

As Foster stood in his living room looking out of the
window he noticed that there was blossom on some of the
trees in the garden and one of the guards was mowing
the grass in the small orchard. He turned when he heard
the knock on the door and Gala came in looking pleased
and excited. 'My father's in town, he's staying at the

Berolina and he's invited us to dinner with Serov and Hartmann. Is it OK with you?'

'Of course. Let me freshen up and then we'll go.'

Sergei Leonov looked more like an American than a Russian. Large in size and – larger still in presence. A big, handsome, Roman emperor's head and a face that was used to being noticed. Outgoing and outspoken and apparently unconcerned that his caustic comments about Moscow bureaucracy could be overheard by diners at nearby tables. He laughed a lot, and shrugged and waved his arms about as if he was still filming in Cine Città. The service they got from waiters was equally flamboyant and enthusiastic.

He obviously knew Serov well and reminisced from time to time about combined operations against the *apparatchiks* in the Kremlin. With Hartmann he seemed more cautious, listening to his responses but refraining from comment. With Gala it was obviously a long-forged affection that showed itself in hugging and patting and reminiscences of times together in Rome, Los Angeles, New York and Madrid. From time to time when someone else was talking Leonov glanced briefly at Foster. The glances were amiable but uncommitted. Foster felt that Leonov was used to observing his daughter's male companions without needing to be judgmental.

They all left the hotel together, like a pride of satisfied lions. Leonov waving amiably at shouted greetings from people who knew him. And it was Leonov who suggested that they should all go back for a drink at Hartmann's place. And it was Leonov who ordered the porter to get the car brought round – Hartmann's car.

At Hartmann's house the radio was playing as they moved into the sitting room. Leonov in the lead, until he held up his hand for silence so that they could hear the music.

219

'Listen. Listen all of you.'

He waved his hands slowly to the beat of the music then turned to look at them.

'What is it? Who wrote it? Come on – come on. You should be ashamed.'

Foster said quietly. 'It's a piece by Glazunov called *Melodie*. It's Opus 20 or maybe 21.'

Leonov turned to look at Foster. 'Good, good . . . the bastards said his music was too sweet – like film music. They gave him the title of People's Artist of the Republic.' He shook his head slowly. 'But he knew they were phonies and he moved to Paris. God rest his soul. Wrote this piece when he was twenty-one or two.' He sighed. 'Ah well.' He turned on Hartmann. 'Come on, Peter. Tell them to bring in the bottles, there's a good fellow.'

As they sat around talking it was obvious that although neither Hartmann nor Serov was overawed by Leonov they had great respect for the man. They were all equals in their own ways but he was equal in a unique way. They all had courage of one kind or another but Leonov wore his courage on his sleeve, openly and defiantly.

It was long after midnight when Foster crossed swords with Leonov. Perhaps not quite crossed swords but there was a hiatus in the conversation that became a silence.

Leonov stared at Foster and said, 'So why do you think they won't throw Honecker out on his arse, along with his cronies?'

'Because he gives them what they want. A quiet life. You've got a job. Maybe you hate it but you're working. Not very hard of course. You've got a roof over your head. Your space is a bit crowded but not too bad. If you're ill you get free medical attention. Very few crimes. Old ladies can walk the streets without getting mugged. It's Germany before the war. Lace curtains and Thomas Mann.'

'Oh, for Christ's sake. You call it a job, making junk

cars and junk goods. Scratching an existence. Spying on your neighbours and spied on in return. Doing what you're told. One boring day after another.' He wagged a finger at Foster. 'You mark my words some bloody Nazi will come out of the woodwork and wave a flag and promise them anything they want. They'll call for freedom. And the sad thing is – if they get it they won't know what to do with it.'

'Somebody will show them what to do with it.'

'Yeah. That's what Hitler did. There's plenty more Hitlers left in the world. Show me a democracy in Africa. Show me one in South America.' He shrugged. 'Show me one anywhere, for that matter.'

Foster smiled at Leonov. 'Maybe we're all too wise to want to live in a democracy.'

Leonov laughed and put down his glass. 'He's right, you know. Just think about it. Government by the majority. The voice of the people? The voice of bloody morons, the thugs, the ignorant, the mobs, the muggers, the football hooligans – the Nazis. Black-shirts, brown-shirts, Jew-baiters – they're the ones you'd get and they'd offer money, power – anything you fancy – to any dumb bastard who'd vote for them.' He shook his head angrily, 'And they probably wouldn't get more than ninety-eight per cent of the vote.'

It was 2 a.m. when Gala and Foster drove back to his house. As they waited for the guards to check them and open the gates, she said, 'They seem to have accepted you as one of them.'

He turned to look at her. 'And what does that make me?'

'One of a group of people who think for themselves and might alter the way the world, or at least Europe, will be in the next fifty years.'

'They'd be kidding themselves if they thought that.'

'They don't. It's just me who hopes they might.'

'Why?'

'Just a feeling in my bones that what we've got is crumbling away. Fast. And nobody seems to be noticing.'

'Give me an example.'

She thought for a moment. 'The so-called neo-Nazis.' She paused. 'I know you think they're just another lot of football hooligans and some of them are. But what they're saying is Germany for the Germans. *Ausländer aus*.' She shrugged. 'And nobody's stopping them. The police just look on. Why? Because they go along with the slogans. You don't have to wear a swastika to be a Nazi. You know that. You've seen the Stasis. Nazis under a different name. A hammer and sickle instead of that heathen cross.'

'And what do you think of them? Your father, Hartmann and Serov?'

'I think you're all fools. Romantic, well-meaning fools. And I love you all.'

'Why?'

'Because you care. That's why Hartmann took you over in the first place. Not just the background. But because you cared about your idiots who'd been arrested.'

CHAPTER 23

Foster was up early the next morning. A quick breakfast and then back to his work-room. He spent the whole day compiling a shortlist of people from his Stasi file whom he intended contacting personally.

He knew from the start that Malins would be his first contact. He was the only one in Berlin. All the others on his list were in West Germany and he wouldn't risk going via West Berlin. He'd have to choose some crossing-point near the border crossing at Helmstedt.

He worked out the lines of his interview with Malins carefully. First the shock of possible exposure and then the friendly scenario that made them into working partners. Nothing forced. Just old pals chatting together from time to time about the world at large.

He spent a couple of hours with Hartmann with his list to make sure that there were no further contacts of any kind between the Stasi officers who had been the controllers of the men on his list. There was also a need for cash in large quantities to be available for him on the other side and some means of coded communication in case he needed special facilities. It was decided that Hartmann would arrange unofficial crossing facilities for him that would avoid any of the identification checks that the regular crossing-points required. It would take a week to ten days for Hartmann to make the arrangements and in that time he would deal with Malins.

* * *

He made the call from Hartmann's secure line and had waited until the early evening when he expected Malins to be at his home. There was no reply the first time he dialled Malins' number but he tried again half an hour later. He recognised Malins' voice. Malins was too experienced an operator to respond with his name. He just gave the telephone number. Foster stayed silent for several moments and Malins cut in impatiently.

'Who's that? If it's you, Kennie, stop buggering about.'

'Is that Mr Malins? Roger Frederick Malins?'

'Who's that?'

'My name's Foster. Charlie Foster.'

There was a long silence while the penny dropped and then Malins said, 'Is this some practical joke?'

'No way, comrade.' He paused. 'I thought we should meet and have a little chat.'

Another long pause as Malins tried to decide how he should react. Foster smiled to himself. It was probably a fight between curiosity and the thought of collaring a traitor but finally Malins said, 'I'm not interested, my friend. You made your own bed and you'd better lie on it.'

'I was thinking we might talk about Seagull. You remember Seagull, I'm sure. Just a private talk. Just you and me.'

More silence, then, 'Where d'you wanna talk?'

'How about the porn-shop on the corner by the crossroads at Zoo Bahnhof.'

A deep sigh from Malins. 'When?'

'Tonight. There about ten, if that suits you.' Foster paused. 'Don't be tempted to play games, Malins. I'd have a lot to tell them if anything went wrong.'

There was a moment's silence and then Malins slammed down the phone. And Foster was relieved at the obvious display of frustration and anger. Malins would be easy.

*   *   *

Foster went through the German crossing-point at Fried-richstrasse on his East German passport in the name of Schultz. Hartmann had given him a note that ensured that he wasn't hindered or searched.

As he walked away from the checkpoint it seemed strange to be back on the other side of the Wall. It was almost 9 p.m. but it was still light and the air was warm enough for the girls to be in dresses without coats.

The S-Bahn train was almost empty. It was too late for East Germans to be crossing the border. He got off the train at the Zoo station and walked up Hardenberg-strasse as far as the art school buildings where he turned and strolled back to Fasanenstrasse and down to Kant Strasse. There was a café opposite the porn-shop and he chose a window table and ordered a sandwich and coffee. It was a wide main road with two lanes of traffic each way, but the overhead bridge cast a shadow across the road so that he could only see the corner shop in-termittently. It was too far away to identify anyone entering the shop and after he finished his sandwich he paid the waiter and walked outside. He looked at his watch. Another ten minutes to go before the shop closed. He walked up to the lights and crossed the road.

A man came out of the shop with a brown paper bag and as Foster got to the door a man stopped him, his arm across the opening.

'Sorry. We're closed.'

'I've got an appointment.'

The man smiled. 'We don't have girls here. But I can give you an address.'

'My appointment's with Mr Malins.'

'Is he the English man?'

'Yeah.'

For a moment the man hesitated. 'You'd better come in. I'll see if he's available.'

Foster stood looking at the shelves of videos and magazines. There were still two or three customers making up their minds. When the man came back he said, 'Down the stairs, past the booths and there's an office at the end of the corridor. Just go in.'

Malins was sitting in a leather armchair. 'Lock the door.'

Foster ignored the order and sat on the edge of an ancient oak desk. Malins stared at him. 'Well, you look just the same, Charlie. I'd have thought you'd at least have grown a beard.'

'Where can we go to talk?'

'We can talk here.'

Foster smiled and shook his head. 'And you work on the tape with your little razor blade for a couple of hours. No thanks.'

'Where do you suggest?'

'How about your place? The one at the garage where you used to meet Steiner.'

With only a slight hesitation Malins said, 'OK. We'll get a taxi.' He stood and put on his jacket from a hook behind the door.

It was only a five-minute journey to the garage and after he had paid off the driver Malins took out a bunch of keys and headed for the brightly-lit office beyond the petrol pumps. As he unlocked a red door Malins said, 'You going back to the other side tonight?'

'Don't worry about me, Roger.'

'The checkpoint's closed at midnight. We'll have to be brief.'

Foster laughed softly. 'I'll be OK.'

Malins switched on the lights in the office. It was clean and well-furnished, with a small bar with a selection of drinks across one corner.

'A drink, Charlie, or you still on the wagon?'

'A fruit juice would be fine.'

Malins pointed to a couple of comfortable-looking arm-chairs.

'Take a pew.'

When Malins came back with the drinks he sat down alongside Foster. He lifted his glass.

'Cheers, mate.' He paused. 'What's cooking?'

'I just wanted a chat with you.'

Malins shook his head, smiling. 'Not any more, old chap. After you phoned me I had a good hard think about it. Decided I'd had enough. Gonna call it a day.'

'It's a lot of bread to chuck away, Roger.'

He saw the quick interest on Malins' face. He'd probably thought that the good times were over now and that a show of sudden virtue was the best face he could put on the situation. He shifted in his chair to look at Foster.

'Why did you want to see me, Charlie?'

'I thought we could make a better deal than the old one. It was a bit hit and miss, wasn't it?'

'It was what they wanted.'

'I thought we could get away from the gossip of SIS and concentrate more on generalities.'

'What's that mean?'

'You're interested?'

Malins shrugged. 'I guess so.'

'They still do those general assessments in London?'

'Yeah.' He smiled. 'Reasoned Analyses they call 'em.'

'How often do they get them?'

'Weekly.'

'They'd pay double the old rate to have copies of those not more than a week old. D'you reckon you could cover that?'

'You mean official copies or just copies?'

'Just copies.'

'Make it ten days and it wouldn't be a problem.'

'A deal then?'

'And that's all you want?'

227

'Yeah. Payment in dollars. Two thousand a week.'

He saw the immediate excitement on Malins' face. 'OK,' he said, nodding for emphasis.

'Tell me. Why did you put money in a porn-shop?'

Malins laughed, more at ease now. 'I didn't. SIS wanted somewhere where informants could go in and out without being noticed. I suggested the porn-shop, and after a lot of discussion they agreed. I pay a rental for the room. That pays the rent for the whole shop.' He looked at Foster. 'Somebody was putting it around that you'd been seen in Dublin.'

'Who was the somebody?'

'I don't remember. There was a bit of a panic when you disappeared but after the official version went out that was the end of it so far as West Berlin was concerned.' He smiled, knowingly. 'How you making out over there?'

'I get by. I've written out a telephone number you can use to contact me. I can be back to you inside a couple of hours if I use this number here.'

'You must have been pretty sure of yourself to have it all worked out before we met.'

'You're an independent guy like me. I knew you'd see the benefits.' He paused. 'You still running your old network?'

'Yeah. Do your people know about that?'

'There's nothing on the records about it.'

'You didn't tell 'em?'

Foster grinned and shook his head. 'What the head don't know the heart don't grieve about.' He paused. 'What are you concentrating on at the moment?'

'The so-called neo-Nazis. London reckons they're going to be a big problem. They're all over the place. Got moles here in the police and your lot too. Most of 'em are just thugs but the people behind them have got contacts all over. In the UK and the States. London are worried about them.'

'You got people inside them?'

'A few. A couple in East Berlin, others in Leipzig and Dresden. That's where it'll start if it does start.' He stood up smiling. 'By the way, old Honecker's one of the porn-boys' best customers. Has 'em sent over by the dozen. All the latest. I always have a smile when I see him on TV.'

He held out his hand but Foster ignored it, reaching into his inside jacket pocket and pulling out an envelope. 'It's in dollars.'

As Malins slipped it into his jacket pocket he grinned. 'Must break their bloody hearts parting with dollars.' He paused. 'You go first, Charlie, and I'll hang on for a bit. Better that way.'

Foster smiled. 'Do you know the kiosk by the *Gedächtnis Kirche*? Sells magazines and newspapers?'

Malins nodded.

'When you've got stuff for me. Leave it there in an envelope marked "Laufer" and it'll be picked up inside an hour. If you want a meeting just phone and I'll meet you here.'

'OK.'

Foster took a taxi back to the checkpoint to avoid the trains and Hartmann was waiting for him with his car.

All he said was, 'It go OK?'

'You bet. No problem.'

CHAPTER 24

The next two names on Foster's target list were Theo Müller a BND man and Franz Lemke a German-Canadian journalist.

Müller was within a couple of years of retirement. As with all Stasi informants he had been paid so that his cooperation was on the record. But the real reason for his cooperation was his previous Stasi contact, an attractive young woman, a teacher, not a full-time Stasi employee. Müller had fallen in love with her early on in the relationship. Despite being much older than her he was an attractive man and although in the beginning she had slept with him in the course of duty the relationship had developed into a genuine love on both sides, and that made her a more valuable pawn in the game than the money. Although it had never been openly discussed they both knew that her safety was now at stake. A promise had been made that when Müller retired he would be given a house and pension in East Germany and they would have official recognition and blessing of their marriage. Müller was a senior in the BND's planning section at Pulach.

Franz Lemke, the journalist, was in his early fifties. Both his parents were Germans who had emigrated to Canada. He had been born in Hamilton, Ontario, and had Canadian citizenship. His father, a successful importer/exporter, had kept many contacts, both business and social with Germany, mainly in the West but he had, from time to time, helped old friends in East Germany obtain bits and pieces of electronics that he was assured were only for commercial use. Nobody was going to be hurt by a couple of hard-disks and a dozen computer chips. When the old man had talked about home he meant Frankfurt.

Franz had gone straight from high-school to the *Hamilton Spectator* and after five years had been promoted to the newsroom handling local events. He had worked hard and conscientiously and three years later he had been hired by the Toronto *Star* as second-string to the journalist handling the political scene in Ottawa. He was soon demanding and getting his own by-line. When he was offered the Paris post he was delighted. When a new deputy foreign editor took over at Yonge Street he knew at the first meeting that his days were numbered. After several of his feature interviews had been spiked he started looking for something new. Because of his bilingual German he decided to try Germany first. He had received three firm offers from newspapers in the first two weeks and he decided that he would set up his own freelance news service covering all aspects of the German scene.

Müller's Stasi contact was Lena Bekker and Foster decided that it would be useful to see her before he made his contact with the BND man. She lived in Halle about twenty-one miles north-west from Leipzig and he made arrangements with Hartmann to visit her in two days' time.

The day before he was due to leave there was a phone-call from Malins and Foster went across himself to pick up the envelope from the garage. It was thicker than he expected but he didn't open it until he was back in his work-room.

The material was eight weeks of the SIS analyses, about twelve pages of single-spaced typing. He phoned Hartmann who came over and they read the pages together. Although they were all classified as Top Secret they were written in general terms rather on the lines of an article in *The Economist*. There was no reference to sources but their conclusions were so positive that they read like history rather than forecasts of the future.

Two strands permeated them all, the dangers of the neo-Nazis, not only in East Germany but in the rest of Europe including the UK. Their controlling leadership was rated as intelligent and sophisticated with connections and funds from the USA. The street-level thugs were compared with the Nazi Brown Shirts. The second thesis was growing evidence of unrest in East Germany. An unrest that was only vaguely related to the neo-Nazis but was widespread among both old and young. The discontent was centred on the lack of freedom to travel and to criticise the leadership. It was ill defined but the analyses saw the discontent as a factor to be borne in mind when planning intelligence operations in Warsaw Pact countries.

The two latest summaries made brief references to the possible creation of a NATO committee being formed to consider reactions to public disorder in East Germany, and the likely reaction of the Soviet and local government to public disorder. The fear was expressed that if the official reaction led to violence against the public there would have to be some response by the West.

When they had both finished reading the material Hartmann turned in his chair to look at Foster.

'What do you think? Are they genuine?'

'I'd say yes. The phrasing is typical. A lot of caution and no positive suggestions.' He smiled. 'The kind of report that you can claim gave fair warning if what you forecast turns out to be true. But if you were wrong nobody remembers what you said.'

Hartmann nodded. 'But underlying it is the same assessment that we have come to. One of the snags of a suppressed public is that you've got no way of judging what they're really thinking. If Serov and I were put on trial we haven't a fact between us. Just trained instincts that smell trouble in the air. SIS are saying exactly the same. We ought to know far more than they do – but we don't.'

'What do you think's going to happen?'

'I don't know. I really don't. It's like the meteorologists talking of vague signs of hurricanes out to sea. They may die away. Or they may come roaring in, destroying everything in their path. You know, animals, even domestic ones, can tell when there's going to be a thunderstorm, hours before it happens.' He paused. 'But the more we can piece together of what others who might be involved are thinking the sooner we can take sensible precautions.' He shook his head. 'Something's going to happen. I can feel it in the air.'

'When did you start having this feeling?'

'When we went into Afghanistan?'

'Why then?'

'Because nobody could tell me why we were doing it. And God knows we still don't know. It's our Vietnam.'

They spent an hour planning Foster's trip into West Germany. Hartmann was adamant that he should not go through any checkpoint where there might be SIS people on security. In the end Hartmann insisted that they would make special arrangements for him to cross the border away from all checkpoints.

When, in 1945, US troops fought street by street to take Halle they destroyed a large part of the town. But there is still a statue of Georg Friedrich Händel in the square.

Fräulein Bekker's address was in a huddle of small buildings behind the St Moritzkirche that had been built after the war for middle-grade employees of the town council. Fräulein Bekker's father had worked in the Employment Department and after his death his wife and daughter continued to live there. She was, after all, a teacher at the infants' school. It was a narrow, cobbled lane at the back of the church. A group of small boys was kicking a football around at the far end and after he had pressed the bell he watched the boys.

It was a few moments before the door was opened. The young woman was in her early thirties and she was more attractive than the photograph in her file had shown.

'Fräulein Bekker?'

'What can I do for you?'

Foster held up his KGB ID card so that she could see it.

'My name's Schultz, Fräulein, and I was told you would understand if I just said *Schwalbe*.' Swallow was her Stasi contact word.

She looked confused and then she said, 'Has something happened to Theo?'

'No. He's fine. I just wanted a few words with you. Is there anywhere we could have a drink?'

'Yes, there's a bar round the corner. I must tell my mother that I'm going out.'

She closed the door in his face and Foster wondered if she was checking up on him, but she came back in a few seconds, a woolly cardigan round her shoulders.

They took a table at the back and Foster brought over two light beers. As he put the glasses on the table and sat down he looked at her and said quietly, 'You look worried. Are you?'

She shrugged, avoiding his look by staring at her hand around the glass. 'Only because of you. That worries me.' She looked up at him briefly. 'Should I be worried?'

He shook his head. 'Not at all. Let's not use any names while we're talking but let me say that I'll be seeing our mutual friend in a few days' time and if you'd like me to take anything, a letter maybe, I'd be happy to take it.'

'And what do you want in return?'

'Does there always have to be something in return?'

'In this strange business the answer is yes.'

'All I want is to ask you about him as a man. I've never met him.'

'You know of our relationship?'

'Yes.'

'Well obviously I find him a wonderful man. Kind, considerate and longing for his retirement to come up so . . .' she smiled '. . . so that we can live happy ever after.'

'Does he like his work?'

'Yes, he does.'

'What are his interests?'

'You mean hobbies?'

'Yes.'

She laughed softly. 'Music – jazz music – and model trains. And fishing in lakes and rivers. He puts them all back.'

'Is he interested in politics?'

'Of course. That's part of his job but he doesn't identify with any party.'

'What about the regime here?'

She shook her head dismissively. 'No comment.'

'And you?'

'No comment too.'

'If you had the chance to live in the West, would you take it?'

'You bet. Do you think that's possible?'

'Not immediately but maybe in a few months' time. What are things like here at the moment?'

She smiled and shrugged. 'Same as always. Great for the top boys and nothing for the rest. Kids who've never even seen an orange or a banana. Neighbours spying on each other. Nobody works hard because there's no point in doing it. You don't get more money and if you did there's nothing to spend it on. But at least you don't have to make decisions – you just do what you're told to do. Human sheep.'

'Do people complain?'

'Not unless they want a spell in prison as Enemies of the State.' She paused. 'Some day the whole lot's going to explode.'

He had learned all he needed and he had walked her back to her place and then walked to the hotel where he was spending the night. He'd told her that if she had anything for Müller to leave it at Reception addressed to him.

There was a small parcel handed to him the next morning. It felt like a book.

It was 2 a.m. when Foster got back to the house and there was a note from Hartmann telling him to phone no matter what time he got back.

Hartmann's news was disturbing. There had been a call from Malins and Hartmann had sent somebody over for the package. The package was just an envelope with a single hand-written note inside. Malins had decided to take early retirement. But he was staying on in Berlin and would still be in contact with SIS Berlin. What did he think was going on?

'There's several possibilities. SIS could have been watching Malins and decided to put him on the back-burner. That meant that either they had no solid proof against him or that they were planting him for their own purposes outside the organisation.'

Hartmann said quietly, 'Or that they hope to use him as a contact with you. Offer you a deal.'

'That's a possibility.'

'I've also heard that your old friend Slaney has been posted back to a desk-job in London.'

'That doesn't surprise me. He must have been in the dog-house when I walked out.'

'And he could come out nice and clean if he was not only able to find you but turn you as well.'

'Too imaginative for Slaney.'

'Could be somebody else's suggestion.'

'You sound worried about it. Are you?'

'Concerned, not worried.'

'Forget it. I made my deal with you and Serov and I'll not let you down.'

There was a long pause. 'One other small thing. My apologies for raising it but I was looking through a surveillance report on the girls who work the Berolina bar. They give reports to the Stasis on all their clients. There was one client the Stasis couldn't identify, but from the description I read it could have been you.' He paused. 'Was it?'

Foster laughed softly. 'Could have been.'

'You should have told me you wanted a girl.'

'Didn't want to embarrass you, Peter.'

'Next time ask me. Yes?'

'OK.'

CHAPTER 25

The night sky was clear and cloudless; there was a full moon. Foster stood a few yards back from the fence with the border guard beside him. He was aware of Hartmann sitting in the car down the path to the woods.

They had laid down reflecting tape along the route across the minefields that he was to follow. To his left he could see the shadow of the watch-tower and a searchlight moved slowly along the edge of the woods on the far side of the border zone. There were flutterings of disturbed birds in the woods behind him and the sharp cry of a vixen was cut short by the nearby snarling and barking of the guard-dogs. As the man beside him looked at his watch Foster looked at his own watch. Another seven minutes to go.

It had all been planned and timed meticulously. He was to go across an hour before dawn. Earlier he and his guide would have difficulty trying to avoid the guards on the other side. The villages near the border were kept under constant surveillance by the West German *Grenz Polizei*. Later they would be too visible in the dawn light.

The fence was four metres high with razor-edged wire stretched between the posts, and every other wire was twinned with a high-voltage wire.

It seemed incredible as he stood there that a government could erect such a deadly defence, not so much against intruders from the other side but against its own citizens so desperate for freedom that they would risk their lives for the privilege of being able to live their own lives in the way that they chose. Or was it just the lights and the shop-windows full of luxuries like soap that lathered, toilet rolls, babies' napkins, books, the Rolling Stones, Chanel No. 5 and genuine Levis.

The guide nudged him and nodded and he led Foster to the fence. The electricity had been cut off at the sub-station but the searchlight was still working off its generator. The guard unhooked one wire after another and then ducked under and Foster followed him. The big light was doused and the guard took his arm, leading him between the reflective tapes across the sand-covered space to the woods on the other side. The sand was there to show up footsteps and would be raked after he had gone.

As they approached the other side a red light glowed for a moment at the edge of the woods. The man was waiting for him, a scarf round his face so that only his eyes were visible. He took Foster's arm and led him down a narrow path in the woods until the trees gave way to undergrowth and then a field with a small wooden bridge over a stream. The man signalled to him to sit down and when they were both seated he took off his scarf and started explaining how they would wait until there were villagers about. There was a car at a nearby inn, the man would drive him to a railway station and he could catch the train to Braunschweig.

It was a long train journey from Braunschweig to Munich and it was 11 p.m. when he arrived at the Haupt-bahnhof. He took a taxi to the inexpensive Pension Schubert and booked into one of the three rooms with private bath. He asked for a wake-up call at 7 a.m. and slept soundly through the night until the phone woke him. He washed and shaved and then dialled Müller's house number. It was answered on the second ring.

'Müller.'

'Herr Müller, my name is Schultz. I was asked to deliver

a small package to you. When would it be convenient to meet?'

'Who's it from?'

'A young woman. She asked me to remind you of the Swallows.'

There was a long pause, then, 'Where d'you want to meet?'

'How about the main lounge at the Hilton in an hour?'

'How will I know you?'

'I'll introduce myself to you.'

As Müller absorbed the fact that his unknown caller knew what he looked like Foster waited.

'Make it half past ten.'

'OK.'

Foster stood by the newspaper kiosk. They were both in the same business and he guessed that Müller would get there early to try and identify his caller and cast around to see if there were any other observers of the meeting. Müller was a big man, he looked overweight but healthy like a long retired beach-guard. There were faint echoes of Strength through Joy. Foster watched him stroll around the foyer, into the bar, a glance inside the almost empty restaurant. A word with the receptionist who checked a computer and shrugged as he shook his head. Finally Müller made his way into the lounge and took a table in the far corner, waving to a waiter and ordering a drink. When the drink was served Foster walked over to him, smiling as he sat down at the table. He passed the package across to Müller and said, 'I've no idea what's in it. I hope it's good news.'

Müller pushed the package to one side; pointing to it, he said, 'Do I owe you anything for bringing this?'

'Maybe just a little of your time.'

'You said something about swallows, what was that all about?'

'Let's not play games. We both know what it means.'

Müller shifted uncomfortably in his seat. 'Has anything gone wrong? Is she OK?'

'She's fine.'

'So why are you here instead of her?'

'Before I go into that . . . tell me . . . would you be interested in you both living here in the West?'

He saw the surprise and interest on Müller's face. 'I guess so.'

'I talked with your friend about the possibility. Not right away but in a few months' time.'

'You could fix that?'

'I think so. So let's talk. I'm not interested in the usual things you and your friend talk about. I'm interested in BND's thinking about East Germany.'

Müller smiled. 'Official thinking or off the record?'

'Both.'

'Officially our instructions are to treat them like any other country. Keep close tabs on what they're up to. Especially the Soviet troops. Make a few contacts. Keep informed on public attitudes to the regime.' He shrugged and smiled. 'The usual crap. Specially for politicians.'

'And unofficially?'

'There's going to be trouble there. The whole damn country is on the boil. If Honecker and his gang put it down with open violence then we shan't stand by and let them get away with it.'

'What if the Soviet troops take Honecker's side and support the Stasis and the East German Army?'

Müller shook his head. 'They won't. That's for sure.'

'Why not?'

'Two good reasons. If Moscow did that then Gorbachev could kiss goodbye to all the praise and cooperation he's getting from the West right now. And the second reason is that in our opinion if East Germany really boiled over they'd only be the first. Moscow could forget the Warsaw

Pact. They'd all rise up too. Better put a smile on your face and do nothing. Play the democracy card and ask for more money from the USA. Anyway, all the information we've been getting in the last six months tells us that the Russians themselves are in a real mess, economically and politically. There's God knows how many factions and interests fighting it out in the Kremlin at this moment. God knows which lot's going to come out on top.'

'Have plans been made to go over the border if Honecker starts shooting his own people?'

'That puts it too high. Let's say that the military have given a great deal of thought to how they would rescue the East Germans from the Reds. Nobody's put a rubber stamp on it. But it's there ready and waiting.'

'How long to put it in action?'

'Four days if we want to go through the hoop with NATO. Two days if we go it alone.'

'What would NATO do?'

'Nothing. That's our opinion. Their publics wouldn't let them.'

'How likely does the BND think it could happen?'

'Right now, fifty-fifty. Goes up by two per cent a month on the possibility scale.'

'Would Kohl be tough enough to give the order to go across the border?'

Müller shrugged. 'It may not be Kohl who'd decide.'

'Who then?'

Müller shrugged. 'No comment.'

Foster knew he had all he wanted but they had talked for another hour before Müller had to leave. He had asked Müller where the BND saw the greatest problems apart from East Germany. He was surprised at the answer that BND opinion was that the neo-Nazis were the greatest long-term problem. Not from the thugs but from the people behind them. When he asked Müller why the BND saw the neo-Nazis as such a problem Müller said that it was on two grounds. Firstly that it could revive old anti-German feelings and secondly, that the neo-Nazis' aims were the encouragement of the worst kind of nationalism and the German government's fear that fanatical nationalism was going to be the great problem of the next decade.

Franz Lemke was based in Bonn but he lived in Cologne. He had a large apartment over a shop that sold artists' materials in one of the busy but pleasant streets at the back of Neumarkt.

There was no problem about contacting him. Foster gave the code-name and Lemke had suggested that he came over straight away. As a journalist he was not much concerned about hiding the identity of his contacts. He had hundreds of contacts and if one of them was a Stasi man he had no particular reason to conceal it. What he passed on to the Stasis was something else; they could get him under Federal German Law for that. If they could prove it. And there had never been anything in writing. He had his apartment swept every day for bugs and after the first couple of times that a microphone had been discovered, whoever it was gave up. He used a portable phone when he was away from the apartment and paid extra for the ability to operate on his choice of three different frequencies.

Lemke was a jeans and denim shirt man. In his early fifties, lean and fit and exuding energy like a magnetic field.

It was a beautiful apartment. Modern painting on the walls and what looked like a genuine Klimt in pride of place over a beautiful antique walnut bureau. The large sitting room on the upper floor had windows that looked across the city so that the three arches of the Hohenzollern Bridge were just visible.

The sofas and armchairs were both large and comfortable. Lemke was obviously not the slightest bit embarrassed by his visit.

'What happened to your predecessor?'

Foster shrugged. 'He's in a different section now.'

Lemke laughed. 'They send him down the salt-mines or what?'

Foster smiled. 'Or what.' He paused. 'Could I ask you to give me some idea of how you see German politics from a Bonn viewpoint?'

'Jesus. What do you want? SPD politicians with their mistresses on their office payrolls or CDU guys making fortunes out of influencing government contacts?'

'Are those top politicians or the dregs?'

'Both.' He smiled. 'If there's one thing I've learned in a long career mixing with politicians it's not to trust 'em. None of 'em. They lie like flat-fish to hang on to power. Hypocrites the lot of them.' He laughed. 'An American, H. L. Menken, summed up the problem of listening to politicians talking politics. He said, "It is hard to believe a man is telling the truth when you know that you would lie if you were in his place."' He shrugged. 'Liars and hypocrites, but human all the same. You've got to remember they wouldn't be there in the *Bundestag* or the *Bundesrat* if they could earn a living some other way. But it's the power that really gets them.'

'What are the West Germans' problems at the moment?'

Lemke thought, frowning, for a few moments, then said, 'They're beginning to get scared about the unions, especially those covering the heavy industries. Wanting their dane-geld in pay rises. Then there's the self-styled independence of the *Bundesbank* being under pressure from the politicians. The *Bundesbank* says they won't go with rises for anybody – the politicians scream about losing votes.' Lemke frowned. 'What else are they worried about?' He shrugged. 'Too many Turkish *gastarbeiters*.

The bloody neo-Nazis, of course. Not just the thugs but the so-called intellectuals who say there was no holocaust and that the concentration camps were built as holiday camps by the Poles after the war.'

'Do they really need to worry about the neo-Nazis? Aren't they just football hooligans trying to look important so that the media will give them publicity?'

Lemke shook his head. 'No. It's more important than that. And it's not just the Krauts who are worried about that. The Americans are worried. The printed propaganda and cart-loads of dollars come over from the States. They're international – that's the problem. France, Italy, Holland, Belgium, the Brits – they've all got them, beavering away, waiting for the day. If there's ever any uprising in East Germany those bastards will be in the streets egging them on. And don't forget "out with foreigners" means out with the Russians.'

'Does the BND rate them?'

'You bet they do. They've got a special section that does nothing else.'

'You mentioned an uprising in East Germany. Is that a possibility, d'you think?'

'They've been simmering on the back-burner for a couple of years. I'd say they were coming to the boil.'

'What would Bonn do about it if there was an uprising the other side of the border?'

Lemke grinned. 'First you tell me what your people would do if there was an uprising.'

'The Stasis would do whatever Honecker ordered us to do.'

'And what would Honecker want you to do?'

'We think he's stupid enough to tell us to use any means to put down any uprising.'

'The BND had a non-official tip-off from Moscow that if Honecker did use violence then Moscow wouldn't stop him . . .' he paused '. . . and they wouldn't stop the West Germans going over the border to protect civilians.'

'Would they go over?'

Lemke sighed and shrugged. 'I've seen an eyes-only BND analysis of what might happen. They think Kohl would make threats in public but he'd make no move unless NATO came in too.' Lemke smiled. 'He'd love the kudos but he hasn't the guts to go it alone.' He paused. 'The BND analysis said that Honecker was so stupid he'd probably order an armed attack on anybody causing trouble.'

'Do you have a copy of that BND analysis?'

Lemke stared at him, smiling, then he said quietly, 'Is it true that they're fighting it out in the Kremlin as to who takes over from Gorbachev?'

'Yes.'

'Will there be a *putsch* from one group or another?'

'It's very possible.'

'The army, or the party?'

'Neither.'

Lemke looked surprised and very interested. 'Both?'

'It will take time but there are very important people who think Gorbachev's already lost control of the situation both politically and economically. He doesn't know how to work the machinery. Things are worse under *perestroika* than under the old regime.'

'What would make it work?'

Foster remembered something Serov had said, 'Nothing will work until the communist party in the Soviet Union is banned.'

Lemke roared with laughter. Slapping his thigh in delight. 'My God, what a thought. If pigs could fly. That's one thing we'll never see. If that's what they're gonna wait for then Gorby's got it made.'

Lemke turned to look at Foster, saying nothing for several seconds, then, 'There's something odd about you, my friend. Something doesn't fit.' He paused. 'You're not Stasi, are you? I've never met a Stasi who could string two thoughts together. What are you?'

Foster shook his head. 'What does it matter?'

Lemke wasn't diverted. He went on, 'If you're not Stasi you must be our dear boys, BND, or you're KGB. Give me a clue.'

Foster smiled. 'I could be CIA.'

'No. I know all the CIA guys operating in West Germany. They'd never dress as scruffily as you do. And the jeans would be genuine Levis not that crap you've got on.'

Foster stood up. 'Thanks for your time and the chat. I hope I've been of some use to you.'

'You have, my friend, you have. More than you think.' As he showed Foster to the door, he said, 'Come again some time. I love Moscow gossip. Even if it ain't true it's all sellable.'

Müller looked at the man sitting at his kitchen table. He held up a glass bottle, 'Haag coffee OK for you?' The man nodded and took off his jacket, hanging it over the back of his chair.

As Müller handed him the cup of coffee the man, whose name was Jost, said, 'He lost the bastard between here and Düsseldorf. He took a ticket for Düsseldorf and he didn't see him get off before then but he must have changed trains somewhere. He wasn't on the train when it arrived at Düsseldorf.'

'How many on the surveillance team?'

'Just the one.'

'That was a mistake.'

'The real mistake was not realising that the guy was obviously assuming that he might be under surveillance and took all the routine precautions that a trained man does.'

'What about Lena? If he's spotted your man she could be in danger.'

'Do you want her to come over?'

'Yes. And there's her mother too.'

'Leave it to me. We'll get her over in the next couple of days.' He sighed. 'I know it's a pain in the ass but I want to go over his conversation with you again.'

They had gone over the meeting with Foster a dozen times and Müller had confirmed that the man in the photographs taken by the surveillance agent was the man Schultz.

When Jost was about to leave Müller asked him, 'Why are Pullach so interested in this guy?'

'Well firstly he's not your usual Stasi guy, and apart from that he's interested in a higher level of information. Not the crap your usual guy wants. This one is interested in a different kind of intelligence. The intelligence of intention. A different ball-game. He doesn't fit. They want to find out more about him.'

CHAPTER 26

The guide had left him and Foster stood in the shelter of the trees at the edge of the woods. It was a typical late June evening. The setting sun was casting long shadows across the border strip but there was no movement on the other side. Just an occasional glint of the reflection on binoculars in the watch-tower. It would be at least half an hour before the guard came over for him from the other side. Hartmann would be waiting for him in the car down the rutted pathway through the fir trees and the clumps of wild blackberry bushes. Another couple of months and the guards would be picking the ripe berries and taking them home in their lunch-tins.

It had seemed odd to be on the other side of the border again. The liveliness of the people, the fantastic selection of food, the luxury furniture and clothes and all those adult electronic wonders like VCRs, TVs and hi-fis. An acronym for everything. In the East he had hardly bought anything beyond newspapers and magazines. There was so little to buy and what was available was so poorly made that it wasn't worth buying. Even the little money the people earned wasn't worth anything either. He slid his hand inside his jacket and the paper crackled as he checked the small packet. He had only bought two things on this side and they were both for Gala. A genuine Hermès scarf and a small bottle of Chanel No. 5. Not very imaginative but both of them icons of femininity, a tribute rather than a gift. He had missed her mixture of affectionate banter and perceptive comments. They would have got on well in other circumstances but in the limbo in which he now existed even real relationships seemed strangely artificial.

As he stood there, waiting, he wondered how it would all turn out. What had been done so impatiently had gone far beyond what he had intended. And that was because he had given no thought to what he would do after he had paid for the release of the couriers. Even if he hadn't become entangled with Hartmann, Serov and Gala's father he would still have been left needing to decide what to do. Staying with the Stasis or the KGB had never been part of his vague scenario. He hadn't seen Checkpoint Charlie as his version of the Rubicon, but sooner or later he'd have to think about what he was going to do. Then he saw the light flash briefly on the far side of the fence.

It wasn't Hartmann who had been waiting for him but Gala. Flinging her arms around his shoulders and kissing him. When he handed over the package she unwrapped it carefully and looked at the scarf and the white and gold box of the perfume. She looked down at them for so long that he wondered if she was disappointed. Then she looked up at his face and there were tears on her face. When he asked her what was the matter she shook her head and wiped her eyes with her hands. When they were half-way back to Berlin she pulled off the road, switched off the engine and turned to look at him.

'How did you get on?'

'It was useful.'

'I can't bear to think of you taking extra risks to buy me these presents.'

He smiled. 'There wasn't any risk, honey. You've got to remember that I'm more at home over there than I am here.'

252

She looked at him for a long time then kissed him gently as she turned the key in the ignition.

They went to Hartmann's place and the two of them talked through the night about his meetings with Müller and Lemke. As he was leaving Hartmann said, 'They're right, both of them, there's going to be real trouble here. Honecker doesn't believe it, he's such a fool.'

He had slept for only a couple of hours when he was woken by the phone reserved for Malins' calls. The message was brief. 'We've got problems on your vehicle. You'd better call in as soon as possible.' Then Malins hung up.

It was two hours before Foster got to the garage and Malins was waiting for him in the back office.

'They're looking for you, sonny boy.'

'Who's looking for me?'

'SIS Berlin. Ever heard of a chap named Tarrant?'

Foster shook his head. 'No. Is he MI5 or SIS?'

'SIS. Sent over from London.'

'How do you know?'

'He's talking to everyone who knew you. Came to my place.'

'What did he want?'

'Just a fishing expedition. What you're like. Why you went. Where did you go.'

'Where do they think I went?'

'They're bloody sure you went over the border.'

'Did he say why they were suddenly interested in me?'

'He didn't give anything away but I've asked around and I gather they want to get in touch with you.' He shrugged. 'Maybe they wanna do a deal.'

'What was Tarrant doing before he came to Berlin?'

'No idea.'

'What's he like?'

'About the same age as you. Smooth and quiet on top

but I'd say he was a tough bugger underneath. His old man was in the business.'

'Can you find out any more about him?'

'Like what?'

'Where he hangs out? Why they're looking for me?'

'I'll see what I can do.'

Back at his house there was a message for him to go round to Hartmann's place as soon as possible.

Hartmann looked worried as he handed Foster a mug of coffee.

'Got some worrying news, comrade. Somebody's looking for you.'

'So I heard. Malins just told me. What did you hear?'

'We don't know his name but a guy's been trying to trace Uschi Bayer. Asking her girl-friends where she is. Trying to find out her address.' He paused. 'We put a stop on one particular source but it seems the guy knows that she's married to a Soviet and that he works for the KGB. So far as we know that's all he knows. But he's still ferreting around.'

'How do we know this?'

'The woman who runs a students' lodging house near the University is an informant for the Stasis. She told him and we've been watching Uschi's girl-friend. The SIS guy's using her for checking around. We let Uschi meet her and chat to her. She thinks she put the girl off but it won't put the guy off. He'll keep looking.'

'Why do you think he's looking for me?'

'There can only be two reasons.'

'Like what?'

'Maybe they want to try to turn you. Double you up.'

'Or?'

'Or maybe they'll just try and grab you. Take you back and put you on trial.'

Foster smiled. 'Thanks for being so tactful.'

'How?'

'For not saying that maybe they'd just as soon knock me off.'

Hartmann shook his head. 'No. If that was what they had in mind they would have used a local. Think of the risk they'd run. If we caught this guy with a weapon we'd put him on trial and there would be an international scandal. Imagine the headlines . . .' he waved his hand in the air . . . 'MI6 man sent into East Germany to kill another MI6 man.' He smiled. 'No. They'd use a local. Probably one of those neo-Nazi thugs we've been talking about.'

Hartmann stood up and stretched his arms as he looked at Foster. 'When are you going to give young Gala a break?'

Foster looked surprised. 'I don't understand.'

'You're kidding.'

'I'm not.'

'You're playing hard to get, aren't you? You don't need to – she's crazy about you.'

'I don't believe it. You're mistaken.'

'Why do you think it was Gala who came to meet you at the border and not me?'

'I assumed that you were too busy to come yourself.'

Hartmann leaned forward in his chair, his face serious. 'She loves you, my friend. It's been obvious to everyone else. Of course – you don't have to do anything about it. It's up to you.'

'Does she know that you're telling me this?'

'Of course not. Forget it. I shouldn't have mentioned it, but I thought you might be hung up because of the circumstances. The stupid lives we lead.' He paused and stood up. 'She's a nice girl so take care of her, treat her gently.' He smiled. 'I don't need to tell you, I know you will.' He sighed. 'Would you have still come over if you'd known it was going to lead you to this strange existence? One could hardly call it a life.'

'Who knows? I did it – so I'd better learn the lessons.'

'And what *are* the lessons?'

Foster shrugged. 'God knows.' He grinned. 'Maybe I ought to say that it's nice to be wanted.' He sighed, 'I'll get Gala to bring in the girl this guy has been talking to. She won't know much but there might be a clue somewhere in his contact with her.'

Gala stood waiting for him to speak as he looked around the room. Then he turned to her, shaking his head slowly as he said, 'It's too big, honey. She'll be overwhelmed. It's not an interrogation and it must be gentle and friendly. No formalities. Just the three of us. You, the girl, and me.' He paused. 'Do you agree?'

She smiled, ignoring the question as she said, 'I'll bring her over in about an hour. Is that OK?'

'That's fine. No rush. And tell Frau Schmidt to bring us tea and sandwiches as soon as you get here.'

She was very young and very pretty and she was trying to hide her nervousness. He chatted to her about her studies at the Humboldt until the tea had been set out on the coffee-table and Gala settled down on the sofa beside the girl.

'I told Ingrid that you wanted to talk to her about the Englishman.' She turned to the girl. 'Is that OK, Ingrid?'

'Yes. I'm not sure that he was an Englishman. He sometimes hinted that he was a Canadian.'

'You're sure he wasn't a German?'

She frowned. 'He spoke really fluent German but it was a little old-fashioned.' She smiled. 'He sometimes didn't understand current slang.'

'What was he like physically? What did he look like?'

'He was quite attractive. He was rather like the film-star who was in *Butch Cassidy and the Sundance Kid*.'

Gala chipped in, 'Do you mean Paul Newman?'

'Yes. But this one had red hair. He seems about the same age and build as you.' She looked at Foster and smiled. 'In fact, come to think of it he looked like you, period.'

Foster saw Gala's broad smile and ignored it. 'What was it he wanted from you?'

'He wanted to know about Uschi Bayer. What had happened to her and where she lived. I told him that she'd been arrested by the Stasis as a spy. He wanted me to ask around about her and I learned that she was out of prison and had been seen coming out of an apartment block that was taken over for the Soviets. There was a rumour that she'd married a KGB man, so I watched the place where I'd heard she lived and I saw her and she was with a young man in KGB uniform. I only saw them once.'

'When are you seeing the Englishman again?'

'I don't know. He said he had to go home for two weeks.'

'Where was home?'

She smiled and shook her head. 'He didn't say.'

'Did he pay you for helping him?'

'No, but he hinted that if I went on helping him he might arrange for me to live in West Berlin.'

'Did you want that?'

She didn't reply, obviously scared, and Gala intervened. 'Of course she did, anybody would.' She smiled. 'Including me.'

Foster handed the girl a photograph. It was a small group standing on the steps of a church. 'Was that the man?'

She looked at it and then looked up at him. 'Yes, that's the man and that's Uschi. I don't know the other people.'

'When the Englishman contacts you again will you let me know immediately?'

'Would it mean trouble for Uschi?'

'No. I promise you.'

'And for the Englishman?'

'I'd just like to meet him and talk to him.'

'Would he be arrested?'

'I don't think so.'

'He's a nice man. I wouldn't like anything to happen to him. The Stasis or someone like that.'

'Where do you meet him?'

'At the Arkade Café on Französischestrasse.'

'Well, thanks for your help. Don't forget to let me know if the Englishman contacts you again.'

When the girl had left Foster said, 'I'll have to ask Hartmann to put an interception team at the café.'

'Will you have the man arrested?'

Foster shrugged. 'Depends on what Hartmann wants. The Brits would raise hell if we did.'

Gala smiled and shrugged. 'I don't think Hartmann would worry very much about that.'

'Be a mistake not to bear it in mind.'

CHAPTER 27

When Johnny Tarrant landed at Gatwick Tony Martin was at the barrier waiting for him. Tarrant was in no mood for small-talk and as Tony Martin shook his hand he said, 'What's it all about, Tony?'

'Let's get a coffee and I'll tell you.'

As the waitress cleared away the debris of the previous customers and wiped the table Tarrant's impatience was barely concealed. As soon as she left he said, 'Now. What's going on? And why couldn't you have told me on the phone? And why drag my old man into it, whatever it is?'

'I spoke to your father to ask his opinion about whether I should get in touch with you or not. He said I should.'

'It's about Jenny, isn't it?'

'Yes.'

'Trouble?'

'Not the kind of trouble you mean. She's written a couple of letters to you in the last couple of months. She sent them to your father. I gather he sent them on to you. Yes?'

'Yes.'

'Can I ask what she said in the letters?'

Tarrant shrugged. 'They were only a couple of pages each. Just the kind of letters kids write to their parents from boarding school. What she'd seen on TV. The view from her room. Pigeons on the window-sills. Hoped I was OK. That sort of stuff.'

'Did you reply?'

'I sent her a post-card – painting of Paris. Hoped she was well and settling down OK.'

Tony Martin shuffled a salt-cellar and a pepper-pot around before he looked up at Tarrant again. 'She's very ill, Johnny. I'm at my wit's end what to do.'

'How ill?'

'I think she's dying.'

'From what?'

'She's just given up the ghost. She's still at my secretary's place. Still in that room. She's never been out. Just watches TV and reads Mills and Boon romances – and talks about you. Makes you sound like a cross between Clint Eastwood and Mother Teresa. It's like an obsession. I've had a psychiatrist talk with her a few times. He says she's got a guilt complex about you a mile wide. The GP who visits her says there's nothing clinically can be done for her. It's like those young girls who won't eat – anorexia. No explanation. No apparent reason for the behaviour. Just wasting away.' He shrugged. 'Some people say that that's some kind of guilt reaction. But nobody really knows.' He paused. 'I hate dragging you into all this – but will you help?'

'How?'

'Will you see her and if you can bring yourself to do it will you pretend you care for her and that there might be a chance to get together again in the future?'

'Did you tell my old man what you had in mind?'

'Yes. He went to see her about three weeks ago. Mavis, my secretary, was there. She said he had tears on his cheeks as she showed him out. I asked him to persuade you to do this but he refused. Said you'd gone through enough already. But he didn't object to me contacting you.'

'I've got four days' leave, that's all. I'm in the middle of an operation, I've got to get back to Berlin. Let me think about it. Give me an hour. Can you hang on?'

'Of course. Let's meet in an hour at the bar in the Airport Hilton.'

When Tony Martin had left, Tarrant got himself another coffee and a chicken sandwich and went back to the same table. As he ate he looked around him at the people. Parents with excited children heading for a week in Albufeira. Young girls with sleeping babies cradled in their arms. Businessmen with Samsonite briefcases looking through papers and tapping away on lap-top computers. Indians and Pakistanis heading back for a couple of weeks at home to show off their rings and clothes. Young couples back-packing through Europe on Student Railcards. Seven or eight countries in three weeks. They all looked so sure of what they were doing. Got their lives all sorted out. And for some unknown reason he remembered those lines of a poem, 'Oh what can ail thee, knight at arms, alone and palely loitering'. He couldn't remember who wrote it but he guessed it was either Keats or Wordsworth. He had always taken airports in his stride, his thoughts on where he was going and what he would be doing. Not aware of the lives that went on around him.

His mind went back to when he'd first known Jenny. All those pathetic fantasies about her background that he had never questioned. It seemed crazy that he, a trained professional, who never trusted what anyone said, should have been so easily deceived. But he could remember on his original training course the instructors emphasising that you should never behave in your private life as you were trained to do in intelligence work. Digging camouflaged holes for opponents to fall into. Do that with your wife or girl-friend and it wouldn't last long. But she'd been so pretty and so lively and that had been enough. He'd been a fool. But he wasn't guiltless. He was so frequently away and had to be so secretive about where he had been and what he had done. A pair of costume ear-rings from a Duty Free shop didn't make up for it. She had been jealous and suspicious and no doubt she'd been lonely. Far too dependent on human company to survive a husband who was away more often than at home. He had told her a little of what he did but she was obviously not impressed. She was used to concocting better fantasies herself and took it for granted that his explanations were merely cover for a life of sex and booze. In her background those were the things men lied about or boasted about according to the company.

He looked at his watch. Another twenty minutes, but it would take him ten minutes to cross the bridge to the hotel and find the bar. Not that there was any point in hanging around. He'd known right from the start that he'd do what Tony Martin had suggested. The thought of his father shedding tears for Jenny had been enough. They were much the same temperament despite the age difference. He wished he had his father's charm and easy self-confidence with people. He'd take her out to a show and dinner, one of the musicals, *Cats* or *The Phantom*.

Tony Martin came with him in the taxi to the Special Forces Club and waited as he booked a room for the night and dumped his travel bag. Tony Martin had phoned his secretary to warn Jenny that she would be having visitors in an hour or so. When he told Martin that he was going to book tickets for a show Martin looked at him and shook his head sadly. 'She's not capable of going out, Johnny. She hasn't got dressed for a long time. Just chat her up for half an hour and that'll be enough for today.'

He had stayed for just over an hour and when she was obviously exhausted he put her to bed, promised to see her the next day, kissed her and walked down the narrow stairs to the street, glad that Tony Martin had left after only ten minutes. He walked down to the Embankment and leaned against the parapet looking at the lights on the far side of the river. Part of him wished that he hadn't gone there and part of him was glad that he had seemed to bring her some comfort.

He had been shocked when he saw her. She had made the effort to get dressed. But a black sweater and skirt couldn't hide the emaciated body. Nor the lipstick and mascara the thin drawn face. She was like the pictures of the people who had been liberated from concentration camps. And she had put on a brave effort to talk, responding to his stupid jokes and all the time holding his hand as if it were a life-line. He had only two choices. He could see her the next day for a couple of hours and then fade out of the picture, or he could make a genuine attempt to get her back into the world again. And this was the girl who once wore that silk dress with the roses on it, the girl who walked barefoot along the sandy beaches of the Algarve, the girl who liked him to send her to sleep by reading her poems from Palgrave. The girl whose favourite record was The Shadows playing the theme from *The Deer Hunter*. The girl who missed him when he was away. She was also the girl who had dragged him through the courts with a farrago of lies and innuendoes.

He saw a taxi with its lights on turn onto the Embankment and waved it down. The night porter let him into the club and took his order for a wake-up call and the *Daily Mail*. Berlin seemed a long way away.

The next morning he phoned his father and asked if he could bring her down to the cottage for a couple of days.

'Sure. It's your home, my boy.' He paused. 'You're sure you want to do this?'

'No. But I feel I should try and help.'

'Fair enough. But remember – it's OK to be the Good Samaritan but it ain't OK to try and play God. It never works.'

'What's all that mean?'

'What's wrong with Jenny was done a long time ago. Long before you came on the scene. Just tread very carefully – for her sake as well as for your own.'

His father was his usual charming, easy-going self with Jenny and she had obviously enjoyed the two days in the country and the company of the two men and when he took her back to her place he felt that he had genuinely helped her to start her recovery. He hadn't talked about getting together again. Neither had he slept with her but he made it clear that there was an amiable and continuing relationship and that seemed to satisfy and encourage her.

His father had driven him to Gatwick and waited with him until his flight was called. As they shook hands at the gate he said, 'Thanks for helping things along.'

'I'm your old man, Johnny. That's what I'm there for. But remember what I said – Good Samaritan fine but don't try working miracles. When someone is floundering in the water you stay on the bank and hold out your hand and pull 'em out. You don't jump in the water with them.'

He smiled. 'I'll remember.'

Peter Waring was waiting for him at Tegel and taking his bag he led him over to the coffee place. When they were settled Waring said, 'The BND have been in touch with London, asking what you're up to.'

'Who did they contact?'

'They tried Slaney but he passed them on to Powell.'

'What did he tell them?'

'Said you were doing some research on conditions in East Berlin.' He smiled. 'I gather they weren't impressed. They got on to me and I told them the truth – you are operating for London not me. There were hints that unless we came clean we couldn't expect cooperation from them in future.'

'Are they bluffing?'

'No. They've already backed out of a joint operation comparing notes on illicit border-crossing sites. Not vitally important but a bloody nuisance.' He stirred his coffee slowly as he looked at Tarrant. 'They've obviously got their eyes on you so bear it in mind.'

'Why are they interested?'

Waring shrugged. 'Touchy about not being informed or maybe they've guessed that you might be looking for our old friend.'

'Were they told he'd done a moonlight?'

'Only the official version. Found negligent in his operation and had flounced out. The BND always said that anyone who'd done that would go over the other side sooner or later.'

CHAPTER 28

It had been a traditional August day. Long hours of sun-shine, red admirals and peacocks fluttering on the heavy fronds of buddleia and the smell of cut grass everywhere. The windows were open and the net curtains moved lazily with the early evening breeze. Hartmann, Serov and Gala were drinking lime-juice as Foster played on the piano. They were waiting for Gala's father to arrive for dinner. He was due to land at Schönefeld early evening and come straight to Hartmann's place. But it was already after nine and there had been no message.

Serov was a bit testy at being kept waiting and, to pacify him, Foster was playing all the ballads that were popular when the war was getting to its end.

Serov called out, 'There was a song that went, "*Dein-etwegen muss Ich manchmal leiden . . .*".' Foster nodded and played and sang the next line. '". . . *Deinetwegen muss das Glück verneinen . . .*".' He laughed but went on playing. 'I can't remember any more words.'

'How is it you know all those old songs? You can't have been alive then?'

'My mother used to sing them. "*Deinetwegen*" was one of her favourites along with "*Hörst du mein heimliches Rufe . . .*".'

There was the sound of a car in the drive, the banging of a car door and then their awaited guest came storming in. 'Why are you sitting around like nothing's happening.

You've got a dish, haven't you? Why aren't you watching CNN?'

Hartmann stood up, smiling. 'Calm down, Sergei.' He paused. 'A whisky or champagne?'

Leonov stood there, looking from one to the other. 'What's the date today?'

Serov said, 'Fifth August.'

Leonov said quietly, 'It's a date you'll never forget, my friends.'

Serov shrugged. 'What's biting you, old friend?'

'You haven't heard anything?'

'Come on. Don't play games,' Hartmann said as he handed a glass of champagne to Leonov.

'I've just come from Budapest . . .' he looked around for an empty chair and sat down slowly '. . . there are over a quarter of a million East Germans trying to get out of the bloody country. The West German embassy in Budapest has been occupied by refugees and the rest are camping out along the frontier with Austria. Right there on the barbed-wire fences.' He took a sip of his drink, looked at the glass and then at Hartmann. 'The Hungarians are going to open the frontier tomorrow and let anyone through who wants to go. There are film crews and TV crews from every Western country – interviewing people who are openly criticising Honecker and the whole damn set-up. This is it, my friends. This is the beginning of the end. I was told that the East German embassies in Warsaw and Prague have thousands of people climbing the fences, camping out in the grounds. Being fed by the Red Cross. All with the same story – they want out.' He shook his head slowly. 'And no bastard's going to stop them.' He turned to Hartmann. 'Have you got a scrambler I could use to phone Moscow?'

'Come with me.'

As Leonov left with Hartmann, the others sat in silence until Hartmann came back.

'The lines to Moscow are all overloaded. He's going to try Kiev but he'll be some time.' He looked at Serov. 'I'm going to make some contacts here in Berlin, but carry on with dinner.' He smiled at Gala. 'You be mother, my dear. Get them started. I'll be back as soon as I can.'

Serov didn't want to eat and had stayed alone in the sitting room, and Gala took Foster into the kitchen where they ate soup and cold chicken.

She smiled and said, 'I feel like when I was a kid and they wanted to have a row so I was sent into the kitchen with the cook.'

'Did they have many rows?'

'God, yes. You've seen my father. Fantastic creative talent but he's like a volcano waiting to erupt. They loved one another completely and they almost understood one another too well. But any outsider who criticised one of them would be savaged by the other.' She paused. 'Is it as bad as daddy says?'

'Yes. Perhaps the worst part is that nobody knew in advance that it was going to happen. Honecker's people obviously didn't know. The Stasis didn't, the KGB didn't. There was nothing. One day all was normal and the next day – this.'

'What will Honecker do?'

'God knows.'

'D'you feel like a drive into town? We could have a look at the Western embassies and see if anything's happening here in Berlin.'

'OK. I'll tell Serov we'll be back in an hour or so.' He smiled. 'They'll want to talk all night, that's for sure.'

They stood looking at the West German legation. Inside were fifty or sixty people, some sitting or lying on the grass inside the tall iron gates and a few, mainly men, standing right up against the railings. They were shouting insults at the Volkspolizei who were guarding the legation gates. The gates had been padlocked from the outside and the guards were armed with AK 47s, fingers on triggers and faces grim as they ordered sightseers away. Any sign of disobedience meant having to show identification papers and notes made on official report pads.

As more and more people filled the pavement across the street from the legation the guards became more aggressive. They were taking orders by portable radios and five minutes later six or seven police vans swept up the street and more police came tumbling out of the vans. And now the police moved on the crowd of watchers. By now there were several hundred people. A man shouted something at the police as they moved in and they seized him, rushing him to the back of one of the vans and bundling him inside. More angry voices were raised from the crowd and before Foster and the girl had left there had been at least fifty people shoved into the police vans. Then there was the sound of a portable generator being started up and cables were being laid out, and a few minutes later two searchlights were trained on the watchers and a man with a large video-camera was recording the faces of the watching people.

As they drove back to Hartmann's he said, 'Did you notice that they didn't disperse even with the camera identifying them?'

'They can't arrest two hundred people just for standing there looking.'

'Don't you believe it. They fired on a peaceful crowd of protesters in 1953. There wasn't even a Wall in those days. They killed at least two hundred innocent, unarmed civilians.' His voice rose as he said, 'They don't give a shit about people. They never have. That's what communism's all about. You don't like someone – you have him killed. *You* don't kill him. You *have* him killed. Understand?'

She looked surprised. 'That's the first time I've seen you or heard you angry.'

'I'm sorry. I didn't mean to sound off but seeing those goons at the legation really gets me. People who don't care about other people – whether they're happy or sad, alive or dead.' He shook his head. 'They sicken me.'

'Was that why you did the deal for Uschi and the others?'

He shrugged and sighed and said quietly, 'I guess so.'

She sighed. 'I expect they're waiting for you back at Hartmann's place.'

And Gala was right, they were sitting around the TV waiting for him.

Serov turned. 'The bastards are jamming all the outside TV stations.'

Foster could see the thick white bar lines flickering on the screen. They had tried to get CNN or one of the West Berlin stations but they were all jammed. Gala told them what they had seen but they made no comment. She shrugged, kissed Foster on both cheeks, Russian style, and walked off, saying as she went, 'Are you coming or shall I take the car?'

Hartmann turned to look at Foster. 'We need to talk. How about tomorrow? Come over about nine, OK?'

'OK.'

CHAPTER 29

One of the servants at Hartmann's place took Foster up to a room he had not seen before. Hartmann, Serov and Leonov were sitting around a table where a place had been left for him. After the standard chat had been disposed of Hartmann turned to Foster.

'Let me bring you up to date. I've spoken to General Schumann at Stasi counter-intelligence. It was all off the record but he tells me that for the last three months his department has given warnings in writing both to Stasi HQ and unofficially to KGB liaison here in Berlin. There was no comeback and no interest shown by either party. In informal chats at both places it was obvious that they didn't believe him.' He paused, looking at Foster 'Why the smile?'

'Stasi HQ wouldn't want to admit that there was trouble and the KGB wouldn't trust it because it came from the Stasis.'

Hartmann smiled wryly. 'I spoke to two very senior colleagues of mine in Moscow and the impression they gave me was that they had so many similar problems at home that they didn't give a damn what was happening here. And they were absolutely positive that if Honecker starts shooting people here that Moscow will not help him in any way. They've warned him against violent action against the general public and if he goes down the pan – too bad. No, repeat no, help from Moscow.'

Foster nodded. 'And if the West Germans used the

attacks on civilians as an excuse to come over the border to protect the population, then what would Moscow do?'

'All the signals from Moscow say that they wouldn't lift a finger to stop it.'

'It doesn't sound possible. It would be the end of the Warsaw Pact.'

Serov said, 'My contacts in Moscow seem to be accepting that.'

'But surely they'd fight like hell to stop it happening.'

Serov shook his head. 'They reckon that they've got all the problems they can handle in keeping things off the boil in the Soviet Union.'

Leonov intervened. 'Mine's only gossip but the people I talked to say much the same. It's like there's been some virus that's developed overnight. Everywhere. Like the world's gone crazy. If I'd put it up as a film-script they'd have said I was crazy. Not just Moscow but Los Angeles too.' He shrugged. 'Like you, I can't really believe it even now. But it's fact not fiction. The Hungarians have closed down their film institute, so have the Czechs. The Poles threw the Commies out at their elections in June. I fished around my contacts in LA and Washington and not a murmur. All they care about is the World Series and Jimmy Connors. It's like somebody's lit a fuse and it's working its way through the whole of Europe. But who lit it – and why the hell has nobody noticed?'

There was a long silence and then Hartmann looked at Foster. 'I think we'll have to change our thinking. There are more urgent considerations now.'

Foster frowned. 'Like what?'

'We need to be in a position to bring pressure to bear, if it's necessary. On your computer you've got the details of West Germans who have been Stasi informants and collaborators. I can give you access to KGB records that give details of their collaborators. Americans, British, French, most European countries. Politicians, journalists, theatricals, influential individuals . . .' he shrugged his shoulders, '. . . the same kind of people you have on the Stasi records.' He paused. 'How long would it take to input the KGB data?'

'Is the data on paper or disks?'

'Both.'

'How many disks that are relevant?'

'According to what I'm told it would mean copying just over one hundred disks.'

'That's no problem. I could do that in a couple of days if I work straight through.'

'It might have to be done only at night.'

'OK. Say four nights.' He was silent for a few seconds and then he said quietly, 'How would they be used?'

Hartmann shrugged. 'In several ways. As a way to bring pressure on governments not to take precipitate action or we shall reveal their people's involvement. And as a form of insurance to protect those people who have striven to keep the peace.' He looked at Foster. 'And as a weapon against tyrants.'

Foster said quietly, 'A kind of blackmail.'

Serov said, 'No. A kind of diplomacy when all else looks like failing.'

Foster turned to Hartmann. 'When can you get me the KGB data?'

'I can't bring it here. You'll have to copy it at the Stasi communications centre. But for God's sake don't let them have an inkling of what it is you're copying. I can hand over half the disks tonight but they'll have to be back in Karlshorst by 6 a.m. tomorrow.'

Foster stood up. 'I'll start on the Stasi material during the day. I'll keep in touch and wait for you to contact me about the KGB files.'

Alter Simpl on Türkenstrasse in Munich is a café-bar that attracts a wide spectrum of the local population. Once famous for its sharp-edged satirical revue it's now more likely to be remembered as the café frequented by Lale Anderson who made the song 'Lili Marlene' famous.

Klaus Gutmann had taken his new girl there for a Wiener Schnitzel and a few beers. She was young and pretty and was impressed by both the Porsche and his apartment. The signs were that tonight might be the night. His intentions were strictly honourable. Well – honourable enough. It would be charm not booze that seduced her and he would be quite happy if it turned out to be a long-term relationship.

It was almost 2 a.m. when they left and there'd been no problem when he invited her back to his place for a last drink before driving her to her home.

He had poured her only a small whisky and handed it to her before he made the mistake. Without thinking he had switched on his answering machine. It was a message from Pullach telling him to phone them urgently. Everyone in Munich thought they knew what went on at Pullach, the HQ of the West German intelligence service. It was a successful and resourceful organisation and its members were respected by other intelligence services. But its air of mystery and secrecy made the local population a little chary of getting close to the inmates of that establishment in the small outlying village 10 km south-west of the city.

He didn't turn immediately to look at the girl but when he did he knew that tonight *wasn't* going to be the night. She was amiable but very cautious, but the kiss on her parents' doorstep was friendly enough.

As he walked back to his car he looked at his watch: 3.30 a.m. and Pullach was on the other side of town. It was crazy. Dachau was only a few kilometres outside the city but nobody suspected you of being a monster because you lived in a nearby village. He'd phone when he got home.

There was a message for him with the night duty officer.

Contact Schildt next morning if he was calling after midnight.

The meeting with Schildt was brief and he was handed half-a-dozen grainy black and white photographs as he sat down. They were all of the same man. In a bar, a restaurant, in various streets and at the ticket counter at the Hauptbahnhof.

He looked up from the photographs. 'Who is he?'

Schildt said, 'That's what we want you to find out.'

'Any clues?'

Schildt outlined the meeting with Müller and their concern about the man not only not being the regular Stasi contact but interested in policy rather than details.

'I've had a thought, Klaus. Maybe the guy wasn't a Stasi agent. Maybe not even a German. I wondered if you could use your charm on the lady at the CIA office and see if he might be one of theirs.'

'Doing what?'

'Oh – just playing games. You know what the Americans are like.'

'What makes you think he's one of theirs?'

'Just a hunch. I could be wrong.'

'Does he speak with an accent?'

'No. He's German, that's for sure.'

Gutmann sighed and stood up. 'OK. I'll see what I can do.'

Teresa Gordon was in her mid-thirties, an attractive woman who the BND were sure was intended by her employers, the CIA, as a lure for unsuspecting BND junior officers. She had had several BND boy-friends in the two years she had served in Munich but they had all been honest enough to report that she was great company but nothing more.

Klaus Gutmann had taken her out several times, paid

for out of the BND's imprest account, but despite his good-looks and charm he had been no more successful than the others. The difference was that he had continued to take her out to dinner or a week-end drive to a country inn and at least both organisations had made tentative use of the relationship to exchange minor items of information.

It was at least a semi-official enquiry and he saw no reason why he shouldn't see her at the CIA office. In the interview room he handed her the photographs and she looked at them carefully.

'Why don't you guys use decent cameras, like a Leica or something? These look like they were taken with an original Box Brownie.'

'It was a fast film and poor light. They're just a bit grainy, that's all.'

'Who is he?'

Gutmann gave her just the basic facts and she looked back at him when he'd finished.

'And you think he's CIA? You must be out of your mind.'

'We thought he might be one of your local agents or informers.'

'But your guy Müller would surely have known him if he was a local.'

'It was just an outside chance. Maybe you could pass them around and see if any of your people come up with anything.'

She sighed. 'OK. Just for you, Klaus. Leave 'em with me. If you don't hear from me it means you've drawn a blank.'

'How about dinner on Saturday?'

'Thanks, but I've got two days' leave in Paris at the week-end.' She smiled. 'Some other time, OK?'

'I'll call you next week.'

*　　*　　*

It was Cassidy, inevitably called 'Butch', who was last to look at the surveillance photographs. It was only a cursory look before he put them to one side on his desk. It was four days later that he looked at them again but in that four days he had been impressed by the BND's persistence and their grounds for thinking that there was something wrong about the man who had contacted Müller. It was good thinking. But the CIA wasn't the only intelligence unit operating in Munich and West Germany. It could equally have been the Brits. They too liked playing games. He didn't like the SIS people. In fact he didn't like Brits at all. The SIS people were arrogant bastards and snobbish with it. Faintly amused at Americans trying their prentice hands at what the Brits had been doing for hundreds of years. But the new Brit at SIS's Munich office had talked about cooperation between the two services locally and had said that London's attitude was now cooperation whenever national interests were not in conflict. And he liked the new fellow. Murphy was Irish and built like a New York cop. A bit of a joker but those piggy eyes didn't miss a thing. And about the first thing he had done on taking over was to warn Cassidy about an American who was laundering money for one of the local drug barons. He'd passed over the whole file and said it was up to Cassidy what happened. The Brits would pull out and leave it to him. He didn't believe it but the gesture was well meant. And the DEA had been grateful for the information. At least it would show willing if he contacted Murphy about the photographs.

Cassidy and Murphy met for a coffee at Cassidy's offices. Cassidy showed him around their facilities and gave him an expurgated run-down on their general operations. When it came to the photographs he gave them rather more importance than they deserved and handed over a set of copies for Murphy's records.

Murphy recognised the man in the photographs straight

away but he said nothing, just putting them back in the envelope before he shook hands and Cassidy took him through the electronic security lattice. Murphy told his driver to take him to his house not his office.

Murphy laid the photographs out on the kitchen table and went to his study for the magnifying glass. As he looked again at the photographs there was no doubt in his mind. It was Foster, all right. He had seen him almost every day in Berlin for a couple of months. Foster was running a line-crossing network when Murphy had been Peter Waring's admin officer. Slaney was back in London and Murphy had only heard the official version of Foster's sudden departure. But gossip said that Foster might have gone over the border. And gossip said that the guy sent over from London was looking for Foster. And here he was, in Munich, pretending to be a Stasi contact agent.

The problem was, should he tell Berlin or London? Protocol said Berlin as the line of command but it was London who'd sent over the man to find Foster.

Experience had taught Murphy not to rush into making decisions when policy was involved, so he went back to his office and put the problem to one side.

Mid-morning the next day he used the scrambler to speak to Waring, who didn't sound all that excited and told him that he'd call him back in a couple of hours.

Peter Waring had no intention of getting involved in the Foster business and when he had the report from Murphy he contacted Powell in London immediately. And Powell said he'd get back in the hour.

Powell had never had any doubt about Foster going over to the other side. There was no alternative if he wanted to do a deal for his three couriers. In his brief interview with Foster when he'd come to London to plead his cause, Powell had recognised what Slaney and the rest

of them had missed. Foster was an old-fashioned romantic. The kind who tilted at windmills along with Don
Quixote. The kind who voted Liberal or, these days,
SDP. Indifferent to winning or losing. Just intent on being
the knight in shining armour. Probably had Rudyard
Kipling instead of the Gideon Bible as his bedside reading.
And Powell knew, from long experience, that there was
nothing more dangerous than a born-again romantic on
the loose.

He phoned his old friend Schumacher, the head of
Abteilung 1 at Pullach. It was time to cash in a few old
favours. Like the Mafia always said, 'A favour done is a
favour earned'. Schumacher was glad to cooperate. He
wasn't all that sure as to what Powell expected to achieve
but he wanted the BND to be in on it whatever it was.
Promising cooperation was supposed to be the norm in
relations with both SIS and CIA. When the French were
involved Bonn had to give the nod.

Powell called Tarrant back to London and told him to
use every effort to find Foster. The photographs and the
circumstances surrounding them finally established that
he was working for the other side. And now he had the
cooperation of the BND to call on. If he became really
hard pressed he could contact Powell who would arrange
for Waring to provide whatever help he needed. But his
brief was still to operate on his own.

Tarrant did the return trip in a day and privately wondered why Powell hadn't just gone over the situation with
him on the phone. When he got back to his place at Kant
Strasse he decided to go across to check whether there was
any message for him at the café from Ingrid Schumann. It
was already mid-evening but it was a week since he had
last contacted her.

It was 9.30 p.m. as he went through Charlie, buying
the compulsory Ostmarks and standing there as the guard
looked through each page of his Canadian passport. When

it was handed back the guard reminded him that his right of passage only ran to midnight.

As he slid the passport back into his inside jacket pocket he walked on up Friedrichstrasse and took the east-bound U-Bahn to Alexanderplatz. When he came up into the square he looked up at the sky. It was September and the sun was beginning to have that golden hue that had always been the symbol of the harvest. He stood outside the station, looking towards the fountain. There was a boy sitting on the low wall there, playing a guitar and singing, surrounded by a dozen young people, an elderly couple, looking and listening, standing away from them as if they didn't want to be connected with them. He could just hear the guitar and the tune had a Western rhythm and the boy's voice was plaintive and sad.

There were few people in the square and the wide roads were empty of vehicles. He wondered what it had been like for Foster after moving over the border. He could never have done it himself. It was such an empty landscape. It had advantages of course. It was Germany before the war. Lace curtains, little crime, because people were scared of the Stasis, no need to make decisions, Honecker and his cronies would make them for you. Where you lived, what you earned and what you thought. It was crazy that a group of men could draw a line on a piece of paper, and build a wall that divided a nation into two different nations. The same people, ordinary Germans, made to be different, made to be each other's enemies. And the same men could make them into virtual prisoners in their own country. Foster must have been crazy to walk into the prison camp with them.

There were still a few people at the tables on the fore-court of the café but it wasn't the girl at the cash register machine, there was a man taking the money. There were girls in the background but Gerda, Ingrid's girl-friend, wasn't one of them. There was no way he could contact the girl. He couldn't risk going to her rooms, the landlady was an informer and he wasn't prepared to risk harming the girl. But he would have to think up some alternatives. Back to dead-drops. He'd have to look around for suitable places. Somewhere near the tennis courts maybe. He hung around until the café closed and then headed back to the checkpoint.

For a week Tarrant observed the café every day at different times from when it opened to when it closed. Neither the girl-cashier, Gerda, nor Ingrid herself ever appeared. There was no way of arranging a dead-drop system without first contacting the girl and that could lead to the landlady getting her arrested.

CHAPTER 30

Eddie Foster saw the man as he came into the shop and waited for him to ask for him. It was the ritual they always used. His assistant brought the man over and he took him into the small back office.

He looked at the man and said, 'What can I do for you?'

The man half-smiled as he said, 'D'you remember when Pongo Waring played for the Villa?'

'Yes. Billie Walker was captain in those days.'

The man reached inside his jacket and took out an envelope, handing it straight to Eddie Foster who slid it into the pages of a Sony catalogue on his desk.

'You got anything to go back this time?'

Eddie Foster shook his head, only once out of the six visits he had had did he send anything back. It was too dangerous. It was inevitable that they'd keep some sort of watch on him.

'No. But say I'm grateful for the contact.' He held out his hand instinctively and the man took it, gripping it tight as if it was some secret sign. Eddie Foster opened the side-door and watched the man walk across the yard to the alley that led to the main road. He had no idea who the man was but from his accent he could be a local.

When he locked up the shop at closing time he went back into his office and opened the envelope. It was just a single A5 sheet and half a dozen lines of typing. It was so badly typed that he guessed that Charlie had typed it himself. He sat down and read it again. He looked forward to getting the messages but they always upset him. It was such a waste. A gesture that was meant to make a point about loyalty. It was a bit like a book he'd read when he was a kid, called *Beau Geste*. But in Charlie's case people didn't see it that way. To them he was either a romantic fool or just a defector – a traitor. It angered him that they had put round the rumour that Charlie had been sacked for endangering his network people. It was the only time when a message from Charlie had made him sleepless for days on end. They didn't care who they trampled on so long as they came out of it all right. This message just said that he was OK. There had been no hint of what he did over the other side but Eddie felt sure that he was probably working for the East Germans.

He took the cigarette lighter that he kept on his desk for visitors and walked into the toilet where he watched as the paper burned to ashes as he held it over the wash-basin. He ran the cold tap and waited until the last of the ashes had swirled down the drain.

Way back he had had two visitors who claimed to be Special Branch who had gone through a pathetic probe to find out if he had any contacts with Charlie, or even if he had some idea of where he might be. Charlie must be valuable to the people over the border or they wouldn't go to the trouble of arranging for him to get the messages. He had no idea who the man was who brought them. They just phoned. If they said Tuesday it meant they'd come on Monday and the time was always two hours before they said. The first time he'd offered the man a fiver for his trouble but he'd refused it. Said it was for the sake of the workers' struggle. He wondered if Charlie had had to go along with that rubbish. He smiled at the thought. Charlie was too much a loner to go along with any dogma whether it was political or religious.

* * *

They were in Foster's work-room, Foster sitting in front of the computer checking what was on the screen. He read it carefully and then sighed and leaned back in his chair as he switched off and unplugged a small device with a plastic cover about the size of a paperback book.

Hartmann said, 'Why the deep sigh?'

Foster turned to look at Hartmann. 'You're sure that you've no more KGB material we need?'

'Quite sure. And even if there was more I daren't take any more.'

'In that case we've finished the job.' He pointed at the device. 'Everything's been transferred on to that.'

Hartmann frowned. 'You mean everything off the disks is now on one disk? It's not possible. There are tens of thousands of pages on those floppy-disks.'

'What we've got there is called a CD-ROM and just one of those holds three hundred thousand pages of typed or printed material.' He waved at the array of equipment alongside the computer. 'The equipment I've had to use is rather crude but I've made it work. For professionals it would be considered slow access – like nearly half a second.'

'And you can attach that to any computer and access those records?'

'The computer has to have a CD-ROM drive but you can buy those for external use if the computer doesn't have one.' He paused and went on. 'I thought it would take me a week but as you know it took nearly three weeks.'

'Why was that?'

'Because to be useful to us it has to be code-indexed. The KGB material, the Stasi stuff and what I've classified as miscellaneous are all in discrete sections. And then there's a list of access codes covering names, status, payments, type of information, recruitment and so on. And with all that the CD-ROM is only half used.'

'Can we make copies?'

'If I can use the Stasi equipment, yes.'

'They mustn't know what you've got on that CD thing.'

'You arrange for me to have four hours unsupervised and I can do you copies.'

'OK. Ten copies. I'll fix it for tomorrow night.'

'I think you'd better come with me.'

'Why?'

'I've had several phone calls from Stasi people in the last few weeks. People who were antagonistic when I was working there are suddenly very chatty. Do I need any help or equipment? – maybe we could get together – combined efforts and all that.' He paused. 'They don't even know what I'm doing, so how do they figure we could combine our efforts?'

'D'you think they have any idea what we're doing?'

'I've gone over it in my mind. What clues they have can only be from equipment I've used or taken over. They could deduce that I'm extracting and copying files – but they wouldn't know which files or why I was doing it.'

Hartmann was silent for some moments then he said, 'When we've got the copies tomorrow night we'll close down, at least for a few months.'

When Tarrant woke in the middle of the night he switched on the bedside light and looked at his watch. It was 3.15 a.m. He put on his bathrobe and walked into the kitchen and switched on the electric kettle. When he was pouring the boiling water over the coffee granules in the cup he suddenly thought of a way to contact the girl. He was the problem. Somebody else could contact her, preferably a girl. Leni owed him plenty of past favours – if she would just make one contact it would be enough. There would only be a very slight risk. What could they prove? A girl contacting another girl. A relative or a friend. The trouble was that in the GDR you didn't need proof. You put people in the slammer and thought about it afterwards. He'd talk to Leni and see if she'd go along with it. Play up the helpless young victim bit. She had always been a sucker for sob-stories.

She wasn't smiling as she said, 'Come on, Johnny. Level with me. What's it all about?'

He tried to look indignant but it wasn't very effective despite the shrugging.

'Like I said, I just want you to ask for the girl at the address I give you. And if she's not there ask where she is.'

'But why? Why don't you do this yourself?'

'Because there are problems.'

'Is this business or pleasure?'

He smiled. 'A bit of both.'

'And the bit that's business is to do with what you do?'

'More or less. She's just a young girl. No parents. I just want to help her.'

'And before you help her she has to help you. Yes?'

'In a way. It's not James Bond stuff, if that's what you mean.'

'Sounds more like *Funeral in Berlin* to me.'

'I promise you on the Bible or anything else you want that the girl has nothing to do with espionage.'

'Except that she knows you.'

Tarrant knew then he wasn't winning and for a few moments he was silent as he collected his thoughts. And when he spoke his voice carried an air of sincerity that was very nearly true.

'If I tell you more, will you promise me never to tell anyone what I've told you? Whether you help me or not.'

She hesitated and then said, 'I guess so.'

'Like I said the girl has nothing to do with my kind of work. All she is is the friend of another girl who knows where a man is who I'm looking for.'

'To kill him?'

'For Christ's sake, Leni. Do I look like a killer?'

'You're tough enough, Johnny. Killers often have lots of charm when they want something.'

'I just want to talk to the guy.'

'OK. Tell me what you want me to do.'

Leni wore an old sweater, a leather jacket and skirt for her trip into East Berlin. Through the Friedrichstrasse checkpoint and then walking to the address that Johnny Tarrant had given her.

The landlady was holding a plate and a tea-towel in her hand as she stood at the open door. She brushed loose hair from her face with the back of her free hand.

'We're full. There's no vacancies.'

'Is Ingrid around?'

'Ingrid who?'

'Ingrid Schumann.'

The woman closed her eyes for a moment, trying to remember the exact words the man had rehearsed with her.

'She'll be at the café tomorrow. She's not here.'

'What time will she be there?'

'From mid-day till closing time.'

And with that the woman closed the door, trembling as she tried to recall if she'd said it like they had told her. She'd done her best and that's all the bastards could expect. The whole thing was like some film story. The girl Ingrid gone weeks ago only to be followed up by the young Russian who looked like the one who had been prancing around Uschi Bayer. Somebody told her she'd married him. More like his tart. But that's how they all were these days. Ready to open their legs for anything in a uniform. Too much TV from the other side of the Wall.

* * *

Tarrant was quietly pleased that his little plan had worked. With another meeting with the girl he could show her the dead-drop he'd decided to use in the cemetery near the university. It was a step forward anyway. He bought her a pair of fur mittens at a shop in the Ku'damm and had them gift-wrapped.

He planned his contact carefully. He would arrive just after 2 p.m. and he'd ask for a cheese sandwich. Then he'd notice the girl and stroll over to her at the table and go through the motions of chatting her up and then they could go off in different directions and meet at the cemetery.

As he arrived he saw that there were no tables in the forecourt. It was after all half-way through September and there was a distinct chill in the air. It was the same man at the cash register but the usual student crowd had obviously eaten and left. The windows were slightly steamed up but he could see vaguely that there were people at the tables inside. The bell rang as he opened the door and the man at the cash desk nodded to him amiably as he looked around for the girl. As he hesitated at the door somebody came through the door behind him and a voice said in bad German, 'Just walk on through to the door at the back and don't try any games.' He half turned to look behind him to see the man and he felt the gun ram into his kidneys and the hot pain went down to the back of his legs as the gun jabbed again at his sciatic nerve. His mind went back to his training at Ashford when it had been demonstrated again and again that you never shoved a gun in a man's back because he just turned and swung with one arm and the gun would fire into empty space. They'd demonstrated it with live ammunition and once you'd learned the trick it was infallible. But doing it on the grass at the edge of the parade ground was one thing and doing it in a crowded café in what amounted to enemy territory was another. There were probably other guns trained on him too. As the man behind him shoved him forward he made his ungainly way through the tables with their startled occupants to the door at the back. He found himself in what looked like a store-room and there was another man there leaning against a stack of empty crates.

They were both in civilian clothes but they looked as if they would be more at home in uniform. The older man looked at him and then said, 'Show me your papers.'

Tarrant shook his head. 'Not until you identify yourself. You've no right to see my papers. I'm just a tourist here for the day.'

The man shrugged. 'OK. If that's how you want to play it.' He nodded to the other man and reached out to take his gun. Tarrant noticed that it was a Czech copy of a Luger.

The other man grabbed his wrist and clamped on a handcuff pulling both his wrists together and squeezing the ratchets tight so that they dug deep into his flesh.

There was a black Zil outside and he was bundled into the back seat alongside the older man who now had the gun. Tarrant was aware of people standing, watching what was going on, curious rather than concerned. People being arrested and pushed into cars was not so unusual a sight.

There were never many vehicles on the main roads in East Berlin and the driver was keeping alongside the Wall until they got to the T-junction at Eisenstrasse where he turned left into a series of back streets to Hans Lochstrasse and then Tarrant knew where they were heading.

They weren't Volkspolizei or Stasi, they were Soviets and they were heading for their HQ at Karlshorst. They wouldn't be Red Army men on a mission like this, they'd be KGB and that meant that something had gone terribly wrong somewhere. They knew too much about him for it not to mean real trouble. And he wasn't going to have a knight on a white horse like Foster to rescue him. Waring wasn't responsible for him and London would swear they'd never heard of him. And because of the looseness of his arrangements it would probably be at least a week before anyone rumbled that he wasn't around any more. And if you're SIS the old name, rank and number ritual didn't work. KGB interrogators had a lot of experience in making men talk and there had been no training sessions on how to cope with rough stuff. All that SIS asked of you was that if you were involved with others try and stick it out for forty-eight hours so that they could head for the hills, and after that it was up to you.

CHAPTER 31

Sergei Leonov had swept into town in his usual fashion, seemingly oblivious to what was going on in the Democratic Republic and bringing a breath of fresh air into the Hartmann group. He had just completed a movie, filming in Moscow and Dresden, and was now on his way to Rome to discuss a joint Soviet/Italian film that was to be an exposure of corrupt politicians in Milan. There was no problem about raising the budget. The problem was how to find a substitute location for Milan whose officials had refused any facilities in the city with barely concealed threats of violence against the crew. He had taken them out to lunch at a villa that was always made available for him when he was in the GDR.

After lunch they walked together to the lake that marked the limits to the estate. At the lakeside they stood watching as hundreds of starlings wheeled and swooped across the water in their ritual gathering before they flew south for the winter.

As they walked he said, 'They're early to leave this year. They usually stay until the first week in November. Two weeks ahead of the time-table.' He shook his head. 'Wise birds who leave early this year. Wise people who leave early too.'

Hartmann smiled. 'You're not usually so pessimistic, Sergei.'

'I'm not pessimistic, my friend. I'm a realist. You should

295

go to Dresden or Leipzig. For the last three days I was in Dresden there were demonstrations every day. Not just a few hundred but tens of thousands. Shouting for freedom to travel. It wasn't just a demonstration, it was a boil bursting, decades of frustration, decades of oppression. They don't even know what they want. But they do know what they don't want. And that's Honecker and his gang. The Stasis. The Soviet occupation forces.' He turned to look from one to the other and settled on Gala. 'What's the date today, my love?'

She looked at her watch. '18th, October 1989.' She smiled as she looked back at him, 'And it's a Wednesday.'

He waved his hand, shaking his head. 'Remember this day, my friends. Ten years ago Frank Coppola made a film called *Apocalypse Now*. What you're going to see before long is our Apocalypse Now.' He waved a thick forefinger at them, shaking his head and speaking softly for a change. 'It's going to happen. And soon.'

Serov smiled. 'What's going to happen, Sergei?'

Leonov shook his head. 'I don't know. I really don't. It's in the air. You can smell it everywhere. Moscow, Prague, Budapest, Sofia, here. Like a lot of cooking pans on a giant hotplate, all at the boil, their lids bouncing and rattling from the steam coming out. Mark my words.'

Hartmann said quietly, 'And what can we do?'

'To stop it – nothing. No more than you can stop a hurricane.' He paused. 'If any of you have somewhere to go – then go. Anywhere.'

'And if we stay?' It was Foster who said it.

'If you stay you can watch a dream turn into a nightmare.'

'But if people get the freedom they want, why the nightmare?'

'Because you need to be trained for freedom and our poor bastards haven't had any training. They are lazy and slipshod in their work. They haven't made a decision for themselves for fifty years. The West will eat them – you'll see.'

He turned away impatiently and headed for the villa as the others followed him.

Hartmann and Foster had gone back to Hartmann's place and were sitting in his study. There was a cardboard shoe-box on the coffee-table between them. It held all the copied disks.

Hartmann pointed at the box. 'It seems crazy to say it but that shoe-box is our personal insurance. But you have to remember that dear old Sergei is a film man. They live in an exaggerated world. A world of fantasies. Everything has to be larger than life.'

'But if he's right?'

'God knows. It depends on how it all comes out. But whoever it is they'll want to suppress what's on those disks of yours.'

'So where do we keep them?'

'One copy each for you, Serov, Gala, Sergei. Two for colleagues of mine in Moscow. And I'll keep the rest in reserve. OK with you?'

Foster shrugged. 'Whatever you say.'

Tarrant had been left for three days in the grim cell. A concrete slab to sleep on and a thin mattress stuffed with straw. A plateful of thin stew each day with a piece of off-white bread. But no contacts apart from the guard who opened the cell door to give him his food. No interrogations. He recognised that it was the old routine, ignoring a suspect so that his ego was deflated. Make him feel unimportant. Even forgotten.

On the fourth day he was escorted down a long corridor, up several flights of steps to another floor and then showed into an office. There was just one man in the office as

Tarrant heard the key turn in the lock of the door behind him.

The man pointed to a wooden chair and Tarrant sat down. He guessed that the man was in his mid-forties but there was no clue to his nationality. His English was fluent but heavily accented. The whole installation at Karlshorst was Soviet so he could only assume that the man was a Soviet. He saw his passport and various other items from their search laid out on the desk. He had no network so he had nothing to worry about on that score. They must know that or they would have been interrogating him non-stop from the moment they picked him up. He wondered what else they knew and how they knew anything at all.

The man sat on the edge of the table looking down at him.

'Your passport is in the name of Lucas. John Lucas. Why did you choose that name?'

'Because that is my name.'

The man smiled. 'It's not important, Mr Tarrant. I ask out of simple curiosity. The John is obvious. That is your real name. But Lucas – I don't see the connection. The passport is quite good. Genuine passport but phoney details.' He smiled again. 'Place of issue given as Toronto. But the serial number was issued in 1940. I don't think you were born then, Mr Tarrant.' He paused. 'Another of London's cock-ups, I guess.'

Tarrant said nothing but suddenly he realised that things had gone horribly wrong. The indignant, innocent tourist scenario was no longer a runner. The whole thing was leaking like a colander. The Russian had good reason to smile. Must be deciding whether he'd have him on or off the bone.

'So, Mr Tarrant. What do we do with you? False documents to gain entry into the GDR goes down as espionage with our laws. The Canadians too aren't going to like being dragged into an affair like this. And London swearing they've never heard of Johnny Tarrant. Poor old Slaney will be posted to Kabul or some other God-forsaken place to keep him out of the limelight.' He smiled. 'What a mess.' He paused and shrugged. 'So like I said, what shall we do with you? Any suggestions?'

Tarrant said nothing.

'And if we just shove you back into West Berlin and tell them not to play silly games they'll assume that we've turned you. Months of debriefing to try and find out if you're now a double-agent. Whatever you say they won't believe you.' He smiled. 'We never believe ours either. Remember Colonel Abel who the CIA exchanged with us for Gary Powers, the U2 pilot? Abel was debriefed in Moscow for a year. He'd been the most successful KGB operator in New York we'd ever had. But the boys in Moscow weren't taking any risks. Why should the Americans trade a top KGB man for a pilot who confessed in court to being on a spy mission? When you go back you have no friends. Not even a guy like Abel. The poor bastard spends his time reading *Newsweek* and *Pravda* and playing chess with his minder.' He paused, quite a long pause. 'I really don't know what to do with you.'

Peter Hartmann edged off the table, walked towards the window and stood looking out. After long moments he turned to look at Tarrant.

'Are you interested in a deal, Johnny?'

'What kind of a deal?'

'Have you ever met Charlie Foster?'

'No.'

'If you had made contact with him, what were your orders?'

Tarrant just shook his head.

'Were you supposed to kill him or try and turn him?'

'Neither.'

'Come now. You weren't concerned about the state of

299

his health, for God's sake. So what was the object of the contact?'

'Just to locate him and inform London. No contact required.'

'Ah yes. And then dirty-tricks take over, yes?'

'What would be the point?'

'Wipe him out so that everybody knows what happens to anybody who might be thinking of changing ideas.'

For once Tarrant smiled. 'Nobody's crazy enough to want to come over here.'

'Foster did.'

Tarrant shrugged and smiled. 'Some would say he was crazy anyway.'

'That's rather ungenerous, isn't it?'

'Why?'

'I'm sure they briefed you on why Charlie Foster came over.'

'So what?'

'So loyalty and courage doesn't count with you?'

'It was his inefficient running of his operation that caused the problem.'

'That's SIS's cover story. His couriers were blown by a man who had a marital problem. Just luck so far as we were concerned.' He paused. 'And your mission was defused for exactly the same reason. A chance piece of gossip from an informant on your side of the Wall. One of your own people.'

'You mean someone in SIS Berlin?'

'Of course.'

After a long silence Tarrant said, 'What's the deal you had in mind?'

'Just answer me one question first.'

'Try me.'

'Tell me why you think that London are so interested in Charlie Foster. Not what London said – but your opinion.'

'How long can I have to consider if I can reply?'

'How about overnight? We'll meet again tomorrow.'

Tarrant shook his head. 'What does it matter? London are very worried about the situation here in the GDR. They think there's going to be real trouble. Talk of revolution and so on. They thought that Charlie could be persuaded to fill us in on what he knows. That's what London said and I believe them. But in the first place all I was to do was locate him.'

'Maybe you should meet Charlie Foster. If he's willing to meet you, that is.'

'And then?'

'And then we'll think about what to do with you.'

Hartmann pressed a bell on the wall and Tarrant heard the key in the lock and saw the guard come in.

'Tell Captain Rykov I want to see him. Don't lock the door.'

Captain Rykov was a man in his fifties and Hartmann spoke to him in Russian and made arrangements for Tarrant to be moved to better accommodation.

Hartmann, Foster and Gala had dined together at Hartmann's house and they were at the coffee stage, still at the table, when Hartmann said, 'Do you know an SIS man named Tarrant. Johnny Tarrant?'

Foster thought for a moment. 'I've heard the name but the man was before my time. I think I'd heard that he had retired.'

'Maybe this is his son. He's about your age. Red hair, blue eyes and tough.'

Foster shook his head. 'Can't help you, I'm afraid.'

'SIS sent him through the Wall to find you.'

Foster looked amazed, and it was several seconds before he spoke.

'To find me? Why should they do that?'

'Tarrant says they are very worried about what's

happening here in the GDR and they think you could put them in the picture. Tell them how it is.'

'The cheeky bastards. I can't believe it.'

Hartmann laughed. 'You Brits have always been like that. You stab some colleague in the back and later on you ask him for his vote as if nothing had ever happened.'

'Where is this chap?'

'He's in a cell in Karlshorst.'

'Do you want me to see him?'

'I don't know. I'd like to think about it.'

Gala said angrily, 'Charlie ought to have a lot more protection from now on. This man Tarrant could have been sent to kill him.'

'I don't think so but we'll double the guards at your place if that's what you want.'

'That's the least you can do, Peter. You should contact the people who sent him and tell them that if anything happens to Charlie then it's goodnight for their man. The bastards.'

Hartmann smiled at her fondly and reached out for her hand, patting it gently as he said, 'I'll look after your boy, my dear. Dry those eyes. All will be well. He's well capable of looking after you and me as well as himself.'

And it was only then that Charlie saw the tears trembling on the edge of the girl's eyes.

As he held the car-door open for her she stood up, facing him and without thinking he put his hands on her shoulders as she looked up at him. And he said quietly, 'Thanks for caring about me, but Peter's right. I can look after you two better than you can look after me.'

'Charlie, without Peter around the Stasis would have you in jail in an hour.'

'Did he give you your copy of the disk?'

'Yes.'

'Where is it?'

'In my bedroom.'

'Did he tell you what's on it?'

'Yes.'

'Well that's your insurance, but you must put it somewhere . . .' he shrugged '. . . a locker at a railway station or a bank.'

She laughed. 'The Stasis regularly check lockers at banks and stations.'

'So bury it somewhere. In a churchyard or a cemetery or in a park. We'll do it together tomorrow. It's important. Could save your life.'

She sighed. 'Don't you get tired of all this? The gloom and doom, the coming disasters, revolutions, the black-mail material on those disks. It makes me want to leave it all and go somewhere where the sun shines and people are mostly happy.'

He smiled. 'Where've you got in mind?'

She frowned. 'San Francisco, Buenos Aires, Hawaii – somewhere like that.'

'We'd better ask Peter to get you a US passport.'

'I've got one. Daddy got it for me when I was a kid. He's got American citizenship and half a dozen different passports. And lots of money stashed away in various tax havens. I have too if we need it.' She wondered if he had noticed the 'we'.

'I must have some money somewhere. I've never drawn my pay. I'll have to ask Peter how to get at it.'

'I checked last week for you. You've got over a hundred thousand dollars in actual dollars. He's drawn it for you. It's in his safe.' She paused. 'How soon before you'll need it?'

'If I need it at all it will be sometime in the next six months. Maybe less.'

'What do you think will happen?'

'A massive uprising. Honecker will order it to be put down by the police and the army. When enough people have been slaughtered the West Germans will move in. And if we're all very unlucky the Red Army will fight the West Germans.' He shrugged. 'Something's going to happen. Your father's right. You can smell it in the air.'

'I can't.'

He smiled. 'I'm glad you can't. You're the only sane one among us.' She smiled and said softly, 'Do you like me, Charlie?'

'Of course I do.'

'Why do you like me?'

He shrugged. 'I don't know, I just do.' He paused. 'Do you like me?'

'Does it matter?'

'It matters to me.'

'Why?'

'Because I feel we're a pair. When I think about leaving this set-up I always imagine you being with me.'

She smiled. 'I'm cold. Let's go inside.'

She made them hot chocolate and they sat at the kitchen table.

'The others all seem very worried about the situation, but you don't. Why not?'

He thought for several moments and then said, 'I guess it's because this whole thing is artificial so far as I'm concerned. I don't belong in this picture. It's like watching a film. It's nothing to do with me. I have an obligation to Peter and I carry it out. When I've paid the debt I shall leave. I should have left even if there hadn't been all these disturbing events.'

'Where would you go?'

He hesitated for a moment and she assumed that he didn't want to tell her. 'You don't have to tell me, Charlie.'

He smiled and shook his head. 'I hesitated because I'm not sure whether I'd go to Amsterdam or the USA.' Still smiling, he said, 'Unlike some people I don't have an American passport.'

'Hartmann or my father could fix that for you.'

'Do you fancy coming with me?'

She smiled. 'You're a funny man, Charlie Foster.' She paused. 'Can I ask you a personal question?'

'Sure. Go ahead.'

'Do you think I'm attractive?'

He laughed softly. 'Of course I do. You must know that.'

'Most men who find me attractive make a pass at me. Why haven't you?'

'It's hard to explain.'

'So try.'

'Well if we'd met socially, or accidentally, outside this thing with Peter Hartmann, it would have been different. But I felt that you'd been put here as a duty, an obligation. You were stuck with me, not because you wanted to be but . . .' he shrugged '. . . like I said – kind of forced to do it. And in those circumstances you might feel you have to go along with anything I want as part of some deal. So although I thought you were very beautiful right from the first time I saw you, and later I grew fond of you for other reasons, I thought it would be the action of a real creep if I made even the mildest pass at you.'

'You know, Charlie, under that tough outside of yours, you're really rather a puritan, aren't you?'

He shrugged. 'Who knows? Whatever you say, honey.'

'Say that again.'

'Say what again?'

'Say honey again.'

He smiled as he said, 'Honey' and she kissed him on the mouth as his arms went round her.

It was 3 a.m. when Foster switched the TV on and moved the dish so that they could watch CNN.

The first item on the news was that Erich Honecker had resigned the previous evening. There was a rostrum picture of Egon Krentz who had taken over from Honecker. The second item was that Hungary had declared its independence from Moscow and the Warsaw Pact.

Foster looked at his watch. It was less than twelve hours since Leonov had forecast what was going to happen.

'Your old man ought to be a fortune-teller. He says something impossible is going to happen and a few hours later it happens.' He stood up, reaching for her hand.

'Time to go to bed, honey.' He smiled. 'Again.'

The next day demonstrations in Leipzig and Dresden were each more massive and for the first time they were shown on East Berlin's TV station. The next few days seemed like the fulfilment of all the demonstrators' dreams. There were discussions on TV between the ruling politicians and the opposition who clamoured for their immediate resignations. The party boss in Dresden panicked and promised immediate concessions, and on October 23 half a million protesters filled the streets of Leipzig. The opposition christened itself the New Forum and the Communist government announced that it was dropping the charge of Enemy of the State which it had declared was the crime of those who had used Hungary, Austria and Czechoslovakia to flee the country.

CHAPTER 32

Eddie Foster opened the small package and read the note.

Dear Dad,
    All OK with me. Put this in your office safe for me.
    All the best.

He looked at the small plastic container and had no idea what it might be, but he opened the safe and slid it inside into the small metal drawer where he kept his will, bankbook and insurance policies. He vaguely thought of changing the combination but decided against it. Charlie knew the combination, it was a six figure number using the date of his mother's birthday, and he might need to use it some time.

Pouring himself a cup of tea from the Thermos he always brought with him he pulled out the visitor's chair and sat down. There was a folded copy of that evening's *Birmingham Mail* on his desk and a copy of *Shortwave Magazine*. As he sipped the tea he wondered how Charlie really was. He must be out and about or he wouldn't be able to post things and pass messages to him. It was no life for a young man. He should be settled down by now with a decent girl and maybe a child on the way. He'd got enough money to buy them a small house and give Charlie a substantial share in the prospering business. Tomorrow would be November 1 and then it would be Christmas. They had always tried never to miss the family Christmas together. Charlie had flown back from Cyprus one year and had arrived dead on midnight as they were just switching on the Christmas lights. His father wouldn't bother about the lights this year.

It was Stan Richards who first sounded the alarm about Johnny Tarrant. Dolly had suggested that Johnny came round for dinner and Richards hadn't been able to contact him. Nobody seemed to have seen him for several days. When he asked Peter Waring if he knew where Tarrant was it had set the alarm bells ringing. A quick check revealed that Tarrant had not been seen for at least two weeks.

Waring had no intention of being drawn into something that London had insisted was not under his control. He phoned Powell in London but was told that Powell was in Washington. He found Powell at the number that Century House gave him. When Powell had heard the news he had said that he was too involved in something at Langley, would Waring please do him the favour of phoning Willis in London, apprising him of the situation and asking him to take the matter in hand?

Willis was on leave but was traced to his hotel in Portofino. Cursing Powell angrily he said that he would come direct to Berlin the next day.

Ross Lindquist, Deputy Director of CIA Special Operations, read through the report and transcript of Powell's telephone conversation with Waring that NSA had sent him. It wasn't clear enough what it was all about but a missing SIS man in Berlin was worth a few man-hours of checking-up. Instructions and details were sent through to CIA Bonn and Berlin. It was given only routine priority.

Electronic surveillance at Pullach had routinely monitored the radio message to CIA Bonn and with its usual efficiency the BND's correlating system threw up two additional reports. One concerned a Turk who worked for the BND who had gone missing a year ago. The other was the file on Foster with details of Munich office's cooperation with Tarrant. Pullach sent reminder copies of their material to Waring in Berlin who left it pending for Willis. Waring wondered why Pullach had suddenly revived the matter and ordered Signals Security to give him a report on the security of SIS Berlin's radio and telephone traffic. There was either a leak somewhere or Powell was playing footsie with Pullach.

Foster had felt no compulsion to meet the man who was looking for him.

He looked through the observation slot in the cell-door and was aware that his time in the solitary cell had had quite an effect on Tarrant. He was sitting on the low bed his elbows on his knees and his face in his hands. He noticed the rich red hair and the broad shoulders. They had taken away his jacket and his shoes and Tarrant had draped the rough, grey prison blanket round his shoulders. There was no heating in the Karlshorst cells. He felt no sympathy for the man in the cell. Like the instructors always said – he knew the rules of the game. But he was aware that if Hartmann had not been involved from the first day he came over, the man sitting in the cell could have been him.

Foster walked back to the room where Hartmann was waiting for him.

'I'll get the guard to bring him up here and I'll wait in the lawyers' office – the guard can bring you there.'

'What do you intend doing with him?'

'I haven't decided. I'd like your views when you've talked to him. Meantime he'll do no harm where he is.'

It was ten minutes before the guard came up with Tarrant and when the guard had left Foster pointed to a metal chair by the table. Such furniture as there was

was all metal and all of it was bolted to the concrete floor.

Tarrant had the pale complexion that frequently went with red hair and Foster guessed that the scatter of freckles made Tarrant look younger than he really was.

He perched himself on the edge of the small table and stared at Tarrant.

'You must be Tarrant. All the way from Century House and my old friend Slaney. How is he these days?'

'There's going to be a God almighty diplomatic incident if you don't release me in the next couple of days.'

Foster laughed and he was genuinely amused. 'You must be out of your mind, Tarrant, if you think that they'll lift a finger to get you out.' He paused. 'If they weren't like that I wouldn't be here.'

Tarrant stared back defiantly. 'They'll get you, Foster, sooner or later.'

Foster smiled. 'Don't scare me or I might just run away and leave you to the KGB.' He paused. 'What were you supposed to do when you found me?'

Tarrant just shrugged.

'Is Peter Waring controlling you?'

'No. Control was London. They just wanted me to locate you, not make contact.'

'What had they got in mind after that?'

'I've no idea.'

'Who briefed you in London?'

'Powell.'

'But Powell's political not operations.'

'I got shoved sideways from operations and Powell gave me this job.' He sighed. 'I think it was just a time-filler.' He paused. 'By the way, I contacted your old man. He didn't give an inch but he said if I ever contacted you to give you his love.'

'Where did you interview him?'

'At the shop in Sutton Coldfield.'

'How was he?'

'Seemed very chipper but wasn't going to talk to the likes of me.'

'Why should London let somebody like Powell use an operations guy on a surveillance job? It's a waste of a specialist.'

'I'd put up a bit of a black and I think this was like I said – a time-filler.'

'What sort of a black?'

'A messy divorce that got into the papers.'

And for the first time Foster felt a spasm of sympathy for the rather pathetic figure in front of him.

'Is there anything you want?'

'I wouldn't mind a decent meal and another blanket.'

'I'll see if I can get you moved.'

And as if the brief touch of domesticity revived him Tarrant said, 'People back there think you're working for the Stasis – are you?'

Foster pressed the bell for the guard and told him to take the prisoner back to his cell.

Hartmann had Tarrant transferred to slightly more civilised quarters at the prison section of the Stasi complex at Normannenstrasse where Foster had a more relaxed conversation with his would-be pursuer. Tarrant told him about his stormy marriage and Foster had been shocked to hear of the death of Slaney's wife. Tarrant had asked him about his life in East Germany and Foster had found himself defending the ordinary people against the standard capitalist criticisms. He came to no conclusions about how to deal with the prisoner. Maybe they could use him in some way. But Foster didn't intend to probe about SIS. It wasn't part of his bargain with Peter Hartmann. If Hartmann wanted to play games with Tarrant that was up to him.

* * *

They had arranged to eat that evening in the kitchen at Foster's place and Hartmann had kept them waiting for nearly two hours. He looked worried and preoccupied when he arrived and when Gala had poured him a whisky Hartmann held up the glass to them.

'*Na zdrovye*.'

They both smiled and responded in Russian but Hartmann shook his head.

'No cause for rejoicing, my friends. I've just had several hours on the phone to Moscow. It sounds like the knives are out and the shredding machines are working overtime destroying what guilty consciences feel might be damaging evidence of corruption, subversion, treason or plain stupidity.'

Foster said quietly, 'Who's doing the shredding?'

'Sounds like everybody's under suspicion. There's talk of a coup against Gorbachev, an attack by him against the old guard. The army split from top to bottom by who was a communist and who wasn't. Either way there's going to be some group or other ready to throw anybody they don't like into Lefortova.'

'Are you affected?'

'I'm sure I am – or will be.'

'Why?'

'My God, they don't need reasons. It just depends on who comes out on top. I've always tried to be independent but in these times that's the worst crime of the lot.' He paused. 'By the way, Honecker's on his way to Moscow. Needs one of those diplomatic medical check-ups that only Moscow can perform. That means the local troubles are about to turn nasty.'

The next day, November 9, was one of those cold but sunny autumn days that brighten up the drab buildings and streets and gave no hint that it was to be memorable in any way. As late as mid-afternoon neither the authorities nor the opposition had any idea that they were about to make history. It was as if somebody pulled on a dropped stitch and slowly unravelled the whole sweater. But although nobody recognised it, half a dozen old sweaters were unravelling at the same time.

CHAPTER 33

It seemed an ordinary day. There were protesters in the streets demanding the right to travel outside East Germany, particularly to West Berlin, but the police and the border guards had become used to that. Anyway, that was a problem for politicians. There had, in fact, been a meeting the previous evening of the eleven members of the Central Committee where Egon Krenz was unanimously elected as Honecker's successor. The meeting had gone off without incident despite a crowd of 50,000 outside shouting their discontent while the meeting went on. There was a change in their shouted demands, a change that nobody in authority appeared to notice. It was no longer a demand for travel outside the GDR but a demand for an immediate election.

Then on the evening of November 9 there was an announcement that nobody subsequently admitted to having authorised. The announcement was made during a press conference by the Politburo member Günter Schabowski. There had been a new law passed, Schabowski announced. From now on citizens of the GDR may travel wherever they wished, including into West Berlin, without permits or passes and without interference by the police or the border guards. The announcement was made at 7.30 p.m. on both TV and radio, and at first people thought it must be a hoax but it was repeated several times.

When a young man at the Bornholmer Strasse

checkpoint heard the announcement on his portable radio there were only twenty or thirty people waiting to pass through the control. The watching police and border guards took it for granted that it was a mistake which would be swiftly corrected. But ten minutes later there were a thousand people waving, laughing and shouting, demanding that the barrier be opened immediately.

For over an hour senior officers on the spot phoned to their superiors at the Frontier Control HQ in Schnellerstrasse, but they were told to act on their own initiative. Then a Stasi colonel told the milling crowd that the law only came into use the next day and identity cards would be stamped. He hinted that there was no guarantee that people who went into West Berlin would be allowed back. But the colonel, like a good many other people, had not realised that everything had changed that night. The people were cursing them for what they were, cursing Honecker and the Party, cursing them for years of oppression. They stood there shocked, and disbelieving what they saw and heard.

It was two Stasi captains who realised that if the barriers were not opened they would be smashed open by what was now tens of thousands of people as far as the eye could see. They moved aside the barriers and what had been an ugly crowd was transformed into ordinary people laughing and crying, dancing and singing as they crossed the bridge into West Berlin. The border guards and the police stood watching, stony-faced and disapproving, trying not to hear the obscenities shouted in their faces by women and men who so obviously hated and despised them.

Hartmann, Foster and Gala watched it all on Sat Eins on their satellite dish as shocked as the border guards and police, but shocked for different reasons. They took Foster's car and watched at two of the crossing-points as people embraced relatives and lovers from the paradise on the other side. They drove back in silence aware that they had seen a piece of history in the making. Nothing was going to be the same again.

When the Stasi sergeant brought Tarrant his late-night bowl of thin soup he told the prisoner what had happened but Tarrant didn't believe it. A thing like that would take months of planning, it couldn't come out of thin air, however rarefied it might be.

By the week-end 500,000 East Germans had made the trip into West Berlin. Some never went back, but others had children and wives and jobs that were their lives. Video-recorders, Sony Walkmans, TVs and porn magazines were the most purchased items. A few romantics bought perfume and a few modest entrepreneurs stocked up with genuine Levis. What confirmed that the dream was in fact reality was the fact that at what had been the checkpoint nobody tried to inspect or appropriate their booty.

CHAPTER 34

The windows in the small conference room had been deliberately set at a height that made it impossible for anyone sitting at the table to see out. Igor Serov was standing at one of the windows looking out at the double row of dachas that were part of the comparatively new HQ of the KGB's First Chief Directorate at Yasenevo. The previous day's light fall of snow had frozen overnight and the vehicles on the Moscow Ring Road were moving very cautiously. General Serov intended moving cautiously himself at the meeting that was due to start in ten minutes.

It went through his mind that despite those newly hyped words – *glasnost* and *perestroika* – nobody had taken up the cause of one old-fashioned word – *pravda*. 'Truth' had long been limited to the title of the Soviet's best selling daily newspaper. It was a virtue long abandoned by those who controlled the Soviet Union. It was a word that only peasants used. But since Gorbachev had opened Pandora's box 'truth' had been used as an excuse for exposing past misdeeds by Soviet rulers. Truth was spreading like a virus through every mechanism of the system. God knows how many open or secret factions there were in the Kremlin, the Red Army and Air Force, the Soviet Navy and the *apparatchiks* who worked the levers of the huge, ungainly machine. Today's meeting was the usual weekly meeting that brought together representatives of the intelligence areas of the armed forces, the KGB, the Border Guards and the Foreign Ministry. All with their axes to grind, apparently oblivious to the fact that the whole edifice of power was galloping away, out of control. As the independent observer he was the permanent chairman of what was called the Joint Intelligence Committee. Everybody had such a committee – the Brits and the Americans at least. Every member intent on passing nothing to his colleagues, each committee passing on its filleted intelligence to its government.

The meeting was drawing to a close after less than an hour. It was a broken-backed meeting with cards held close to the chest. Optimism covering ignorance, and enthusiasm used as a protection against being accused of lethargy or indifference.

When the last of the nine had given his report Serov looked at Ustenko who was responsible for Soviet forces outside the Soviet Union whether they were on active service or merely occupying forces.

'Comrade General, tell us about morale in our forces in the Democratic Republic now that travel is unrestricted.'

Ustenko was an old China-hand, well used to the vagaries of Kremlin politics and with a keen sense of which way the winds were blowing.

'I'm glad to say, Comrade General Serov, that our people there are in a good state of readiness for any eventuality but preserving an outward calm in public with no interest in local politics.'

'They haven't been paid for four months, comrade. Are you telling me that they don't care about their pay?'

'They accept the exigencies of the service, comrade General. I have had no formal complaints.'

'I've made frequent visits to Berlin in the last six months, as you know. I spoke to many servicemen. They were seething with anger at the way they have been treated.'

Ustenko shrugged. 'When the coffers are empty, comrade?'

'I was there last week, comrade. I was offered a Kalashnikov for two hundred D Marks and as many rounds as I could pay for.'

'They must have been new recruits, comrade . . .' he smiled '. . . and impressed by your medals and uniform.'

'I was in civilian clothes, General, and I spoke German. The soldier was a veteran from our army in Afghanistan.'

'If you can give me details, comrade General, I will institute an intensive investigation when I get back to Karlshorst.'

Serov caught a glimpse of the barely perceptible glance between Ustenko and the KGB colonel who was the liaison officer between the KGB and the Stasis. He wondered what those two were cooking up. His unofficial estimate was that the Red Army in the GDR was so well established in the black market that 3,000,000 roubles a week were being sent back by troops to the Soviet Union. Serov's sympathies were with the troops but not with the bastards who kept back their pay and used it to speculate in goods. The coffers in Moscow may be empty but the pay and cost of the occupation troops was paid direct to Karlshorst by the Germans. Rape and theft had always been the victors' rewards but what the crooks at the top were doing was indefensible. He'd given them a warning shot and if they didn't toe the line he'd hang the lot of them.

Peter Waring was angry and frustrated. Angry because Joe Willis had come over to supervise the Tarrant affair. Most desk officers had at least had a couple of years out in the field. But you don't get drafted to a desk if you were any good on operations. They tended to be failed academics or so-called born administrators. Waring had parked Willis in the flat in Kant Strasse that had previously been occupied by Tarrant. There was nothing for Willis to do. There was nothing for any of them to do. Tarrant had gone down the tube and that was that.

On top of the Tarrant business the opening up of the Wall had meant that everything they had been doing for the last couple of years was in ruins. There had been contingency plans for every foreseeable situation, but the opening of the Wall was neither foreseeable nor capable of even the most elementary security measures. The crowds coming daily through every checkpoint could be KGB, Stasi or Arab terrorists to a man, but there was no way of weeding them out. There was no law that allowed him even to run random checks. And Willis had filled in his time contacting London behind Waring's back with wild suggestions of closing the checkpoints on the Allied side of the Wall.

Georg Steiner moved the black queen and looked up at Tarrant's face. 'Check. Check-mate.'

Tarrant looked for a few moments at the huddle in the corner of the board. He wasn't a good chess player but even he knew that he should have castled four moves before. He smiled as he looked at the Stasi guard. 'Thanks for the game, Georg.'

'Herr Schultz is coming over here at mid-day. You'd better shave before you meet him.'

Tarrant smiled. 'Don't worry. He's all right. He's on my side.'

'You're a lucky man, he's very important.'

Tante Olga is a typical workman's pub on Linienstrasse. Its customers are mainly labourers and artisans working on the seemingly endless reconstruction sites in the centre of the city. There was usually a huddle of journalists at the table in the far corner. Nobody could explain why the pub had first been adopted by the newspapermen but they were accepted by the rest of the customers rather like a herd of gazelle accepting the surveillance of a group of gorged lions.

For Georg Steiner the journalists were the main attraction. To be precise, just one of them, Alwyn Lewis, who was a freelance correspondent for several British newspapers and a couple of agencies. They moved to a table in a small annexe that was put aside for regulars.

When Lewis had fetched the beers Steiner said quietly, 'Can we do a deal?'

'Depends on what you've got, Georg.'

'It's about one of the prisoners.'

'Go on.'

'He's an Englishman. Been charged for espionage.'

Lewis shrugged. 'Your people reckon you're spying if you want to look up a number in a telephone directory.'

'This one's a *profi*, a professional. Sent over from London. He's at the Stasi HQ but it's a German working for the KGB who's handling him now. The Englishman's collaborating.'

'What's his name – the Brit.'

'Tarrant. John Tarrant.' And Steiner spelled out the name. Watching as Lewis wrote it in his notebook.

'How long have you had him?'

'About two weeks. A few days before they opened the Wall.'

'What's he supposed to have done?'

'I don't know that yet.'

'OK, my friend.' Lewis reached into his coat pocket and took out a folded note. 'A hundred Westmarks and more when you've got more. OK?' He paused. 'Why're you telling me this?'

'I want an introduction to the British intelligence in West Berlin.'

'Why?'

'To cooperate.'

Lewis smiled. 'You thinking of changing sides?'

Steiner smiled too. 'Maybe. Will you help?'

'Let's see how it goes.' He stood up. 'You've got my contact number?'

'Yes.'

The Night-Duty Officer at Century House pulled over the usual pile of the first editions of the next day's papers. He usually went through the tabloids first. They seldom had anything of interest to SIS. MI5 were the ones who were interested in the peccadilloes of MPs, trades union bosses and tycoons, not MI6. But there was a flyer on the front page of the *Daily Mirror* that said 'British spy held by Krauts – page 2'. He opened the page. There was a large headline but not much text. But what he read was enough to make him reach for the phone. When the operator responded he said, 'Get me Mr Powell wherever he is.'

'He's listed as at home.'

'Wherever – doesn't matter.'

Powell was seeing off the last of his dinner-party guests when his wife came out to tell him that he was wanted on the phone.

'Who is it, Marion?' He looked at his watch. 'For God's sake, it's nearly one o'clock.'

'It's the firm.'

He waved his guests' car on its way and went inside. He picked up the phone in the hall.

'Yes?'

'Duty Officer, sir. Are you on the scrambler?'

'No.'

'I think it would be advisable, sir.'

'Hold on, I'll go up to my study and ring you back.'

'Right, sir.'

At his desk Powell pressed the red button on the scrambler and picked up the receiver, listening to the twittering as it sorted through the coding. When he got the DO he wasted no time.

'What is it?'

'There's a piece in the *Mirror* with a big headline and a couple of paras in the *Guardian*. The headline in the *Mirror* says "Brit spy held by East Germans" and then there's about twelve column inches of copy.'

'What's it say? Just the gist of it.'

'Usually reliable sources – British spy named John Tarrant – arrested by Stasis – cooperating with KGB – another intelligence cock-up. No by-line.' He paused. 'The *Guardian* piece is . . .'

'Get my people together – the emergency team. An hour from now, and send a car for me. I'm at home. Putney, not the cottage.'

'Right, sir.'

It was light now and they were sprawled in chairs, shirt-sleeves rolled up, ties loosened and the detritus spread across the long conference table of the night's parade of Coke, tea, coffee, and a dozen varieties of sandwiches. Powell stood at the windows looking out across the roofs of the buildings on the other side of the street. He looked at his watch, they'd got maybe an hour before the phones started ringing. Then those smart-arse voices firing question after question, interrupting the responses before they were complete – looking for some short phrase that could provide another crisp headline.

He turned and looked from one to the other of the four men who lounged exhausted in the leather chairs.

'OK, Roger, we'll do it. I don't see we have any choice. You take all the calls up to editors I'll deal with pro-prietors if we get any.' He waved a hand like a conductor in front of an orchestra. 'Calm – surprised at the inaccur-acies – we speak more in sorrow, etc., etc. – Tarrant not one of ours – a freelance who worked for various governments – sometimes for us – too inexperienced for us – loyalty unknown – a mercenary. Sad story but that's how it goes.' He pointed at one of the men. 'OK, Roger? You happy with that?'

Roger nodded. 'You and I had better do some mock interviews together while we eat some breakfast. Time spent in reconnaissance and all that jazz.' As he stood up Roger said, 'We gotta decide whether we rate him as a defector or just a cock-up merchant. Which d'you fancy?'

'We say we don't know. But if he is a defector then now the Wall's open we'll go in there and get him and put him on trial.'

Roger laughed. 'Bang on, Tony. Stupid bastards – all of them.'

The mid-day TV and radio news broadcasts didn't go overboard. It was the fifth item by what seemed common consent. The next morning's newspapers all gave it a mention. Five paragraphs or less. It was all there, but Century House seemed to have successfully made its pass at the media bull with its subtle waft of the red muleta.

The item was in the West German papers the next day but it didn't make the TV news. But the piece in the *Frankfurter Allgemeine* stated that when they contacted an official in the East German Foreign Ministry there had been an angry denial.

When Hartmann showed the British newspaper report to Foster he was surprised by Foster's anger.

'How the hell did they find out about Tarrant and the rest of it?'

'It was leaked to a journalist by one of the guards at the cell-block in Normanenallee. He's already in the prison down at Cottbus.'

'I suppose he did it for hard currency.'

'No. He only got a few D Marks but he was promised

an introduction to the SIS detachment in Berlin. There are a lot of Stasis panicking now the Wall is open. There have been raids by the public on many Stasi offices looking for their records. Even demands for prosecutions especially for Border Guards suspected of shooting people trying to get across the Wall.'

'Serve the bastards right.'

'You'd better see Tarrant. I'm told he's taken this badly.'

Foster sat patiently for five minutes as Tarrant's angry tirade washed over him. When eventually the flood subsided he said, 'There's no point in getting worked up about it. You were messing about in East Berlin on intelligence business, trying to locate me. You got caught. You've nothing to complain of there. The fact that when it was published London sold you down the river is par for the course.'

'It bloody well isn't, Charlie. I was carrying out orders to locate you. Their orders.'

'And you got caught. You must have been told dozens of times. If you get put in the bag they'll swear they've never heard of you. Yes?'

'I guess so. But they didn't leave it at that. They left me looking like a defector.'

'They did the same to me. So what?'

'But you *were* defecting. For a decent reason I admit but you actively helped them once you'd come over. Your couriers had you to help them.'

'I can help you too if you calm down.'

'How? Everybody who knows me will have seen the stuff in the papers. Nothing's going to put that right.'

'Well – first things first. Do you want to get out of jail?'

'Of course I do. But not if it means working for these bastards over here.'

'So let's say you were set free tomorrow, where would you go and what would you do?'

Foster was aware of the long hesitation before Tarrant replied, aware now of what it was all about.

'I guess I'd go home,' he said without conviction.

'And then what?'

Tarrant shock his head slowly. 'God knows.'

'Let's get down to basics. I'm willing to get you released. You can go back over the border – up to you. But they'll nail you over the other side. They've got to to save their faces.

'But there's an alternative. Just accept that they won't stomach you wandering around in the UK. You'll get picked up in no time. But I think I could put pressure on them to let you go to some other country – say for a couple of years – full pension paid. And after two years you go back if you want to.'

'Why the hell would they agree to that?'

'Would you go along with it if I could pull it off?'

'And guarantee no harassment?'

'Yes.'

'OK, then, I guess I don't have any choice.'

'What languages do you speak apart from German?'

'Spanish and Swedish.'

'OK. What about Argentina?'

'I'd go with that.'

'It'll probably take me a couple of weeks.'

'Why are you helping me?'

'Just Auld Lang Syne, my friend.'

CHAPTER 35

When the print-out got to Powell he read it only once before he reached for the phone. It was no longer something for desk people. It needed quick action or it would get out of hand. It was a job for McBride.

There were still three long bell-shaped flowers on the datura in the conservatory but the nursery had said it had to be pruned hard before the month was out. At least a third had to come off and all the thin branches in the centre. As he loosened the catch on the secateurs his wife came to the open French windows that led inside the house.

'Wanted on the phone, Mac.'

'Who is it?'

'A chap. Didn't say.'

Taking off his gardening gloves which he wore because the beautiful datura was poisonous on contact, he walked to the white phone on the table in the hall.

'McBride.'

'It's Powell, Mac. I need to see you in a hurry. Can you come up?'

'Be an hour plus parking.'

'Make it the Travellers, OK?'

'OK.'

He hadn't shaved but he slipped the Philishave into his holdall along with the morning paper. It would be quicker by train and it was easy parking at Frant Station.

At the station he ignored the notice that required him

to pay 70p to park his car and after buying his first-class ticket he stopped to chat to Peter at the ticket-office. Peter made beautiful violins in his spare time and they spent the five minutes before the Hastings train came in discussing the pros and cons of Nigel Kennedy.

He had a carriage to himself and had finished a leisurely shave before they got to Tunbridge Wells. At Charing Cross he took a taxi to the Travellers' Club. It was walking distance really but there was a brisk wind sweeping down the Mall and across Trafalgar Square.

A club servant showed him to a private room where Powell was waiting for him. After Powell had poured him a Glenfiddich they sat in facing leather arm-chairs.

'I've got a problem, Mac. I need to use you and your people. And it's desperately urgent. How're you fixed?'

'How long will it take?'

'I've no idea but if it takes more than two or three weeks it'll be too late.'

'You'd better tell me what it's all about.'

Powell went over the recent scenario covering Foster and Tarrant. Answered a few questions and then said, 'This morning I got a message from Foster. Briefly it said he had the records of all Stasi contacts and informants in West Germany, the BND, SIS and the UK. He would release a continuous flow of the details, names and so on, unless Tarrant was paid a full pension and allowed to go to South America and we guaranteed no action or harassment against him.'

McBride raised his eyebrows. 'That's a lot of Semtex, Tony, for one man to use. Any idea of what he's got?'

'No, but it looks as if he's been working for both the Stasis and the KGB. A lot of heads could roll. There'd never be an end to it. It's like a blackmailer who sells you the photographs but keeps the negatives.'

'And?'

'And we want it stopped. Letting Tarrant go to Buenos

Aires or Rio doesn't matter. But those records – that's the crux of the matter. Foster's got to be dealt with – soonest.'

'Finally?'

'Yes. And Tarrant too.'

'Do you know where either of them is?'

'Just East Berlin so far as we know.'

'What form did the message come in?'

'By radio, in Morse, and in a code. Foster was in Signals Security before we took him over.'

'Was a tape done of the message?'

'I believe so.'

'We'd better go back to your office and I'll get started.'

'We'd be very, very grateful, Mac. Three times as grateful as the usual rate. All expenses, no questions asked. Any technical help you need . . .' Powell shrugged '. . . any questions.'

'Guaranteed no bullshit from Facilities and Finance?'

'Absolutely – direct to me.'

'And entirely my discretion?'

'Yes.'

Powell had an official Daimler and driver waiting and they were back at Century House half an hour later. It was Friday and the week-end traffic was already building up.

Powell was relieved that it had gone so smoothly. McBride could be very touchy but he knew his job.

Powell gave McBride the annexe to his own office and his secretary to look after him. She fixed him up with a computer and a cassette player.

He sat at the table in his shirt-sleeves and switched on the tape. As he heard the familiar 'cheep-cheep' he guessed it was either Sitor-A or Sitor-B. But what really mattered was that it wasn't machine traffic. It was done by hand with a Morse-key. He'd get Farmer on it. He reached for the phone and while he waited for an answer he read through the decoded message. It was brisk and military. No please-and-thank-you. He wondered who Malins was. Then Farmer came on the line.

An hour later he went in to see Powell.

'How's it going, Mac?'

'It's rolling. But from now on forget it. Keep your nose clean and out of it. Just one thing I want you to take care of. I don't know why this Foster guy used radio when he could have used phone. Maybe because he was trained on radio. Anyway there's just a chance we could use an old-fashioned DF check on his transmissions and locate him. So I want you to keep the traffic going for at least a week. Sound willing but there are problems. What about this and that, how pay pension, what name, what pension – you can haggle about that for days. OK?'

'OK. Will your people handle the traffic?'

'Yes. But you supply the words.' He paused. 'One other thing. I want you to put the BND in the picture. They'll be as uptight about it as you are and they could help me a lot and still claim they had nothing to do with it if anything goes wrong. Give me a BND name. Got to be right at the top.' He smiled. 'I've asked your girl to fix me a bed for the night in the annexe. I'll want one of the suites on the top floor for my people from tomorrow a.m.'

Powell nodded as he made notes.

Back in the annexe McBride told the girl to run Foster's name through the IBM and give him print-outs of everything no matter how insignificant it seemed to be.

At 8.30 p.m. he phoned home and told Julie he wouldn't be home. Didn't know when he would be back but would keep in touch. Reminded her that the oil-tank for the central heating needed topping up.

By midnight there were four of them. McBride, Farmer, Walker and Hooper. Farmer had contacted Signals

Training at Catterick and asked them to find any tape they had on Foster transmitting. They found it in an hour and played it back down a land-line. There was nothing of any use to them. It was too slow to provide any identification but Farmer confirmed that Foster's traffic was sent by key not machine. Siemens made a converter that could have looked after the coding.

They snatched a few hours' sleep and went for breakfast at a café near Victoria Station. It was Friday and there was a lot of work to be done that day because Saturday meant only skeleton staff and services at Century House. By 9 a.m. they were at work. McBride got Powell to get them two ICOM 751A multi-band transceivers, a Universal M-7000 terminal and two radio compasses. Farmer and Hooper were flying to Berlin at mid-day to set up stations for a direction-finding exercise on Foster's transmitter.

McBride followed two hours later with an introduction from Powell to Max Keller at the BND's Berlin office, and a note to Peter Waring requiring any cooperation that McBride might need.

Nobody from SIS met him in at Tegel but he was used to that. They needed him but they didn't want him. When he was brought in it meant that all else had failed. And they didn't want to know how he had dealt with the problem. He was a professional, and they respected him. But they didn't want to know him.

There was a note on the board that just said 'MAX' and then a number which was obviously a Berlin phone number. He got change at the magazine stall and dialled the number. Palmer answered and gave him the address of the flat they had rented in Kochstrasse right against the Wall.

In the taxi he read through Foster's message again. As some kind of indication that he had what he was claiming he had given the financial details and dates of payments made by the Stasis to an SIS man named Malins. When he had queried this with Powell he had been told that Malins had been under suspicion for some time and a few months back he had been 'retired'. It seemed that Malins had stayed on in Berlin and was the owner of a travel business and several bits of real estate in Berlin.

Palmer had already fixed a discone aerial on the roof and Walker was in the top-floor studio of a house at the far end of Oranienstrasse. The angle of convergence was narrower than they wanted but it was the best that they could do in the time and still be as close to the Wall as possible. He phoned through to Powell to give him their telephone number. The original message had been picked up by GCHQ at one of its London detachments and the transmitting frequency had been recorded automatically and both ICOMs were locked on the frequency, 7.658 KH.

McBride composed the first response which acknowledged receipt of the initial message and asked for clarification of the pension required and some form of proof that Tarrant was in the sender's custody. Could they give the licence number of Tarrant's car and its year and make? They transmitted the message at the same time that the original message was transmitted and asked for an immediate acknowledgment of receipt. It came through ten minutes after transmission.

The compass readings crossed in the area of Stasi HQ at Normannenallee but not in the complex itself. McBride knew then that unless they could operate much nearer the transmission area it would be impossible to identify accurately where the signals came from.

The response came at the same hour the next day. All the information asked for was provided. Tarrant would require a tax-free pension of £4,000 a month. The details of the car were passed to Powell for checking. When McBride spoke to Powell he asked for the file on Malins to be sent to him urgently. Powell told him that SIS Berlin had a copy of everything on Malins.

Waring would not release the file or allow McBride to photo-copy it. He could have phoned Powell and Waring would have had to turn over the file but McBride needed the information on Malins urgently.

The file on Malins was only six pages but the more he read the surer he was that Malins was the key to finding Foster. The details of the payments to him from the Stasis went back over two or three years and the details given of recent payments and the cooperation Malins gave in return made it easy to check. McBride copied out several items including the address of the garage used as an RV by Malins, and the address of his travel agency. The radio intercepts were a waste of time if he could get what he wanted from Malins.

McBride made two phone calls to England, to a man who kept a pub in Brecon and the other to a man who ran a farm just outside Chichester. They were both of them ex-Paras.

It was late afternoon when McBride left Records at SIS but before he left he phoned the BND contact Powell had given him. Max Keller sounded cautious but willing to see him straightaway. He suggested that they met in the bar at the Savoy in Fasanenstrasse in half an hour.

The bar at the Savoy was rather like the bar at a London club. Old-fashioned and cosy. They had both asked for straight malts and until the drinks had arrived they chatted about Boris Becker and Steffi Graff. Keller was a member of Berlin's BlauWeiss club, where Gottfried von Cramm had played so often.

But with the drinks they drew their chairs a little closer together and got down to business.

'Did Powell fill you in on the background?'

'Yes. I think so.' Keller smiled. 'You never can tell, of course.'

'I wanted to talk about a Brit, Malins. Used to be SIS Berlin.'

'And now a D-Mark millionaire and successful business-man.' But Keller had an amused, disbelieving smile as he said it.

'Is the business real?'

'Oh yes. Very real, very successful.'

'And the fortune?'

'German banks, Swiss and French and real estate in Berlin and Frankfurt.'

'Did you know that he was, or is, working for the Stasis?'

'We suspected it, and we've carried out surveillance on him from time to time. But no joy.'

'Why did you suspect him?'

'He was a captain but off-duty he lived like some Arab oil-sheikh. We traced his banks and the money was being deposited in very large sums. He's got a porn-shop by Zoo Bahnhof, a gas station and auto repair shop, four or five houses on good estates in Berlin, a fine house right on the Havel at Grunewald. We thought it might be coming from drugs. The KGB has been pushing drugs and SIS have penetrated their ring and Malins was at one time part of the SIS team. But there was no evidence that indicated that he was involved other than officially.'

'What about family, girl-friends and business associates?'

'You can forget business associates. He's a loner. No partners, no shareholders. A very nice wife and I would guess it's a genuine, quite affectionate marriage. There have been one or two episodes with high-class call-girls but not many. And such as there were were just sex not real relationships.'

'Is his phone tapped?'

Keller smiled and said, 'No. Of course not.'

'You get anything?'

'Powell told me when he phoned about you that Foster claimed that the Stasi *treffpunkt* was at the gas station. That fits in with what we taped. Malins always talked very guardedly when he phoned there. We put a surveillance team on the gas station but got nothing.'

'Is Malins involved in politics in any way?'

'No. He's just a businessman.'

'What do you know about Tarrant?'

'Well, as you know, he contacted me officially. We chatted amiably. He told me nothing and I did the same for him.'

'Any surveillance?'

'We put a random surveillance on him as soon as he arrived.' He smiled. 'We always do on SIS new-boys. Nothing special. He's been in Berlin before, knows his way around. He contacted an ex-girl-friend of his named Lena. She lives in Marburger Strasse. He rented a room from her but as far as we know he never used it. Probably had it in mind for Foster if he cooperated.'

'The threat about revealing Stasi stooges in West Germany – how do your people feel about that?'

'That's why I'm here, mister.'

'Do you want to join in my operation to get Foster?'

'Help, yes. Join, no. With those kinds of games it's the fewer who know what happened the better.'

'What sort of help?'

'Anything short of participation. Signals, surveillance, transport – you name it.'

'Weapons?'

'Yeah. We want him fixed just as much as you do – probably more. I've been ordered by Pullach to hand over everything to my assistant and concentrate on cooperation with you.'

'I'm gonna need a house where I can keep somebody who doesn't want to be kept. Any ideas?'

'No problem. You can move in tonight. It's near the

Wall, in its own grounds. We use it for training but it's not in use at the moment.'

'How about we eat, Max? I haven't eaten since last night.'

'The food here in the hotel is very good.'

'OK. Let's go.'

A large man opened the door and there was another in the background and they respectfully acknowledged Max Keller who showed McBride around the house.

There were five bedrooms, one large room on the ground floor and several smaller rooms. And three prison-type cells in the cellar. And in one of the smaller rooms was an array of computers, radios, scrambler phones and fax machines.

McBride turned to the BND man. 'By the way, did you know I was in Berlin?'

'Yes.'

'How did you know?'

'Customs at Tegel phoned us about the equipment you brought in. We tailed you from the airport. But we had no idea what you were up to. We thought it might be communications for a high-security network over the other side.'

McBride shook his head. 'Security Signals would have looked after that. We were trying to pinpoint where he was transmitting from. But it was too wide a beaten zone.' He paused. 'The two men – are they BND?'

'One BND, the other's police.' Keller smiled. 'Advises us when we're breaking the law. Advises us on how best to do it.'

They moved into the kitchen and sat drinking coffee.

'I'm going to send my two chaps who are here back to the UK tomorrow . . .' he smiled '. . . complete with their equipment. I've got two more friends coming over, they'll be here tomorrow and they can move in here with me.

I'm going to start on the man who runs the petrol station. He must have seen Malins meeting his Stasi contact.' He reached into his jacket pocket and put an envelope on the table. 'There's photos of Tarrant and Foster in there. I'd like a dozen copies of both.'

'What are you going to do with Tarrant and Foster if you find them?'

'Tarrant doesn't matter. He doesn't know anything. But Foster's different. He's a traitor whichever way you look at it. And now he's into blackmail.'

'The blackmail's not for his personal gain.'

McBride looked surprised. 'Is that what Bonn feel about it?'

'No. They're scared same as your people. Probably because West Germans will be more involved. It would probably bring down the government. It wouldn't do the BND much good either.'

'So why don't Pullach take over from me?'

Keller shrugged. 'I guess the truth is they know London have put you on the job and Foster's a Brit.' He sighed. 'There have been continuous meetings about the situation, believe me. If you weren't already on the job I guess we would have done something.'

'Are you going to move in here with me?'

'If you want me to.'

'I do.'

McBride stood watching as the passengers came through Customs and Passport Control. Baird and King were at the back of the queue. They were both ex-Paras and had met at the basic training squadron at No. 1 PTS and had moved on together for their final training at Brize Norton. They had seen service in the Falklands followed by a long stint in Northern Ireland where McBride himself had served with SAS. Baird and King worked from time to time for McBride. Totally silent about their work, a week's work bringing in more than they earned in a year at their normal occupations. McBride provided about four weeks' work a year. King was the son of an army officer and was brought up in Germany, so he spoke fluent German.

They saw him as they came through but only acknowledged him with an almost imperceptible nod of Baird's head. They followed him out to the taxi-rank and took a taxi themselves, ordering the driver to follow McBride's vehicle.

He settled them in the house, introduced them to Max Keller and then took them all out for a meal. When he briefed them he only told them the barest details of what he was going to do.

Keller drove them to the gas station and they got out, stretching as if they'd made a long journey. There was a shop behind the petrol pumps selling polishes and sprays and the usual things that motorists wanted, and there was a large display of sweets alongside a cash-register. Behind the shop was an office with slatted blinds that were closed, and outside, next to the office, were the toilets.

The porn-shop was a mass of magazines and videos all set out on shelves. There was a table covered with various sex-aids and a notice pointing down some narrow stairs to peep-show booths. There were at least a dozen men looking at the displays but the shop was as silent as a church. The man taking the money and sliding the purchases into brown paper bags was tall and thin with a shaved head and a two-day black stubble. The T-shirt claimed that he was an alumnus of UCLA.

It took forty-five minutes to drive to Malins' house in Grunewald. It was a beautiful, white villa, its lawns sloping down to the Havel with its own wooden jetty and a 35-foot motor cruiser tied up to the old-fashioned iron bollards. There seemed to be no special security measures. No high wall or razor wire. Just a pair of ornamental wrought-iron gates that stood open to the gravel drive that led up to the house itself.

Max Keller said quietly, as they sat in the car, 'I've got photographs including aerial shots and the architect's plans of the house itself.'

It was beginning to snow heavily and the journey back was difficult because even a Merc's windscreen wipers couldn't clear the snow quickly enough. It was only the screen heater that allowed any visibility at all against the driving snow.

Back at the house they sat around the kitchen table. McBride said, 'The garage was a meeting place for Malins and his Stasi contact. From the detail Foster put in his piece on Malins I've got a feeling that Foster himself was the contact over the last few months. I'd like to go late tonight and talk to the manager at the gas station. I'll show him a photo of Foster. He might recognise it.'

Baird said, 'What if he won't cooperate?'

McBride shook his head. 'He will.' He turned to Keller. 'Will you come with us? You at least look like somebody official, which is more than we do.'

Keller smiled. 'You want me for the heavy?'

'You got it, Max.'

CHAPTER 36

It was 11.30 when they drove into the gas station, parking alongside one row of pumps. There were lights on in the shop. Baird was in the driving seat and he switched off the ignition as McBride, Keller and King got out.

They walked slowly to the shop and McBride went in first. The man was drinking coffee from a Styrofoam cup and he looked over the rim at McBride.

'It's self-service, mister.'

'What's your name?'

'Who wants to know?' the man said, putting down the cup and reaching for the telephone on the counter.

'Don't do that, friend. Could damage your health.'

And the man saw the gun poking out of McBride's coat pocket. He moved his hand away from the phone.

'What's it all about?'

'I wanna talk to you.'

McBride spoke bad but fluent German with the confidence of a man not trying to impress.

'What about?'

McBride nodded to King who put a photograph of Tarrant on the counter, turning it to face the man.

'You ever seen that guy?'

The man shook his head. 'No. Never.'

Then King took back the photograph and replaced it with one of Foster.

'What about him?' McBride said. 'You ever seen him before?'

343

The man touched the photograph tentatively and it was several seconds before he looked at McBride and said, 'No. Never saw him either.'

McBride nodded. 'OK. Now lock up the shop and we'll move into the back office.'

'I don't have a key for it.'

'That's OK. We can bust it down but the key saves the repair bills.'

The man reached for the cash-till but the gun jerked and McBride said, 'Don't. Put your hands on the counter.'

'I was just going for the key.'

McBride nodded to King who lifted the counter-flap, walked round and pushed the key that opened the till. He held up the only key in the till for McBride to see.

McBride turned to the garage man. 'You married?'

'Yeah.'

'Phone her and tell her you won't be home tonight. You'll call her in a few days – maybe.'

The man sighed. 'OK, OK. I've seen the guy, the second one.'

'What colour hair did he have?'

'He's got red hair.'

McBride looked at him. 'You gonna cooperate?'

The man nodded vigorously. 'Yeah.'

'OK. Forget the wife. Lock up and we'll talk in the office.'

They watched as the man fixed the two locks and the security alarm. King opened the office door, switched off the shop lights and then switched on the office lights before the assistant was shoved into the office by McBride.

McBride pointed to a chair and the man sat down as King walked round closing the blinds on the windows.

'Right, now. Your name?'

'Franz.'

'OK, Franz. Tell me about the guy in the picture.'

'He came here sometimes.'

'How many times did you see him?'

'Five, six times, maybe.'

'What happened?'

'He just came in here and talked with the boss.'

'You mean Herr Malins?'

'Yes.'

'What was the guy's name?'

'Schultz.'

For a moment McBride was taken aback. He hadn't expected a positive answer. He knew from the tension coming from the others that they hadn't expected a name either.

'How do you know that was his name?'

'I heard the boss call him that.' He paused. 'They seemed to know one another very well.'

'Did they speak German or English?'

'I don't know.'

'When Schultz was coming here, did you get advance warning?'

'Only on the same day.'

'How long did they talk?'

'Two, maybe three hours.'

'Who told you Schultz would be coming?'

'The fellow at the porn-shop.'

'Anything else you can remember?'

'No. I never took much notice.'

'OK. Now listen carefully. You don't tell anyone, not even your wife about our visit and our little talk tonight. You get me?'

'Yes, sir.' He hesitated. 'You're cops, aren't you?'

McBride said, 'What makes you think that?'

The man shrugged. 'You look like cops.'

'Remember what I said, Franz. If you were stupid enough to tell someone we shall hear about it and you'd be in deep, deep shit. You understand?'

'Yeah.'

* * *

Back at the house McBride said, 'We've got no choice, we've got to put the arm on Malins. The guy at the porn-shop just does what Malins tells him. Agreed?'

King and Baird nodded but Keller didn't respond. McBride looked at him. 'You disagree, Max?'

'Not necessarily. But this is the bit that has to be thought out well in advance. No just barging in like we did tonight. If it didn't work we'd all get our heads chopped off. Me in private down at Pullach. You in public and being charged with God knows what. The police won't cooperate with this kind of game. Not even for the BND. If we do the heavy stuff it has to be shit or bust. There's no half-way. And no pleading the national interest.'

It was quite a time before McBride spoke.

'Do you think Malins has any pull with the police?'

'Hard to say. Hard to say. He's very rich, but he's a Brit. He'll have had some contact with the police when he was SIS. But somehow – I'm not sure why – I don't think he would have made friends in the police.'

'How about you? Have you got friends in the police?'

'Of course I have. I work closely with them, here in Berlin particularly.'

'How high up?'

'All the way.'

'If you were the chief of police and somebody told you that there was an official record of all Stasi agents and informers in West Germany and that record was going to be published in the world's press unless the man behind it was eliminated. Would you turn a blind eye or would you have your informant arrested?'

Keller smiled. 'You really are a bastard, aren't you, McBride?'

McBride smiled back. 'I hope so. What's your answer?'

'I think maybe you're pitching your insurance too low.'

'What's that mean?'

'Why not get it so that the politicians are with you. Get

Powell to talk to our Foreign Ministry. Official blessing.'

'If I suggested that to Powell he'd tell me to forget the whole damn thing.'

'Why?'

'The reason why I'm here is because they want something done but they don't want to know how I do it or what I've done. Your politicians would be the same. They'd be shit-scared about what can come out, same as my people. They don't want to be involved in any dirty stuff. Who can blame them?'

Keller shrugged. 'Maybe you're right. Maybe I'm being too German, too official.'

'No. You're just an honest guy who chases spies but takes them to court. Powell is the same. You can know a guy is spying but it's a lot different in a court and you've got to *prove* he was a spy.' He paused and shrugged. 'Maybe you'd rather back out at this stage, Max.'

'No. I've had orders to help you and I will.'

McBride smiled. 'What is it you guys say? *Befehl ist Befehl*. Orders are orders.'

Keller said quietly, 'I guess that's one way of putting it. Let's get some sleep.'

It was an hour before the four of them went to bed but by that time McBride had worked out what they had to do. There were some holes in the plan but they could be filled later.

McBride had an early breakfast alone with Keller. As he explained carefully and in detail the various steps in his plan it was obvious that Keller was relieved to hear what he had in mind.

A taxi dropped them at the lights just before the crossing by the Gedächtnis Kirche and they had to wait for the traffic to move on and the lights change again so that they could cross the street. It was bitterly cold with a wind that seemed to be coming straight from the Arctic.

At the travel agency McBride pushed open the door and Keller followed. Two young women were arranging their desks for the day's work. Removing plastic covers from word-processors and punching in the latest exchange figures for foreign currency on their computers.

The nearer girl looked over at McBride. 'Be with you in a moment, sir.'

'We've come to see Mr Malins.'

'He won't be long.' She looked at her watch. 'Not more than five minutes.'

Almost as she spoke the door opened and Malins came in, stopping to stamp the snow off his shoes as he said 'Good morning' to the girls.

The girl said, 'These gentlemen would like to see you, sir.'

Malins looked towards them, shaking his head. 'Sorry, gentlemen. You'll have to make an appointment. Susie will see to you.'

As he bustled forward Keller said, 'Just a moment, Mr Malins.'

Malins turned angrily. 'You heard what . . .'

Keller had opened his ID wallet and was holding it out for Malins to see the photograph, the embossed stamp and the page with the red diagonal stripe across the letters BND. Malins leaned forward, peering at the wallet. Slowly he straightened up. 'I'll see you in ten minutes,' he said as he turned and walked briskly through to the rear of the office. McBride and Keller sat on a bench for customers and the two girls got on with their work.

As he sat there McBride knew he was going to enjoy himself. There was nothing so satisfying as cutting down to size a pretentious little man who is used to throwing his weight about.

The phone on the nearest desk rang and the girl nodded as she listened. Still holding the handset to her ear she smiled at McBride. 'He'll see you now. Go up the stairs and his office door will be open. Just go in.'

Malins was sitting behind his desk and McBride thought that even sitting down he managed to look pompous.

Malins waved to the chairs in front of his desk and as they settled down a young woman came in with a cup of coffee and a plate of fancy biscuits which she put in front of Malins. Nobody asked the visitors if they would like a coffee or a sponge finger.

'So,' Malins said, 'what's this all about? And who the hell *are* you?'

McBride said, 'My colleague is an officer of the BND. His name is Keller. My name is McBride and it doesn't matter who I am.'

Malins slapped his hand sharply on his desk. 'You cheeky bugger. Don't come the old acid with me.'

'Or what, Malins?'

'Or your fucking feet won't touch.'

McBride replied in kind. 'Cut out the bullshit, Malins, nobody's impressed. And . . .' he wagged a finger '. . . and if you don't behave I'll take you in for interrogation at your old home at the Olympiad.' He paused, waiting for a reply, but Malins said nothing. 'Tell me about Foster.'

'Who's Foster?'

'The guy you've been meeting at the gas station. The guy who pays you your Stasi money.'

'Get out . . .' Malins shouted '. . . get out or I'll throw you out.' He stood up aggressively, mouthing obscenities, puffed up like a mating frog, his fists clenched, his mouth literally frothing.

McBride watched him for a moment then, only half rising from his chair he reached across with both hands, clutching Malins shirt and dragging him face down across the desk. His right hand pulled up Malins' head and he put his face close to Malins' face. Malins was gasping for breath as McBride stared at him and said softly, 'Just sit down and behave, Malins, or I'll hand you over to Waring.' He pushed Malins away who staggered back into his seat. When he had got his breath back Malins said, 'You'll pay for this. I swear you'll not get away with it.'

'Foster has given London the dates of meetings and the money paid. Not only for *his* contacts with you but all your previous meetings. You know what a British court would do for you. I came here to do a deal with you, Malins, but you're not an easy man to talk to.'

Malins was straightening his tie, his chest still heaving from his exertions. 'What's the deal?'

'It's very simple. You cooperate with us and there will be no action from London about your relationship with the Stasis.'

For a few moments Malins didn't speak, and then he said, 'What's the cooperation?'

'We want you to go through your standard routine for getting Foster to meet you over here.'

Malins closed his eyes, leaning back in his chair, then he opened his eyes and looked at McBride. 'How long have I got to think about it?'

'How about you order us a cup of coffee? You can have till we've drunk the coffee.'

'Is Waring doing this?'

'No. He's got nothing to do with it.'

'Slaney?'

McBride ignored the question.

'How about the coffee?'

The coffee came and they drank it slowly but McBride knew that Malins had decided to cooperate even before he pressed the bell for the girl.

'When do you want this?'

'How long does it usually take?'

'Could be a couple of hours if it's urgent. Otherwise the next day.'

'D'you have a password?'

'Yep.'

'What is it?'

Malins sighed before he said, 'Seagull. In German. *Möwe.*'

'Why that – any significance?'

'No idea. That was the password long before Foster came on the scene.'

'You met Tarrant, didn't you?'

'Is that the guy who was looking for Foster?'

'Yes.'

'I only met him once.'

'You know they've put him in the bag?'

'I read the stuff in the papers. Sounded to me like somebody was playing games. Either that or an unbelievable cock-up.'

'Have you seen Foster since then?'

'I don't remember. I don't think so. If I did he never mentioned Tarrant being in the nick.'

'How do you arrange meetings with Foster?'

'I've got a special phone number.' He paused. 'By the way, he uses the name Schultz now.'

'Why Schultz?'

'No idea.'

'So, you phone the number, then what?'

'Sometimes he answers. Sometimes they take a message. I just give a time and day.'

'What about when he wants to contact you?'

'He phones my chap at the sex-shop and he phones me.'

'Right.' McBride looked at Malins' face and Malins was aware of the stone cold eyes. 'Do you cooperate with us or not?'

'And you don't do anything about past events so far as I'm concerned?'

'That's it.'

'OK. I'll go along with it.'

'No games.'

'No. Just tell me what you want.'

'First I want you to make an urgent RV with him. Notify me as soon as it's arranged.'

'What do I say when we meet? I've got to have a reason.'

'Tell him you've heard that London have sent out a team to get him because he isn't cooperating. If he asks about what cooperation you say you don't know. It was gossip you heard from somebody in SIS Berlin. Maybe it isn't true but that's what you heard.'

'OK. What else?'

'A couple of days later you contact him again. An urgent RV.'

'And what do I tell him when we meet?'

McBride half-smiled. 'You won't meet. You'll have done your part. You'll be out of it.' He paused. 'Write me out the number you call him on.'

Malins wrote out a number on a message pad by the phone and passed it to McBride. 'Where can I contact you?'

McBride gave him a picture postcard of the Brandenburg Gate. 'It's on the back. Any time. Just the RV time and day.'

Malins held out his hand but McBride ignored it.

'Just do as I said and you'll be OK.'

When McBride got back to the house he cursed himself for not instructing Malins to make the RV at night. But when the call came through it was OK. The meeting was to be at 9 p.m. that night.

They studied the map until they knew every route that Foster could take to get back to East Berlin and they took the VW to look over the gas station again. There was no street parking nearby during the day because the traffic was too heavy but they found a place by the British Council offices in Hardenbergstrasse that was likely to be possible in the evening.

The plan was that they would use a pair of portable radios using UHF on 452.750, with King on the other side of the street, McBride in the back seat of the car and Keller driving because he knew the street layout in East Berlin better than the others.

They arrived just before 8 p.m. and the small parking area in front of the British Council was empty except for a watchman who shrugged and waved them inside when Keller showed his ID card. King moved over to the other side of the street, strolling up and down from the Federal Court building to the Berliner Bank, with his coat collar turned up, stamping his feet in the frozen snow on the pavement. Keller reckoned it was too cold for any more snow that night, but it would be tricky driving in East Berlin where they didn't clear even the main roads. They switched on the car engine from time to time to use the heater.

Just before 9 p.m. the radio bleeped.

'Subject has just arrived in a black BMW. Another guy is driving . . . subject getting out of car . . . driver staying behind . . . subject on gas-station forecourt . . . goes in shop . . . speaking to attendant . . . opening door to office . . . office lights on but blinds are closed. Over.'

McBride pressed the transmit button.

'OK. Keep surveillance on driver. No need to report unless he leaves car. Which way is car facing?'

'Came from direction of Budapesterstrasse now facing direction Reuterplatz. Over.'

'OK. Out.'

It was almost fifteen minutes later when King reported that Foster was leaving the gas station and heading for the BMW which now had its lights on and the engine running.

When the BMW moved forward they let a few cars pass before they edged on to the main street. They could see the BMW about a hundred yards ahead. They watched it turn right at the Reuterplatz roundabout and followed it with two cars between them up Strasse des 17 Juni. The Brandenburg Gate was no longer closed and they followed the BMW up Unter den Linden and on to Karl Liebknecht Strasse passing Alexanderplatz and turning right into Karl-Marx-Allee. After that only Keller knew where they were. He was sure that they were heading for Karlshorst, the Soviet military HQ. It was going to be a long journey.

The BMW finally stopped at a house standing in a large garden and McBride cursed quietly as he saw two armed soldiers in Red Army uniform swing open the double gates to the drive. There were lights on all over the house and several floodlights in the garden. They stopped at the next side-street and McBride and Keller walked back slowly to have another look at the house. But McBride knew that the first part of his plan to pick up Foster and search where he lived was no longer a runner.

He and Keller gave a passable performance as a couple of drunks as they went slowly past the house. One of the guards was standing at the open gates and he shouted a flow of obscenities in bad German. There was a faint sound of music coming from the house. It sounded like someone playing the piano. The kind of music you got at tea-time at the Inn on the Park in Mayfair. McBride often used the hotel as a meeting place with clients. Sometimes, if they were Americans, they bought the pianist a drink and always asked him to play 'Manhattan'. Right then he wished he was anywhere in Mayfair rather than trudging round the block in the snow to where the VW was parked.

It was after midnight before they got back to the house. Baird wasn't waiting up for them with a warm drink. He was in bed.

CHAPTER 37

If the Chancellor of the Federal Republic had been an American the media would have cast Gunter Vass as a 'crony'. There is no German word for crony but there was no doubt that he was very close to the Chancellor. They had known one another since their schooldays, and they had kept up their relationship despite their very different careers. Vass had been a journalist. A shrewd commentator on politics at home and abroad, and gradually he had been assimilated into the powerful inner circle that a critical press referred to as 'the kitchen cabinet'. Most of them were not politicians but they had all been successful in some sphere of business or the law. None of them were paid by either the Chancellor's political party or the government. They had no axe to grind so they were listened to by the Chancellor who took notice of what they said. It was never advice. That would have been impertinence. If the group had a theme, which they would have roundly denied, it was nostalgia. Nostalgia for a time that they had never experienced in their own life-times. A time when music, painting, the theatre and literature were at least as important as business, economics and the Bundesbank.

It was to Vass the Chancellor turned for comment on the thin file from the BND that was labelled 'Miscellaneous II'. They were sitting in the Chancellor's private room with only the night staff on duty outside.

Vass read the half-dozen pages carefully then looked at his friend.

'Should have been labelled – Dynamite.'

'You think so?'

'Of course. Don't you?'

'With all due respect to our BND friends I tend to treat reports of coming disaster with a certain amount of reserve. Let's say . . .' he smiled '. . . I don't inhale.'

'And you intend leaving it to the British to deal with this man?'

'Why not?'

'They have too little to lose if they fail.'

'Go on.'

'If this information is true, and there seems no reason why it should not be true, the Stasis will have had very little contact with the British. The East Germans are only interested in what *we* are doing. They will have hundreds, maybe thousands of contacts out here. Some casual, but many will be working arrangements. Espionage. Treason. It would bring down a government of saints.'

'What would you do about it?'

'I would set up a special team at once. To find this man.'

'And what would you offer him?'

'Nothing. He is a blackmailer. You never finish with blackmailers. Ask the police. I would eliminate him.'

'Others could provide the same information.'

Vass smiled. 'It's a question of authenticity, like with works of art, its provenance. People would believe a Brit. An intelligence officer. Who would believe the same information coming from a Stasi General let alone a minor official? It could be word for word true but nobody would believe it. They have no substance. The Britisher has.' He paused. 'That information coming out from a Stasi background you could kill with ridicule. An attempt by a discredited government to make trouble. Envy of our economic success, envy of our leadership in Europe.' He shrugged. 'Remember what Dietrich Bonhöffer said in his book on *Resistance and Submission*. "It is the nature and the advantage of strong people that they can bring out the crucial questions and form a clear opinion about them. The weak always have to decide between alternatives that are not their own."'

The Chancellor smiled. 'You generally quote Aristotle on Ethics. Makes a change anyway. It's time I went to the theatre. It's a Brahms night.'

Pullach decided against putting together a special team. They already had a good man inside the British group and all that was needed was a couple of men to work on the side under Keller's instruction. The only problem was that so far McBride would never discuss what he intended to do with Foster. But Pullach had made clear to Keller what the end result had to be. It wasn't said in so many words but the message was clear enough. Just a 'yes' on the phone, the information, if it was available, to be destroyed without being read and nothing in writing.

Foster took Gala to the Rathauskeller for a meal. It was a basement restaurant under the East Berlin town-hall. It was called the Rotes Rathaus, the Red Town Hall, not because of the communist government but because it was built from red bricks. The restaurant had two separate sections, one specialising in beer, the other in wine. They chose a table in the wine restaurant.

When they got to the coffee she put her hand out to touch his as it rested on the table.

'You look worried. What is it? Can I help?'

Foster shook his head. 'I am worried. I heard last night that London have sent some kind of hit squad to track me down.'

She frowned. 'For God's sake. It sounds like some ridiculous American gangster film. I think it's called the A-team. Do you believe it?'

He sighed. 'Yes. At least it's possible and I don't see any point in them pretending.'

'Have you told Hartmann?'

'Yes. But he's got his own problems at the moment.'

'Like what?'

'It's almost like civil war in Moscow right now. Pro-Gorby groups, anti-Gorby, KGB takeover groups, Red Army takeover group. Old style communists who want the party back in power. It's all been simmering for months but it's on the boil now and everybody's waiting for the lid to blow off.'

'Will it affect Hartmann?'

'He's been recalled to Moscow.'

'Will he go?'

'I don't think so. I think he's making plans to get out.'

'Where will he go?'

'I think he'll head for the United States or Canada.'

'It's like the end of the world. The Wall down. Communism grinding to its end. Nothing seems solid.'

Foster said, 'You're right. There are some lines in a poem by W. B. Yeats – "*Things fall apart, the centre cannot hold, mere anarchy is loosed upon the world.*" It goes on. "*And what rough beast, its hour come round at last, slouches towards Bethlehem to be born.*"'

She looked at his face. 'And what about you?'

'I think it's time for me to move on.' He paused. 'Are you sure you want to go with me?'

'Of course I'm sure.' She smiled. 'I can quote too – "*Whither thou goest, I will go and where thou lodgest I will lodge, thy people shall be my people, and thy God my God.*"' She stroked his hand. 'When I was little I wanted to change my name to Ruth but it would have hurt my father.' She paused. 'So where do we go? I'll need a couple of days to collect a few things – especially money – yours as well as mine. Do we tell Hartmann?'

'Yes. Let me tell him.'

'That news about a hit-squad. Is that why the guards on the house have been doubled?'

'Yes.'

The snow had settled and frozen on the windows so that the light in the room was that soft, even light that photographers use in fashion shots. But it did nothing for the man sitting on the chair by the table. Foster watched Tarrant sipping a glass of milk, waiting for him to finish. When Tarrant put the glass on the table his hand shook and the glass rattled.

'So what do you want to do?'

Tarrant sighed. 'Tell me again. I'm so tired it doesn't sink in.'

'I think London are playing games. They don't seem to be responding to my offer. My guess is that they want to wipe the slate clean of both of us.' He paused. 'You understand what I'm saying?'

Tarrant nodded but didn't speak.

'The Wall is over so if I let you go you can go across into West Berlin. Have you got somewhere where you can go that SIS don't know about?'

Tarrant sighed. 'Yes. I've got a room they don't know about. But they'll still be after me, won't they?'

'I guess so. But you could get out of Germany. A train to Amsterdam or Vienna.'

'And then what?'

'Have you got any cash at the room?'

'About five hundred D Marks.'

'I'll give you a thousand US dollars but you'll have to look after your own life after that. OK?'

Tarrant nodded. 'When can I go?'

'Probably tomorrow. They'll give you your documents back later today. You'd better get some rest.'

Foster waited for a few moments but there were no thanks and no response from the figure in the chair. He couldn't see him lasting long. London's betrayal of him had hit too hard.

Foster spent two hours with Hartmann and then went back to his place where Gala was waiting for him. There were sandwiches and coffee and she seemed optimistic and lively despite what was happening.

'Did Hartmann tell you about the money?'

'He just said you were dealing with it.'

'A quarter of a million dollars in hundred dollar notes. All guaranteed genuine. Many of them used notes.' She laughed. 'And all out of KGB funds.'

'Thanks.'

'Anything else you want to take?'

'Just shaving stuff and a change of clothes.'

'I've bought you shirts and slacks but you'd better buy another pair of shoes tomorrow.'

'OK.' He smiled. 'Guess where Hartmann's going.'

She smiled. 'San Francisco?'

'He told you already.'

'No. I just guessed.'

'How?'

'He's gay. Didn't you realise that?'

And slowly it settled in his mind. The good looks, the charm, the gentleness, the unusual kindness. He had always seen it as genuine but convenient for Hartmann's role as an antidote to the usual potato-faced KGB colonels. Suddenly it all seemed so obvious. He could well understand young men loving such a man.

'Ah well,' he said at last, 'we live and learn. I owe him a lot. Probably my life. I hope he's happy in San Francisco.'

She smiled. 'If it's any consolation all the girls fall for him too.'

McBride was with Malins at his office in the travel agency.

'Press him for tonight. Sound like it's good news. And it's urgent. Very urgent.'

'What if he wants it tomorrow?'

'Lower your voice. Very confidential. London are going to offer some sort of deal. You don't know what it's about. But you'll know more by the time he sees you. OK?'

'I'll try.'

'Don't fucking try, my friend. Do it.'

McBride took the call and gave a thumbs-up sign to Keller who was reading a paper-back. Foster's meeting with Malins was for 10 p.m.

The plan was much the same as the first time but this time they would pick up Foster before he went into the gas station.

McBride went to his room and sat on his bed with his pistol, an oily rag and a can of WD40. His pistol was a .45 1911A1 automatic made in 1945 by the Ithaca Gun Co. He took the cap off the canister of WD40 and remembered the days when the only suitable cleaning and oiling liquid was Singer sewing machine oil. He didn't intend a complete field strip but he did want to check and clear the recoil spring. He took out the magazine and checked that there was no cartridge in the chamber. Easing out the plug he put his hand over the spring barrel to stop the spring flying out. He checked the spring carefully, sprayed inside the barrel and pushed in the plug. Slowly and carefully he loaded seven rounds into the magazine and pressed it home until it clicked. Pulling back the slide as far as it would go he loaded a round into the chamber and pushed up the safety with his thumb. As he sat there cleaning and loading the spare magazine he was singing very quietly to himself, '*Jesus wants me for a sunbeam to shine for him each day . . .*'. Finally he put the pistol on the bed beside him.

They spent an hour with a sheet of paper where Keller had drawn the roads around the gas station on a large scale, and they used two packets of cigarettes for cars and three matchboxes and a couple of egg cups representing people.

Keller would sit in their parked car and McBride and King would pick up Foster and bundle him into the back of the car with McBride. Then straight back to the house, where Baird would be waiting for them.

They were in place by 9.15 p.m. and this time the car had to be parked in the street. They couldn't risk being seen taking him as far as the place they had used to park at the British Council offices. But at least they could wait and watch in the car. They sat listening to a jazz programme from RIAS until McBride said, 'Here he is, he's slowing down to park.'

They waited until Foster got out of the BMW and was locking the driver's door as he looked towards the lights of the gas station. McBride and King moved behind him and McBride said, 'Don't make any noise, Foster. Just walk with us to the VW.'

Foster turned quickly, looking at McBride and then down at the pistol in his hand. With McBride and King pushing him along they got to the car. Keller leaned over from the driver's seat and pulled forward the passenger seat. They shoved Foster inside and McBride followed him, hurriedly closing the door as the car moved off.

'Take off your coat, Foster.' And McBride gestured with the pistol. Slowly Foster took off his coat and McBride watched him intently all the way back to the house but Foster didn't speak or move.

Baird was waiting for them and they took Foster down to one of the cells in the basement, showing him inside and locking the steel door. There was a mattress in the corner, a chair and a slop-bucket. In the ceiling was a 40 watt bulb with a metal grille over it. Baird sat in an old armchair outside the cell door. It was a standard prison door with steel rods about six inches apart and four horizontal bars.

They had set up one of the bedrooms for interrogating Foster. It was just before midnight when McBride called for Baird to bring up Foster.

McBride pointed to the spare chair and Foster sat down, his eyes away from McBride. There were all the personal items taken from Foster laid out on the table. 20 US dollars, 30 Ostmarks and 50 DMarks. A part-used pack of paper tissues and the receipt for a meal for two at the Rathauskeller. There was a ring with five keys including the keys for the BMW.

'This deal you offered about Tarrant, Foster. Why are you interested in Tarrant?'

Foster shrugged. 'He'd been stupid, nothing more. But when your people put out the story that he was a defector you showed what shits you all are.'

'Where is he now?'

Foster smiled and shook his head. 'You're too late, mister.'

'The information you talked about. Where is it?'

'What's your name?'

'My name doesn't matter. Where's the information?'

'Don't be stupid, mister. That's my insurance.'

'Not with me it isn't. Is it at that place you live near Stasi HQ?'

He saw the momentary surprise in Foster's eyes.

And just at that moment Keller came in, waving his hand to indicate that he should be ignored. He stood leaning against the wall behind Foster's chair.

'Where's Tarrant?'

'Get it straight whoever you are. We probably had the

same training in interrogation and the same training in resisting interrogation. So you know the score.' He half-smiled. 'We don't even have to bother with name, rank and number.'

For fifteen minutes McBride tried to get Foster to talk but there was no response. But McBride noticed that Keller shook his head when he asked Foster if he wanted to do a deal with the information he had.

Foster was put back in the cell and Keller and McBride headed for the kitchen which was where they always seemed to end up.

As they sat with a plateful of cheese sandwiches and a jug of coffee McBride quizzed Keller about his headshaking when he'd mentioned a deal to Foster.

'There's no point, Mac. It could all be a bluff.'

McBride smiled. 'You don't think it's a bluff, do you?'

Keller shrugged. 'Who can tell?' He paused and looked at McBride as he put some extra cheese into his sandwich. 'What are your feelings about friend Foster?'

'I think he's an arrogant bastard.'

'But he defected to save the skins of his couriers.'

'That's a perfect example of his arrogance. He was part of a group, the others don't go along with his thinking so he walks out on them. Who the hell does he think he is, God?'

'He just has a chip on his shoulder about authority. Especially SIS here and in London.'

'Balls. I don't like authority either. That doesn't give me just cause for ignoring everyone's orders if they don't suit me. I don't necessarily know some of the facts that they have. Baby has to do it his way.'

'It was just divided loyalties. Choosing between loyalty to his team or loyalty to SIS.'

'No way. He chose to go over to the other side. He was a defector. And that's just a soft word for a bloody traitor. No different from George Blake or Philby. They play both ends against the middle. And when the chips are on the table they do a bolt to the other side.'

'So what are you going to do with him tomorrow?'

McBride shook his head. 'I'll let you know when I've done it and we can all go home. If he wants to play the bloody hero so be it.'

'You could maybe find out what he was doing over the other side.'

McBride shouted with obvious anger, 'I know what he was doing – he was working for the bloody enemy. That's enough for me.'

'You've probably got enough on him to convict him in court.'

'Oh sure. A real Christmas for the fucking media. No way.'

Then they heard the phone ringing downstairs. McBride looked at his watch. It was 4.30 a.m. 'Who the hell can that be? Nobody's got this number.'

Keller stood up. 'I gave my people the number for emergencies. Could be them.'

It was ten minutes before Keller came back, fuming with anger.

'Did you know that Tarrant had a hidey-hole in Berlin?'

'He used the SIS place in Kant Strasse.'

'He had another place, rented it from an ex-girl-friend of his. My people were keeping it under surveillance.' He paused. 'Am I right in thinking Tarrant's got red hair?'

'Yes.'

'He let himself into the room at 3 a.m. My guys say they couldn't get hold of me. They let him settle in and then they knocked on the door.' He sighed. 'Cutting a long story short they shot him. He had an electric razor in his hand when he opened the door. My chap thought it was a gun. And he thought it was Foster.'

'Is he dead?'

'No. A wound in the shoulder. My chaps contacted

Pullach who contacted Waring. Tarrant was taken under escort to the British military hospital and sorted out. Waring contacted SIS London and Tarrant's on his way to Gatow and is being flown back in an RAF plane.' He paused. 'Do you want to contact London?'

McBride shook his head. 'No. They can sort out Tarrant. I'll deal with Foster tomorrow and get back.' He looked at Keller. 'What about the press, have they got wind of it?'

'No. Only the girl who owns the flat knows anything happened and she's been warned. She won't talk.'

McBride made a phone call to London the following morning. Powell agreed that it would be better for him too to fly back courtesy of the RAF and then there would be no airline bookings on the record. A flight was arranged for that night at 11 p.m. from Gatow.

It was a week later when an unidentified body was found in the basement of one of the disused blocks of workers' flats which had been abandoned when the Wall was built. The autopsy indicated that there was a possibility that the man had died from asphyxia caused by strangulation. A police spokesman hinted that the victim was probably a Turkish guest-worker who had been involved in some gang rivalry.

CHAPTER 38

Peter Hartmann didn't make it to San Francisco. When he heard that Igor Serov had been arrested in Moscow he knew that he didn't have time to make suitable arrangements for US documentation. He went to Spain and lives in a small but pleasant villa on the hills outside Javea. He is much liked and respected in the small community and it is thought that he is writing a novel.

Gala moved out of the house the day before Hartmann left for Spain. She left a note for Charlie Foster pinned to the door of the house and stayed with friends for just over a month when her father persuaded her that she should leave with him and stay with him in a house he owned on the Costa Ligure between Portofino and Santa Margharita.

Six months later she and her father moved to California. First of all to Los Angeles because of her father's work, but a year later she moved to Carmel having acquired both skill and recognition as a photographer. She set up her own studio and made enough money to live comfortably. For a long time she thought of Charlie Foster every day. She knew long ago that he must be dead. She played tapes of Fats Waller and Nat King Cole and wished that she had told him how much she loved him. The studio was on the top floor of the flat-roofed house and she sometimes stood at the big windows, looking across the valley trying to think of him without thinking about what had happened to him. She had many friends, some of them men, but none of them close.

In the garage was an aluminium case with reinforced edges and a scrawl in black paint that said – Arriflex Camera + Accessories. Inside the case was a quarter of a million dollars in hundred dollar bills. Sometimes she wondered why she had loved him so much. He had never even asked her the date of her birthday. Hartmann had said it was his training had made him like that. Whatever it was she missed him.

When Eddie Foster had had no message for over a year he had phoned Century House with no great expectation of help. Personnel passed him to Willis who passed him to Sir Anthony Powell, who seemed to be genuinely surprised to be reminded of Charlie Foster and was very 'cut up' not to be able to help.

The business was doing well and Eddie Foster decided after a couple of years with no news of his son that he had had enough. So he sold the business and the house at the top of the market, bought a pleasant town-house in the centre of Chichester and a Broom 33 which he kept at Birdham Pool, and sometimes ventured as far as Honfleur.

When he was packing up before moving he had opened the package in his safe. He sold CDs and cassettes in the shop and he thought he recognised what was inside the packet. It had no label and when he slid it into the CD player of one of the shop's hi-fi units there was no music and no sound. He hesitated for a moment about throwing it away and then chucked it into the black plastic garbage bag.

Johnny Tarrant was taken by ambulance from Brize Norton to Sandown on the Isle of Wight. The house was well guarded but Tarrant was allowed reasonable freedom inside the grounds. Slaney had contacted Tarrant's father and after much anger and recrimination a deal was reached. Another couple of months for the arm and shoulder to heal properly and articulate, and then Johnny would go to Ireland. His father would buy him a cottage and SIS would provide a pension. A scale-pension. Nothing extravagant. After five years he would be free to do whatever he wanted.

When Tommy Tarrant drove on to the ferry he was not best pleased. In his opinion his son had been a fool and his son's superiors were not only incompetent but irresponsible and devious. It would take more than a lunch at the Garrick to calm him down but at least he had come out with a better deal for his son than the bastards had intended.

He had driven down in the MGB and planned to leave it for Johnny to use when he was able to drive. It would cheer him up to have his car. Tarrant looked at his watch. He'd got an hour to get through before he would be allowed in to see Johnny. He walked down to the quay. Most of the boats were under cover for the winter but there were a few big gin-palaces with their decks under several inches of snow. He scuffed the snow off a bollard with his boot and sat down on it and fished in his anorak for his cigarettes and then remembered that he had stuffed them in the canvas holdall. He unzipped it and pushed aside a rolled-up pair of thick woollen socks. Then he saw the cigarette packet alongside the bundle of mail that he had brought for his son. He had thrown away the obvious junk mail – the chance of winning a fortune if only you opened the envelope immediately. The bundle of envelopes was held together with a rubber band and as he moved it aside he remembered the letter in his pocket. The one addressed to him, but about Johnny. He took it out of his pocket and unfolded it. He had read it a dozen times. It was from Johnny's friend Tony Martin, the solicitor. It was quite short.

Dear Tommy,

As you know I have made countless unsuccessful attempts to contact Johnny but he seems to have vanished.

However, in case you are more fortunate I thought I should let you know semi-officially what happened.

Johnny's time spent with Jenny was a great help but as time went by she continued to deteriorate, and I have to inform you that she died a week ago from an overdose. The inquest was as you could expect.

Obviously no blame attaches to anyone. She was a sad victim of her upbringing. I thought Johnny should know.

     Yours aye,
      Tony.

PS. The personnel chap I spoke to at Century House said that he had never heard of Johnny. Strange people.

                Lamberhurst
                November '92.

TED ALLBEURY

SHOW ME A HERO

Andrei Aarons was just twenty when he became a spy.
Quiet, idealistic, a true believer, always able to justify
the imperfections of the Revolution. Picked, trained
and sent off to New York to begin his extraordinary life
as the most successful espionage agent the Russians
ever had.

So why did six American presidents trust him?

'One of the masters of espionage has come up with
another winner.'
Sunday Telegraph

'Master craftsman among thriller writers.'
Edinburgh Evening News

HODDER AND STOUGHTON PAPERBACKS